CONSTANCE O'BANYON

PIRATE'S PRINCESS

ZEBRA BOOKS
KENSINGTON PUBLISHING CORP.

ZEBRA BOOKS

are published by

Kensington Publishing Corp.
475 Park Avenue South
New York, NY 10016

First printing: August, 1989

Printed in the United States of America

A NIGHT MADE FOR LOVE

Cord's lips touched Jahane's, softly at first, exploring, tasting, reveling in the tender feelings. Then he crushed her in his arms, needing and wanting her with an ache deep inside.

Jahane was unaware when Cord lifted her into his arms, until she felt the softness of the bed beneath her. When Cord lay down beside her, she allowed him to pull her against him.

Cord had denied his love for Jahane for so long that he was overwhelmed with feelings he could not understand or control. When her soft hand caressed his cheek and she breathed his name, his control snapped completely.

"Jahane, how long have I felt this way?" he asked more of himself than of her. "How long have you lingered at the back of my mind?"

"I cannot remember a time when I did not love you," she replied. "When I think back to my childhood, yours is the face that comes to me."

He looked down at her, noticing that her eyes were brightly shining. "Jahane, are you certain you love me as a woman loves a man, and not as a sister would love her brother?"

"I love you so deeply it hurts, Cord. Please, make me yours, tonight . . ."

Dedication

To the three who made being a grandmother a wonderful and rewarding experience and made the word love reach a new depth for me: To Jeffrey Scott Gee, bright, witty and intelligent. To Brian James Gee, who charms me with his sweet smile. To Caitlyn Dae Melton, who wound herself around my heart.

One

Balmarhea

Chapter One

Balmarhea Island, 1842

The night shadows hid the lone figure which moved swiftly but cautiously along the walls of the city. Dressed simply in the rough black robes of a humble priest, Serafimo Beaudette, the Archbishop of Balmarhea and youngest brother of King Alfons, was taking great pains to conceal his identity. Pausing every few moments to look about and make certain he was not being followed, he hurried toward the castle, where he knew his brother, the king, anxiously awaited his arrival.

Serafimo wondered what crisis had prompted Alfons to send for him in the middle of the night. The written message had been brief but urgent: *Come at once. Do not fail me. Pray God it is not too late.*

Though the words were grim, it was what the message did not say that filled the archbishop's heart with dread. He knew that ominous forces were at work in Balmarhea and danger was everywhere, and as both brother and loyal subject, he had long feared for the safety of the king and his family. Their island and its tranquility had gone undisturbed for six generations, but now the jealousy and greed of their middle brother for that which belonged to the firstborn son had set in motion the turbulent wheels of

9

civil war.

In the distance, the sporadic sound of gunfire split through the quiet of the city, reminding the archbishop of the urgency of his mission. Just ahead he heard the sound of men running, and he flattened his body against the wall, clutching the shadows. Though his position as head of the Church should be enough to safeguard him from rebels and loyalists alike, he had no inclination to find out if the men were friend or foe. There was every reason for caution because the city was surrounded by traitorous rebels, and even those still loyal to the king were more apt to shoot first and then wonder about one's allegiance.

Now the gunfire appeared to be coming nearer, and the archbishop wondered how much longer the royal troops could hold out against such a powerful enemy. He had to believe that the king's troops would be victorious; after all, were they not superior in strength and number to the rebels? Did they not have God on their side?

Only last week it had appeared certain that the hostilities were nearing an end and the rebels would be defeated. But instead of surrendering, the traitors had evaded capture and attacked the capital city, almost annihilating the royal army that stood in their path.

Where were the king's generals now? he wondered. Why hadn't they repelled the attack upon the city? Serafimo did not have the mind of a warrior, but even he knew the generals had blundered badly. And, yes, he had to admit that Alfons was also to blame. The king was an honorable and compassionate man who loved his subjects, and since there had never been a war in his time, Alfons had made bad judgments in dealing fairly with the rebels, only to be met with treachery in return. He had wanted to heal the country's wounds and bring all the people together again, but that was not to be.

Serafimo cursed the generals who had failed in their duty, and he cursed Reynard, his brother, who had betrayed their king and country.

The archbishop was not even ashamed of the anger that flamed within him. The last few days had reintroduced him to many emotions that he thought he had left behind when he had entered the Church. He longed for the time when his island kingdom would again know peace, but at what cost? So many had died already, and more would surely die before this night ended.

Serafimo rushed noiselessly down the cobblestone streets, breathing a sigh of relief when the castle, with its white towers and cupolas, loomed out of the darkness like a beacon of hope to him on this grievous night of despair.

Avoiding the front entrance to the castle, which was heavily guarded, the archbishop rounded a corner and moved along the shadows of the wall until he came upon a secluded iron gate. After he paused and glanced back over his shoulder to make sure he hadn't been followed, Serafimo inserted his key, and the gate swung inward on well-oiled hinges to reveal the royal family's private gardens. Hurriedly, he closed and locked the gate behind him.

As the archbishop moved down the garden path, he was reminded of happier times when his father had been king, a time when he and his two brothers had been good friends. No, the passing of time and the teachings of his chosen profession had dulled his memory. Had not Alfons, who had then been the crown prince, and heir to their father's throne, always been generous with Reynard; and had Reynard not been spiteful and vindictive in return? No, Reynard had not been satisfied with the title of Duke of Maxime. He had always wanted to be king.

The archbishop's black robe flapped against his legs as he hastily entered the castle by a door that was cleverly hidden behind a box hedge.

Torches burned low in their sconces, casting grotesque shadows on the walls of the long, narrow hallway. Serafimo's footsteps echoed through the empty corridor that

11

should have been occupied by the king's own guards.

Stepping from behind an age-old tapestry and into the great hall, he saw that not only was the king awaiting his arrival, but also Queen Eleanor, Prince Alexander, and the young Princess Jahane were there. Surely there must be grave matters at hand if Alfons had felt compelled to awaken his children in the middle of the night.

Serafimo's presence had not yet been detected, and he stood respectfully waiting to be acknowledged while he assessed the royal family. His brother, the king, was tall and stately, his gray hair adding just the right distinguishing touches to his unlined face. Before Reynard incited a civil war, the people of the island of Balmarhea had loved their king well, for he was a kind and honorable man whose rule was always tempered with compassion.

Serafimo's eyes moved on to Queen Eleanor. To say that the queen was beautiful was to say too little. She was tall and willowy, with golden hair bound around her head in a coronet. He was saddened to see that her lovely face was now creased in a worried frown.

Serafimo glanced fondly at his nephew, the young Prince Alexander. Although only in his eleventh year, Alexander had already displayed a sense of fairness and honor as well as other important leadership qualities. Serafimo knew the young prince well, since it had been his honor to tutor Alexander from the time he had left the nursery. The boy had a quick mind, but his one failing was learning to conquer his impatience, which Serafimo had tried to instruct him to temper with forbearance. Always arrogant and aloof, the prince now seemed to stand apart from the other family members.

Serafimo couldn't keep from smiling as his eyes moved to the young princess, Jahane, who lay upon a padded bench, sleepily resting her golden head upon her mother's lap. Angelic and lovely, Jahane was no more than three years of age, but she possessed a shiny disposition and a happy temperament. There was a promise of great beauty in her even features, and already her father had been besieged with offers from the rulers of other, more powerful countries to betroth her to their sons, but Alfons had refused all offers in response to the queen's wishes to wait until their daughter was of a marriageable age.

Serafimo's attention was directed back to the king, who had by now discovered his presence and motioned for him to come forward.

"Where are the guards?" Serafimo asked in concern, noting that no one stood guard over the royal family.

"I sent them to reinforce the front gate. In any event, I wanted no one outside the family to witness what must take place in this room," Alfons answered. "Thank God you've come, Serafimo, for I have much to say to you and little time to say it."

"I came as quickly as I could without arousing suspicion, Your Majesty," Serafimo said with respect. Although the two men were brothers, Serafimo always paid the greatest homage to the king. "When your messenger came, our brother, Reynard, had just arrived at the cathedral, and I had to deal with him before it was safe to come to you."

Although the king's eyes sparked with anger, there was also a touch of sadness in their blue depths. "Inasmuch as I cannot yet prove Reynard is behind this, I cannot act. But it is my belief that he is more than a little involved in this war. I feel it in the depth of my heart, however much it grieves me to admit it."

"It is not my wish to speak ill of our brother," Serafimo replied, "but I am almost certain that Reynard is the real power behind this insurrection, sire. It is no secret that he has tried to cause trouble for you."

The king focused his whole attention on Serafimo. "Yes, you are right," he agreed sadly. "And Reynard alone stands to gain by my death and the deaths of my children."

"But surely the war will turn in our favor, Alfons," the archbishop said, forgetting to be formal in his brother's presence. "I have prayed for the worst to be over."

King Alfons shook his head. "I fear your prayers have not been answered, my brother. My generals have all been duped. They were drawn away from the city with the thought of thrashing the enemy and ending the war. Fool that I was, I listened to them. I now know my troops were drawn to the far side of the island, leaving the capital unprotected. This city is doomed," the king said sadly. "Before help can come, we will be finished."

Serafimo's face whitened. "But, Your Majesty, surely this cannot be!"

"I can assure you it is true. We have very little time before the enemy breaks through the city gates. That is why I sent for you. Were you challenged on your way here?"

Serafimo's mind was still reeling from the shock of what his brother had told him. "No, sire, I encountered no one face-to-face." Serafimo shook his head as if to clear it. "You must all flee at once," he said urgently. "I can smuggle you out of the city, or offer you sanctuary in the cathedral if you would prefer. No matter how treacherous Reynard may be, even he would never violate the sanctity of the Church."

"No, Serafimo, my place is here. I will not be driven out of my city like a fugitive, and I cannot rule from your church. I am king as long as I draw breath, and I will behave accordingly. If my subjects see me leave, they will panic, and many will lose their lives unnecessarily."

"But, Alfons, surely—"

"No, and that is my final word on the subject, Serafimo. Surely you do not expect me to play the coward?"

The archbishop turned to his queen, hoping to enlist her aid. "Help me convince my brother to flee to safety with you and the children."

She shook her head sadly. "My husband's duty keeps him here, and my place is beside him; so there you have it, Serafimo."

Suddenly the sound of cannon fire erupted. The archbishop knew that the brave guards at the front gate would hold their position until the last man, but they would be no match for the heavy enemy artillery.

The truth of the situation finally hit him full-force. The king and queen were prepared to die! Did they also plan to sacrifice their son and daughter to the enemy? "Surely not the children, Alfons?" he said in disbelief.

The king reached out and touched his sleeping daughter's cheek. He had become a father late in life and doted on his two heirs. Serafimo could only guess at the thoughts that were going through his brother's mind at this time.

"No, not my children," he answered, glancing at his wife, a sad-sweet smile lingering on his lips.

"Thank God for that," the archbishop said, crossing himself as he waited for his brother to continue.

"It is my belief," the king went on, "that Reynard will cause you no harm, Serafimo. He will not see you as a threat. Besides, he will need to have you beside him so he can convince the people of Balmarhea to trust him."

"I will never stand beside him. I am loyal to only you. But I agree that he knows it is in his best interest not to harm me."

Alfon's eyes sparkled at the declaration of his youngest brother's loyalty. "Yes, you will be safe, so therefore you are the one to take my children to safety."

Fealty and admiration burned in the archbishop's heart. "Your Majesties, I stand ready to aid you with my life if the need arises. You have only to tell me what you want accomplished, and with God's help, it shall be done."

Alfons bestowed a smile on his brother. "I counted on that, Serafimo. That's why I am placing the prince and

15

princess in your care. I charge you to keep them safe at any cost. Do what you must, but do not allow them to fall into Reynard's hands. And when the time comes, help them to lead our people. Is that understood?"

Serafimo felt honored that his beloved brother had entrusted the future of Balmarhea into his keeping, and a flame ignited in his eyes. "They will not be taken as long as I live, sire; this I promise you." Strong conviction gave believability to his words. "You have my solemn oath that while there is breath in my body, I will keep them safe."

"Good, good. Now, I want you to trust no one with the whereabouts of Their Highnesses, with the exception of my prime minister, Count Chapin d'Arcy. You can place your trust in him. I have instructed him to aid you in any way you deem necessary."

"As you wish, sire. Have you a plan in mind?"

"Yes, I do. It seems d'Arcy has contacted an American sea captain friend of his who will aid you in getting the children away from Balmarhea. I am informed that the American's ship is concealed off our shores, and her captain only waits for Their Highness to be brought to him."

The king moved to his wife's side. "It is time, my dear. You must bid our children farewell. Haste is of the utmost importance."

Serafimo watched the queen raise her head proudly. The only evidence of the pain she was suffering was the telltale tears that beaded on the tips of her golden lashes. She lifted the Princess Jahane in her arms and cuddled her closely before placing a soft kiss on the rosebud mouth. Reluctantly, she handed the child to the king.

Prince Alexander stood with legs apart and arms folded defiantly across his chest. "I will not be going with you, Uncle. Take my sister to safety, but my place is here with my father and mother." The angry young prince turned to his father. "I will not be sent away like some child. I am

16

your son; I will stand with you until the end. We must fight, Father, not meekly wait for death." A look of disbelief was etched on his face. Why was his father giving up without a fight? "Our people need you to guide them, and I do, too, Father."

Pride brightened the king's eyes as he looked upon his heir. "Your courage does you much credit, my son, but it is foolishly spent, since defeat is certain. You will not die here tonight to prove your contempt for injustice. Rather, you will live to one day claim the throne which will rightfully be yours."

The young prince stood his ground. "You cannot make me leave, Father. I belong with you. Send Jahane away with our uncle so that she may be safe, but allow me to stay with you."

The king now frowned at his son. "You will do as you are told, Alexander. I am still king, and I have issued you an order. Go with your Uncle Serafimo."

Rebellion sparkled in the prince's eyes. "No, I will not obey you in this, Father. How can you ask me to walk away and leave you and Mother to die?" Prince Alexander dashed across the room, and before anyone could guess his intention, jumped on top of a table and tore one of the ancestral swords off the wall. "If you will not fight, I must fight for us both."

The royal family watched as the prince paused at the door for one last look at his mother before disappearing through the secret exit behind the tapestry.

The queen, seeing tears running freely down her son's cheeks, lost her composure and slumped down in a heap. Holding on to her last bit of courage, she offered her hand to her husband with an apologetic light in her eyes as he helped her to her feet. Now, her courage had returned, and she raised her head proudly. With a last kiss on her sleeping daughter's face, she turned away to stand at the window.

17

King Alfons clasped his daughter to him so tightly that she stirred and opened her eyes.

Unaware of the drama that was being played out around her, she spoke in her childish voice. "Papa."

The king smiled sadly. He would never see his Jahane grow to womanhood, never know the kind of woman she would be without her lovely mother's influence. Perhaps he was wrong to allow his wife to stand with him tonight. Unwilling to dwell on his tormented thoughts, and knowing nothing he could say would make Eleanor leave him, he turned back to Serafimo.

"There isn't much time, so listen to me carefully. As you are aware, no one can be crowned sovereign of Balmarhea without the great scepter."

"That is so," Serafimo agreed.

Every citizen of Balmarhea knew the legend of the ruby scepter, which was reputed to contain a sliver of the Holy Cross. The law bestowing absolute power on the ruling monarch had been enacted by Henri the Brave, who had been King of Balmarhea during the Crusades. Afraid that one of his three brothers would try to take the throne away while he was fighting in the Holy Land, Henri had taken the scepter with him to ensure that he could not be deposed.

"Since Reynard knew that the scepter was kept in the secret panel behind the throne, and since he may be in power before this night is over, I have chosen a new hiding place. Unfortunately, I had no opportunity to show it to Alexander, so I am now forced to reveal it to my daughter instead."

"But she is too young to understand the importance of the scepter," the queen protested.

"Yes, perhaps too young to comprehend the significance of what I must show her, but not too young to remember the hiding place of the scepter." Alfons turned to his brother. "Serafimo, go outside the great hall and wait. The

18

queen will join you later," he said.

Serafimo nodded, knowing they needed time alone with their daughter.

He moved out of the room and closed the door behind him. Leaning his back against the cold brick wall in the hallway, Serafimo closed his eyes, unable to comprehend all that had happened in such a short time. How painful it would be to say goodbye to the king and queen, knowing he would never see them again. He felt the responsibility of the princess's safety weighing heavily on his shoulders. It would be no easy task to keep her out of Reynard's grasp. He tried not to think about his nephew. It was probable that the young hothead would get himself killed tonight, he thought with a heavy heart. Therefore, the future of Balmarhea lay with the young princess.

The door of the great hall opened, and the queen stepped out to stand beside her brother-in-law. How proudly she faced him, how regally she would meet her death, he thought.

"Serafimo, make every effort to find my son and take him to safety. While his bravery does him credit, I fear it will not save his life should he fall into the hands of the enemy." She paused before continuing. "And, when she is older, tell my daughter . . . tell her how dearly I loved her. Tell her . . . tell her." The queen's voice became choked, and Serafimo turned away, giving her time to compose herself. "And if her brother should . . . not . . . be found, teach her all that a queen should know."

"You can depend on me, Your Majesty."

King Alfons placed his daughter on a high stool, and she watched curiously while he pointed to the tapestry near the stained-glass window. The ancient needlework was of galloping steeds and knights in armor upon a background of the royal crest.

King Alfons spoke to his daughter in an urgent voice. "Jahane, you must remember this tapestry with the horses. Remember, remember." He shook his head. "But then you are so young."

"Horse," she said, pointing to a rearing steed which had been sewn with red silk. "Horse."

"Yes, Jahane. Now watch what I am about to show you. But it is a secret, and you must tell no one. Watch me. I have pushed the tapestry aside."

Curiously, the child observed her father's actions.

"Look, Jahane, this stone looks like all the others, but it is hollow in back. Look, Papa will remove the stone."

When the stone had been withdrawn from the wall, the king reached inside the hollowed-out space and pulled out the golden scepter, holding it out to his daughter. "Look at this, Jahane. Feel it. See the pretty stones—they are rubies."

Quickly removing the dagger at his waist, he dug out one of the rubies and placed it in the child's hand. "Keep this safe so all may know that you are the true princess. The twelve rubies are perfectly matched. There are no others like them anywhere in the world, so no one can ever substitute an imitation for the genuine stone."

"Pretty," she said, clasping the red stone in her chubby hand as if she had been given a precious gift. Soon losing interest in the ruby, she looked back at the tapestry. "Horse, Papa, horse."

Her father shook his head ruefully. "You are too young to remember the secret. But you must, Jahane." He took the ruby from her and dropped it in a leather pouch which he tied about her neck. "Jahane, if only I could be sure you would remember the scepter's hiding place."

Suddenly the king's eyes narrowed as he remembered the time he had fallen out of a carriage at age two. Everyone said he was too young to recall the incident, but he did, because of the pain of his broken arm. Pain was a great reminder, he thought, abhorring the idea of intentionally hurting his young daughter—but he must. She had to remember this night, or Balmarhea would never again have a ruler with absolute power.

Gathering her up in his arms, Alfons gripped his dagger. His hand trembled as Jahane looked at him so trustingly, and he knew that to wound her would be the hardest thing he would ever be called upon to do. With a deep resolve and a determined mind, he slashed the knife across the palm of her right hand, which he thought would be the least painful place he could cut.

Jahane cried out in alarm and panic, and looked up at her father in disbelief. The cut was deep, and blood ran from her hand, trickling through her fingers and splashing on the sleeve of her father's garment.

Filled with remorse for what he had been forced to do, Alfons clutched his beloved daughter to him tightly and spoke to her soothingly, while he instructed her to watch him place the scepter in its new hiding place.

"Remember, my daughter—remember this night! Remember the horses, the tapestry, and the scepter. Remember, Jahane, but tell no one our secret."

Hurriedly he scribbled words on a parchment, affixed his seal to it, and tucked the document under his arm.

As Jahane continued to sob in pain, her father carried her out of the great hall to where his wife and brother waited for them. Time was running out, and the child had to be safely out of the castle before the enemy broke through.

Sadness encased the king's heart, and he was overcome with a fierce protectiveness to save his daughter. Most probably his son, in his brave but reckless way, would get himself killed this night. And Jahane would one day be queen.

Serafimo took the child from his brother, staring at the blood that dripped from her hand and the bloodstains on his brother's sleeve.

The queen looked at her husband in horror.

"I had to," the king said in explanation. "She may now remember where I hid the scepter." Alfons then handed the parchment to his brother. "Keep this safe, Serafimo, for it tells how I gave the princess one of the rubies from the royal scepter. Since she has to flee from Balmarhea, charge her to return when she is older and produce the stone I have given her and the scepter we have hidden. And bid her to rule our people wisely."

Serafimo bowed. "It will be as you say."

The queen lifted her daughter's bloody hand and gently wrapped it with her lace handkerchief. Pressing her cheek to her child's, the queen refused to cry. "Always remember that your father and I love you, my dearest one. I pray God will keep you safe." She looked for the last time upon her daughter's face, then turned to be enfolded in her husband's loving arms.

Even though Jahane's sobs had subsided, she was still disturbed by what her father had done. But comforted by her mother's soothing voice, and clasped in the arms of her uncle, who was dear and familiar to her, her eyes fluttered shut and she fell into a fitful sleep.

Heavy gunfire now appeared to be concentrated inside the castle courtyard, so the king cautioned Serafimo to leave the same way he had entered.

Serafimo knew that he was looking for the last time upon the face of his brother and sister-in-law. That they would meet death honorably, he had little doubt, though he wished he could save them from the fate that awaited them.

As the archbishop hurried down the hallway, carrying his precious burden, he heard the echo of the queen's anguished cry, and it tore at his heart. He did not look back, even though the temptation was great. Instead, his footsteps quickened. He knew if Reynard were to come upon them, neither the fact that Jahane was a child, nor the fact that she was Reynard's niece, would stay his hand from slaying her. Reynard was in league with the devil, and the quest for power ruled his life.

Serafimo slipped out the hidden door and cautiously made his way across the garden, mindful of the child he held in his arms.

Anger burned in his heart toward his brother, Reynard, and the thought of Cain and Abel came to his mind.

Chapter Two

In a secluded lagoon off the island of Balmarhea, looming out of the darkness like some great shadowy ghost, the ship, *Boston Clipper*, rode at anchor.

The night was without a moon. Even the stars seemed dim and cast no light on the scene below. The only sounds that could be heard were the ship's timbers creaking and the warm breeze that rippled and snapped her canvas sails.

Below, in the captain's cabin, eleven-year-old Cord Meredith watched as his father, who was owner and captain of the ship, studied a map of the island with two members of his crew.

They conversed in hushed tones, and Cord knew something out of the ordinary was happening because his father was being secretive and had directed that all lanterns be extinguished and all portholes be covered so no light would penetrate the night to give away their presence.

As Cord looked on, Captain Jonah Meredith straightened up to his full height and crammed a pistol into his belt before motioning for his men to precede him on deck. After the others had departed, Jonah turned to his young son.

"Cord, I know you are curious about the strange activity that has been taking place since we anchored, but I cannot tell even you what is afoot because I am sworn to secrecy.

Should anything out of the ordinary occur tonight . . ." he hesitated before continuing, ". . . I have left instructions with Thadeus to set sail at once. I'm telling you this merely so you will be prepared should the worst— But I don't foresee any trouble, Cord, so do not be concerned."

Cord stared at his father, unable to comprehend his meaning. "Father, if you are going into danger, please allow me to accompany you. I can shoot a gun as well as any man here, and I'm not afraid."

Jonah looked into his son's dark, troubled eyes and rumpled his black hair playfully.

"No, you aren't afraid, are you? But I cannot take you with me, Son. Your mother would never forgive me if anything happened to you. I promised that if she allowed you to ship with me for a year, I would not endanger you in any way. Of course, when I made that promise to her, I had no way of knowing that I would receive a desperate appeal from an old friend, and that for friendship's sake, I would be forced to put this ship and you in jeopardy."

"But why, Father?"

Jonah smiled at his son. "Because Count Chapin d'Arcy asked me," he explained, as if that was reason enough. "Until now, Chapin has never asked me for a favor. After all he's done for me, I could hardly say no, now could I?"

"That would depend on what Count d'Arcy has asked of you."

"I can't tell you any more, Cord. Not even the men who accompany me ashore tonight know what we are about. It is enough for you to know that Chapin is a friend and he needs my help. There's no more time to explain, so don't ask me any more questions, Son."

"But, Father—"

Jonah pressed the boy to him for a moment in a rare show of affection, then abruptly released him with a look of regret in his eyes. "If anything should happen . . . if . . . well, just see that your mother gets this letter."

Cord was confused and frightened. What had his father been asked to do in the name of friendship? What kind of danger was his father talking about? Cord took the sealed letter and tucked it inside his coat pocket.

"Must you do this, Father?"

"Yes. Chapin d'Arcy and I have been friends for a very long time. As you know, he's the one who helped me buy the *Boston Clipper,* and he made arrangements for me to trade in Balmarhea. Because of his assistance, I am a wealthy man today. I owe him a great debt of gratitude, Cord."

"But, Father, you paid him back all the money," Cord reasoned.

"That is so, but the debt of friendship is never paid. As you grow older, you will realize this."

Suddenly the boy had the strongest feeling that he would never see his father again. "I beg you, Father, allow me to go with you. Whatever you have to do, I'll be able to help, I know I will. And you don't have to break your word to Count d'Arcy by explaining anything. I have to go; Mother made me promise to look after you, too."

His father's eyes darkened with a determined look. "For the last time, Cord, no! You will remain on board the *Boston Clipper.* Is that understood?"

"Yes, Father, I understand, or . . . no, I don't think I do."

"Accompany me on deck, Son. It's time for me to leave," his father said kindly. "I promised to meet Count d'Arcy two hours after sunset, and it's about that time now."

Cord trailed behind his father, wishing he would reconsider and allow him to go ashore. In the inky darkness, he stood by silently as his father and two companions slipped over the side of the ship and dropped into the longboat below. The sound of swishing oars soon faded into silence, leaving Cord shivering with some unknown dread. What would he do if his father didn't return? What would he say to his mother?

Cord was so deep in thought that he was startled when Thadeus Kramer, his father's second-in-command, came up beside him.

"My father wouldn't take me with him, Thadeus. Why?"

The first mate clamped his teeth down on his unlit pipe. "I suspect your pa wanted you to stay here and look after things, Cord," he said matter-of-factly.

"I don't like to be spoken to like a child, Thadeus," Cord replied in anger. "You and I both know this ship will float with or without my help."

Thadeus smiled to himself. "I do so humbly beg your pardon, young Cord, and if I gave you the impression I was talking down my nose at you, I wasn't."

"I am not as young as you and my father seem to think. I am a more than fair hand with a gun, and I am tall for my age. I have always been capable of handling myself well enough in a scrap."

"Aye, that you have. But you are forgetting the first rule of the sea."

"Which is?"

"That the captain's word is law. And your pa's the captain."

"I know that, Thadeus, but it doesn't change how I feel . . ." Cord's voice trailed off into silence, and after a moment of thoughtfulness he spoke in a composed voice. "Tell me about this island, Thadeus."

"Well, the Island of Balmarhea is ruled by a monarch named King Alfons, and the spoken language is French. If it wasn't so dark, you could see the towers of the king's castle, which would be about an hour away from here, in the city of Montique."

"Since my father is a friend of the prime minister, does that mean he also knows the royal family?"

Thadeus smiled. "I don't believe he is acquainted with

27

them."

"What can you tell me about Count d'Arcy, Thadeus?"

The old sailor pulled on his yet unlit pipe. "Well, now, I can tell you he's the prime minister and a mighty important man on Balmarhea. I believe I overheard your father to mention that the count has a wife and a young daughter."

"How did my father come to be acquainted with such an important man?"

"As I recall, Count Chapin d'Arcy was on board a ship that went down off the coast of France, and your pa, being the captain of a small vessel at the time, pulled him out of the ocean, saved him from drowning, and nursed him back to health. d'Arcy and him have been friends ever since."

"I know Count d'Arcy has visited our home in Boston on several occasions." Cord stared into the darkness, his real questions still unanswered. "Are you sure you don't know why he sent for my father and why everything is so secretive?"

"Nay, and I don't ask questions either. As first mate, I just do as I'm told."

Cord knew that Thadeus was more than a hand on the *Boston Clipper*. He was a man his captain could depend on and also a friend. Cord also had a feeling Thadeus knew more than he was telling.

With a heavy intake of breath, the boy filled his lungs with jasmine-scented air. He wished the night would pass so he could see this island his father had so often referred to as paradise. They had sailed into this cove under cover of darkness, and if they sailed away before dawn, it wasn't likely he would even catch a glimpse of Balmarhea.

Periodically Cord could hear the distant sound of gunfire, and he concluded that the island was under siege!

As Cord stared into the darkness, fear for his father's safety gnawed at his insides. How could he stay on board

28

ship when his father was probably in danger?

With his mind made up to join his father, Cord wished Thadeus would leave so he could put his plan into action. The first mate would prevent him from leaving if he realized what he had in mind.

After a long moment of silence, Thadeus moved away, leaving the boy alone with his thoughts.

Cord waited until the first mate was out of hearing before springing into action.

First he stashed the letter his father had given him under one of the longboats, then he cautiously climbed over the railing, knowing that the man on watch would be alert to any unusual sound. Silently he dropped into the water below, and with strong strokes, he swam toward the island and the sound of gunfire.

On the island kingdom of Balmarhea, in the capital city of Montique, another young boy, the same age as Cord Meredith, faced the dangers of war.

Prince Alexander knelt before the altar in the family chapel, silently praying for the survival of his mother and father. Raising his head to the golden, jewel-studded cross, he blinked tears away.

Realizing the sounds of battle were drawing ever closer, Alexander crossed himself and jumped to his feet, reaching for his sword. The flame of disillusionment burned brightly in his blue eyes, and to his way of thinking, the sword of justice was clutched in his hand. He was ready to do battle, to take on any enemy who dared cross his father's threshold.

Charging into action, the prince hurried past the large chamber that led to the royal family's private apartments. Pausing before the massive doors of the entrance hall, he could hear the sounds of battle coming from the main courtyard, and he knew that the enemy had broken through the lines of defense and had now penetrated the castle itself.

Riddled with indignation at the rebels who had invaded his castle, Prince Alexander slid back the iron bolt, swung open the heavy door, and boldly stepped outside.

To Alexander's astonishment, hungry flames were leaping into the sky, and the courtyard was ablaze with burning carts and wagons. Even the royal carriage was on fire. He saw men battling in hand-to-hand combat and heard the clashing sound of their swords echoing through the walled courtyard.

He shuddered when he saw the dead and dying who littered the ground. Some bodies were hanging from the walls, and still others had fallen into the fountain — the water of the fountain was blood-red in color!

Almost immediately the prince was recognized by the five loyal guards who stood watch in front of the entrance, and they gathered about him like a protective shield.

Alexander, not wanting to be singled out for special treatment since he much preferred to be accepted as a warrior, pushed his way past the guards and leaped into the thick of the fighting.

Swinging his sword and having it clash with an enemy sword sent the heat of battle coursing through his veins. Soon perspiration blinded him as he swung his sword with stunning accuracy. He had been instructed by a master swordsman, and he felt pride in the fact that he could defend himself quite well. With a powerful thrust, his sword slashed across an adversary's face, and the man screamed out in agony before falling to the ground.

Alexander stepped over the man's body to face another enemy. He had no time to dwell on the fact that he had just taken one man's life and would kill many more times today, if he survived long enough. With no thought of his own safety, only conscious that he was protecting his mother and father, his sword swung out with the mastery of one trained to kill.

The battle in the courtyard had been raging for over an hour. Alexander's muscles ached, and he was sick of the sight of blood. His stomach churned when he made a forward thrust at a faceless enemy and he felt his sword slice through bone. He had never been in battle before, and he knew he would never be the same person after today—because he had now killed.

It was becoming apparent to him that the few loyal troops that still fought beside him could not hold back the tide of the enemy forces that swept through the gate like a flood of humanity.

With renewed strength, Alexander wielded his ancestral sword, fighting like a man possessed. He knew that once the enemy got past him, and the few remaining loyal guards, they would reach his mother and father.

The acrid smell of smoke stung his lungs and burned his eyes. His hand was covered with blood from enemies who had fallen victim to his sword. There were no more than a dozen royal soldiers left, but they bravely fought alongside their prince, each knowing in his heart they could not win.

Now Alexander was being driven backward toward the castle door. He wondered why he had not already fallen, since the ground around him was littered with dead bodies. He realized the enemy did not know his identity or he would have either been slain or taken prisoner long before now.

Backing to the door, he suddenly felt a hand on his shoulder.

He swung around, his sword poised and ready to strike, until his eyes met and locked with those of Count Chapin d'Arcy. Relief flooded through his body.

"Come with me, Your Highness, you cannot fight the whole of the enemy army by yourself. I had orders from the king to take you to safety."

Alexander was about to refuse when a new wave of

adversaries flooded through the gate, and he realized Count d'Arcy was right.

"I will not run away," he said in a voice that reminded the prime minister of King Alfons.

"There is no shame in retreating when one is outflanked. A great leader will often fall back and regroup, in order to fight another day, Your Highness."

Prince Alexander, seeing the wisdom in the count's statement, finally nodded in agreement. "Let us take up our positions with my mother and father."

The count pulled Alexander away from the door and into the shadows of an alcove where they would attract less attention. "Your Highness . . ." he paused, going down on one knee. "Your Majesty, I regret to inform you that . . . the king and queen . . . are dead. You are now king." Grief shadowed the prime minister's eyes. "Long live the king," he said with conviction.

The heavy hand of anguish permeated every emotion in Alexander's young mind, while inside he battled with pain too horrible to deal with. He could not bear to think about his gentle mother's eyes closed forever. How could death claim his father, who had so much strength and courage? He wanted to lash out at the enemy who had deprived him of his beloved parents.

"No, it cannot be!" he raged. "I will kill them all for this."

Chapin tried to take the young king's arm, but Alexander spun away from him.

"I am very grieved on behalf of our country and yourself, Your Majesty. But surely you can see it is imperative that you leave with me now. The best way you can strike back at the enemy is to live to be crowned."

Alexander stared down at his blood-covered hand, and shook his head in bewilderment. "I do not want to be king. I would have been satisfied to serve my father for the rest of my life." At the moment, he appeared more like a young boy seeking comfort than a king. "How can I live if they are dead?"

"You will live because you must, sire. It is what your father would have expected of you."

Alexander's eyes met the prime minister's. "My sister, Jahane . . . is she safe?"

"Yes, for the moment. She is with the archbishop. He asked me to take you to join them."

Alexander stared blankly at Count d'Arcy. "I must not give up the fight," he said, his hand tightening on the hilt of his sword. "I must avenge my mother and father!"

Chapter Three

Alexander saw the last of the loyal defenders cut down and the enemy finally break through to the castle. He had no will to resist when Chapin d'Arcy shoved him into the shadows and penned him against the wall, warning him to remain silent.

When the enemy had disappeared inside the castle, the courtyard became strangely quiet, and Chapin drew his grief-stricken charge across the courtyard, hoping to get him away to safety. He paused when he heard the sound of approaching riders, and he pulled Alexander back into the shadows, waiting to see if the newcomers were friend or foe.

Alexander's hand tightened on the hilt of his sword when he saw his Uncle Reynard, Duke Maxime, ride up at the head of a column of soldiers.

Unlike the other members of the royal family, Reynard was dark complected, with black hair and steel-gray eyes. Women had always flattered and spoiled him, for he was handsome of face. He was a vain man who usually dressed in black since he thought it complimented his coloring.

The duke dismounted and glanced around at the destruction with satisfaction. Then he raised his voice, and it rang out through the courtyard with jubilation.

"Neatly done, the battle is ours." Reynard raised his

gloved hand. "We are triumphant!"

Chapin d'Arcy had to hold Alexander back by sheer force.

At that moment, several of Reynard's soldiers came rushing out of the castle. They were led by Count Jacques Arville, a despicable man of small intellect, who was always ready to do Reynard's bidding. Bony, and looking very like a skeleton, with yellow skin stretched taut over his sunken face, his eyes glowed with excitement. He could hardly control his elation as he made his report to the duke.

"The king and queen are dead, but I couldn't find the prince or princess."

"Have the bodies of my brother and his wife prepared for a state funeral," Reynard ordered. "I'm sure the people will insist on having their day of mourning before we celebrate our victory."

Alexander's body shook with rage, and Count d'Arcy could no longer hold him back. Breaking free, the boy leaped atop a burning cart and catapulted onto the wall so he stood above his uncle's head. "Not yet a triumph, Uncle. You still have me to deal with."

Reynard turned cold eyes on his nephew, then an evil smile curved his lips. Snapping his fingers, he motioned to his men to take aim on the boy.

The duke's men hesitated, knowing Alexander, by rights of succession, was now king.

That gave Chapin d'Arcy time to draw his pistol and train it on Reynard. Stepping forward, the count placed his body between Alexander and his uncle. "Hold, Your Grace. Would you murder your brother's son, and the rightful heir to the throne, before a witness?"

"Ah, the good prime minister. I should have known you were at the bottom of the mysterious disappearance of my niece and nephew. Are you still playing the faithful watchdog?" Reynard sneered.

35

Chapin d'Arcy's eyes were cold with contempt. "Yes, a watchdog to ferret out a traitor in our midst."

Reynard's eyes narrowed. "Careful, Prime Minister; I will be your king."

"Never *my* king, Your Grace. You killed *my* king. And now Prince Alexander is the rightful ruler."

Reynard's white teeth flashed when he smiled, and he worked his fingers into his black leather gloves. "Surely you are mistaken, d'Arcy. I have killed no one. And as for Prince Alexander," he shrugged, "he is but a boy and unprepared for such a tremendous responsibility."

Alexander drew himself up proudly. "Unprepared or no, I am king, Uncle." With the desire for vengeance burning in his eyes, the boy raised his sword, taking aim at his uncle's heart. "It may have been another who killed my father and mother, but it was your treacherous mind that plotted their deaths. For this you shall die, traitor!"

A sinister smile transformed the duke's face. "I will not die by your hand, Nephew." He nodded to his man, Count Arville, who stood on his right. "Shoot him."

Several things happened at once: Chapin ran toward Alexander; a volley of shots rang out just as Alexander's sword sailed through the air, and the blade slashed across his uncle's face, the impact knocking Reynard to the ground. Then Alexander reeled from the bullets that riddled his body. He teetered on the edge of the wall and fell backward, down the cliff, lost in the swirling sea that hammered against the castle walls.

Chapin, in several leaps, reached the top of the wall, glancing down in horror. He knew that even if the bullets had not killed the young king, the surging tide would have smashed his body against the rocks. No one could have survived such a fall!

The duke gained his feet and ran a hand down his cheek where the blood was flowing from the gash on his face. "Bring the prime minister to me," he ordered, turning away and walking purposely toward the castle.

A voice boomed out, stopping Reynard in his tracks. "And ye shall bear the mark of Cain, for ye have slain your brother," Serafimo, Archbishop of Balmarhea, cried out. "Will you not slay me as well? I am also your brother."

Reynard spun around, staring at his younger brother with hate-filled eyes. Serafimo, seeing the bloody, open gash on Reynard's face and the malignant glint in his eyes, witnessed a side of his brother he had never observed before.

Reynard walked slowly toward Serafimo, his eyes piercing and cunning. "Will you condemn me without a trial, Brother?"

"I am sickened at the sight of you. I was witness to the death of our nephew just now, and I blame myself for being too late to save him from your villainy."

Reynard noticed for the first time that Serafimo held a small, blanket-clad figure, and his eyes gleamed. "So, *you* have the child."

Serafimo drew back a step, blaming himself for jeopardizing his niece. Thinking he would be able to prevent Reynard from harming Alexander had caused his anger to overrule his good judgment and expose their presence to Reynard.

"Even you would not dare to harm the Princess Jahane while she is under the protection of the Church," Serafimo declared. "Have you not killed enough of your family today? Do you also want the blood of your innocent niece on your hands?"

"Give the girl to me, Serafimo. You have my word no harm will befall her. I may even see that she is placed on the throne."

Now Serafimo smiled. "Yes, you would place the princess on the throne so you could rule through her. But you cannot have her, Reynard. Jahane will be taken to a place

37

of safety, and one day she will return and take her rightful place as queen of Balmarhea."

Reynard smiled maliciously, wiping the blood from his cheek as he slowly advanced toward his brother. "And who will aid you in your folly?" he asked silkily, throwing Serafimo off guard.

Without any warming, Reynard sprang forward, grabbed the child, and leaped away.

The sudden movement awoke Jahane, and in her confusion, she smiled up at her Uncle Reynard, who had always been kind to her; but his eyes were cold as he glanced down at her now.

Turning back to Serafimo, Reynard smirked. Then his voice rang out loudly as he addressed his men. "The Archbishop of Balmarhea is under my protection. He is harmless enough now. As for the prime minister," Reynard ordered, "slay him!"

Captain Jonah Meredith and his two men passed through the near-deserted streets of Montique without being challenged. When they approached the open gates that led to the courtyard of the castle, they proceeded cautiously.

Jonah heard shots being fired, and he quickly motioned for his men to take cover. He watched in disbelief as a young boy, about his son's age, plummeted from the castle wall into the churning surf below.

In the shadows of the great tower, with his two crew members at his side, Captain Meredith then saw his old friend, Chapin D'arcy, fall to his knees, mortally wounded.

Without pausing to consider the danger to himself, the captain rushed forward.

Avoiding the dead bodies that littered the ground, Jonah made his way to the prime minister's side, cursing himself for not arriving in time to prevent Chapin's death.

"Jonah," the count murmured through a haze of pain. "I knew you would come tonight — but you are too late . . . too late, my friend."

"For God's sake, what's happened here?" Jonah demanded.

"The king and queen . . . are dead. The prince, too." Chapin raised up and grasped the front of Jonah's jacket. "The child, you must save the child."

"What child?"

"The daughter. Take her away to safety. Please, I ask you in the name of friendship." Chapin pointed to Reynard. "There, see, the duke has her. He will kill the child if you do not save her."

"If it can be accomplished, it shall be done, my friend," Jonah assured him.

With a sigh, as if his mind were at rest, Chapin went limp, and Jonah knew he was dead!

Pushing his grief aside, the captain stood up, ready to face the duke. "I'll take that child," he insisted, his voice coming out in a hiss, for he believed the child to be his friend's daughter.

Reynard stiffened, glaring at the stranger. "Who are you?"

"Never mind who I am," Jonah snarled. "Just hand that child over to me."

Reynard stared past the stranger, noticing the two heavily armed companions who stood just behind him. Since his own men had disappeared inside the castle, and he was unarmed, Reynard stalled for time. "What right have you to demand anything from me? This child belongs to me now."

"No! You have no right to her," the archbishop spoke up. "Give her over to his man, Reynard. For the love of God, do not use her in your vicious game."

Reynard glanced at his brother before landing a heavily

39

booted foot in the archbishop's midsection. The force of the blow sent Serafimo sprawling down the steps, where he landed in a heap.

Jonah heard the child scream in fear as she tried to struggle out of the duke's arms. Always a man of quick action, he stepped forward and rammed his pistol against Reynard's heart.

"I have neither the time nor the inclination to argue with you, so hand the child over. I have no love for people who murder children and brutalize men of the cloth."

At that moment Count Arville saw that the duke was in trouble and hurried to the rescue. "Say the word, Your Grace, and this man is dead." The count aimed his weapon at Jonah.

"Call your man off," Jonah warned.

"He will kill you if I give the order," Reynard threatened.

"Even if he does, you will not live to celebrate." Jonah cocked the hammer on his pistol. "Hand her over—now!"

"You'll regret this," Reynard said in his silken voice.

"Perhaps, but that's not your concern. What should concern you is that you just killed my friend, and that I intend to rescue this child because he asked it of me with his dying breath. Now, relinquish her or die!"

Reynard watched the cold eyes that met his unwaveringly, and he knew that the man would not hesitate to shoot. He could see his plans to be king thwarted by this foreigner. He had no alternative but to do as the man ordered.

Angrily thrusting the child forward, Reynard was further enraged when Jahane stopped crying as soon as the stranger took her in his arms.

"This isn't finished," Reynard warned, carefully studying the man's face so he would know him the next time they met.

"Probably not," the captain agreed.

"I'll find her wherever you take her. And there is not a

40

corner in the world where you will be safe from my wrath."

Jonah ignored his threat. "Turn around," he ordered.

Reynard's smile was sinister, but he complied. Once his back was turned, Jonah brought the handle of his pistol down on the duke's head and watched him crumple to the ground, unconscious.

Seeing that his men had taken aim on the duke's man, Jonah clutched the child in his arms and quickly moved to the fallen priest.

Bending down to him, the captain asked with concern: "Are you in danger here? May I help you escape, Father?"

Serafimo painfully raised up on his elbow and struggled to his feet with Jonah's assistance. "Are you Count d'Arcy's American friend?"

"Yes," Jonah answered sadly. "But Chapin is dead."

"I know — I saw him fall. That's why you must take the child to safety as he would have had he lived. Leave this island immediately, and do not stop until you have put an ocean between her and Reynard."

"I don't understand what has happened here," Jonah confessed.

"There's not time to explain, my son, but I will caution you to hide this child well. God will reward you for what you do tonight."

"Tell me why the duke wants Count d'Arcy's daughter."

"She is . . . is . . . It is enough for you to know that men died here tonight so she might live. If Reynard gets his hands on her again, he will slay her. You must go — Hurry," Serafimo urged.

"But why is she so important?"

The archbishop had no choice but to trust this man. "The child is the Princess Jahane," he admitted. "She is heir to the throne of Balmarhea. Reynard had her entire family killed tonight, and by rights she is now queen. You can see why she must be protected."

41

Jonah glanced quickly at the fair-haired child who had fallen asleep in his arms. He felt the heaviness of the responsibility that had been thrust upon him. He could not leave her behind if this man, Reynard, was going to kill her. So he made a quick decision. "You must come with me also, Father, for I do not believe the man will allow you to live, either."

"I am safe enough, my son. Do not be deceived by these humble robes. Reynard would not dare kill the Archbishop of Balmarhea. He will want me alive because he will be unable to control the people without me."

Serafimo placed his hands upon the head of the sleeping princess, giving her his blessing. "Take care of my niece, Captain. The future of Balmarhea rests in your hands." Tucking the blanket securely around Jahane, he quickly placed a kiss on her brow. "Go, now. When it is safe to bring her home, I shall come for her. Where will I find you?"

"I am Captain Jonah Meredith of the *Boston Clipper*. My home is Boston."

"Not anymore," the archbishop said regretfully. "Not if you value the lives of your family. Do not underestimate Reynard, for after tonight he will want you dead. He will find out the name of your ship, and he will follow you to Boston. I implore you to hide the child from him."

"You can trust me, Your Eminence. Reynard will not find us," Jonah vowed, already concerned for the safety of his own family.

Glancing down at Reynard's unconscious body, Jonah once again cocked the hammer of his pistol. "If this man is dead, the princess does not need to flee, and my family will not be in danger."

The archbishop intervened. "No, my son. Neither you nor I can have his death on our conscience. I do not believe you have ever killed an enemy who could not defend himself, and I— Reynard is my brother."

42

Serafimo saw the captain's face freeze in amazement.

"There is no more time to explain, Captain Meredith. Leave quickly, and I will try to hold Reynard's men here until you are safely away. Whenever you are able, let me know where you have taken Jahane."

Aware of the need for haste, Jonah could do no more than nod. With an urgency in his step, he moved toward the gate, his men falling in behind him after knocking the luckless Count Arville unconscious.

They moved out of the castle gate, barely avoiding being seen by the horsemen who rode into the courtyard.

As the three Americans ran through the deserted streets, shots rang out, and Jonah watched one of his men fall with a fatal head wound.

Running past the city gate, he hurried in the direction of the *Boston Clipper,* his progress hampered by the child in his arms.

Jonah did not hear the bullet that tore into his flesh. He was unaware that he had been shot until he felt a stinging sensation, and then weakness slowed his steps. In spite of his attempt to stay on his feet, he fell to his knees, taking care not to drop the child.

Several more shots rang out, and his other crew member fell. Jonah, too weak to go to his aid, called out. There was no reply. He did not have to be told that his man was dead.

The child began to whimper, and Jonah regretted that he had not the strength to take her to safety.

Chapter Four

When Cord reached shallow water, he waded ashore, almost stumbling over the longboat that his father had abandoned earlier in the evening.

The darkened night, which had aided Cord in escaping the ship unobserved, hindered his progress now that he was on land. Shadows enveloped him, and he was surrounded by unrecognizable animal sounds. And of course, there was always the distant discharge of gunfire, reminding him that his father could be in danger.

Cord's clothing was dripping wet and clung to his strong, young body. He shivered more from fear of the unknown than from being cold. He wasn't sure what he should do next, only that it was important that he find his father without delay.

He was unfamiliar with the island, and uncertain which direction his father had taken. Choosing the obvious path, he walked in the direction of the distant lights that surely would prove to be a city.

It certainly would have helped had he known what his father had been planning to do on this island.

Cord pressed on for what seemed an eternity, ignoring the discomfort of his wet clothing. His steps were unsure as he hurried across the unfamiliar terrain.

When he finally reached a well-worn path, he paused,

staring at the flames that licked at the sky. What he had believed to be lights from a city were in fact fire! It appeared the whole countryside was ablaze!

Suddenly the sound of gunfire ripped through the night air, and bullets went whizzing past Cord's head. Quickly, he ducked behind the trunk of a palm tree, his heart pounding, his eyes straining in the darkness. Hearing muffled voices nearby, he flattened his back against the palm tree so his presence would not be detected.

The moon chose that moment to come out from behind the clouds, casting a pale light upon the land.

Cord could make out the figure of a man, who was obviously heading in the direction of the *Boston Clipper.* When the man stumbled and fell, Cord recognized his father. He watched as his father attempted to rise, only to fall again to his knees. What was the blanket-wrapped object his father was carrying that seemed to impede his progress?

Jonah struggled to his feet, knowing the child would die if he did not make it back to the ship. Unsteadily, he moved in the direction of the longboat, praying he would make it before the threatened dizziness engulfed him.

Cord heard a loud voice call out in French: "Stop the American!" This was followed by a loud volley of gunfire.

Realizing his father was being pursued, Cord ran down the path to aid him.

The boy was grateful that the clouds moved across the moon once more, and he blessed the blackness which would surely conceal his father from the men who chased him. His lungs burned and his breath came out in painful gasps, but his footsteps did not lag.

There was no time to wonder why his father was being fired upon, but where were the two crewmen who had accompanied his father ashore tonight?

When he reached the water's edge, Cord came upon the empty longboat, and realized frantically that he would have to backtrack, for he must have passed his father in the darkness. He dared not call out lest he draw the attention of the men who were chasing his father.

When Cord heard the sound that resembled a child crying, his astonished footsteps led him in that direction. Stumbling through the darkness, he tripped over a prone body and quickly scrambled to his feet.

With a pounding heart, he whispered urgently, "Father, is that you?"

"Cord, Son" came the weak reply. "You'll have to help me. I'm wounded."

"The others, Father—where are they?"

"They are dead."

Without further urging, Cord reached out and took his father's arm and tried to pull him to his feet, but his father was too weak to stand and slumped down once more.

When the boy felt a hot, sticky substance clinging to his hands he knew it was his father's blood!

"Don't worry about me, Cord," Jonah pleaded weakly. "You must take this child to the ship and tell Thadeus to set sail at once."

Cord was too concerned about his father to wonder what child his father was talking about. "No, Father," he said with determination. "Don't ask me to abandon you."

"Then put the child in the longboat and come back for me . . . but hurry, Son."

Jonah shoved the bundle at him with his last bit of strength. Confused, Cord's arms closed about the child. He was aware of the need for haste, so he ran toward the longboat, quickly placing his charge in the bottom of the boat. He then hurried back to his father.

Jonah Meredith was a big man, so it took every ounce of Cord's strength to assist him down the beach and into the longboat. Now the French voices were growing louder and more angry, and several random shots were fired with dangerous accuracy.

"Will no one else be coming, Father?" Cord asked, glancing back up the beach, but of course seeing nothing in the obscure darkness.

"No, Cord. I told you they were dead," his father answered, reaching out and pulling the child into his protective arms. "My God, they were all slain," he moaned. "The king and queen, the prince, Chapin, my men . . . all dead."

Cord could not understand his father's mutterings. He wondered who this child was and why they were taking her to the ship. There were many unanswered questions, but he pushed them to the back of his mind so he could concentrate on getting them safely aboard the *Boston Clipper*.

Running beside the boat, he pushed off until he was past the waves that threatened to drive him back to shore; he then jumped in the boat, took the oars in hand, and rowed toward the ship. Straining against the tide that surged into the lagoon, he made slow progress.

Just behind him, Cord could hear the confusion of their pursuers, who must have spotted them by now. Amid flying bullets, he applied the oars, steadily moving the longboat toward the ship while fear ate at his mind. He had to get his father to the *Boston Clipper* so the ship's doctor could help him.

The sound of gunfire must have alerted the crew, because when the longboat finally bumped against the ship, helpful hands pulled them up the rope ladder and onto the deck.

After Captain Meredith had given the order to set sail at once, he thrust the child into Cord's arms and collapsed at his feet.

Several men lifted their captain and carried him below to the doctor's cabin, while Cord hurried after them, unmindful of the sleeping child he carried in his arms.

Dr. Bridey bent over his captain. Seeing the severity of

47

his wounds, his eyes met Thadeus's and he shook his head grimly.

"I know it's bad," Jonah gritted out as the doctor cut away his bloody shirt and tossed it aside.

"The best I can do is give you something for the pain," the doctor said regretfully. Even as he bound the wound, blood was soaking through. "The bullet's gone clean through, Captain. Being it's a stomach wound, you know what that means."

In a voice weakened by pain and loss of blood, the captain spoke so softly that the doctor had to lean forward to catch his words. "I don't want anything to dull the pain. I have to keep a clear head . . . there is so much to do. Everyone leave now; I want to have a private word with my son."

Moving closer, Cord laid the baby down on the bunk beside his father and stared in horror at the blood-soaked cloth that bound his wound. The lad knew little about medicine, but he was afraid his father's injuries were serious indeed.

Cord's mind splintered in pain and confusion, and his heart felt as if it had been trampled on. He refused to believe what he knew in his heart—his father was dying.

"Let me call the doctor back, Father. He can do something for you." Cord wanted to cry, indeed his eyes burned, but not one tear did he shed.

"No, Son, no one can help me now. The sooner you realize that, the better it will be for us both."

Unbearable grief sharpened Cord's mind, and now the tears rolled down his cheeks unashamed.

"Cord, listen to me," his father said with urgency in his voice. "It is imperative that you keep a clear mind and do exactly as I tell you."

"I . . . the doctor . . ."

"No, Cord, the doctor cannot help me now." He grimaced in pain, then his hand came down to rest on the child

48

that was apparently fast asleep and oblivious to the turmoil in the cabin. "You must take this child to your mother, in Boston. I will write a letter instructing her what to do."

Cord shook his head to clear it. His father was depending on him, and he couldn't fail him now. "Who is this child, Father?"

Jonah closed his eyes for a moment, and when he opened them, they were glazed with pain. "This child is very important, Son. I promised Chapin . . . I will be unable to keep that promise, but you shall keep it for me. Do you hear me, Cord? Protect this child with your life."

"Yes, but, Father—"

"Listen to me. The streets of Montique are littered with the bodies of men who died tonight so this baby might live." His voice deepened. "Tell anyone who asks that this is Count Chapin d'Arcy's child. Do you hear me, Cord?"

"Yes, I hear you, but I don't understand anything you are trying to tell me. Why did you risk your life for a child you don't even know?"

Jonah's voice had an edge to it because his strength was waning, and he had to make Cord understand the importance of what he was trying to tell him. "Cord, I already told you, Chapin asked me to."

"But, Father—"

"Cord, heed me well. You are going to be the man of the family now. You are a son whom any man would be proud of. When I am gone, this ship will pass to you. It is the only heritage I can leave you. This is a great responsibility to put on your young shoulders, but I charge you to take good care of your mother—and guard this child well."

Jonah Meredith looked deeply into the eyes of his son, regretting he would not see him grow to manhood. Neither spoke until at last Cord choked out, "I promise I will do as you say, Father."

Jonah nodded, his hand resting on his son's arm. "Take

49

the child away now, Son, and send Thadeus to me. I just want to remind you that Thadeus is my man and you can always look to him for help and advice."

Cord did not want to leave his father, but he had to obey his wishes. "I will remember to look to Thadeus when I need help," he agreed, unable to deal with the grief that lay heavy in his heart.

"Tell your mother . . . tell her that—never mind, she knows how I feel about her." Jonah could feel his strength waning, and the pain was fogging his brain. "Go now, Son," he said weakly. "And God go with you and keep you always."

Cord gently picked up the child and backed toward the door. "I love you, Father."

"I know, Son."

Reluctantly he stepped out the door and closed it softly behind him.

Jonah now allowed a moan of pain to escape his lips. His vision blurred, and he knew he didn't have much time before he lost consciousness. He had sent Cord away, not wanting his son to watch him die. No son should have to witness his father's death.

He had to hold on until Thadeus came—he just had to. There were so many instructions to give. So much to do.

Cord's steps were hesitant as he entered the captain's cabin, where he had been so happy for the last few months at sea with his father. He was in shock, and he could not understand what was happening to his safe little world.

Since it was dark, he carefully felt his way to the cot he had been using and laid the sleeping child down. Then he sank down himself, burying his head in his hands, at last allowing his grief to spill out.

He could hear the wind snapping at the canvasses and feel the ship moving out of the lagoon. Had it only been a short time ago that he had been laughing with his father? How quickly human life could be snuffed out. How vulnerable was the human spirit. Grief was so sharp and cutting that he felt a physical hurt surround his heart.

The child stirred and cried out. Cord picked it up and held it close to his body, rocking it back and forth, giving comfort, while seeking comfort for himself.

Had his father mentioned if the child was a boy or a girl? He couldn't remember.

For over an hour he held the child until it fell asleep. Finally, in a state of exhaustion, he placed the child down and curled up at its side. The swaying of the ship soon lulled him to sleep, but even in his sleep he kept the child close to him. Restless, he would awaken and pull the child into his comforting arms. Thus they slept.

The morning sun streaked across the cloudless sky, penetrating the crack in the porthole covering and falling across Cord's face. He stirred, opened his eyes, and then gazed in astonishment at the child beside him. There could be no mistaking that the child was a girl, for her long golden hair was a mass of ringlets, and her clear blue eyes stared back at him with open curiosity.

He blinked his eyes as the lovely child smiled and patted his face. He realized she was speaking to him in French, a language in which he was proficient.

Suddenly Cord remembered that his father was gravely wounded, and he jumped to his feet. Poking his rumpled shirt in his trousers, he ran his fingers through his hair while he quickly moved to the door.

When he would have left, the girl began crying and holding her arms out to him. With resigned patience, he gathered her to him and moved up the companionway. His footsteps were hurried as he ran to the cabin where his father had been taken the night before.

Thadeus called out to him, "Hold on, Cord, I want to talk to you."

Impatient to see his father, Cord waited for Thadeus to approach. When he saw the first mate's face, he knew without being told that his father was dead. He saw it on the faces of the helmsman and the ship's doctor, who gathered around to bring him comfort.

Cord shook his head in disbelief. No, it wasn't supposed to end like this.

He and his father had started this voyage in high spirits. His father had been his teacher and his friend. Now he was gone.

He pushed against the cabin door, needing proof of his father's death, but Thadeus stopped him.

"He ain't there, Cord. We had him all laid out in his dress uniform for the ceremony."

Shifting the child in his arms, Cord fought against his tears as the heavy hand of sorrow settled on his shoulders. He prayed for the strength to get through this day. He refused to allow the crew to see him cry. His father would expect him to act like a true seaman.

"We are preparing for a burial at sea," Thadeus needlessly informed the lad.

With great inner strength, the young boy met the older man's eyes, knowing that his father would have liked being buried at sea, since he loved the sea so well.

"When will the ceremony begin?" Cord wanted to know, his mind reeling away from the thought of never seeing his beloved father again.

"If it pleases you, we should begin almost immediately. We have just been waiting for you to awaken." For the first time Thadeus glanced at the lovely little girl in Cord's arms. "Here now, let me take her from you. I'll have Cook give her something to eat."

When Cord handed the child to Thadeus, she started screaming at the top of her voice, and she would not be quieted until Cord took her back. She clung to his neck while her sobs subsided, and a defiant glance from her blue eyes dared anyone to try to take her away from him.

Cord found a strange kind of solace in the child's need for him. "It was my father's wish that I keep her with me. I will not be parted from her."

Cord stood dry-eyed as his father's body was tilted toward the water to slip from beneath the American flag and plunge into the unusually calm sea.

When he turned away, the child that had been entrusted to Cord still clung to him. The weight of his charge was light, for she had been placed in his care by his father as a sacred trust. As he glanced into her big blue eyes, he saw adoration reflected there, and his heart melted.

The ship's sailmaster had been most helpful in providing the child with hastily sewn garments.

When Cord had discovered the deep wound on her hand, he had cleansed and bandaged it, wondering what kind of monster could have done such a thing to this lovely young girl.

Cord did not even know this child's name, or anything about her, but he felt a strong bond developing between the two of them. Had not his father lost his life so that this child might live?

Cord made himself a promise that he would never allow anything to happen to her.

She was his responsibility—she belonged to him.

Chapter Five

Reynard swore at the physician who was cleansing the gash on his face.

"I fear you will have a permanent scar, Your Gr— Grace," the man stuttered, knowing how vain the duke was about his appearance. "As for the lump on your head, I believe it is nothing to be concerned about."

The duke pushed the physician aside and ordered him out of the room.

When the doctor had fled, Reynard turned to Count Arville. "Have you found the Princess Jahane?"

"My men are in pursuit of the American sea captain now. I expect it is but a matter of time before they catch up with him, Your Grace."

Reynard glared at the man. "You had better not fail me this time, Count."

Count Arville blinked his eyes, knowing the duke was displeased with him. "Shall I have Her Highness brought to you here at the castle?"

Reynard whirled on the man. "Good God, can I not depend on you to think on your own?" His eyes narrowed angrily. "I want only proof of my niece's death. Make it look like the American killed her."

"What about the prince, Your Grace?"

"Imbecile!" Reynard thundered. "Alexander's body will never be found. You saw him fall into the sea."

Count Arville nodded quickly. "I will see that all is

done, Your Grace."

Reynard smiled in satisfaction. "Leave me now. I have matters that require my attention."

When he was alone, Reynard glanced around the great hall, a malevolent smile on his lips.

"All mine," he whispered, with the feeling of power and possession surging through his body.

His eyes fell on the throne, and he moved around to the back of it, touching the lever which had been cleverly concealed among the rose carving. His hand trembled as he turned the lever and waited for the secret panel to slide open.

His heart stopped beating as he reached inside the compartment. He had the world at his fingertips. The scepter would give him absolute power and untold wealth!

A great oath issued from his lips. The scepter was gone!

Boundless rage ignited within his mind, and his agonized cry rose up to echo around the great hall.

Why had he not foreseen that Alfons would find a new hiding place for the scepter? Without the scepter, he could only be a figurehead, never the king.

Pounding his fists against the wall, he realized that Alexander probably knew where the scepter had been hidden. What a fool he had been to order the boy's death before he had the scepter safely in his hands.

Again he reached into the secret panel and discovered a parchment wedged in the back. Staring at the paper, his eyes narrowed as he read the words written in his dead brother's bold hand:

If you read this, Reynard, then my worst suspicions will be confirmed, and your hands will be stained with my blood. You have betrayed me, but my satisfaction will be knowing you will never find the scepter or rule Balmarhea. May God have mercy on your soul, for you have sinned against Him and me.

It seemed his brother had won once again—even after death. A wild cry rose from Reynard's throat, and he shook his fist toward the heavens.

"I will have the scepter, Alfons. I will be king!"

It was several hours before daylight when the disheartened Archbishop of Balmarhea dismounted and lit his lantern before making his way down the sandy beach below the castle.

His heart was heavy with dread. He owed it to his dead brother to find Alexander's body, if he could, so he could place the boy beside his mother and father and give him a Christian burial.

As Serafimo watched the waves crash forcefully against the rocks, his small hope that his nephew might have survived was destroyed.

After searching diligently for over an hour, he reluctantly admitted defeat. One last time his eyes ran over the rocks and then out to sea, and he decided Alexander's body must have been washed away with the outgoing tide.

His heart was heavy as he turned back to his horse, and he wondered what this day would bring.

He had little doubt that Reynard's plan was to loudly proclaim that he would find and punish his family's murderers. And some of the people would believe him innocent; while many others would know that Reynard's was the hand that had wrought death and destruction to this land.

Of course, no one would ever put their thoughts into words, for to do so would bring death to them and their families.

Although Serafimo knew the truth, he would have to remain silent, because to speak out would continue the civil war, and there was no need for more bloodshed now.

These were troubled times, and Serafimo knew the

people would need his comfort and guidance. Let the wounds heal. He would bide his time until Jahane was old enough to return and rule Balmarhea.

His foot was in the stirrup, and he was remounting, ready to abandon his search, when he heard a soft moan.

With heart thundering in anticipation, he quickly leaped to the ground, and his footsteps hurried in the direction of the sound.

As he approached two huge rocks that came together in a vee, he swiftly moved over them until he found the battered and bleeding body of his nephew.

"God save us," Serafimo cried, going down on his knees, with hope stirring in his heart. "I would never have thought that you could have survived such a fall," he said, more to himself than to his unconscious nephew. "God in his mercy must have decided to be generous and save your life, Alexander."

He gently raised Alexander's head and almost cried out at the bloody, bruised face.

The boy was unconscious and blood was oozing from several gunshot wounds. His lips were swollen, and it was hard to tell which bones had been broken since he was laying like a tattered rag doll.

Anger burned in the archbishop's heart as he looked upon Reynard's handiwork. He had to keep reminding himself that vengeance belonged to God.

As he touched his nephew's fevered cheek, he realized the boy's injuries must be treated at once. Serafimo knew that although it would be dangerous to move Alexander until the extent of his injuries had been determined, it was equally dangerous to allow Reynard to find him still alive.

Removing his robe, and placing it across Alexander to keep him warm, the archbishop hurried toward his horse, knowing he had to have assistance to remove Alexander to safety.

Two hours later, just as the sun made its appearance for the day, Serafimo and his servant, Everett, placed Alexander's battered body on a stiff board and carefully lifted him onto an ox-drawn cart.

"Where can we take him, Your Eminence," Everett inquired, "where he will not be discovered? He is extremely weak, and his wounds are so severe that I fear he may not live out the day."

"I have decided we will take him to the monastery in the northern hills. The monks there are well-versed in healing and they are loyal to the Church. As for the prince's condition, I do not believe God has spared his life to have him die on us now, Everett."

"But, Eminence, the monastery is occupied by monks who have taken the vow of silence. They wear hair shirts, and do little but work hard and pray."

The archbishop glanced down at his nephew's pale face. "Perhaps therein lies the prince's salvation. The good monks will not be inclined to ask questions, and they will be even less willing to answer them should others ask."

It was late afternoon, and the sun was sinking in the west as the ox-drawn cart rattled up steep mountain roads.

Serafimo gently held Alexander's head on his lap, cushioning his battered body from the jolts of the rough road. He prayed constantly that the boy would live to one day ascend the throne of Balmarhea.

A wistful smile touched the archbishop's lips as he watched his young nephew's face.

"Your father would have been so proud of you, Alexander." The boy moaned in pain as the cart hit a bump and his body was thrown against Serafimo.

A tear rolled down the archbishop's face as he raised his eyes to the heavens. "If you will allow this boy to live, God, I vow to you that I will have patience and wait for your guidance concerning his future."

He glanced down at Alexander, who was so pale he looked more dead than alive. "He is a good and faithful boy, Lord, and he will make a good king. Spare his life, so he might grow up to serve you and the people of Balmarhea."

A sudden feeling of peacefulness descended on the archbishop, and he smiled. When he placed his hand on Alexander's brow, it felt somewhat cooler.

"Fear not, my king, for you are in God's hands, not Reynard's, and it is my belief that God has a purpose for you."

Reynard pointed his jeweled finger accusingly. "You dare to come before me, Count Arville, and tell me you allowed the American to sail away with my niece?" he snapped. "You simpleton, must I do everything myself? Am I surrounded by imbeciles?"

Arville ducked his head in remorse. "I am most distressed, Your Grace, but—"

Reynard moved across the room, his black cape flying out behind him, the bandages on his face giving him a sinister appearance.

"Spare me your excuses, Count. You carelessly allowed the Princess Jahane to escape, and I will hear none of your sniveling."

"I am sorry, Your Gr—"

"Silence!" Reynard snarled. "Leave me now. I have no wish to look upon the face of incompetence."

"Yes, Your Grace, but first, may I ask what you want done with Count d'Arcy's daughter?"

Reynard whirled around to face Count Arville. "Why should I care what you do with the prime minister's daughter? She is of no use to me." Suddenly his eyes filled with interest. "How did you come by the girl?"

"When you sent men to the prime minister's house, he was not at home—" Arville looked uncertain for a moment, cleared his voice, and continued. "It seems they were rough with the prime minister's wife . . . and . . . well, she died."

"Get on with it," Reynard said impatiently.

"They brought the girl to me, because at first they thought she was the Princess Jahane. It is uncanny how much the two girls look alike. Both have the same coloring and the same—"

"How old is the child?" Reynard wanted to know.

"I am not sure, Your Grace. I would guess somewhere around the Princess Jahane's age."

Reynard's eyes took on an inner glow, and his features sharpened. "So, you say d'Arcy's daughter looks much like my niece." He stroked his chin, a malevolent smile on his face. "You are mistaken, Count." Laughter rolled off his lips. "Surely that girl is the Princess Jahane."

Arville protested. "But, no, Your Gr—"

Reynard held up his hand to silence Count Arville. "Take the girl to the convent outside the city, and tell the good sisters that it is my wish they look after her. Tell no one her true identity, and see that she is kept hidden until I say otherwise."

Count Arville did not understand the duke's sudden interest in d'Arcy's daughter, or why he was mistakenly insisting she was the Princess Jahane. But what did it matter as long as the duke had forgotten to be angry with him?

"It will be as you say, Your Grace. No one will ever know what happened to d'Arcy's daughter."

As an afterthought, Reynard added, "Instruct the sisters that the girl is to be well-educated. I have plans for her future."

Chapter Six

Boston

Thadeus balanced the dainty porcelain teacup on his lap, feeling most uncomfortable. He sat on the satin slipcovers, wishing this interview was over.

He cleared his throat before taking a sip of the tea, trying not to wrinkle his nose in distaste at drinking what he considered to be a woman's brew.

His eyes swept the face of his dead captain's widow. It was obvious that Cord got his dark coloring from his mother, Thadeus observed, as he watched Maggie Meredith pour herself a cup of tea. Her eyes were a soft brown, and her dark hair, though drawn away from her face severely, did not detract from her loveliness.

Thadeus was impressed, as he had always been, by her gracious manner. The captain had once told him that his wife had come from an elite Boston family and had been disinherited when she had gone against their wishes and married him.

"Would you say my husband suffered before he died, Mr. Kramer?" she asked, predictably.

"No, madame," he replied, seeing no reason to add to her grief. "The captain didn't suffer overmuch."

She broke the seal on the letter Thadeus had just delivered to her, and shook her head in confusion as she read it. "I do not understand some of my husband's meanings. Can you enlighten me, Mr. Kramer?"

"I will try, madame."

Thadeus noticed the circles under Mrs. Meredith's eyes, and he knew that the news of her husband's death had been devastating to her. He felt pain at her grief, but did not know how to comfort her.

"I stayed away until now, madame, to allow you time to grow used to your . . . to the captain's . . . death. I promised him the night he passed away that I would relay to you his wishes concerning your future."

She touched the letter lovingly. "I have been most anxious to know about the charming little girl that Cord brought home. My son could tell me very little about her, except that he believes she is Chapin d'Arcy's daughter."

"I fear I cannot enlighten you as to her identity, and anything I might say would only be speculation, since the captain didn't confide in me, madame."

"May I assume my husband knew he was dying when he gave you this letter?"

"Yes, madame, you could assume that."

Maggie Meredith glanced down at the letter, trying to decipher the remainder of the scribbled message.

While Thadeus looked on, she read the words that had been written the night Jonah had died.

Suddenly she gasped. "Dear Lord, the child is . . ."

She fell silent as she read the next line, where her husband warned her to tell no one the identity of her charge. She could hardly credit that the little girl she had taken into her home was a royal princess!

Maggie read on.

Jonah warned her that the child's life would be in danger if the wrong people were to find her.

She glanced up at Thadeus's serious expression, knowing she could not even tell him the child's identity.

Realizing she had been silent for a long time, and that she was making Thadeus uncomfortable, she smiled at him apologetically.

He smiled back. "Everyone on the ship grew quite fond of the little lady, Mrs. Meredith, and I told them I'd ask you how she's faring."

"Oh, Mr. Kramer, the child has been quite a joy to me. She is so lovely, but she is withdrawn most of the time and is happiest when she is with Cord. I can only imagine what she must have suffered. Sometimes at night she will awaken screaming, and only Cord can comfort her. I admit it near breaks my heart to see her so frightened. After reading my husband's letter, I think I understand why."

For a moment her eyes wandered around the room, her thoughts elsewhere. Then she spoke softly. "Did my husband tell you anything about the large red stone she has with her?"

"No, I know nothing about that."

"I am not an expert on precious stones, but I am almost certain that it is a ruby." She shrugged. "Anyway, it seems to mean a great deal to the child, although I cannot imagine how it came to be in her possession. She insists on keeping it with her at all times."

"She's a lucky little girl to have you, madame."

"It hasn't always been easy. At first she had no knowledge of English. It is fortunate that Cord and I know French, or we would have had trouble communicating with her. However, she is very bright and is learning English."

"What do you call her, madame? We never knew what her name was."

Maggie paused, her husband's warning still clear in her mind. But what harm could it do to tell Thadeus the child's name?

"We have discovered her name is Jahane," she finally answered. "Is that not unusual?"

"Yes, most unusual, madame." Thadeus agreed. "But

then I suspect that name's French, don't you?" Thadeus said, as if that explained everything.

"Yes, I suppose it is."

"Me and the crew was wondering if you are planning to keep her with you, then?"

"Yes, it was my husband's wish."

Now Thadeus shifted in his chair uneasily. "I am most distressed that it falls to me to pass the captain's last instructions on to you, and I hope you will understand them, for I do not."

"Tell me what he said."

"I know this will cause great hardship on you, Mrs. Meredith, but this is what he told me. You are to sell the house and property as secretly and as quickly as possible. The captain suggested that his attorney would be able to handle the details for you. He wanted you to then take young Cord and the girl and leave Boston, telling no one of your destination."

She did not flinch at his harsh instructions. "Sell everything and move away? There must be urgent cause if my husband has asked this of me."

"He told me that it was important that you hide the child, because there will be those who will try to find her—desperate men who have it in their minds to kill her, though he didn't say why."

Maggie Meredith nodded. She knew why.

"The captain said to impress on you that this would surely happen if certain unscrupulous villains got their hands on her. He seemed to think that you and Cord might be in danger as well." Thadeus hesitated, and then, after drawing a deep breath, continued. "Now, Mrs. Meredith, I know it might sound like the captain was delirious and didn't know what he was talking about, but I believe he had a clear head, no matter how incredible this all sounds."

"I believe so, too, Mr. Kramer."

Maggie stood up and took the teacup from the first mate. "I want to thank you for your kindness in coming here today. I know it had to be very difficult for you."

"I'd do anything the captain asked me, madame."

"Even to the extent of pretending to like that tea, Mr. Kramer?" Her laughter was soft. "You will find brandy on the sideboard. Help yourself." She smiled knowingly. "I believe it will be a drink more to your liking."

Thadeus looked at her gratefully.

She was lost in thought as she watched him pour a small amount of brandy into a crystal glass. "Did my husband have any other message for me?"

"Yes, he implied that San Francisco might be a good place for you to settle. The captain said to remind you that he had a second cousin there who would be of help to you."

"Yes, I remember him," she replied as calmly as if they had been discussing the weather, instead of disrupting her whole life.

She showed no pain at being asked to move away from Boston and everything that was dear and familiar to her. She did not cry or question, but accepted her dead husband's decision with a clear understanding. Thadeus could easily see why his captain had loved her so well.

"Were there any other instructions?" she wanted to know.

Thadeus nodded. "Not instructions exactly. The captain said it might be wise to change the name of the *Boston Clipper*, and he said if you were in agreement, I could captain her until Cord was old enough to take her helm."

"Yes, I would like that, Mr. Kramer. I know my husband placed great trust in your ability, so we must see that his orders are followed explicitly."

Thadeus finished the brandy and set the glass down. "I'll be making the ship ready, madame. Should you need me, Cord will know where to find me. I'll be waiting to transport you to San Francisco, or wherever you desire, as soon as you are ready."

Maggie walked Thadeus to the door and watched him mount his horse and ride away. With a heavy sigh, she turned back into the house and stood at the window, glancing at the park across the street.

She would honor her husband's wishes, even though she did not understand them.

She pressed her face against the windowpane, remembering when he had brought her to this house as a bride. "Oh, Jonah, how grievously I shall miss you, and how painful it will be to leave this house you built for me."

She smiled and dabbed at her eyes with a handkerchief. "But you will always be with me, won't you, my dearest love, no matter where I go."

Chapter Seven

Balmarhea, three years later

Alexander took an unsteady step, felt the room whirl, and fell to the floor.

Learning to walk again had proven to be a painfully slow process. At times he would be discouraged, but some driving force always pushed him onward.

He held out his hand for Brother Lazarus, his sole companion, to help him to his feet.

"I will not give up!" Alexander exclaimed with determination, not expecting an answer, since the monk who assisted him back to bed had taken a vow of silence. "I will walk again. The day will come when I will leave this place forever."

After the prince was propped up against two pillows, he looked at Brother Lazarus, whose primary duty for the last three years had been to nurse him back to health. "Do you realize I have never heard the sound of your voice?" he said in irritation. "It has been months since I have heard anyone's voice but my own."

Brother Lazarus merely smiled indulgently.

At times Alexander would become impatient with the monk because he was always so amiable. He would even have welcomed the man's anger if only it had been put into words.

"Why can't you tell me what is going on in Montique?" he questioned. "Have you any word of what is happening on Balmarhea, Brother Lazarus?"

The monk only shook his head, his eyes sadly sweeping Alexander's face, then he smiled with kind forbearance, and walked toward the door, his coarse brown robe flapping against his legs and his sandals moving noiselessly across the stone floor.

When Alexander heard the door close, he felt the ache of loneliness. It was sometimes unbearable not knowing what was going on in the island; it was worse not being able to leave this room.

There were days when the young boy thought he would go mad if he didn't hear the sound of another human voice. But in his helpless state, Alexander was forced to endure the loneliness of the monastery's existence.

In the past three years he had existed in a haze of pain. There had been times when he had prayed for death. Though much of the physical pain had subsided, the pain of his parents' deaths was still with him.

He had questions that demanded answers, and there was no one he could ask.

Where was Jahane? Had she suffered the same fate as his mother and father? His Uncle Serafimo had assured him that she was safe, but he had no proof.

Alexander glanced about the room that had been his home for the past three years. Accustomed to silken bed hangings and plush rugs on the floor, he detested this sparsely furnished room. The walls were bare but for the wooden cross which hung above his bed. The trappings consisted of a cot, a straight-back chair, and a stand near his bed where his medicines and a water pitcher were kept for his convenience.

In frustration and anger, Alexander picked up the water pitcher and flung it across the room, feeling some satisfaction when it shattered against the wall.

"Why will no one talk to me?" he shouted. "Why must I be forced to endure this silence? I am not a monk—I am a man!"

The door was suddenly whisked open, and Alexander stared into the shining blue eyes of his uncle Serafimo. The archbishop looked stiff and majestic in his silken regalia, but the smile on his lips softened his austere expression.

The archbishop had only visited twice in the three years the young prince had been at the monastery.

Alexander had long ago decided he would not talk to his uncle when he finally made his next visit, but that decision was forgotten at seeing Serafimo.

"Uncle, I thought you had condemned me to a life of poverty, silence . . . and celibacy." Alexander's eyes were searching. "Am I not forgotten?"

Serafimo looked the young man over. The archbishop could see from the stubble on his chin that Alexander now shaved. He had grown, and his health had obviously improved, though his temper had not.

"How could I forget you? Though you do not yet wear the crown, you are my rightful king, sire. If I have stayed away, it was not from neglect, but rather because Reynard has me watched day and night, and I dare not lead him to you."

"I was not meant to be an invalid, Uncle," Alexander declared, still not pacified. "I have few pleasures to pass the time. I do not enjoy the company of monks."

The archbishop glanced at the broken fragments of the smashed water pitcher. "I see you are keeping your sword arm exercised."

Alexander's lip curled in scorn. "There is no one here who knows anything about swordplay, so I cannot practice. I could be dead for all these monks care."

Serafimo arched his eyebrow. "It seems your spirit has healed more quickly than your body. Knowing your temperament, I can only imagine how sorely you have taken to your convalescence."

"I don't wish to discuss my infirmities. Tell me instead what is happening in Montique," Alexander growled fervently. "What deviltry is Uncle Reynard up to?"

"Reynard has set himself up as head of the Council of Lords, but, as you know, their power is limited." Serafimo shook his head. "Reynard is still trying to find the scepter. He has had many walls torn out of the castle and stones taken out of the floor, but without success."

Alexander raised up on his elbows. "I must go to Montique. I will never allow Uncle Reynard to sit on my father's throne."

"Patience, Alexander. There will be a time to face Reynard, but it is not yet. We must be sure when you stand before him that you have the means to bring him down."

Alexander's eyes spit fire. "My sword will bring him down."

"No, Alexander. To act prematurely would only be folly, for Reynard will not easily relinquish his hold on Balmarhea."

Alexander's eyes gleamed with fury. "The people will assemble around me, for I am their rightful king. I will take the throne by force if there is no other way. It would please me to run my sword through Uncle Reynard's evil heart."

Serafimo was saddened to see that Alexander was eaten up with bitterness and hatred. The boy had too much time to brood. "It is true that most of your subjects will stand with you, Alexander. They will fight for you to the end. But is this what you want for them?"

"What do you mean?"

"I mean a good king thinks of the welfare of his people first."

Alexander's eyes were cold. "I have thought of little else."

"My advice is to wait until the moment is right before you strike. You must mend, and then we must find your sister before we do anything else."

Alexander's expression softened. "The last time you were here, you said you were sending Everett to Boston to find Jahane. How is she? Is she well? When will you bring her back to Balmarhea?"

"I have not yet heard from Everett, but his instructions are to find Jahane and stay near to keep watch on her. Be assured that your sister is in good hands for now, and well out of Reynard's reach. It is better to leave her where she is for a time than to risk her falling into Reynard's hands."

"But what do you know about the American captain who took her away? What if he surrenders her to Reynard."

"No, that will not happen. I saw the captain risk his life for your sister that night he took her to safety. Captain Meredith was Count d'Arcy's friend. I have made some discreet inquiries, and I discovered that he once traded here in Balmarhea, and he is a well-respected gentleman with a son about your age. So, Alexander, try not to worry about Jahane."

The boy nodded, knowing his uncle Serafimo would do what was best for his sister. "But I do miss Jahane, Uncle. She is all I have left."

"I know, Alexander. Have patience just a bit longer. One day the two of you will be reunited."

"You said something that puzzled me, Uncle. You said Reynard had torn down walls trying to find the great scepter. Is it not in its usual hiding place behind the throne?"

A smile lit Serafimo's eyes. "No, your father moved the scepter to a new hiding place, which my brother has been unable to locate. That is why I am urging you to be patient. Reynard cannot be crowned king without the scepter."

71

Alexander's eyes gleamed with interest. "I cannot be crowned king without the scepter either, Uncle. Do you know where it is? My father did not show the new hiding place to me."

"He would have, had you not run off that night, you young hothead. Only Jahane knows where it is hidden. After you had gone, he was forced to show it to her."

"But she was only a child. Suppose she should forget?"

"I believe your father took steps to ensure she will remember," Serafimo answered, remembering the child's bloody hand. "No, she will not forget."

"I wonder if she ever misses me?"

Serafimo looked with sympathetic eyes on his nephew. "I am sure she does."

"How much longer must I remain at this monastery?"

"For a while longer, because you are safe here. No one, save the abbot, knows your true identity. Try to curb your temper and your impatience. Our day will come, but if we are ill-prepared, you will not gain back your father's throne. Learn tolerance and patience from the monks, Alexander; those two qualities will stand you in good stead."

"I would sooner have a strong sword arm so I can make Uncle Reynard pay for what he has done."

"And so you should, but just have patience." Serafimo passed on to another subject. "I have brought Father Joseph with me. I believe he will prove to be an amiable companion for you, and hopefully make your days less lonely."

Alexander curled his lip in disgust. "Another monk who is sworn to silence. I find it exceedingly difficult to care about this."

Serafimo smiled indulgently. "No, he has taken no vow of silence. He is a priest, but you might find to your surprise that Father Joseph is unlike most priests."

"What makes him different?" Alexander asked with little

72

interest. His only companions of late had been holy men. And they had not helped him feel less lonely.

"Father Joseph is a fair arm with the sword. He will help you recover your strength, and you can also practice the sword with him. Also, I have been concerned that you still cannot walk. He has worked with the lame with remarkable success."

"I am not lame," Alexander declared stubbornly.

"Even so, it will take many painful years for you to get your strength back, Alexander. Deep inside you know this. You were almost fatally injured, and it is only with God's help that you have come this far."

"I do not need this priest to help me walk. I can do it on my own."

Serafimo smiled. "It never hurts to have help, Alexander. It does not make you less strong to depend on others."

Alexander stared at his uncle, feeling ashamed of his outburst. He thought of how different his uncle Serafimo was from his Uncle Reynard. Serafimo was as good as Reynard was evil. "Forgive my ill temper, Uncle, and do not think me ungrateful. Promise you will not desert me."

"Even when I am not with you, my prayers are. Take heart, Alexander. One day you will have that which you desire."

Alexander had heard all this before. He wasn't interested in some day—he could not look past today. With a heavy sigh, he met his uncle's eyes. "How long can you stay?"

"I must leave straightaway. I cannot visit this monastery more frequently than I do the others. It would not be well for Reynard to become suspicious. I shall come whenever possible. Meantime, watch after your health." He took his nephew's hand, knowing he could do little to heal the pain in his tortured mind. "Look to the future and not to the past, Alexander, and God be with you."

"Assure me again, before you go, that my sister is safe."

"I will send you word of her as soon as Everett reports

73

back to me."

Alexander nodded. "I will wait to hear, and I will try to learn patience, Uncle. But I will not like it."

Serafimo laughed. "I know, Alexander, but one does what one must." His eyes cleared. "I can see you have made a remarkable recovery."

"What good does it do? I cannot yet walk."

"But you will. Try not to think where you are now, but how far you have come since that night you fell from the castle wall. There was a time when I thought you would not survive—but, with God's help, you did. You are a fighter, with the blood of kings flowing through your veins."

"I will try to remember that."

Serafimo's heart ached for Alexander. He was now fourteen, and at an age when young men learned about life and living, Alexander had been exposed to grief, pain, and betrayal.

The young man looked at his uncle, wishing he did not have to go away. "Will you give me your blessing, Eminence?" he asked earnestly.

Serafimo reached out and placed his hand on the golden head, asking for God to bless the young uncrowned king and help him learn forbearance for the years of suffering that were yet ahead of him.

Alexander watched his uncle Serafimo leave with confusion in his young heart. Revenge burned like a slow fire within his breast, and he gripped the coverlet so tightly that his body trembled.

One day, in the not too distant future, he would revenge his mother and father's deaths. One day his uncle Reynard would pay for his treachery.

As he drifted off to sleep, his last thoughts were of his sister, Jahane.

Six-year-old Jahane slipped her hand into Cord's. Looking up at him, she blessed him with a smile and gazed at him adoringly.

She spoke English with just the slightest French accent. "Cord, do you love me?" she asked solemnly.

"Yes, Jahane, I love you."

"Am I the only girl in the world for you?"

The handsome young boy laughed, delighted with the little minx. Was Jahane unusually bright and much more interesting than other girls her age? he wondered. Yes, he was sure she was. It was for certain he was never bored while she entertained him with her wit.

"You are my only girl, Jahane. Will you remember that?"

"Yes. Because I belong to you, don't I, Cord?"

He laughed again and took her small hand in his. "Yes, Jahane. You belong to me."

"Because your papa gave me to you," she said, repeating the limited version of the story Cord had told her about the night he had first seen her.

"Yes," he agreed. "And since you were placed in my care, you will always belong to me."

Cord, now fourteen, was not too old to be charmed by this little enchantress. When he dropped down on the sofa, she climbed up beside him and spread her pink gown out about her, tossing her golden head flirtatiously.

He hated to see her happy smile fade, but he had to tell her that he would be going away. "Jahane, honey, I want you to know that I will be going to sea. I will be sailing to many different places, and I will be away for a time."

Her blue eyes widened. "Will you take me with you?"

"No, Jahane, because where I am going is no place for a little girl."

Her face fell and she placed a trembling hand on his

cheek. "You will come back?"

"Yes, I will come back," he assured her. "While I am away, you be good for Mama, will you?"

Her eyes filled with tears as she fought to be brave. "Yes, I will be good for Mama."

He straightened the pink bow in her hair. "What would you like me to bring you?"

She said without hesitating, "I would like a doll. And bring yourself back."

He chuckled. "All right—myself and a doll."

Suddenly she climbed in his lap and grabbed him about the neck and cried out in desperation, "Promise you will return, Cord. Promise!"

He hugged her to him, thinking how she had wound herself around his heart. "I promise, little one, and you know I always keep my word."

She laid her head over on his shoulder and blinked her tears away. She loved mama, but Cord was her whole world. "What if I have one of my bad dreams while you are away?"

His arms tightened about her. "Then dream only of me, Jahane."

She raised her head and looked at him with a serious expression. "One day I will grow up, Cord. If I promise to become beautiful and well mannered, and to always mind Mama, will you marry me?"

His laughter was warm because she seemed so sincere. "I shall marry you even if you are only passingly pretty," he teased.

"I am going to be very beautiful, Cord, I promise. And you will keep me with you always. We will be married, and live in a castle, and I will be queen, and you will be my consort."

"Don't you mean I will be king?" Cord asked, trying to keep a straight face.

"No," she said solemnly. "That could never be. The

people would not allow it."

He stood up and set her on her feet. "Then I shall have to be satisfied with being a mere prince."

She frowned. "I do not think you can be a prince, either, because you do not have royal blood." Then she smiled, as if a new idea had occurred to her. "But do not worry, Cord. If you cannot be my consort, I will not be queen."

He held out his hand and she placed her small hand in his. "Well said. But I believe Della has been reading you too many books and filling your head with mythical kingdoms."

Her brow furrowed. "But I am a princess," Jahane insisted.

"You are my princess, but perhaps you will have to be satisfied to be a mere sea captain's wife."

She looked at him questioningly. "Are you going to be a sea captain, Cord?"

"I am."

She nodded. "Then I will be a sea captain's wife."

Chapter Eight

Balmarhea

Prince Alexander pushed his heavy cowl aside and bent down at the mountain stream to quench his thirst. With a muttered oath, he slung his leg over his ancient mount, remembering a time when he had ridden the finest-blooded horses.

Over the years Alexander had learned patience. He had learned how to keep himself under tight control and to bide his time. There had been years spent regaining his strength and learning how to walk again and with the help of Father Joseph, years of practicing with his sword so he would be ready when he faced his Uncle Reynard.

Here on this mountain he rarely heard anything about the outside world. Only occasionally had he wandered past the shelter of the monastery walls. Even on rarer occasions did his Uncle Serafimo pay him a visit.

The monastery that had been his only home for many years he likened to a prison. The rest of the world thought he was dead, and sometimes he felt he was. The only thing that kept him from losing his sanity was his Uncle Serafimo's assurance that they would one day take back the throne of Balmarhea.

Alexander was wise enough to know that to act prematurely would be to lose everything. So he counted off the days, and restlessly looked toward the west where his future lay.

The sun was white-hot above Alexander's head when he rode into the monastery gates. He was greeted with a stiff nod from Brother Lazarus, which reminded him of the solitude of the life he lived.

A year ago Father Joseph had left, and Alexander reluctantly slipped back into his solitary existence. The silence of this monastery lay on his shoulders, like a cross to be borne. At times he talked to himself just so he could hear the sound of a human voice.

Alexander longed for the feel of silk shirts next to his skin, rather than the rough robes he was forced to wear. He thought about the food he had taken for granted as a boy, when he ate the thin broth and hard bread which was the brothers' daily fare.

Sometimes he wondered if the monks knew his identity. If they did, he saw no indication that they revered him as their rightful king.

Dismounting, the prince walked with a slight limp as he led his horse in the direction of the stables. After rubbing the animal down and seeing to its feeding, he made his way to his quarters, hating the loneliness he would find there.

Alexander had few possessions to call his own. He had the feeling that when he was gone from this place, he would leave nothing of himself behind. There was no affection in his life, no love or caring from anyone. Indeed it was a lonely existence.

Opening the door to his room, he was surprised to see his Uncle Serafimo seated in the straight-back chair, watching him closely.

"Uncle, to what do I owe this untimely visit?" There was sarcasm in his voice. "You do not usually call on me twice in the same month. Or have I been here so long that I have begun to lose track of the time?"

Serafimo assessed his nephew. Alexander had grown straight and tall, with a powerful build. He walked with a slight limp, the only lasting effect from his perilous fall down the cliff. Of course there were scars from the bullet wounds, but the scars that Serafimo was concerned about were those that did not show—the scars left on his nephew's heart and mind.

In spite of the drab monk's robe, there was still a regal air about Alexander—a nobility that showed in the lines of his face. The young man looked like someone exceptional, even though his blond hair needed trimming and there was stubble on his chin which indicated he had not shaved in several days. It was not difficult to visualize the crown of Balmarhea on the young prince's head.

The archbishop spoke at last. "I have grave news, Alexander. I thought it best that you and I decided together what we should do about this new occurrence."

Alexander removed his outer robe and tossed it on the bed. Dousing his head in the cold water he poured from the pitcher by his bed, he washed away the dust before turning back to his uncle. The years of solitude had taught him self-control if nothing else.

"I'm listening," he said at last.

"As you know, Reynard has been unable to have himself crowned king, because he still cannot find the scepter."

"Yes, this I know. You and I also discussed that I may have the same problem myself, since I do not know where it is hidden."

"Never mind that now. We have other pressing matters at hand. It seems Reynard has produced a young girl, and he claims she is your sister, Jahane, who was miraculously saved when the rest of the royal family was slain. He is grooming her now to introduce her to the country as the rightful queen."

Alexander's eyes hardly flickered, but his body was tense. "Go on."

"It is not Jahane he has in his clutches, you may be assured of that. But strangely enough, I fear the people of Balmarhea may be willing to believe that this impostor is Jahane. They will most probably lay their hearts at this pretender's feet, wanting to believe she is their true princess."

"You could convince them otherwise. The people will believe anything you tell them, Uncle."

"Perhaps even I will not be able to dissuade them if Reynard presents her to the people. I find one often believes what one wants to believe."

Alexander slowly sank onto his bed. "Is it not possible that the girl is Jahane?" he asked, torn between wanting to know his sister was alive and well and having her in Reynard's power.

"No, the girl is a impostor."

Alexander's heart was pounding. "Are you certain of this?"

"Yes. And I will tell you how I know. The night your father was killed, he took Jahane with him into the throne room and showed her the hiding place of the royal scepter. To ensure that she would not forget its hiding place, he gave her one of the rubies from the scepter. He then slashed a deep gash in her hand so she would not forget."

Alexander found it hard to believe his father would inflict pain on his sister. "What are you telling me?"

"I am telling you that I had an occasion to examine this impostor's hand, and she has no scar. If she were Jahane, there would be a scar!"

"How were you able to get in to see her?"

Serafimo smiled. "I am the archbishop, and she is being raised at a convent I have visited on occasion."

"I see. Does my Uncle Reynard know that Jahane was shown the hiding place of the scepter?"

Serafimo looked uncertain for a moment. "No, I do not believe he does. But all the same, he has been relentless in his search for her. I suppose he has given up ever finding her, thus his reason for producing the impostor."

"What does my Uncle Reynard propose to do with this impostor?"

"He intends to set her on the throne and rule through her. He cannot make the impostor Queen of Balmarhea without the scepter, but through her he can have a great deal more power than he does now if the people accept her as Jahane. It is rumored that he intends to wed her to his eldest son, my nephew Damerou. You never knew your cousin, but a more undesirable young man I have yet to encounter, even if he is my own flesh and blood." Serafimo's eyes softened. "But then, you are the nephew of my heart."

Alexander placed his hand on his uncle's shoulder. "You and Jahane are the only family I have left—at least the only ones I care about. At times it's hard for me to realize that Uncle Reynard caused the deaths of my parents and wanted me and my sister dead. It seems like a bad dream, that night my mother and father were killed and Jahane was lost to me."

The archbishop's eyes saddened. "I often wonder about your sister. Where is she? Does she know who she is? And if so, does she ever long to return to her homeland?"

Alexander's eyes softened. "Jahane would be a young lady now. It's hard to think of her as other than the charming little girl who made everyone love her."

"Yes, I remember. We all adored her."

"My desire to find her is as strong as my desire to take

82

back the throne." Alexander jumped to his feet and began pacing the floor. "You are not blameless in Jahane's disappearance, Uncle. You should have hidden her away instead of trusting her fate to strangers. How can I be sure that you have made every effort to find her?"

Serafimo looked sorrowfully at the prince. "I have never given up trying to find your sister. At the time I sent her away, I had no choice. It had to be done to save her life. As you know, Everett has searched diligently to find the Meredith family. No one seems to know what became of them, and no one ever recalls them having a young child with them. It is said that several years ago, they just sold everything and disappeared from Boston. No one knows where they went."

"Could Reynard have had his hand in Jahane's disappearance?"

"No, Reynard has had men searching for her as relentlessly as we did."

"I assume Uncle Reynard still believes I died the same night my parents were assassinated?"

"Yes, he has never questioned that you were dead. If he thought you had survived the fall, he would have been searching for you, as well." Serafimo glanced about. "Here, inside these walls, you have been well protected from prying eyes. The good brothers have guarded you well."

"Does anyone here other than the abbot know my identity?"

"They have never been told. However, I believe they have a strong intimation of your importance."

"Tell me how you know of Uncle Reynard's search for Jahane and his plans for this girl he would put in her place?"

"Why, I have spies in his household, of course, he has them in mine."

Alexander's eyes narrowed with a dangerous light. "Where is this impostor?"

"She is at a convent outside the city where Reynard is having her prepared for her marriage to Damerou."

Alexander felt hatred burn in his heart for this girl who dared to stand in his sister's place. "I will confront this girl and have her tell me to my face that she is Jahane. Take me to her now so that I may prevent her from stealing my throne."

"I thought you might feel this way, and that is why I am here." Serafimo's eyes softened. "I know your life here at the monastery has been hard, Alexander. But you have been groomed and tempered for what you must now do." He laid a comforting hand on his nephew's shoulder. "Our people would probably never believe what an onerous burden it is to be king. All they see is the wealth and power, not the responsibility and the danger to which you were born and the sacrifices that you have made for them. I am sorry that your life has been so hard. The time is growing near when you must fulfill your destiny. And if God is willing and I am able, I shall help you in every way I can."

Alexander had waited for this moment, but now that the time had come, he felt unsure of himself. He had not seen the world outside this monastery and its environs in a very long time. He had not been near a woman since he was eleven years old, and he did not even know how to talk to one.

"What shall we do with this girl, Uncle Serafimo?"

"We must get her away from the convent and out of Reynard's clutches. I have a place prepared to imprison her until we can make Reynard give up his plans to present her as Jahane. Even though she is heavily guarded, I have made it possible for you to get into her quarters. But we must leave at once, Alexander, for to delay could result in disaster."

"Will you come with me?"

"No, it is better if I am in Montique when the girl disappears. One of my men will lead you to her. You can trust him as you would me."

Alexander moved to the chest at the foot of his cot and removed his sword. It was the same sword he had ripped from the castle walls on that fateful night so long ago; the sword that his ancestors had used to slay their enemies, the sword that would one day end his Uncle Reynard's life. Reverently he touched the hilt before strapping it about his waist.

"I hope you have furnished me with a decent mount, Uncle. I cannot keep up with you on the swaybacks they call horses in this monastery."

Serafimo smiled. "Yes, of course. I have brought you my swiftest horses."

Alexander picked up his black cowl and reluctantly slipped it over his head. Serafimo had lapsed into profound silence, so Alexander turned to face him. "Do you have more to say?"

"Just be careful, Alexander. I do not want Reynard to find out you still live. The time is not yet come for you to face him. But it is soon."

"I live for the day when I can stand before my treacherous uncle and run my sword through his black heart. He has much to answer for."

"All in good time, Alexander. But first we must deal with the false princess."

Alexander's hands ached to choke the life out of the girl who would pretend to be his sister Jahane. What kind of woman would play a puppet to his evil Uncle Reynard? "Yes, I shall first deal with this impostor," Alexander said, in an icy voice. "She will rue the day she joined my Uncle Reynard in his evil game."

The young woman glanced at the bed which was piled high with gowns, shoes, bonnets, and jewels. But there was no gladness in her heart for the finery which had been so generously lavished on her.

She picked up a green velvet gown and ran a delicate finger down the skirt, wondering what it would feel like to be dressed in such a grand manner.

As far back as she could remember she had lived at the Lord of Creation Convent. While there, she had worn only the garments of a novice. Then suddenly, three weeks ago, her whole life had changed. Instead of being the foundling she had always thought herself to be, she had been told that she was Princess Jahane, the heir to the throne of Balmarhea.

She had always been called Brynn by the nuns. She examined her mind, trying to recall any fragment of memory that would remind her of her past. She could never remember being called Jahane, or being treated as royalty. Her earliest memory was of fire—violence and death!

She could remember crying for her mother, who lay in a pool of blood, but had her mother been the Queen of Balmarhea? No, it couldn't be. But why else would Duke Maxime have made such a claim? She remembered him charging her to call him Uncle Reynard, but she could not remember ever having had an uncle Reynard.

Brynn glanced down at the huge diamond ring that circled the finger of her left hand, and trembled in fear at what it represented. It was the betrothal ring given her by Duke Maxime, who was acting on behalf of his son. She yanked the ring off her finger and placed it on the dressing table. Somehow it was abhorrent to her.

Brynn wondered what her intended husband, Lord Damerou Beaudette, would look like. She knew so little about men, or what they expected out of marriage. Her mind refused to dwell on that unpleasant aspect. The sisters at the convent had never prepared her to be any man's wife.

Since the evening was so hot, she moved out of the room to walk in the airless garden, hoping for a breath of fresh air.

She had grown up occupying a cramped little cell with one of the sisters. Then, three weeks ago, she had been moved to these spacious quarters with a lovely little courtyard garden.

Believing herself to be alone, Brynn did not see the dark figure that quickly moved into the shadow of the nearby wisteria bush.

Prince Alexander watched the young girl move about the garden. Her face was hidden from him at the moment so he couldn't see her features. She was dressed all in white, and he surmised she wore some sort of nun's habit. She was not tall, and he could see from her hands that she was delicately built.

Unexpectedly, she turned. Alexander stared not at the face of an evil witch as he had expected, but the sweet face of an angel. He could not see her hair since it was covered with a wimple, but her lips were full and her eyes held a wistful expression, although he could not make out their color in the dying sunlight.

Alexander's jaw clamped in anger as he reminded himself of the deceit this imposter was practicing. She was the means with which his uncle Reynard would try to ascend the throne of Balmarhea at last. Hatred burned in his heart like a torch as he stepped into her path, blocking her way.

A startled gasp escaped the girl's lips, and she shrank back in fear at the figure that towered over her. Since he wore a dark cowl, she could not see his face.

For a long moment, neither of them spoke; then at last Alexander said, "What are you called?"

"I . . . what?" she asked in confusion. "Surely you have been told my name."

"What is the name you have used all these years?" he asked in irritation.

"I . . . Brynn," she answered, for some reason taking a quick backward step.

"I thought you might have been called Princess Jahane," he said in a hard voice.

"Yes . . . I have been called that, but only of late." Suddenly she smiled, thinking she knew who this stranger must be. "You must be Lord Damerou. But I was not told to expect you this evening. And why are you dressed as a monk?"

Alexander was glad she had mistaken him for her intended bridegroom; this would make it easier for him to question her and get the right answers. "Shouldn't a man take whatever disguise is at hand so he can look upon the face of his future wife?" he asked, playing her game of deceit.

Reaching up, Alexander pushed the wimple from her head, and golden hair spilled down her shoulders. He was so struck by her beauty that he was unable to speak. He had not expected her to be so lovely. A widow's peak added just the right touch to her heart-shaped face. Now he could see the color of her eyes, and they were soft blue, not unlike his sister's.

Against his will, he was drawn to her because she seemed so delicate and vulnerable. He could see just the touch of fear in her eyes and knew she was frightened of him.

Why was she not ugly? he wondered. Did not deceit and dishonor show on one's face? What right did she have to look so young and pure?

His anger reached a new height as he dismissed her innocent appearance. "Will we be disturbed here?" Alexander asked. He realized he could not linger for long. "Dare I hope we can be alone for a time?" he said softly, gritting his teeth to keep from wringing her neck.

For some reason a thrill went through Brynn's body at the sound of his deep voice. Oh, how she wanted to like her future husband. But she was also a little apprehensive because she could not see his face. It was most difficult to talk to one whose identity was concealed.

"No, we will not be disturbed, lord. I have been alone all day, in what the sisters call my time of meditation. No one is allowed to disturb my solitude." She shyly lowered her head. "Except you, of course, my lord."

Repulsed by the part he was playing, Alexander forced himself to speak more kindly than he felt. "Tell me about yourself," he said, nodding to the wooden bench in the corner of the garden, and indicating they should walk in that direction.

Brynn seated herself on the edge of the bench, and the man still towered above her. "There isn't much to tell, lord. I have lived all my life, at least that which I can remember, in this convent. Before now, I have never been alone with a man." She lowered her head again, and he could swear he saw a blush tinge her cheeks.

"So you believe yourself to be the Princess Jahane?" He could not keep the contemptuous note from his voice.

"Nay, lord. It is you and your father, Duke Maxime, who believe me to be the lost princess. I have no such remembrances."

Alexander was not to be put off by her act of innocence. Plans had been made for the abduction of this impostor, and he would carry them through. He had thought he would be forced to take her against her will, but since she believed him to be Damerou, he would lure her away instead.

With grim determination, Alexander pointed toward the horizon. "That is what I would call a magnificent sunset, and it is yet an hour until dark. How would you like to take a ride with me, Princess Jahane?"

Her eyelids flickered. "Do you mean horseback riding?"

"Yes, of course."

She looked uncertain, but her heart raced at the thought of riding with this man. "Do you think it is permitted, lord?"

"Of course, if I say so, and I do say so. Can you ride?"

"Yes, lord. But I am not properly dressed to ride a horse."

"No matter," he said, taking her arm and steering her out the garden gate, anxious to be away before they were discovered.

Alexander suddenly found his mission distasteful and wanted to have it over with. He found little satisfaction in the lie he was spinning. He had to keep reminding himself that this woman was not as innocent as she would have him believe, that she was in league with his evil Uncle Reynard.

When they were safely away from the garden, he led her down a slope and past a clump of bushes where two horses were tied to a fallen tree.

Brynn was surprised when he gripped her waist and plopped her on one of the horses. Before she could protest, or even settle herself on the saddle, another mounted man joined them.

The man she thought to be her betrothed mounted his horse and took her horse's bridle, leading her forward at a fast pace.

Brynn had no time to consider what was happening to her, for it took all her concentration just to stay in the

90

saddle.

Glancing at the stiff back of the man who was to be her husband, she wondered why he was acting in such a mysterious manner. She hadn't really seen his face, but there seemed to radiate from him a feeling of unrest.

Suddenly Brynn realized she was in danger. If this man was her intended husband, he had no love in his heart for her. She kicked her mount in the flanks, wrenching the reins from his hands and knowing she had to escape.

Alexander watched the girl turn her mount away, and he easily overtook her. With a wide sweep, he lifted her in his arms, swinging her onto his horse.

"Did you think I would set you on a horse that was swifter than mine?" he questioned angrily. With a swift kick in his horse's flanks, they raced forward.

With one last glance back at the safety of the convent that was quickly fading in the distance, Brynn felt the helplessness of her situation.

"You have every right to fear, impostor," Alexander hissed in her ear. "You will pay a great price for your part in this treachery."

She shivered with fear, wondering what he was talking about. She had a feeling it would do no good to ask. It occurred to her that no woman could ask this man anything and expect a reply.

Chapter Nine

Prince Alexander's horse thundered after the man his Uncle Serafimo had sent along as his guide. They had been riding at a fast pace for hours, and he knew they must be cautious in case they were being followed. It would be easy to spot them here in open country. He shifted the trembling girl in his arms, looking back over his shoulder.

Up ahead were dense woods, and he breathed more easily when they were under the cover of the trees.

When the girl tried to wriggle out of Alexander's grasp, he tightened his hold on her. "Be still, you little fool. Do you want to fall beneath the horse's hooves and be trampled to death?"

"Why are you doing this?" she asked. "What are you going to do with me?"

He glanced down at her. "You might well ask, Brynn, or whatever you call yourself. I wonder what the penalty is for masquerading as a royal princess."

There was no time for Brynn to answer, for they were on a narrow trail, and when she looked to her right, all she could see was a deep crevice and open space. When the horse's hooves kicked rocks over the side, it seemed to her that it took a very long time for them to reach the bottom.

Holding on tightly to her captor, she buried her face against the man's chest so she wouldn't have to look down.

It was long after sunset when they finally stopped to make camp.

While Alexander kept a wary eye on the girl, he helped his uncle's servant unload the packhorse. He asked no privilege because he was the king. The years at the monastery had taught him to do his share.

While the servant unsaddled the horses and hobbled them so they wouldn't go too far astray, Alexander spread a blanket on the ground and motioned for the girl to sit down.

Brynn huddled against a huge rock, her frightened eyes following the man dressed as a monk as he moved about making camp. It was unnerving that his face was hidden by the cowl. If only she could see what he looked like, she might fear him less.

When he walked toward her, she cringed away from him. With an angry hiss, he spoke. "Since we dare not light a fire, you will have to make do with this dried meat."

She shook her head, and moved still closer to the rock. When he took her hand and placed the jerky in her palm, his voice was angry. "You can eat or not, it is of no importance to me. But if I were you, I would consider it might be the last meal you will have until we reach our destination."

"What is our destination?" she wanted to know.

Without bothering to answer, he turned away, spread his blanket close to her, and lay down. Brynn glanced down at the meat in her hand and raised it to her lips. With a tug on the leathery substance, she chewed and swallowed, thinking if he was taking the trouble of feeding her, perhaps he wouldn't kill her.

Silence settled over the camp. Since there was no campfire, the only light came from the moon. Brynn watched the servant return and lean against the trunk of a tree, his eyes watchful. Obviously he would stand guard tonight, for every so often, she could feel his watchful gaze burn into her.

The man who was dressed as a monk had apparently fallen asleep, for he hadn't moved since lying down.

Brynn finally tossed the meat aside and pressed her back against the rock. She was very sleepy, but too frightened to close her eyes.

Finally, with the hooting of the night owl sounding in her ears, her head fell backward, and she was caught in the sweet arms of sleep.

The next morning Brynn was awakened by a heavy hand on her shoulder. The servant stood over her, motioning that she should prepare for the day's journey, but the man in the cowl was nowhere in sight.

Just when she began to hope he might have gone, he appeared, leading the horses. Still not allowed to ride by herself, since she had tried to escape, the man lifted her on before him and they rode away without eating.

Along midmorning, Brynn was so hungry she began to wish she had eaten all of the meat she had been given the night before.

All day they rode until Brynn thought she would drop from exhaustion. The woods became so dense the horses could not go forward, and they had to get off and walk, leaving the animals behind.

"How much farther?" Alexander asked his uncle's servant, when the girl stumbled and he had to lift her in his arms and carry her. "Shouldn't we already be there?"

"The cabin is just ahead" came the reply. "Just past that last bunch of trees."

Brynn shivered, not knowing what horrible fate awaited

her after they reached their destination. Through the dense trees, she could see a faint light. When they moved into the clearing, she saw a cabin and what appeared to be a barn.

The guide opened the door, and when Alexander carried his burden inside, the man left, saying he would return to care for the horses they had left behind.

Alexander set the girl on her feet and glanced about the cabin. There was only one room, but it was spacious and clean and seemed to contain everything the girl would need — a cookstove, washbasin, table and chairs, and a bed. There was even a green rug on the wooden floor. A lone candle rested on the table, its faint light doing little to light the dark room.

Brynn strained her eyes, trying to see what her abductor looked like, but his face was still in shadows.

"Where is this place?" Brynn asked, glancing at her surroundings. "Why have you brought me here?"

Alexander looked at her with angry eyes. Seeing the bruises on her smooth cheek, he felt no remorse for her. Not even when he noticed the burrs that were tangled in her long golden hair did he pity her. In his way of thinking, she deserved far worse than she had yet received.

"What are you going to do with me?" she asked through trembling lips.

He wanted to ignore her, but he remembered the years when he had asked questions of his companion in the monastery only to be met with a wall of silence, so he spoke resentfully. "You are full of questions, and I have no intention of supplying you with the answers. All you need to know is that you will remain here until it pleases me to let you go."

"But I don't understand," she bravely continued. "What have I done to you. It is for certain you are not the man I am to marry, for he would have no cause to treat me so."

His lips curled in contempt. "No, thanks to God, I am not he. But, if I were you, I would make no further wedding plans. By now the hue and cry will have gone out, and I'm sure your bridegroom knows you are missing, perhaps dead." His blue eyes hardened with distaste. "Do you seriously believe that Damerou would grieve for your demise, impostor?"

Again she tried to see his face, but it was as if he was purposely staying in the shadows. "Are you going to . . . kill me?" she asked in a frightened voice.

He motioned that she should be seated at the table so she would be in the light, while he moved his chair in the shadows.

"Kill you?" he said at last. "No, not unless you give me cause. I want no more than to detain you until your bridegroom gives you up for lost. Then you will be free to go your way."

"But why?"

"Be silent," he said heatedly. "I told you before that you ask too many questions."

Alexander watched as her soft brown eyes clouded with misery. "I need to understand why you are doing this," she persisted. "I haven't known anything that has been going on in my life for the past few months. Now, since you abducted me, I know even less. Why don't you leave me alone?"

"Why did you not ask Duke Maxime why he thought he could put you forth as the Princess Jahane?"

"I . . . know nothing about his reasons. Just as I don't know why you are doing what you are doing. I am learning that men think they have the right to dominate a woman and she has no say in the matter."

He was silent, but she knew he was watching her as a hawk watches a rabbit, and it was most unsettling.

"Please," she said, hoping he would have mercy on her. "I am so very weary. Could I not lie down?"

"You can take the bed" came the gruff reply. "But don't try anything because I'll be watching you. Don't think you can get away, because you cannot."

Brynn stood up on shaky legs and moved to the bed. She was still frightened of the man, but her tiredness overcame much of her apprehension.

She slumped down on the bed, wishing he would say something and stop staring at her. At last he did speak, and she wished he had remained silent, for she could hear the hatred in his tone.

"How can someone like you, who looks so innocent, be so evil?"

"I am not evil," she remarked wearily, knowing nothing she said would change his opinion of her.

Alexander wished he could dismiss the girl as unimportant, but he could not. "Why did you allow Duke Maxime to use you in his plans to tighten his evil hold on the people of Balmarhea? Why did you give your consent to wed his weak-minded son?"

"How do you know his son is weak-minded," she countered. "Do you know him so well?"

"No, we have never met," he admitted. "But I do know about him."

"Then how can you judge him when you do not even know him? How can you judge me when we had never met before yesterday?"

He ignored her questions. "Tell me about Damerou," he pressed. "Have the two of you decided to ascend the throne of Balmarhea?"

"I told you, I do not even know him," she said in a pitiful, soft voice. "If you will recall, I thought you were he, when you came upon me in the garden. Why do you torment me when I don't even know you?"

"Perhaps it's just guilt you are feeling."

She faced him with courage. "I have nothing to feel guilty about."

97

"Haven't you?"

Daringly she spoke. "If you are a priest, then perhaps I shall make my confession to you and you will give me absolution. But I do not think you are a priest at all. You call me a pretender, but are you not the real pretender?"

He laughed deeply. "You are right. I am not a holy man or a priest. Therefore, you should not expect any compassion from me. And perhaps I should not expect any confessions from you."

Suddenly she was overcome with panic she could not control. With a quick leap, she headed for the door. But before she was halfway across the room, strong hands circled her waist and she was lifted into the man's strong arms.

Fighting and kicking, she tried to free herself, but he only laughed at her puny attempts. At last she managed to slip out of his arms, and he pushed her to the floor. Straddling her, he held her arms over her head.

"Try that again, and you will regret it," he said in a cold voice. "You would do well to do as you are told."

Her eyelashes fluttered in desperation, and she held herself still. "Please let me up," she whispered in desperation. "I promise not to try to escape again."

Alexander wasn't listening to her. His eyes were drawn to her heaving breasts, and he felt a tightening in his loins. He had never been this close to a girl before, and he felt as if someone had just branded him with a hot iron. His eyes moved across her face, noting the fear in her eyes. Her golden hair was tangled in knots, and he was appalled that he had not even allowed her time to groom herself during their journey.

His touch softened, and he stood up and pulled her up with him. For a moment he was unable to catch a deep breath, and his heart was racing as if he had been running.

Closing his eyes, he tried to remember who she was and

who he was. After a moment, he glanced back at her and saw she was rubbing her wrist. The red welts he saw had been caused by him.

Alexander moved to the table and raised the water pitcher to his dry lips, needing time to regain his composure.

He did not like what was happening inside his head, and he would not tolerate what was happening within his body. After taking a long, cleansing drink, he moved to Brynn and offered the pitcher to her. At first she refused with a shake of her head, but he poked it at her again and she relented. She drank thirstily and then handed the pitcher back to him.

"Are you hungry?" Alexander asked, thinking she looked unusually pale. Seeing the basket of fruit on the table, he chose an apple for himself and then offered one to her. The last thing he wanted was a sick girl on his hands.

She shook her head no and retreated step by step as he advanced toward her.

"If you would only allow me a moment to rest." In exhaustion, she slumped over on the bed. "I am so weary."

He watched as her eyes closed and her breathing deepened. In the time it took Alexander to eat an apple she was fast asleep.

Alexander stood over the girl for a long moment, wondering who she could be. He smiled with irony when he thought of the look on his Uncle Reynard's face when he got the news that his bird had flown her cage.

He sat down on a wooden chair and propped his booted feet on the edge of the bed. He had waited a long time for this day. He had found a way to strike out against his Uncle Reynard by removing from his grasp this lovely tool he would have used in his evil plan to take over Balmarhea.

Now the wheels had been set in motion that would eventually show up his uncle as a traitor, and Alexander was anxious to proceed with the unmasking. His uncle had been allowed to go unpunished far too long.

Unable to get comfortable, Alexander stood up and paced the floor, feeling like a caged lion.

Now that he had the girl, what in God's name was he going to do with her?

Looking in her direction, he noticed how the moonlight shining through the window played across her golden hair.

With grim determination, he tore his eyes away from her, wishing he had not been so quick to volunteer to abduct her.

Glancing at the mantel clock, he saw it was past the midnight hour. Wearily he sat down in the chair, emptying his mind. He tried to stay awake so he could keep watch on the girl, but weariness overcame him and his eyes closed and he fell asleep.

Chapter Ten

Alexander fought his way back from sleep. The hard chair he sat in reminded him that he would get little sleep tonight. He had been a fool to fall asleep, for the girl could easily have escaped. He could hear her even breathing and felt relief that she had not tried to flee but was still asleep.

He tried to stay awake by thinking about his sister. Alexander could envision himself and Jahane standing together before their Uncle Reynard and denouncing him as a traitor. What would be their uncle's punishment? Should he sentence him to death—or would it be better to make him rot in some dank, dark prison so he could reflect on his past misdeeds?

Wearily Alexander closed his eyes, trying to remember what Jahane looked like. He could recall golden hair that curled around her face and beautiful blue eyes.

He smiled, remembering how Jahane had always begged him to take her horseback riding. She had been so young—only three years old when their parents had been killed. If she were still alive, would she remember him? he wondered. No, probably not, he concluded.

With a deep intake of breath, he tried to settle in a comfortable spot, but the chair was too uncomfortable. Leaning his head back, he closed his eyes and soon drifted off to sleep in spite of his discomfort.

Alexander awoke in total darkness. It took him several seconds to realize where he was. Apparently the candles had gone out and dark clouds blocked out the moonlight.

Suddenly he remembered the girl and feared she might have fled while he slept.

Feeling around in the dark, his hand came in contact with Brynn's soft flesh. He jumped back when she screamed out in fright.

"Leave me alone," she cried. "Do not touch me. I am frightened of you."

He swore under his breath. "You have nothing to fear from me. I merely wanted to know if you were still here, or if you had taken it into your head to escape."

"I considered leaving when I awoke to find you had fallen asleep," she admitted. "But I knew I would soon be hopelessly lost in the woods and probably be devoured by some wild beast. You have me at your mercy, monsieur."

Alexander laughed. "Yes, I do, but I must confess you have wild imaginings. So, you thought my company preferable to some wild beast?"

"I do not admit that you are better than any beast. You have abducted me against my will, but thus far you have not tried to harm me."

Alexander sat back down in the hard chair, wishing he had a soft bed to lie upon. "Ah, but you should fear me, Brynn. I would not hesitate for a second to break your pretty neck if you do not do exactly as you are told."

"I do not believe you would harm me, or you would already have done so."

"There you are mistaken. If you test me too far, you will find out how wrong you are."

"I was raised by the sisters to believe that all men are

102

good, only situations create evil."

"A fanciful dream. Greed makes men evil. When a man covets what belongs to his brother, he has been known to kill, lie, and cheat, and many other despicable doings."

"Do you covet your brother's wealth?"

Alexander, so accustomed to the silence of the monastery, found himself conversing with the girl almost against his will. He knew he was talking too much, but he found it easy to talk to her.

"No, I do not covet my brother's wealth. Of course, I do not have a brother, and I only want what rightfully belongs to me. And I will have it, make no mistake about that."

Alexander felt the hard chair biting into his skin, and when he tried to find a comfortable position, he bumped his leg on the table, muttering a frustrated oath.

"Are you hurt, monsieur?" Brynn inquired.

"And what if I am," he said sourly. "You should lose no sleep just because I am uncomfortable."

There was a note of patience and kindness in her voice. "What is your name?"

Before he realized what he was saying, he answered, "Alexander."

She was quiet for a moment. "Well, the way I see it, there is only one bed, and there are two of us. I feel guilty being the only one to sleep in comfort. If you wish, I will share this bed with you."

He was suspicious of her motive. "You would like that, wouldn't you. Then when I fell asleep, you could knock me over the head and escape to freedom."

As a mother would speak to a misguided child, Brynn now spoke to Alexander. "I was awake for a long time while you slept. Had I been of a mind to, I could have easily done you harm and run away. It is not in my nature to hurt another human creature, not even if he happens to

103

be my tormenter, as you are."

It had been a long time since Alexander had been near a woman. There had been no softness in his life, and no spoken kindness since his mother's death. There was a note in this woman's voice that reminded him of his gentle mother.

"Perhaps I shall lay beside you, if you have no objections."

"Do I have your word as a gentleman that you will stay on your side of the bed?" she asked.

"I do not profess to be a gentleman, but I shall stay on my side of the bed, if for no reason than I have no desire to seek your side of the bed."

"All right, come ahead," she said, moving as close to the wall as she could possibly get.

When Brynn felt the bed sink beneath Alexander's weight, she almost wished she had not been so generous. She had never been this close to a man, and this man was very disturbing to her peace of mind.

Alexander turned his back to her, wondering if he dared trust her. "So," he said, wanting to find proof that she was trustworthy, "you were raised in a convent?"

He thought of his mundane existence at the monastery and wondered if her life had followed a similar pattern. "What was your life like with the holy sisters?'

"It was not unpleasant, although it was often lonely. But if one is not prepared to take up the habit, one can feel cut off in many ways."

Alexander hoped he could trap the girl into admitting who she was. "What was your life like before you lived at the convent?"

"I can remember very little before the sisters took me in."

"Do you really believe that you are the Princess Jahane?"

"I have never felt that I was she. But Duke Maxime assured me I was indeed his niece."

Alexander's lip curled in disgust. "I suppose you wanted to be the princess."

"No, never," she stated vehemently. "The thought of being Princess Jahane is very frightening to me. I would much rather live my life in the convent than be the princess."

Suddenly Alexander rolled over on his back, just as the clouds moved away from the moon, and bright light fell through the window and across his face. Brynn sucked in her breath and she could hardly breathe.

She knew who this man was! He was Prince Alexander! But no, how could that be? Everyone knew that the prince had been killed the year of the rebellion.

Her soft hand moved out and she could not resist touching his arm. He did not draw back as she spoke. "I know who you are. I think deep inside I knew it from the first moment we met. Even though I had not seen your face until now, I sensed you were someone important."

Alexander scowled at Brynn. "You are mistaken. I am no one of importance, and you could not possibly know me. How could you, since we have never met?"

"Oh, yes, I know you, Your Highness," she blurted out. "You are Prince Alexander. I am sure of it. I would know you anywhere."

Alexander stiffened, cursing himself for telling her his name when she had asked. "And what makes you draw that conclusion?"

"I once heard the sisters say that Prince Alexander's body was never found. Everyone, at least at the convent, hoped that meant he still lived. Oh, I do hope you are he. You are the prince, are you not?"

Her sweetness was reaching out to him, and he tried to resist. He had lived so long without kindness in his life that he felt drawn to her. If she was trying to trick him, he would be hopelessly lost, for even now his body gravitated toward her.

"What if I am he?"

"Then I should rejoice within my heart, as would the rest of the country. I have heard of the unrest in the city. I have heard the plight of the farmers, shopkeepers, and fishermen. I know they remember a time when King Alfons ruled Balmarhea and there was peace and plenty. We would all trust that great king's son to bring stability back to Balmarhea."

There was still caution in his voice. "You sound very sure that I am the prince."

"It's just that . . . no, I cannot tell you. You would not believe me anyway."

"I am willing to listen."

"I am embarrassed to say this to you. You will think it presumptuous of me . . . but when I was smaller, I had a make-believe playmate."

"I do not believe that is unusual."

"No, but, my playmate was . . . was . . . you."

He smiled at her admission. "I see." But he didn't see. Was this some cruel trick she was playing on him? Was she pulling at his heart, trying to draw all his secrets out of him so she could tell his Uncle Reynard? He decided to change the subject. "Did the sisters at the convent educate you? You seem very well versed for a girl."

"Yes, they did. I was taught about courtly manners, how to walk, eat and sit. The reverend mother paid particular attention to my manners, which I thought strange. Mostly, however, there was very little for me to do at the convent so I passed much of the time reading in the great library." She shifted her weight away from the rough wall. "That's why I know who you are. I have seen your portrait in a book of heraldry. Of course, you were much younger then, but it was the same face, the same hair, the same arrogance about you."

Brynn could not admit to him that she had worshipped the young prince and had spent hours gazing at his likeness. She had often pretended that he was her prince, and she had spent long hours fantasizing about him.

Alexander's voice was laced with steel. "You realize after your little confession that I cannot allow you to leave? You will not be allowed to tell my Uncle Reynard what you have discovered."

Her heart skipped a beat as he admitted who he was. Her happiness knew no bounds as she realized the boy she had worshipped as a child was alive! "Yes, Your Highness, I do know that."

No one had called Alexander by his title in a very long time. He reached out and gripped her shoulders. "Brynn, if you have used your wiles to trick me, then you will live to rue this night."

"Nay, Your Highness, I have no tricks. I would like to help you if you would allow it."

His grip tightened, and he knew he was hurting her, but she did not cry out. "Tell my why my Uncle thought he could pass you off as my sister?"

"I am not sure. Tonight, as you slept, I was thinking about that. I believe your uncle has been my benefactor all these years. I also believe he has kept me hidden away waiting for just this occasion."

He loosened his hold on her, beginning to trust her. "What makes you say that?"

"It's just that now I have had a chance to fit the pieces together, I have finally come to that conclusion. I remember your Uncle Reynard once came to see me when I was twelve. Of course, I did not know who he was at that time. When I was brought before him, he questioned me at great length. As he was leaving, I overheard him say to his servant that I would do nicely for the plan he had in mind. For some reason I never forgot him saying those words. I now know what he meant."

Alexander's arms slipped about her shoulders, and he jerked her forward. "Would you be willing to say this before the courts?"

"Yes, Your Highness."

He shook her and her hair tumbled about his face, the sweet scent filling his nostrils and filling his mind with new, disturbing thoughts. "Do not try to beguile me, Brynn. I promise you that you will not like me if you ever think to cross me."

He was hurting her, but it was heaven to be in his arms. "I . . . would not."

Suddenly he felt something wet on his hand, and it took him a moment to realize she was crying. Emotions such as he had never known took hold of him, and he felt his tight grip on her soften to a caress.

"I am deeply grieved if I have hurt you, Brynn. It was not my intention to cause you pain or make you cry. God, I just do not know how to treat a woman."

"I . . . you must have been with many women. Any woman would be honored to . . . I mean . . ."

He laughed softly. "I have no intentions of admitting or denying my prowess with women, Brynn." His voice became serious. "Did I hurt you? Is that why you were crying?"

"No, it isn't that," she said softly. "I was just thinking about all you have lost in your life. Your family was all killed, and you have been forced to pretend to be dead, also. I do so wish I could help take away some of your pain."

Alexander was touched by her kindness, and he gravitated toward her. When he pulled her against him, she did not resist. Inexperienced about how to make love to a woman, he did not know what to do about the fire that had ignited within his body. His hungry lips sought hers, and he felt her readily yield in his arms.

Sweet feelings sang through his body as she pressed her soft body against him tightly.

Alexander felt as if his whole body was coming alive as never before. He was aware of her every intake of breath, her sigh of surrender, her sweet lips softening beneath his.

As inexperienced as he was, age-old primitive instincts now guided his movements.

Chapter Eleven

Like streaks of lightning flashing across the sky, like a rainbow arching across a green valley, Alexander found beauty in touching the woman he was supposed to hate. Sweetly, his lips sought hers, and they fused together in a kiss that left them both breathless.

"Brynn, I never intended for this to happen," he admitted, breaking off the kiss.

Her hands moved down his shirt and she unfastened it, running her fingers across his chest. "If this is all the comfort I can give you, then I give it gladly."

Alexander felt his body tremble, and he fought to regain control of the situation. If she was practiced in wooing a man, she was certainly rendering him her babbling fool.

When he would have pushed her away, her lips found his, and instead, he twisted her around and buried his lips against hers. Hot flashes rampaged through his body. He was on fire, and primitive need heightened his senses. Instinctively, he knew how to excite Brynn and fulfill his own needs.

Alexander scarcely moved, and he could not breathe when Brynn pressed her soft body against his. He guessed that she was as innocent about making love as he. In the back of his mind, Alexander realized that if he did not put a stop to this now, he would soon lose control. Sliding his hand between them, he gently pushed her away. "Again, I apologize," he told her in a thick voice. "It seems I allowed your beauty to rule my head."

Her voice was soft when she said, "I did not know I had beauty."

He laughed. "Apparently the sisters failed to enlighten you on several points. Did they never tell you not to entice a man beyond mindlessness?"

Her hand came forward to rest against his chest, and he grabbed it, clutching it tightly.

"I was taught that vanity was a sin, and that the way of flesh is the way to hell," she admitted. "But I know in my heart if you love someone, love can be beautiful."

"Love?"

For her answer she moved forward and pressed her lips to his. At first Alexander tried to resist, but he soon gave in to the inevitable. His hot breath fanned her hair, and he had the feeling he wanted to take her inside his heart and hold her there forever.

Alexander was only vaguely aware of slipping out of his clothing between hot kisses. When they lay naked in each other's arms, their hot flesh melted together. Where there was no experience on Alexander's part, human nature took over. His hands were smooth and caressing on Brynn's satiny flesh, and she moaned her pleasure when he touched her.

He loved the feel of her body beneath his hands, and he explored each part of her. When he touched her firm young breasts, his breath quickened and he dipped his head so his hot mouth settled on a swollen tip. Groaning at the tantalizing sweetness, Alexander knew he could not stop until he possessed all of her.

Mindlessly, Brynn moaned his name, and his lips covered hers, silencing her for the moment.

Aching and burning with need, he slid his hand down her thigh and spread her legs so he could slide into her. His body trembled and shook as he felt her hot flesh close in around his swollen shaft.

Slowly at first, he moved inside her. Then, when aching, trembling feelings guided his movements, he took them both to the point of ecstasy when he pressed deep inside her.

He kissed her lips, he called her name, he touched her quivering breasts with his lips. A blending of their minds and bodies gave added pleasure.

With a shuddering release, with blinding white lights, his body reached the ultimate surrender. As her body quaked, he held her to him, wondering if one could fall in love in just a matter of one day.

"Brynn," he whispered against her ear. "Sweet, sweet Brynn."

"I never felt like this before," she said in a dreamy voice. "But I have never been with a man. It was . . . it was beautiful beyond belief."

"I know," Alexander admitted, feeling his power as a man. He had given her pleasure, and she had surrendered her youth and innocence to him.

"How do you know?" she asked, running her hands over his chest and allowing the mat of hair to tickle her palm.

"I am wise enough to know that I was the first to be with you. Why did you allow me to go so far with you when you had never made love to a man before?"

"It was right that you should be the first man to lay with me," she said without shame or remorse. "You, or—rather your picture is—" She blushed and hid her face against his chest. "When I was young, I tore your picture out of the book and kept it with me always. I had to keep it hidden so the sisters would not take it from me. Through the long, lonely years, your image

112

was my only companion."

He took a deep breath. "Are you sorry for what happened between us tonight?"

"No. If I never see you again, I will keep the memory of tonight with me always."

He agonized over the thought of never seeing her again, and it caused an ache deep inside him. But he was a man with a mission, and he could not allow any woman to sway him from his course. He was thoughtful for a moment. Suppose she had set out tonight to keep him from his set path?

But, no. Had she not grown up in innocence as he had? Had her life not been filled with loneliness so deep that the days were an ordeal to get through?

"I will have to leave you soon," he told her.

"I know."

"Will you miss me?" This statement surprised him as well as her.

"I will always miss you, Your Highness. But I will take joy in knowing you held me in your arms for a time."

Pulling her to him, Alexander closed his eyes, allowing her sweetness to fill his heart and mind. Until a few short days ago he had not known this girl existed. Now she had chased away all his loneliness, and he was grieved at the thought of ever leaving her.

"Sleep, Brynn, it is almost daylight."

Brynn clung to him. And long after he had fallen asleep, she watched over him, knowing she was unworthy to love this magnificent prince.

A great sadness descended on her as she softly touched his golden hair. If she never saw him again, she would always remember that tonight he loved her. Her name had been on his lips as he called out in ecstasy. Most probably he would forget her, but she would always remember that for a short moment in time she

113

had made him forget his loneliness.

When Alexander awoke, he reached out for Brynn, but she was not beside him. Jumping to his feet, he ran to the door, fearing he might have dreamed last night.

"I sent her out so I could talk to you," a cool voice spoke up from behind Alexander. He whirled around to face the archbishop.

"How long have you been here, Uncle?"

"Long enough to know you haven't been spending your time in idle sleep."

"Do not say anything about Brynn," Alexander stated daringly.

"With your inexperience, I should have foreseen this happening. Did the girl seduce you?"

"That is no concern of yours, Uncle."

"Ah, youth. One always remembers the first whore one lays with. I still remember when I was an impetuous youth and I — "

"Enough, Uncle Serafimo," Alexander stated in the voice of authority. "Brynn is not a whore. Until last night, she was untouched."

"That is more of a pity, Alexander. You were not sent to seduce the innocent. You were sent to capture the guilty."

"It is I who will be King, Uncle, and I who shall make the decisions."

Serafimo looked at the young man and saw a new maturity about him. "I did not traipse through the woods to give a sermon on the ways of the flesh. I have important matters to discuss with you."

Alexander moved off the bed and slipped into his clothing. When he looked up, he saw the sparkle in his uncle's eyes and knew he was happy about something.

"What has happened?" Alexander asked.

114

"I believe there is a chance that we may have located your sister."

Alexander held his breath, not daring to hope. "Are you certain? Tell me the details quickly."

"As you know, my servant, Everett, has never given up the search for Jahane. I received word from him last night that three months ago he encountered an American captain in the West Indies. The man went by the name of Cord Meredith."

Hope fanned to life inside Alexander. "Go on, Uncle."

"Everett, having so little to go on, made inquiries of the man and his family and discovered that Captain Meredith ships out of San Francisco. So, Everett immediately took ship for San Francisco. On making further inquiries, he discovered Captain Meredith has a sister by the name of . . . Jahane Meredith!"

Silence fell between the two men, and Serafimo watched Alexander's throat working convulsively. "Uncle, there cannot be two girls with the unusual name of Jahane who live with a family with the last name of Meredith."

"Exactly what I thought."

"Has Everett made contact with her?"

"No, I had thought you should be the one to contact Jahane. Since you are her brother, she may remember you, and we don't want to frighten her."

Alcxander's eyes brightened, and for the first time in many years he felt hope. "I will go to San Francisco and see this Jahane for myself. If she has a scar on her hand, we shall know that she is my sister."

"Yes, Alexander, and you must leave at once."

The sun slanted its golden light through the branches of the trees as Alexander and Brynn walked through the woods. Brynn glanced across the meadow, enchanted by

115

the wide purple sweep of heather. The scent of jasmine danced on the wind, and she felt sadness pressing in on her.

"I must leave you now, Brynn," the prince told her.

She turned away, not wanting him to see her tears. "God go with you," she whispered. "May he keep you safe in whatever danger you encounter."

In one swift stride, he was beside her. Turning her to face him, he stared into the beautiful blue eyes that were swimming with tears.

"I will be back for you," he promised.

"I will be waiting," she answered.

Alexander held her trembling body to him, wanting to tell her of his pain at leaving her, but he could not. He bent to kiss her soft lips. Then without a word, he released her and turned away.

Brynn watched him disappear into the woods, fearing she would never see him again. Her heart was breaking, and she knew Prince Alexander walked a dangerous road. She only wished she could help him in his time of need.

She reflected on what part she could ever play in his life. Even if he won against his Uncle Reynard, she could never be anything but a mistress that he would have to keep hidden from prying eyes.

Brynn smiled sadly, knowing she would take anything that the prince handed her, for had she not loved him for many years? He had been her imaginary playmate, her friend, her companion. Now that she had met him in the flesh, he was more wonderful than anything she could have imagined.

"I will wait for you," she said aloud. "Even if you never come back to me, I will always wait for you."

Dressed in the dark, heavy cowl of a monk, Prince

Alexander stood beside his Uncle Serafimo, waiting to go on board the ship that would ultimately take him to San Francisco.

"Have you heard any further word of my sister?" Alexander asked.

"No, nothing. But I have a bit of news that might please you. It seems Reynard and his henchmen are scouring the countryside looking for Brynn, their lost princess. I saw him yesterday, and he accused me of spiriting her away. Of course, I told him I could account for my whereabouts for the last four days."

"Do you think Brynn will be safe at your cabin?"

His uncle arched an inquiring brow. "Yes, I would think so. No one save a few trusted friends knows of my hunting cabin. It has always been my retreat when I need repose from the world's problems."

"Who can Brynn be, Uncle? Have you discovered her true identity?"

"No, not as of yet. But I shall make every attempt to learn who she is."

"I have come to believe she was not privy to Uncle Reynard's evil plot. It is my theory that she is innocent of any wrongdoing. If I should not return, take care of her."

Serafimo studied his nephew's face, seeing more than Alexander could guess.

"Do you think you are the first young man who had fallen into a beautiful woman's trap? Some women have the power to make a man believe anything she wishes. I would caution you not to believe too strongly in this one's innocence. You do not really know her. You must never lose sight of the fact that she was one of Reynard's tools."

"I know that, but she appears to be innocent to me. You will look after her and see that no harm befalls her all the same. I have a feeling she may now be in

117

danger."

The archbishop nodded. "I shall look after her." Serafimo glanced out at the ship. "You have all that you need. I gave you enough money to cover your needs. When you get to San Francisco, first take the letter of introduction I gave you to Father Estevan. Since he is an old friend of mine, I know he will help you in any way he can. You can trust him. You will need to buy clothing in San Francisco so you will blend in with the locals. You know English, so use it. My man, Everett, will meet you when you dock."

Alexander smiled at his uncle, who never left anything to chance. "Have you forgotten anything?"

"I do not believe so. Be sure when you see this Jahane Meredith that you examine her hand so you will know if it is your sister. If she has a deep scar on her right palm, then you can be certain she is Princess Jahane."

"They are calling for the passengers to board now, Uncle Serafimo," Alexander said, turning to face the man who had been his only hope for so many years.

Offering his hand to his uncle, Alexander was unprepared when a sudden gust of wind tore the cowl off his head, revealing his golden hair and throwing his face in sunlight. Alexander quickly pulled the hood back in place, looking to see if anyone had noticed, but apparently no one had.

"Pray that I find my sister and can bring her back with me."

"I will keep you in my prayers every night. Have a care, Alexander. Reynard's men will also be looking for your sister. Remember that her life may be in danger, so try to make contact with her as soon as possible."

"Yes, I will look for her the moment I arrive."

Alexander turned away and moved up the gangplank. As his foot touched the deck and he felt the swaying motion beneath him, he gripped the railing. He watched his uncle fade away into the crowd, feeling alone and uncertain.

When the wind caught at the canvasses, he felt the ship move out of the harbor, and he watched as his beloved country faded in the distance.

For hours he stood on deck, until it was too dark to see. But still he imagined he could smell the scent of jasmine, a scent he would always associate with Balmarhea and with Brynn.

He remembered the night before when he had held Brynn in his arms and made passionate love to her. Even now, with the important mission ahead of him, he yearned for the touch of her hand and the feel of her lips.

"I will come back," he said aloud. "Wait for me, Brynn."

Reynard paced the floor in his bedroom, swearing at the top of his voice. The halls rang with his obscenities, and servants cringed in corners. Having seen him in this mood many times, they knew no one was safe from his anger.

The duke stopped before a mirror and glanced at his likeness. His hand went up to the scar that slashed across his cheek, and his eyes narrowed as they always did when he remembered the night his nephew gave him that scar.

A heavy knock fell on the door, and he waved his valet away and wrenched it open himself. Seeing his son Damerou, his mouth twisted in disgust. Damerou was tall and blond, and a handsome rogue with the ladies, but his father never gave him much credit for being intelligent.

"I can tell by your face that you did not find the girl," Reynard ranted. "Can I not depend on you for anything? Well, speak up, did you find any trace of Brynn?"

Damerou took a deep breath. "No, Father, she just disappeared. No one saw her go."

"No one just disappears. Did you search for tracks leading away from the garden?"

Damerou shrank from the rage he saw on his father's face. "No, I never thought—"

"You never do think. Why did I have to be burdened with an imbecile for a son?"

Damerou dared not disagree with his father; no one ever did. His father had never spoken a kind word to him, and had only acknowledged he was alive the last few months because he wanted him to marry some girl he claimed was his cousin, the Princess Jahane.

"Even though I have not located the girl, I have some interesting news, Father."

"I doubt it. But what is it?"

"My Uncle Serafimo was discovered at the docks seeing someone off to America."

"Why should I care what my brother does?"

"You have been interested in San Francisco of late, and the ship's destination was San Francisco. Do you not think that odd?"

Reynard's eyes narrowed in thoughtfulness. "Yes, very odd indeed. What did the man look like that Serafimo was seeing off?"

"I was told he wore the clothing of a monk. There was something else that my informant thought was peculiar."

"Well," Reynard said impatiently. "Do you intend to tell me, or do I have to drag every word out of you?"

"At some point the monk's hood blew off and my informant says he was not a monk at all. He had long golden hair and looked so much like me I almost called out to him."

Reynard froze, and his voice came out in a sharp whisper. "What did you say?"

"I said he almost called out—"

"No, the part about him looking like you."

"Yes, that was the peculiar part. It's very strange indeed to think there is someone around who looks like—"

Reynard waved his son to be silent. "Have your informant report to me at once." His eyes burned with hatred, and he ran his hand over the scar on his cheek. "I wonder if he could have survived the fall. I wonder if . . ."

An evil smile curved his lips. "I believe I shall call on my brother this evening. It could be that he has secrets that he has not told me."

Two

San Francisco

Chapter Twelve

San Francisco, 1856

Meredith House had been built high upon a hill with a magnificent view of the city and bay area. Because of its location, the mansion had survived the numerous fires that had plagued San Francisco in recent years. The house, on its lofty perch, offered the occupants a spectacular view of San Francisco and the sea beyond.

Jahane Meredith rushed through the front door, handing her shopping basket and cape to the Chinese houseboy, Jojo.

"Is Mama in?" she inquired, stripping off her gloves and dropping them in Jojo's outstretched hand.

"Yes'm, missy," Jojo answered in his singsong English. "Madame is in her chamber with the dressmaker woman."

With a quick stride, Jahane rushed across the hallway and up the stairs, her heart thundering with excitement, her patent-leather boots visible when she lifted the skirt of her pink-and-white candy-striped gown.

Instead of stopping at her mother's bedroom door, Jahane climbed to the third floor, threw open the shutters, and stepped out onto the widow's walk. The widow's walk had been added to the house at Maggie

Meredith's insistence so it would resemble the architecture of New England, where women who married seafaring men could watch them come home from the sea.

Here, Jahane had a spectacular view of the bay, and all of San Francisco lay at her feet. Her eyes scanned the waterway, searching for the *Golden Phoenix*. At last her eyes fell on the ship, which she recognized by its seven sails bleached white from the sun, and her heart pounded with excitement.

He was home — Cord was home! She tried to curtail her anticipation, knowing he would have to oversee the unloading of his cargo before she would see him. She considered going to the dock, but quickly discarded the notion, since her mother would never give her consent.

With a last wistful glance at the *Golden Phoenix,* Jahane moved back into the house and made her way back to the second floor. Standing before her mother's bedroom door, she patted her hair into place, tucked a stray lock behind her ear, and ran her hand down her gown.

Satisfied that her mother would not scold her for her appearance, Jahane rapped lightly on the door and entered when her mother invited her inside.

Maggie Meredith stood on a stool while the seamstress, Rose Coolidge, measured the hem of her gown. Looking at Jahane, Maggie could tell she was excited by the glow on her cheeks.

"You didn't stay long at the market, Jahane. Did you get the apples so Cook can make the apple tarts?"

"Yes, Mama, but I didn't finish the rest of the shopping. I just couldn't!" Jahane whirled around in her delirium. "You will never guess what I overheard at the market, Mama. I rushed home immediately to confirm the rumors. And it's true, I saw it for myself!"

Stepping off the stool, Maggie allowed Rose to unfasten her gown. Smiling, she spoke softly to the girl she loved like a daughter. "It pains me to dampen your enthusiasm, my dear, but I have already been informed that the *Golden Phoenix* has come to port. Cord sent word he would be home in time for dinner. Already Cook is preparing his favorite meal."

Happiness shone on Jahane's face. "Oh, Mama, I cannot wait to see him. It has been one year, six months, two weeks, and three days since Cord left. Can't we go to the waterfront to see him? Oh, Mama, I cannot wait!"

Maggie's eyes softened sympathetically, knowing how eagerly Jahane had awaited Cord's homecoming. The young girl spent most of her evenings on the widow's walk, her eyes scanning the horizon for Cord's ship. "No, dear. You know Cord would rather us not go to the docks. If you use your time making yourself pretty for him, you will find the hours will pass much more quickly."

The seamstress emptied her mouth of pins so she could speak. "One seldom witnesses such devotion between a brother and sister. I was telling my Harvey just the other night how Jahane watches each day for her brother's return. And it's remarkable how Captain Meredith dotes on her."

Maggie's eyes narrowed secretively. "Yes, it is remarkable," she admitted. "My son and daughter are very close."

The seamstress prattled on with the familiarity of one who had worked for the Merediths for several years. "You certainly have a family to be proud of. Your son being master of his own ship and all, and this fine house you live in. And look at Jahane. She is one of the loveliest young ladies in San Francisco. I'm not mistaken when I say she could marry any one of a dozen young gentlemen."

Seeing the blush on Jahane's face, Maggie embraced her. "Careful with your flattery, Rose, or you will fill my daughter's head with her own worth. Her nature is sweet and unspoiled, and that's the way I intend to keep her."

Rose Coolidge adjusted her thick bifocals on the bridge of her nose and looked the young girl over from head to toe.

Lovely beyond words would describe Jahane. Her skin was aglow with health, her cheeks flushed with color. Her hair was golden like the sun. For now she wore it pulled away from her face and tied back with a pink ribbon. Her face, though lovely, was enhanced by the most unusual color of blue eyes. They were so pale in color they appeared crystal-clear and transparent. Jahane was tall for a girl, topping her mother by several inches. Yes, Rose thought, she was exceedingly lovely, and so kindhearted that she was a favorite with everyone.

Rose, being a seamstress, and not on the same social level as the Merediths, could only go on what she had been told about the balls and socials where Jahane was always surrounded by suitors. If there was any special young gentleman in Jahane's life, Rose had not heard mention of him, and in her profession, where she was seamstress for most of the more prominent families in San Francisco, she would certainly have heard if there had been.

Maggie Meredith slipped into her green silk gown and turned for Jahane to hook her up the back, while she instructed Rose to put more lace on the hem of the new ball gown and to have it ready by next week for the Fireman's Ball.

Rose gathered up her sewing basket, and draping the gown over her arm, took her leave of mother and daughter. Descending the stairs, she smiled at Jojo who held her cape out to her.

As always when she came to this house, she was awed by its elegance. Unlike many of their contemporaries, who had obtained their wealth in the gold fields and had furnished their homes with new furnishings, it appeared that the Merediths' home was furnished with family heirlooms. Heavy woods with shiny surfaces, sparkling china, and brilliant chandeliers graced the rooms.

For all their socializing, no one seemed to know much about the Merediths' past. They had moved to San Francisco several years ago, after the death of Mrs. Meredith's husband, but from where they came, no one knew for sure. The Merediths always steered the conversation away from their past life, and most people respected their privacy. Of course, that did not stop the speculations from flying.

Jojo opened the door for Rose's departure, and when she stepped out, she encountered a man on the steps. The seamstress beamed up at the tall, sun-browned Captain Cord Meredith. She noticed his arms were laden with packages, and his brown eyes were warm as they settled on her. Rose, thinking how handsome Cord Meredith was, decided that had she been a younger girl, she would have swooned at his feet.

"Good afternoon, Captain. It's a fine day."

"Indeed it is, Mrs. Coolidge," he answered in a deep voice laced with humor, "a fine day for a homecoming."

Rose's eyes moved over his face, which was clean-shaven, to his strong jawline. His shoulders were wide and finely defined beneath the blue jacket he wore. His dark hair was windswept. Handsome and dashing, she could only guess how the young ladies melted when he paid them the slightest attention. She wondered if he was aware of all the sighs among the young ladies she

129

outfitted when his name was mentioned. Of course he knew. How could he not?

Rose saw his eyes move past her, and he glanced into the house as if he were searching for someone, but still she kept him talking. When she saw the china doll's head peeking out of one of the packages, she remarked, "Another doll for your sister?"

His dark eyes softened at the mention of Jahane. "Yes. I admit it's getting difficult to buy a doll for Jahane's collection that she does not already have."

Again his eyes went past Rose and searchingly to the stairs. Rose saw that it was hard for him to make polite conversation when what he really wanted to do was find his sister.

With a nod, she finally stepped past the captain and down the front walk, almost envious of the love that she could feel in this house.

Pausing at the street, Rose pulled on her knitted gloves and tightened the drawstring on her purse, feeling somehow cheated. She would go home to Harvey, who was an accountant at the bank, and to whom she had been married for thirty-two years. They would eat a quiet dinner, and then he would disappear into his study to do paperwork while she retired to her sewing room, and with her fancy stitches, would create gowns and underclothing for the prominent families of San Francisco.

She sighed, thinking hers was not really a lonely existence, because sometimes, like today, she was allowed to touch the fringes of another world—she was allowed to observe how love could knit a family like the Merediths together with invisible bonds. She hurried down the steep walkway, remembering a time when she and her husband had loved each other. But years of hard work and neglect had made her and Harvey companionable strangers. Deep inside, she longed for more, and hungered for better than the long hours of solitude that stretched before her tonight.

With resignation, she adjusted her bonnet against the hot sun and hurried away, wondering what Harvey would do if she put her arms around him. Shrugging her shoulders, she decided against it, knowing he would probably think her addlebrained.

Jahane drew in her breath while her maid, Della, fastened the back of her yellow organdy gown. When this was accomplished, she stared critically at herself in the full-length mirror.

"Do you think Cord will like me in this gown, Della?" She bit her lower lip. "Does this color make me look older, or should I wear the green gown?"

The maid's eyes widened in reflection. "I think Captain Meredith will like you whatever you wear, miss." She chuckled. "I know of some women who wish he would pay them the attention he showers on you."

Jahane met Della's eyes in the mirror. Della had been with the family since they moved to San Francisco, so no one cared that she always spoke her mind. "I suppose you are referring to Lorraine Scott in particular." A frown knotted Jahane's brow as she felt a pang of jealousy. "I know she expects to marry my brother someday."

Della handed her a lace handkerchief, then spoke with authority. "Well, if you want my opinion, I agree that Miss Scott has her eye on the captain."

Jahane turned to face the maid, and smiled. "Well, she cannot have him."

"So you say," Della remarked, gathering up Jahane's discarded clothing.

The soft rap on the door caught Jahane's attention. Thinking it was her mother, she nodded to Della to admit her, while she glanced in the mirror to straighten the curl that hung over her forehead.

The image of a man reflected in her mirror, and Jahane caught her breath. With heart racing, she turned slowly to face Cord. She hadn't expected him so soon, and now that he was here, she seemed unable to move.

There he stood, with arms outstretched to her, looking more handsome than any man had a right to look. Her feet flew across the floor, and she leaped into his arms. Closing her eyes, Jahane felt his arms tighten about her, comforting and reviving her — bringing life to her once more.

For so long she had gone through the motions of living. Her life had paused, waiting for Cord's return.

"Cord, Cord," she cried, burying her face against his rough jacket, then pressing her soft cheek against his. "I have missed you so desperately that I began to believe you would never come home."

He shook with laughter. "I will always return to wherever you are, funny face. Haven't I told you that many times?" Prying her hands away from his neck, he held her at arm's length so he could look at her.

Seeing she almost came up to his shoulder, he spoke. "I believe you have grown since my last homecoming, Jahane. Turn around and let me get a good look at you."

Jahane turned slowly, hoping he would see that she was now a woman. "The dressmaker had to make my gown a whole size larger this past spring, Cord. Do you like this gown?" she chattered.

Cord looked past the soft curves that now proclaimed Jahane a woman, since he refused to admit to himself that she had grown up. He saw instead the glow on her cheeks and the happiness dancing in her eyes, and his heart melted as always.

"Did you bring me a present?" she asked.

His laughter lightened her heart, and she thought she would burst with happiness. Taking her hand, he kissed it and tucked it into the crook of his arm, saying, "To answer your questions, yes, I think you are taller, and yes, I brought you a present." He winked at Della before moving out the door with Jahane.

"What did you bring me?" she wanted to know as they descended the stairs.

"Now, Miss Inquisitive, wouldn't you like to know? As always, I will present the gifts to you and Mama at the same time."

She smiled up at him, knowing he would not be cheated out of his usual ritual. "I hope you are going to stay a very long time, Cord. I cannot bear to think of you going away again."

"Put such notions out of your pretty head for the time being. I intend to be home for several months. You and Mama will grow so weary of me you will beg me to take ship before the summer is ended."

She turned earnest eyes on him. "I would never grow weary of you, Cord."

He paused on the bottom step and encased her in a hug. "Wouldn't you?" he asked in a deep voice.

"No, never."

For the first time he felt the swell of her breasts pressed against his chest, and he experienced a shock that rocked his world. His body had discovered what his mind would not admit; Jahane was now a woman. His senses whirled with unanswered questions. Why did he want to hold on to her childhood? Why did he want to deny that she was growing up? He tried to think how old she was. He and his mother had decided that Jahane had been no more than three or four when she first came to them . . . that would make her seventeen or eighteen!

With a sweeping gaze, Cord discovered that not only was Jahane grown up, she was beautiful. Did other men find Jahane beautiful? Did gentlemen call on her—ask her to dance, simper like sick calves if she smiled at them? What if they did? She had belonged to him from the moment his dying father had placed her in his care, and she always would.

He shook his head to clear it, deciding to push troubled thoughts to the back of his mind. This was his first night home, and he wanted to be with Jahane and his mother.

Chapter Thirteen

Dinner had been a happy affair. Around the mahogany table, Cord entertained Jahane and his mother with tales of his latest travels and adventures.

Cord swore he had eaten nothing half so good as the chicken roasted with pineapple rings, and he devoured, with gusto, the apple tarts smothered with heavy cream.

Jahane hung on to Cord's every word. She found herself watching the way his dark hair curled at the top of his collar. Her eyes fastened on the sleeve of his blue dinner jacket, and she noted the way his muscles bulged each time he raised his fork to his mouth. She studied his features: his face deeply tanned, his lips sensitive, his eyes, oh, those glorious dark eyes that appeared to look right into her soul.

She loved his crooked smile, because she was certain that was the special smile that he reserved for her alone. Jahane wondered why the other men of her acquaintance were not half so handsome and charming as Cord. Since he had traveled the world, he had a certain sophistication about him that other young gentlemen had not acquired.

Of course, she had to admit to herself that any man she met would have to be at a disadvantage in her eyes, because she loved Cord with all her young heart.

When the family migrated to the parlor, there was a feeling of festivity in the air.

Cord was seated on the sofa beside his mother, while Jahane was seated on a stool in front of him, her eyes bright with anticipation.

This was how Cord had imagined his homecoming. Here, with the two women who meant most in the world to him, he felt he had truly come home. He could feel their love reach out and wrap him in a warm embrace.

His heart was light as he handed out presents. First, he gave his mother a roll of green-printed silk from China and porcelain dishes from Germany, while Jahane looked on expectantly, awaiting her turn.

At last, he placed a fragile Dresden music box on Jahane's lap, and watched as she squealed in delight when the figure of a man and woman danced to the tune of a waltz. She smiled elatedly at the rolls of colored ribbons and the handmade lace from France.

Cord met Jahane's eyes apologetically when he handed her the doll he had brought from England. "You see, I pictured you as I had last seen you. I hadn't counted on you growing into a young lady while I was away."

Jahane's eyes sparkled with happiness as she sat the doll on her lap and adjusted its tiny straw bonnet. "So you admit I am grown up, Cord?"

He tugged playfully at a stray curl that rested on her forehead. "I admit nothing of the sort. I wager you still slide down the banister when Mama isn't looking. And do you still raid the pantry for sweets in the middle of the night?"

She shook her head and raised her chin with an air of indignation. "Not so. Mama says sweets aren't good for a young lady's complexion," she smiled. "As for sliding down the banister, I gave that up when I stopped playing with dolls."

Maggie carefully folded her silk and placed it aside. "You will be pleased to learn that your sister is the belle of San Francisco, if there is such a person. She receives so many invitations, she couldn't possibly accept them all. Her dance card is always full, and she is most sought after by the young gentlemen of our acquaintance."

Cord stared at Jahane, noting the pretty blush on her cheeks, and for some reason it troubled him. "So, I am gone for a while, and you replace me in your heart with another man, or men," he lightly teased, not knowing how to deal with the pang of jealousy that made him feel uncomfortable.

Jahane leaned forward in a flurry of petticoats and kissed his cheek. "No one will ever take your place with me, Cord. You will always be the first man in my heart." She dimpled. "Pity the poor man who tries to win my heart, for he will have to live in Cord Meredith's shadow, and you cast a long shadow."

Feeling somewhat pacified, he smiled down at her, the look in his eyes embracing her as he reached for her hand.

Neither Jahane nor Cord saw the worried frown on Maggie's face. "Jahane, go upstairs and get my light-blue shawl, will you, dear? I feel quite chilled."

Jahane stood up, her hand sliding out of Cord's grasp. "Of course, Mama." She hurried out of the room, while Cord's eyes followed her.

Cord, always observant of his mother's feelings, turned his attention to her. His arm slid around her shoulder, and he smiled down at her. "Do you want to tell me the reason you sent Jahane out of the room, Mama?"

Maggie's brow knitted, and her eyes took on a distressed look. "I have to talk to you about Jahane. Something must be done. Have you thought about her future?"

"In what respect? She seems contented to me. What is your reason for concern?"

Maggie's eyes shifted away from Cord's anxious glance. "I have many worries about Jahane," she said evasively.

His expression became more troubled. "Suppose you share your worries with me."

Maggie leaned her head against the cushion and stared at her son. "First of all, she is beginning to question her past. She wants answers that I cannot give her."

"Yes, I always intended to tell her more about the night she first came into my life, but the time never seemed quite right. Of course, there is not a great deal I can tell her about her real family. But I should answer her questions as best I can. Perhaps it's time you told me more about the letter I delivered to you from Father." His glance was inquisitive. "Do you still have the letter?"

"No, it was your father's wish that the letter be destroyed. Actually, what you don't know is that your father wrote a second letter, which Thadeus brought to me."

Cord was astonished. "I never knew about a second letter. What did Father say in the second letter?"

Maggie's eyes turned misty. Even after all this time, every word in those letters was burned into her brain.

138

"Of course, most of it was . . . how he loved me. And he was most concerned for Jahane's safety and that her true identity be concealed, and that has always been my concern as well."

"Do you think she was not Chapin d'Arcy's daughter? Is that what concerns you?"

She lowered her eyes. "I don't . . . I can't say . . . at the moment. I have kept this secret to myself for so long . . ." Her voice trailed off. "Let me think about how to handle this, Cord. We will talk more on the subject later on. Then, together we will decide how to tell Jahane."

"You are confusing me, Mama. You have always let me believe that Jahane was Chapin d'Arcy's daughter."

"It seemed to be the answer at the time . . . Afterward, it was easier to let . . ." Again her voice trailed off.

"I never told you, this, Mama, but a few years back I did some inquiring about Balmarhea. My informant told me that Count d'Arcy had no family that survived that tragic night when the king and queen and their children were all murdered by rebels. I discovered that Count Chapin d'Arcy had a daughter who would be about Jahane's age. His daughter disappeared the night Father brought Jahane on board the *Boston Clipper*, and no one has found any trace of her since, so I have to conclude that Jahane is his daughter. Are you saying she is not?"

"Cord, please. I cannot talk about this right now. But I do want to impress on you that Jahane might still be in danger because of who she is. Several times in the last few weeks, Jahane has told me she thought she was being followed."

"Why did you not tell me before now?" Cord questioned in alarm.

Maggie was so distressed she could not meet his eyes. "I blamed her feelings on her overimaginative mind. I cannot bear to think, that after all this time, she might still be in danger. She is so dear to me, Cord. I don't know how I would have survived all these years since your father's death without her."

"I believe we can now feel confident that she is safe and discount any danger to her. We very cleverly covered our trail, as Father instructed. Even if someone were looking for Jahane, they would never be able to trace her to San Francisco. When he left Boston we severed all ties. As Thadeus suggested, I even changed the name of the *Boston Clipper* to the *Golden Phoenix*. Except for our names, there is nothing to connect us with the Captain Jonah Meredith, who saved the life of a little Balmarhean girl."

Maggie laced her fingers together, wanting to believe that Jahane was safe. "Yes, I suppose you are right. I am an excessive and needless worrier. Perhaps after all these years without trouble, I should feel more confident."

Cord looked into his mother's troubled eyes, and saw that she was still distressed. "You have other worries, Mama—tell me what they are."

"It's very difficult to tell you this, Cord. But it is my belief that you should let Jahane go."

"What do you mean 'let her go'?"

"I mean, Son, that she lives and breathes for you. Every day your name dominates her conversation. She always turns away from any attentions from young men her own age. As she stated earlier, how could they

140

compete with you?"

Cord could not help feeling pleased. "Do you think this is bad?"

"Yes. She will criticize one man because he is not as tall as you—and another because he does not have your sense of humor. She finds every excuse not to like any of them. Of course, she is always charming, and the men continue to pursue her . . . but . . . I just don't know . . . what to do. If only your father were here to advise me."

Cord clamped his jaw together tightly. "Jahane is too young to be courted by men. I am surprised you would allow it, Mama."

"Open your eyes, Cord. She is a young woman. Most of her friends are already married, while Jahane will not even consider having a young man call on her." Maggie toyed with the lace on her handkerchief. "Of course, her standoffish manner only serves to further intrigue the gentlemen. She is favored, and much sought after, and although I do not want her to marry yet, I want her to give up this preoccupation she has with you."

He frowned. "What are you suggesting I do?"

"As I said, Cord, let her go. Don't devote so much time to her. See other women while you are home. Invite them to the house so Jahane can see you with them. Encourage her to seek the company of other men. Don't misunderstand me, I do not want her to become entangled with another man; I just think if she is courted, she will lose this infatuation she has for you."

Cord felt his heart contract. His mind rejected the thought of pushing Jahane away. She had always been his responsibility; she belonged to him. As for encouraging her to seek another man's attentions . . .

"What you ask is impossible, Mama," Cord said bluntly.

She grasped his hand painfully. "Cord, listen to me. You are my son, my own flesh and blood. Next to your father I love you more than anything in this world, but I love Jahane, too, and I do not want her hurt, either. Believe me when I tell you she is not for you. And, don't let Jahane become too important to you. It isn't fair to either one of you. You know I would not ask this of you without good reason, Son."

He closed his eyes as if he were in pain. Finally he spoke. "I will do as you say, Mama, even though I do not understand why. But it will not be easy. I would much rather spend my time with Jahane than a dozen empty-headed beauties."

"Exactly my point. Jahane is accustomed to receiving your undivided attention. You have spoiled her for other men. Of course, the men she meets can not measure up to her dashing brother. No man ever could in her eyes."

"I am not Jahane's brother," Cord reminded her.

"Yes, but—"

"Here's your shawl, Mama," Jahane said, coming into the room. "I also brought your warm slippers." She draped the shawl across Maggie's shoulders and helped her into her slippers. "Are you more comfortable now, Mama?"

Maggie patted the girl's hand, while smiling lovingly at her. "Yes, dear, much more comfortable." She gave Cord a pointed look. "However, I believe I will retire to my room and make an early night of it. The dress fittings today have caused me undue fatigue."

"Would you like me to see you to your room, Mama?" Jahane offered.

"No, dear, you stay here and talk to your brother."

Cord stood up and placed a kiss on his mother's cheek, while she gave him a look that reminded him of their conversation and his promise to her.

"I'll see you both at breakfast," Maggie said, knowing how difficult it would be for Cord to put Jahane from him. It would be painful for Jahane at first, but it was best.

Jahane's eyes followed her mother out of the room. "I hope she isn't coming down with a chill, Cord. I worry about her sometimes."

Cord scowled. "Worrying seems to be a trait that is inbred in the female constitution. My mother is smitten with the same malady as yourself."

"Whatever do you mean? What has Mama got to worry about?"

"That's what I want to talk to you about." Cord took her hand, and was about to seat her on the sofa when Jojo came to the door with a note which he handed Cord.

Cord quickly read the message and frowned. "I fear we will have to postpone our talk. It seems I have a buyer for my cargo, and the man insists on inspecting the lot immediately."

"Must you go tonight?" she asked wistfully.

"Yes, but we shall have our talk tomorrow." He placed a quick kiss on her forehead, and in long strides left the room.

Jahane sat for a long moment, wondering what had displeased Cord. She looked forward to their talk tomorrow. There was much to be said between her and Cord. She had questions that only he could answer. And she had to talk to him about their future.

Picking up the doll and the music box he had given her, she smiled as her footsteps took her toward the stairs. Surely Cord could see that she was now a woman. If he was unaware of her new maturity, she would just have to make him take notice.

As Jahane reached her room, the moonlight was so bright, she didn't light the lamp. She slipped out of her clothes and into her nightgown and dressing robe that Della had laid out for her.

She then opened the bureau drawer and removed an aged leather pouch and seated herself on the middle of her bed, emptying the contents of the bag into her hand.

She glanced at the blood-red stone that sparkled even in this half-light. Somehow it always seemed to invoke painful memories. A face flashed through her mind—a man's face. She had thought he was her father, but how could she be sure? Jahane remembered thinking the man loved her. But why then had he inflicted her with pain? she thought, glancing down at the scar on the palm of her hand.

Jahane had vague dreams which she could not hold on to in the light of day. For many years she had relived in her nightmares the experience of having her hand slashed by the man she had trusted. Sometimes she would dream instead of a lovely, golden-haired woman who had given her comfort, but that, too, was unclear. And in the dark recesses of her mind she seemed to remember a boy—a brother before Cord, whom she had loved more than anyone else in the world.

She shook her head, knowing her past would always be no more to her than a shadowy dream.

Lying back against her pillow, Jahane wound the

144

music box Cord had given her tonight. As she listened to the lovely tune, her troubled thoughts began to dim.

Finally she closed her eyes, trying to recapture the happiness she had experienced earlier in the evening. There was no reason for her to have troubled thoughts about the past, because Cord was her future.

Did he love her as much as she loved him? Would he remember his promise to wait until she was grown so he could make her his wife? Yes, he would remember. Had he not promised that one day they would be man and wife?

Sleep overcame Jahane and her dreams were sweet, until they turned into nightmares!

Chapter Fourteen

Jahane awoke with a start. She listened for a moment and then smiled to herself. The noise that had disturbed her sleep had been Cord returning from the docks.

She was glad she was awake because she had so much to discuss with Cord.

Scooting off the bed, she retied the sash on her dressing gown and quickly ran a brush through her hair. As an afterthought, she picked up the pouch containing the red stone and left the room.

The hallway was dimly lit by the flickering lamp on the table, so she had no trouble making her way to Cord's room.

Rapping softly on his door, she caught her breath when he opened it and his tall form filled the doorway. Resting his shoulder against the doorjamb, Cord gave Jahane an inquisitive look.

"Shouldn't little girls be safely tucked in their beds at this time of night?"

"We were going to have a talk, remember?" she reminded him.

"Yes, but it's late."

With a shrug of her shoulders, she pushed him aside and entered his bedroom. Jahane could remember as a child, when she had awakened from her recurring nightmare and had come here seeking comfort from Cord—comfort that he had always given.

She looked at the oversize bed, recalling the times she had curled up beside him and he had soothed her fears by explaining them away.

As if Cord had read her mind, he spoke just behind her. "Did you have one of your nightmares and need someone to chase the shadows from your room?"

She plopped down on the bed, crossing her legs beneath her and staring into his eyes. "No, not a nightmare this time—I just wanted to talk."

Cord was exhausted. The sale of his cargo had taken longer than he had hoped. Afterward Thadeus and several other crew members had convinced him to go to the Dockside Inn for a celebration. His head was a bit foggy, and he realized he had drunk too much rum.

His eyes moved down Jahane's neck to where her breasts pushed against the soft dressing gown. Quickly he looked back to her face, wondering what in the hell had come over him. He had never before experienced these agonizing feelings for Jahane. Was he out of his mind? It was the rum, he assured himself. He had definitely had too much to drink.

"We could always talk tomorrow," he suggested. "Perhaps if you are now a young lady, as you have pointed out to me since I arrived home, you shouldn't be in a man's room this late at night."

She looked at him, startled for a moment. "I have always come to this room when I was troubled about something. Please do not send me away now."

He had never been able to deny her anything, so he relented. "What has you troubled now, my little Jahane?"

Cord moved toward her and sat down on the bed, just out of her reach so he wouldn't be tempted to touch her. "Tell me what has caused that frown on your pretty face?"

She raised her face to his and looked deeply into his eyes. "Am I pretty, Cord?"

He started to touch her cheek, but something made him pull back. This wasn't his little Jahane; this was a beautiful, desirable young woman, and he was unsure of how to treat her. "Yes, you are pretty. You always have been," he assured her.

"Prettier than all the other women you met on your voyage?"

He tried not to smile, but was not completely successful. "There has never been another woman who could rival you in looks, Jahane. I suppose knowing you has colored the way I perceive all other women."

"Have you . . . have you ever been with another woman. I mean made love to another . . . woman?"

He arched a dark brow at her. "Hasn't Mama cautioned you about asking men such personal questions?"

"You are not just any man."

"Still, it is an unfair question, Jahane. And one you should not expect me to answer."

"That means you have been with other women," she said in a hurt voice. "I suppose I could not expect you to be entirely faithful to me while you waited for me to grow up."

"Jahane," he moaned, his head swimming from too much liquor.

"All right, Cord. I will rephrase my question. Can you say you have never loved a woman before?"

He noticed the way the lamplight flickered across her golden hair, the red fire reflecting in her blue eyes.

148

"No, I never have, Jahane," he admitted. "And before now, I have wondered why. Tonight I realize that I couldn't love anyone else because my heart is too filled with the little vixen who lives under my own roof."

Jahane's heart was thundering. The light in her blue eyes softened with love as she met his dark gaze. She felt a warmth spread throughout her body. "I have always known that you loved me, Cord. It was but a matter of waiting for me to grow up."

He shook his head to clear it. What had his mother asked him to do tonight? Oh, yes, she had said he would have to let Jahane go, but must he do it now? Could he not bask in the adoration he saw in her eyes for a while longer?

"I love you," she said softly. "I always have."

He tried to resist the need to take her in his arms and crush her to him. "You shouldn't say that, Jahane. You don't know what you are doing? You have never had a beau, how can you know how you feel about me?"

Her chin jutted out stubbornly. "Because I decided at a very young age that I would save myself for you. I do not like other men. To me they are all shallow, boring, and not in the least to my liking. They cannot compare with you, Cord."

Cord found himself being drawn to her in a far more disturbing way. He found himself drowning in her eyes. He wanted to touch her silken hair—to hold her to him until the trembling inside him stopped. He forgot the promise he had made to his mother, and reached out, pulling Jahane to him.

"Oh, little one, what are you doing to me? What am I going to do with you?"

She raised her head and looked deeply into his dark

149

eyes. "I know what you promised to do about me many years ago, Cord. Don't you remember?"

He knew he should release her and put some distance between them, but he could not. He did manage to smile, however. "I made you so many promises. To which one are you referring?"

She was so disturbed by his closeness that she pressed her cheek to his so he wouldn't be able to read the distress in her eyes. "I am talking about the promise you made to wait for me to grow up so we could be married," she whispered through trembling lips, fearing he would turn away from her.

Jahane knew Cord could choose from any beautiful woman he wanted in San Francisco, older and far more sophisticated women, so how could she expect him to honor a promise he had made her as a child?

"But, Jahane, that promise was made in jest. Surely you never expected—surely you must know—"

Now she did meet his eyes. "It was not made in jest, Cord. There has always been truth between us, then and now. If you no longer love me . . . say so, and I will leave."

When he saw the glistening tears swimming in her eyes, his arms tightened around her. "You and I could never wed, Jahane. We may not be real brother and sister, but I will always feel the affection of a brother for you." Even as he said it, he knew it wasn't true. Something inside him had changed toward her. Her softness, the sweet scent of her, was weaving a spell about him, and he found it very disturbing.

Her face drained of color. "Surely you don't mean that, Cord. I have done everything to make myself pretty for you. I have held other men at arm's length, because I wanted only you. I do not believe that all you feel for me is the affection of . . . a sister."

"It has to be that way, Jahane. There can be no future for you and me."

She was crying softly, and it tore at his heart, so he clasped her to him. "Please, honey, don't cry." His hands ran soothingly up and down her back until he became aware of her softness, and he pulled back.

"Jahane, could we talk about this another time? I do not think my bedroom in the middle of the night is the place to discuss your future."

Through tear-bright eyes she looked at him. "I have no future without you."

Her hurt was his hurt. How would he ever have the strength to let her go, when all he wanted was to spend the rest of his life making her happy? Confused and disconcerted by these new feelings, he stood up and moved across the room to stand at the window.

"Will you give me time to think about this, Jahane?"

She dried her eyes on the sleeve of her dressing gown, reminding him of an endearing child. "Yes, Cord, I will allow you all the time you need to think about our future." She smiled. "But I know you will come to the same conclusion that I have. You and I were made for each other. Neither of us would be happy without the other. I have always known this and have waited for you to know it, too."

He took a steadying breath and willed himself not to rush to her and declare his love for her. He wanted to hold her, to never let her go. He shook his head, thinking his reasoning was muddled. He wished he had not drunk so much rum. If ever he needed a clear head, tonight was the night.

"We will talk on this later in the week, Jahane. I really do need time to think."

She nodded in agreement. "All right, Cord, if that is what you want. But can we talk about something else?"

He wasn't sure he could trust himself alone with her. "It's late and — "

"This is important, Cord."

He looked at her tenderly. "All right, Jahane. What is so important that it cannot wait until tomorrow?"

She patted the bed beside her. "Will you sit beside me, Cord?"

He shook his head, took a chair, and turned it around, straddling it. "No, I will sit here, and you stay where you are."

For the first time he noticed she held the leather pouch which contained the red stone that had been her only possession the night his father had rescued her. "Tell me what's on your mind, Jahane."

She emptied the stone into her hand, then ran her finger over its smoothness. "I had this stone appraised last month. The man told me it was a genuine ruby, the size, weight, and color of which he had never seen. He told me it weighed over ninety carats and was priceless. Did you know of its value?"

Cord looked astounded. "No, Jahane. I have often thought it might be valuable, but I never thought it would be priceless. What made you take it in to be appraised?"

"I had to know more about the stone. Do you remember that as a child this ruby was always interwoven in my nightmares, Cord? Remember how I would tell you how the man cut me with the knife the night he gave it to me?"

"Yes, I recall very well the many nights you would awaken crying out in fear and pain. Many's the night I held you while you poured out your heart to me. You

152

often told me about the man removing the stone from a golden rod, and how he hid that rod behind a wall hanging with horses woven on it. I always supposed it was nothing more than a nightmare. Now I'm not so sure."

"Cord, tell me what you know about my past." Her voice took on a pleading note. "Who am I? Who were my mother and father? If you know, please tell me."

"I don't know, Jahane. I have told you many times about the night my father rescued you from Balmarhea."

"Yes, I know this, but who am I?"

"Jahane, the reason I have always avoided telling you about the night you were brought on board our ship was because my father thought you might be in danger. So certain was he of that threat that we moved from our home in Boston and took up residence here in California where no one would know us."

Jahane stared at him in astonishment and her face drained of color. "What kind of danger? Who would want to harm me?"

"All I can tell you is that my father told me that men had died that night so you might live. As it turned out, my father was one of those who died. When we took you off the island of Balmarhea, there were men chasing after us, apparently to get you back."

"Balmarhea. It does not sound familiar to me. Why was I not told this before?"

"You were so young, and there had been so much violence the night you came on board the ship, we wanted to spare you."

"I never knew your father died because of me, Cord. I am so sorry. It's a wonder you didn't hate me. You don't, do you, Cord?"

His eyes darkened with pain. "How could you even ask such a thing, Jahane?"

"But you still have not told me who I am, Cord."

"I am not certain, Jahane. I have always thought you might be the daughter of Chapin D'arcy, who was a friend of my father, and the prime minister of Balmarhea. It saddens me to tell you that he was killed the night my father died. And, if you are his daughter, you have no family left."

Jahane tried to feel grief for the man she had never known—the man who had been her father—but she could not feel anything.

"Cord, can you imagine what it is like to have no past? I am so frightened sometimes."

As she had when she was a small girl, she held her hand out to him beseechingly. "Please hold me," she cried.

Cord quickly came to her, enfolding her in his arms. His voice broke as the words came rushing out of his mouth as if a damn had broken inside him. Words he had not dared voice even to himself were whispered in her ear. "My dearest love, you will always belong to me. Don't you know that by now? You are my heart—you are my life. You will always belong to me alone. Pity the man who tries to take you from me."

Jahane pressed herself closer to Cord, basking in his tenderness. At long last he was admitting what she had always known. Raising her face, she parted her lips, offering them to Cord.

With a painful moan, his lips touched hers, softly at first, exploring, tasting, reveling in the tender feelings. Then he crushed her in his arms, needing and wanting her with an ache deep inside. Now his love had been voiced aloud and it would not be denied.

Jahane swallowed a convulsive sob, as happiness burst forth in her heart. This was what she had waited for so many years. This was what she had lived for.

She was unaware when Cord lifted her into his arms, until she felt the softness of the bed beneath her. When Cord lay down beside her, she allowed him to pull her against him, feeling that everything was all right now that he held her so tightly. Cord would make her demons go away tonight as he always had.

Cord had denied his love for Jahane for so long that he was overwhelmed with feelings he could not understand or control. He trembled inside with the effort he was making to push her away from him, but the effort went for naught, for he only gathered her closer, allowing his love for her to flow through his body.

When her soft hand brushed against his cheek and she breathed his name, his control snapped completely and he crushed her against him, fitting her soft curves to the contour of his hard body.

"Jahane, how long have I felt this way?" he asked more of himself than of her. "How long have you lingered at the back of my mind?"

"I cannot remember a time when I did not love you," she said, glad he had at last confessed his love. "When I think back to my childhood, yours is the face that comes to me. Yours was always the hand that wiped away my tears. Although I love Mama with my whole heart, you were always the one I turned to when I needed understanding."

He looked down at her, noticing that her eyes were brightly shining. Doubts still nagged at him. "Jahane, are you certain you love me as a woman loves a man, and not as a sister would love her brother?"

She touched his cheek, loving him in the very depths

of her heart. "I love you so deeply it hurts, Cord. I want to be your wife. I want to have your sons and daughters. I want to be the woman in your life who gives you comfort when you need it. You have always been strong for me; allow me to be your strength as well."

A tear touched his long lashes and he closed his eyes, thanking God for the precious gift of Jahane's love. Yes, he had always loved her. As he had grown into manhood, that love had nourished and grown into the uncontrollable feelings that now threatened to consume him. This was love deep, strong, and everlasting.

When he felt her firm breasts pressed against his chest, he fought for his sanity. He had always protected Jahane, and now she was in danger from his passion. With a shaken resolve, he untangled her arms from about his neck and stood up, bringing her with him.

Almost regretfully he spoke. "Dearest one, I apologize for allowing myself to lose control." He touched her soft lips with his finger. "You were so desirable that I forgot for the moment that my charge was to protect you, even if it is from myself."

Her brow creased in worried lines. "Don't you want to hold me, Cord?"

He was tense as he stepped away from her, knowing what he really wanted was to possess her. "The trouble is that I want very much to hold you. I believe you should go along to your room now, Jahane. We will talk about this at a more appropriate time and place."

There was sunshine in her smile. "Now that I know you love me, I can wait until another time to talk about our future. I have waited all my life for you. What can it matter if I wait a few hours longer?"

"Are you sure about this, Jahane? Will you have no

regrets?"

"I will be happy as long as you love me."

"Then, dearest heart, get ready to be happy for the rest of your life, for that's how long I will love you."

Now tears of happiness were shimmering in her eyes. "I used to dream about what the time would be like when we would confess our love for each other. I knew when that time came, I would be the happiest of women, but I did not imagine how much more I would love you. It frightens me, Cord, to love you so deeply."

He took a hesitant step toward her and stopped himself. "Be advised that you should leave now. You do not know how adorable you look to me at the moment and how hard it is to keep my hands off you."

She smiled, understanding more than he could guess. "I will go, but only if you kiss me good night."

"Vixen," he said, pulling her into his arms. "Don't say you didn't ask for this."

His lips were warm against hers, and she waited for him to deepen the kiss, but he didn't. With the same restraint he had practiced with her all evening, he broke off the kiss, saying to her in a deeply disturbed voice, "Go to your room before I forget myself. Please, Jahane."

"I will go," she agreed. "I'm sure I shall dream about you and me."

"I'm afraid I shall also," he muttered under his breath. With a firm clasp on her arm, he pushed her out the door. "Sleep well, my love. I doubt that I shall."

He shoved the leather pouch containing her ruby in her hand and closed the door and leaned against it.

His heart was pounding and he felt like a man who had been drowning, only to be rescued at the last moment.

"Jahane," he whispered aloud, "what am I going to do about you and me?"

Jahane ran into her bedroom, feeling as if her heart would burst with happiness. At last Cord had admitted he loved her. She dared to think about the future and how she would soon become Cord's wife. She giggled to herself, thinking how astonished he was at first when she confessed her love for him.

She removed her robe and draped it over a chair and dropped down on the bed. Jahane could hardly wait until she and Cord could tell his mother about their love for each other.

The disturbing questions about her past were over-shadowed by her happy thoughts of the future. It didn't matter who she had been in the past. In the future she would be Mrs. Cord Meredith.

Chapter Fifteen

The next morning when Jahane awoke, she could tell by the strange way the sun slanted through her bedroom window that it was late.

Leaping out of bed, she pulled on her dressing gown as she ran from her room. Taking the stairs as fast as she could, she raced into the dining room, calling Cord's name. When she found the room empty, she hurried toward the morning room, where she found Cord's mother bent over her desk apparently writing letters.

Happiness was etched on Jahane's face. Last night had not been a dream. Cord had truly admitted that he loved her.

"Mama, where is Cord?" she inquired, looking about the room, disappointed that he was not there.

Maggie laid aside her pen and studied Jahane's face. "He left this morning before sunrise. He said to tell you that he had to see to some repairs on the ship, and would not return until tomorrow. He said to tell you that the two of you would have your talk later."

Jahane's face fell. "Are you certain he will not be

back today?"

"No, dear, he made a point of telling me he would stay aboard the ship tonight."

Maggie had decided Cord had left because he was trying to find the courage to talk to Jahane. "Come and sit down, dear; but first, have you eaten breakfast?"

"No, I'm not hungry. I don't think I could eat a bite."

"Nonetheless, you shall have something," Maggie stated firmly. Standing up, she tugged at the bell pull. "What would you like?"

Jahane seated herself on the sofa, wondering if Cord had told his mother about their conversation the night before. She peeped from under her long lashes to see if her mother seemed disturbed—but she appeared to be calm. "I will just have fruit, Mama."

When Jojo entered the room, Maggie sent him for a breakfast tray for Jahane. She then returned to her desk and faced Jahane. "I don't suppose Cord had time to talk to you about anything last night?" she asked guardedly.

Jahane smiled to herself. "Yes, we talked about several matters, Mama."

Maggie knew Jahane would be devastated if Cord had been firm about her seeing other men. Apparently he had not talked to her about that. "I see. Did Cord speak to you about anything of interest?"

"Well . . ." Jahane stalled, wanting Cord to be the one to tell his mother that they wanted to be married. "Cord did tell me that his father was killed the night I left the island. I was so sorry to hear that, Mama. I

160

hope it wasn't my fault."

"Dear child, do not even think that way. You have always been a joy to me. And if I had a daughter, I could not love her more."

"I love you, too, Mama."

Maggie watched Jahane's face. "Did you and Cord talk of other matters?"

"Cord told me that he thought I might be the daughter of a man named Chapin d'Arcy." Jahane was thoughtful for a moment. "Jahane d'Arcy? No, that does not sound right to me, Mama. But tell me what you know about Chapin d'Arcy. Did you know his wife? Did you know me when I was a baby?"

Maggie flexed her fingers and leaned forward, a secretive expression on her face. "I met Chapin on several occasions when he was a guest in our home in Boston. Of course I never knew his wife. You will have to understand Chapin and his family were of the nobility, so we did not visit with them."

"What do you mean nobility, Mama?"

Reluctantly Maggie admitted: "d'Arcy was a count." She knew she was being deceptive by allowing Jahane and Cord to believe she was Chapin's daughter. But if Jahane discovered who she was, wouldn't she lose her?

"Then, Mama, if I am his daughter, would I be a countess?"

"I don't know much about such things, Jahane. But I don't think so."

"It doesn't matter, because I never intend to go back to Balmarhea. I would just like to know."

Maggie glanced searchingly at Jahane. "Is this upsetting you, dear?"

161

"Strangely enough, it isn't. The one disturbing thing about it all is not knowing how old I am or even the date of my real birthday."

Maggie laughed. "Cord and I decided you must have been about three years old when you lost your family. We decided to celebrate your birthday on September the eighth, since that was the day you came into our life."

"I am truly sorry that I never knew my own family, Mama, but I never regret that I have had the privilege of being your daughter. I do love you so, Mama."

Maggie reached out and clasped Jahane's hand. "You are so dear to both Cord and me, and I cannot tell you the comfort you have brought to my life."

"I know, Mama. I have never felt unloved. You taught me with kindness and patience. In my heart you will always be my mother."

"Oh, my dear Jahane, you are the daughter of my heart."

Both of them smiled through their tears. "There, that's enough of that," Maggie said, standing up. "We have things to do today, and the day is already half gone."

"Assign me a chore, Mama," she said with a salute of her hand, "and I shall carry it out. You always said time passes fast if one stays busy. I want time to fly by today."

"All right, dear. As soon as you have eaten, I want you and Jojo to go to the market." She handed a shopping list to Jahane. "But do not linger at the market, for the heat is so oppressive."

Jojo entered with Jahane's breakfast tray and placed it on the desk. Handing her a snowy-white napkin, he

162

bowed his way out of the room.

"Why don't you come to the market with me, Mama? You haven't been out of the house all week. The walk will do you good."

"No, dear, I want to supervise the cleaning of the kitchen cupboards." She handed Jahane several coins. "Be sure the fish seller does not try to pass off inferior salmon on you. You know what to look for. If the scales fall off and the eyes look cloudy, don't buy it."

"Yes, Mama, I know," she agreed laughingly. This was the same caution she always received from her mother before she went to market. Marketing had become Jahane's task, since Maggie did not believe in leaving the household shopping to the servants.

With her head filled with the chores ahead of her, Maggie left the room. Inside she was glad Jahane had so easily accepted her insinuation that Chapin d'Arcy had been her father. She had not expected it to be so easy.

It was only afterward that Maggie, recalling the whole incident, thought that Jahane had acted somewhat fancifully and secretively, but she shrugged it off as Jahane's happiness at Cord's return.

Cord found his mother in the front parlor standing before the window. Coming up behind her, he slid his arm around her shoulder. "I understand Jahane is at the market, Mama."

Maggie turned to glance at the clock on the mantel. "That's right. She and Jojo left not twenty minutes ago." She looked at her son curiously. "I thought you had decided not to come home today."

Cord clasped his hands behind him while his eyes locked with his mother's. "I had to come home. I need to speak to you, Mama."

"Yes, I can see that there is something on your mind. Come, sit beside me on the sofa and you can tell me what is troubling you."

When they were seated, Cord searched his mind, wondering how to tell her of his feelings for Jahane. He decided to be direct. "Mama, I love Jahane and she loves me," he blurted out. "We want to be married."

Her expression did not change. "I have known this for a very long time. But it is not possible for you to have her, Son. Jahane is not for you and can never belong to you. I had hoped you would come to this same conclusion before you discovered that you loved her as a woman and not as a sister."

"I will never give her up, Mama. Nothing can make me give her up. I thought you would be happy about this."

Maggie knew the time she had always dreaded had come. She would have to tell Cord Jahane's true identity, so he would know she could never belong to him. "My dear son, I would like nothing better than to have you and Jahane married to one another, but remember the world believes she is your real sister. Think how the gossip would destroy you both."

"That's not the real reason, Mama. Since you have never cared overmuch what the gossips had to say, there's some other reason. What is it?"

She turned away, not wanting to meet his eyes. "Cord, I have not been truthful with you all these

164

years. I allowed you to think Jahane was Chapin d'Arcy's daughter when I knew she was not."

Cord wished he could stop his mother, for he knew whatever she was about to admit would tear him and Jahane apart. "Don't tell me that Jahane is really my sister," he said in agony. "I don't want to hear that she was my father's daughter by another woman, and, anyway, I would not believe it of my father."

Maggie looked astounded for a moment, then she smiled. "No, Cord. To my knowledge, your father did not have a mistress. And if he did, Jahane is not his daughter."

"Then what could keep us apart?"

"Cord, there were two reasons I never told anyone Jahane's true identity. One was I was afraid I would have to give her up if the truth became known, and I did not want to do that, for I had grown to love her and I think of her as my own daughter. The other reason is that in your father's letter to me, he charged me to tell no one, not even you, who Jahane is."

"You are frightening me, Mama. What is the great mystery?"

"I am sorry, Cord. After keeping my secret for so long, it's hard to let it go now."

Cord had a feeling of doom, and he asked reluctantly, "Who is she, Mama?"

Maggie looked at him beseechingly. "You do understand why I had to lie, don't you, Cord?"

"I don't know. Tell me the truth now, and then I'll judge."

"I . . . Your father . . . Jahane was . . . is . . . the Royal Princess of Balmarhea!"

Cord swallowed past the lump in his throat. He could feel Jahane slipping away from him. "No, she can't be! I will not accept that."

"It's true, Cord. Your father wrote it in his letter. Think, Cord. That would explain why she was in danger, wouldn't it, Son?"

Cord didn't want to believe that his beloved Jahane was a princess, for if she were, she would indeed be out of reach for him. Suddenly he saw a ray of hope. "But even if she is, no one will ever have to know. You have kept your secret, Mama, and now I'll keep it, too. Jahane need never know."

"I have wrestled with this for years, Cord. It's almost a relief to share it with you. But . . ." she paused as if trying to decide how to proceed. "What you don't know is that your father wrote that not only is she Princess Jahane, she is the rightful ruler of Balmarhea—the queen!" Tears poured from Maggie's eyes. "I have kept this secret, though it tore me apart inside. On one hand, I felt I was denying Jahane her true heritage, but on the other hand, I knew I was keeping her safe."

"Are you sure of this, Mama?" Cord asked, hoping there could be some mistake.

"Yes, I am sure. Like you, I did some discreet checking of my own. I discovered that not only was there a Princess Jahane of Balmarhea, but her whole family was believed killed the night your father died. The only thing was that they never found the princess's body, nor the body of her brother, the prince, for that matter."

Cord stood up, his mind staggered from what his

166

mother had revealed to him. "What should we do about this, Mama?"

"I suppose Jahane should be told the truth."

"Yes, I have never lied to Jahane, and I will not start now."

"Yes, Cord, she will have to be told. But you tell her, for I cannot."

Cord walked out of the room, feeling like a man who had just lost everything. Jahane a princess, perhaps even a queen. No, not his Jahane.

Jahane walked from one street vendor to another, making purchases while Jojo walked beside her, placing the items in the basket he carried over his arm.

It was while she was examining the fresh salmon from Oregon that she began to feel uneasy as if someone was staring at her. She'd had this feeling before, but never so strongly.

Turning around, her eyes met and locked with a man whose dark eyes bore into her. With a shiver, she turned back to her shopping, dismissing the notion that he was watching her as improbable.

But as she moved from vendor to vendor, he was always just behind her. Finally, she could stand his staring no longer, and she entered one of the shops, hoping he would be gone when she came out.

While pretending to be interested in a string of pearls the clerk was showing her, Jahane gathered enough courage to glance out the window. The man was leaning against one of the stalls, watching the door of the shop as if he were waiting for someone.

Now she could study him without being seen. He appeared to be a man in his late fifties, and a foreigner, by the looks of his clothing. But that was not unusual, the man being from another country, because there were many foreigners in San Francisco. What was so unusual about him was the way he was dressed. Well-dressed men did not usually visit the market, and, besides, he appeared to be buying nothing. He wore light-colored trousers and a green morning jacket. His elaborately tied cravat, his top hat, and gold-handled cane set him apart from the other shoppers milling about.

Perhaps she was being overly imaginative, she thought. Perhaps she had let her conversation with Cord last night about her being in danger influence her thinking.

Deciding that she was being foolish, Jahane moved out of the shop. Now the man was nowhere to be seen, so with a big sigh of relief, she continued her shopping. She must have only imagined that the man was following her.

Coming to the end of her shopping list with the purchase of plump red strawberries, she turned to leave with Jojo trailing after her.

As she went around the corner onto a deserted street, she noticed Jojo was not with her, so she stopped to wait for him. The street was quiet and she began to feel strangely alone.

Jahane held her breath as the very man whom she had seen at the market appeared from out of nowhere, his dark eyes assessing, a slight smile on his thick lips.

She wanted to run away, but he was blocking her

168

path. Surely, she told herself, he could have no real interest in her.

As the man approached, she drew back. When he stopped before her, she flipped open her sunshade, placing it between her and the man, hoping he would know she was not interested in talking to him. When he proceeded to walk in front of her, she glanced frantically back to see if Jojo was yet in sight.

"Excuse me, mademoiselle," the man said in French. "If you are looking for your servant, someone bumped into him and scattered your marketing on the ground. I'm sure he will rejoin you as soon as he has retrieved everything."

Now she looked squarely into the man's face and found his penetrating glance unsettling—his eyes were strangely catlike and yellow in color.

"Thank you, monsieur," she stated curtly, dismissing him and walking toward the corner where she hoped she would find Jojo.

"Excuse me, mademoiselle, could I but speak to you for a moment?"

She did not stop until he spoke again. "I would like to talk to you, Jahane," he said in English.

She spun around with apprehension on her face. "How did you know my name?"

A strange light came into his yellow eyes, and she shivered. "I didn't know your name for sure until you acknowledged it just now," he admitted.

"I do not know you, sir. And I do not wish to talk to you."

"No, but I knew of you as a small child. Have you ever been told about Balmarhea?"

169

Jahane felt panic rising up in her like a great tide. With her heart pounding in her ears, she turned around to flee — that was when she saw Jojo and relief flooded over her.

"No, do not go, Jahane," the man cried out. "It is imperative that I speak with you."

Jojo, seeing the stranger who had knocked the basket from his arm, and assessing Jahane's distress, rushed between her and the man. "Missy, no talky to you. You go 'way now. Missy no talky."

Jahane rushed away, but she heard the man call after her. "Jahane, I have much to tell you. Do you want to hear about your real family and how they have been searching for you all these years?"

She shut out his voice, not wanting to hear anything he had to say. Soon Jojo was beside her, and he had to run to keep pace with her.

"Missy all right?" he inquired with concern in his tone.

"Yes, Jojo, just a little frightened."

"That man was bad, he knocked basket from Jojo's hand. I did not understand what the man was saying to you, missy. He speak in words I never hear before."

Jahane was astounded when she realized that the stranger had indeed spoken to her in French, and she had not only understood him, but had answered him in the same language!

The fact that the man knew her and she did not know him frightened her most of all. When the house was in sight, she turned back to see if the man was following her, but there was no sign of him.

Her footsteps did not slacken until she reached the

170

front door. With rapidly pounding pulse, she ran into the house, calling for Cord.

"Cord, where are you?" she cried. "Cord, help me. I am so frightened."

Chapter Sixteen

When Cord heard Jahane crying out his name, he ran to her and gathered her into his arms and tried to comfort her so he could find out what had caused her incoherent mumbling.

"What has happened to her?" he demanded, looking at Jojo for answers.

"Missy plenty scared when bad man come after her. Plenty scared."

Maggie stood in the doorway, her hand at her throat. "What man?" she asked the houseboy. "Who are you talking about, Jojo?"

By now, Jahane had calmed down enough to feel a bit foolish over her outburst. "It was really extraordinary. This man followed me through the market. I suppose I am making too much of it, but he was frightening."

"Tell me what occurred, and I'll decide if you are making too much out of it," Cord urged, leading her into the parlor and seating her on the sofa.

"Jojo," Cord said. "Bring Miss Jahane something cool to drink."

"Missy talk to man in strange language. Missy plenty scared, I think," the houseboy stated before leaving the room.

Cord and his mother exchanged glances. Then Cord went down on his knees beside Jahane, noting the still-frightened look in her eyes. "What did this man do or say to put you in such a state?" he wanted to know.

Jahane's eyes were clear and troubled. "It wasn't so much what he said . . . it was . . . it was . . . he knew my name and he knew that I had once lived on Balmarhea."

Maggie gasped, and Cord pulled Jahane into his arms protectively. "I see. Did he say anything else to you?"

"I didn't like him, Cord. I first noticed him at the market, then he followed me when I left. For some reason I was very frightened." She steadied her hands by clasping them together tightly. "Very frightened."

"What else happened?" Maggie asked, sitting on the edge of the sofa, fear eating at her insides.

"He . . . the man said he wanted to talk to me about my real family, and how they had been searching for me for years." Jahane's eyes were questioning. "What can this mean, Cord? Could my family have sent him?"

Cord stood up, suddenly at a loss on how to treat the incident. "I will send Jojo to the ship and ask Thadeus and several of the others to stand guard here at the house." He glanced down at Jahane. "You will not go out of the house unless I, or one of my men, are with you. Is this understood?"

Jahane nodded, not wanting to go out alone. She never wanted to see that man again.

Maggie was wringing her hands. "We must send Jahane away." Her eyes brightened with terror. "That's what we shall do, Cord. You will take her on a long sea voyage, and by the time you return, the man will have given up and gone away. Maybe we should think

173

about leaving San Francisco and moving somewhere else."

"No, Mama," Cord said firmly. "We will not run, and even if we did, the man would not go away and you know it. We have to keep Jahane where he cannot get to her."

Maggie's eyes fastened on Jahane. "I could not bear it if anything happened to you. Convince Cord to take you away from here—at once—today!"

"Cord's right, Mama. I cannot run away from my past. Apparently it is about to catch up with me. Besides, now that I have had time to think on it, perhaps the man was not so frightening."

"That's dangerous thinking, Jahane," Cord cautioned her. "We must remember that my father warned us that you might be in danger. We will always proceed on that assumption."

"That does frighten me, Cord," Jahane admitted, her eyes seeking comfort in his warm gaze.

Cord took her hand in his. "I want you to be frightened, Jahane, so the incident that occurred today will not be repeated."

"Have no fear on my part. I have no intention of meeting that man again," Jahane assured him.

"Jahane," Maggie said, coming to her feet. "You go into the morning room where it's cooler, and I'll have Jojo serve you lunch there."

"But what about you and Cord?" Jahane wanted to know. "Will you not eat with me?"

"I have correspondence to attend to, dear, but Cord will be joining you later, after I have talked to him. Run along, and I'll send him to you shortly."

By now Jahane had calmed down from her ordeal, and she smiled at Maggie, thinking she would keep

174

Cord behind so she could try to convince him to take her on a voyage. "I will wait for you, Cord."

As she turned to leave, he gave Jahane that special smile that was reserved for her. "Give me a few moments to calm Mama, and I will join you." His eyes raked her face with concern. "Are you sure you are all right?"

"Yes. I am no longer so frightened."

As soon as Jahane disappeared down the hall, Maggie looked at her son. "What do you make of this? Could the man have meant to harm Jahane?"

"How can we know, Mama? It could be that he was sent by Jahane's family to find her. Or it could have been that the man has been sent to cause her harm. Either way, I do not want her approached by him again. We must do everything in our power to protect her."

"You can assure her safety by taking her away. Why can you not see that is our best course?"

"That wouldn't solve anything, Mama. If I thought it could, I'd put her on the ship today. Jahane cannot live in fear, always looking over her shoulder."

Maggie breathed in a deep breath. "Well, one thing is for certain, Cord, you must tell Jahane today that she is a princess."

Cord felt a sharp pain in his heart, knowing forces were at work over which he had no control. He glanced up at the ceiling to gather his composure before looking back at his mother. "I agree with you, Mama. I will tell her now."

Jahane was seated on the small settee which was located by a floor-to-ceiling window giving her a sweeping view of San Francisco. Jojo had served her chilled melon, but she had ignored it, waiting for Cord to join her.

When Cord did enter the room, her heart winged its way toward him. She had so much to say to him, and she just wanted him to hold her in his strong arms to assure her that everything would be all right.

She stood up and raced across the room to be enfolded in his arms. How good it felt to have him hold her, how right it was to feel his heart beating beneath her hand.

"I waited lunch for you," she said, looking up at him with love shining in her eyes.

He tried to concentrate on what he had to tell her, and not how beautiful she looked with the sun shining on her golden hair. "You shouldn't have waited."

She looked at him carefully. Did he seem stiff and withdrawn? "I wanted to wait for you, Cord." She smiled, and he felt his heart contract. "I wanted to hear you say again that you love me."

Cord put her away from him abruptly and moved to the window, cramming his hands in his pockets. Coward that he was, he could not bring himself to look at her when he spoke. "Jahane, I want to talk to you about last night."

She came up and locked her arms around his waist and pressed her cheek to his back. "First say you love me, my dearest Cord."

Jahane felt Cord stiffen. She was confused when he pried her hands away from him and moved closer to the window, but still hadn't turned to face her. "Last night, I said a lot of things that I shouldn't have, Jahane. I am sorry if it caused any misunderstanding."

Her heart contracted, and she could scarcely breathe.

176

"You said you loved me last night, and I believed you. There was no misunderstanding between us, Cord."

He closed his eyes, calling on all the strength he had to tell the lie that was forming on his lips. "I do love you, Jahane. But not in the way you need to be loved. Mine is the love a brother has for his sister."

Silence fell heavy in the room as Cord clasped the velvet drapery tightly, fearing he would turn around and take her in his arms as he so wanted to do. He didn't have to see her face to know the hurt that would be etched there.

Yes, at first there would be disbelief in her eyes, and then doubt, then she would think it was all done in jest. He had to stoke the lie to keep it burning, so he struck out at her again.

"Last night I had too much to drink, and you were very desirable in that little thin thing you wore."

Cord forced himself to turn around to face her now, but he could not bring himself to look into her eyes. Instead he studied the back of his hand. "I owe you an apology, but then you are always the first to laugh at a jest, and that is all it was." He laughed for effect. "It was really quite funny when you think about it."

Jahane's heart reeled as he delivered blow after blow to her pride and her heart. She raised her head a little higher, squared her shoulders, and when he looked into her eyes, she was able to smile.

"Yes, Cord, it was all very humorous." Her voice shook with emotions, but her eyes never wavered. "I may die laughing at any moment."

Unable to control her tears, she turned and dashed from the room, feeling like a little girl who had just lost her best friend, or a lover who had just lost her only love.

Cord took a step toward her, but stopped himself just in time. He had never wanted anything as badly as he wanted to rush after Jahane and tell her how deeply he loved her. He had been brutal and cruel, and he hated what he had done to her.

"Damn it," he cried, slamming his fists onto the table and causing the dishes to rattle. "Damn it to hell!"

With his eyes gleaming with the injustice of it all, Cord moved to the door and into the hall. He had to find the courage to tell Jahane her true identity, but it would have to wait for another day. She had quite enough to think about for one day.

Retrieving his cap from the coat rack, he passed out the front door. He would sleep on board the *Golden Phoenix* tonight because he didn't trust himself not to go to Jahane and take back the love she had so generously offered him.

Cord knew he had broken Jahane's heart, but he had to. He had been forced to kill her love, when all he wanted to do was hold on to her and never let her go. Her love had been his most precious possession, and he had been forced to throw it away.

As Cord's long strides took him down the pier toward the *Golden Phoenix,* he paid little heed to the crowd of passengers disembarking from one of the passenger ships.

His mind was on Jahane, and he did not notice the man striding toward him until the two of them collided. Glancing up, Cord noticed the man was dressed as a monk.

"I beg your pardon, Brother," Cord said absently. "I'm afraid I wasn't watching where I was going."

The monk pushed his hood aside and Cord was surprised to see he had long blond hair and startlingly blue eyes.

"Think nothing of it, my son," the man said in heavy French accent. "I have only just arrived in this country and do not know my way about. I wonder if it would be an imposition for you to direct me to the mission of San Francisco de Asis?"

"Not at all, Father." He pointed to the north. "You must follow Market Street until you come to Dolores Street, then go three blocks south and you can't miss it. The best way is to take one of the carriages you see lined up along the docks. Give the driver the name of the mission, and he will have you there in no time."

"Thank you, my son, for your kindness. May God reward you."

Cord watched the Frenchman walk away, thinking he was young to be a priest, and he certainly didn't look like one with his long golden hair. With a shrug, Cord dismissed the priest, and his thoughts returned to Jahane.

Alexander waited patiently for Father Estevan to finish reading the letter from his Uncle Serafimo. He glanced around at the cool stone floors and thick walls, thinking there was something very appealing about this mission. There was open courtyards, golden sunshine, and peace. Indeed, everything he had seen of America he liked.

He turned back to the priest, thinking he seemed to blend in with his environment. His plain brown robe and leather sandals fit the picture Alexander had always had of a Spanish priest. He was white-headed, and even when he wasn't smiling, one could see the laugh lines around his eyes.

Father Estevan glanced up at Alexander. "Do you

179

know what your uncle wrote in this letter, my son?"

"I can guess, but as you saw, Father, the letter was sealed."

"Your uncle and I are very old friends. He once helped me out in my time of trial, and I have long awaited the time I could return the favor."

"I will be very grateful for any help you could give me, Father. How much did my uncle tell you about my situation, and who I am searching for?"

"The Archbishop of Balmarhea has written me your true identity, Your Highness. But I believe we should not call attention to your rank while you are in San Francisco, my son."

"I agree, Father. I was to have been met by my uncle's servant, Everett. Have you any notion as to what may have delayed him?"

"I am sorry to tell you, my son, and I have just written your uncle the sad news. Everett's body was found floating in the bay with a dagger in his back. I am afraid he was murdered."

Alexander experienced a feeling of outrage. "Do the authorities know who killed him?"

"No. There were no clues."

"Tell me what you knew of Everett's movements, Father."

"He often stayed here at the mission, but he was a quiet man and kept very much to himself. The one thing I do know about him is that he was devoted to your family. He did tell me he thought he may have located your sister."

Alexander's eyes were wide with hope. "Have you seen my sister?"

"Until I read this letter, I did not know the identity of the girl Everett searched for. I am happy to tell you that I have often been in the company of the girl, Jahane."

He looked Alexander over carefully. "Yes, you could easily pass for Jahane Meredith's brother. The same coloring," he smiled, "the same obstinate look in your eyes."

"I am convinced this girl is my sister. When can I see her?" Alexander asked impatiently. "I have reason to believe that she is in danger. Now that Everett has been murdered, that merely confirms my suspicions."

"You don't need to worry about Miss Meredith being protected, my friend. Cord Meredith will never allow anything to happen to her while he's around."

"If this should prove to be my sister, that man has much to answer for."

"He is devoted to her."

Alexander shrugged. "For all we know, it could have been Captain Meredith who killed Everett."

"I do not think so, my son. You must look elsewhere for the murderer."

"Father," Alexander said, moving the conversation to his sister. "Did you happen to notice if there was a scar on Jahane's hand?"

"No, but then I would not have been looking for a scar."

"Relate to me all you know about the family Jahane is living with."

Alexander listened while Father Estevan told him about the Merediths. When he had finished, Alexander was thoughtful for a moment. He spoke of Maggie's charity work and her kindness to others. He told Alexander of the respect many families of San Francisco had for Cord Meredith.

"I need some kind of plan, because I cannot very

well go up and knock on the front door and expect the Merediths to let me into their home."

Father Estevan nodded his head in agreement. "I think I may have just the right strategy that will put you and Jahane together."

"I am willing to follow your lead, Father, for I confess I know not where to turn."

"Put your faith in God, my son, and he will guide you through the darkest trials."

Alexander dropped to his knees and bowed his head. "Pray for me, Father. Pray that I will find my sister in time to save her."

Father Estevan laid his hand on Alexander's golden head and evoked a prayer to heaven for God to look after the young prince and help him find his sister.

Silently, Father Estevan also prayed for the Meredith family. He knew it would be very difficult for them to give Jahane over to this stranger.

Later that evening, as Alexander was having dinner with Father Estevan, the priest tried to comfort him. "As I told you, the Merediths are fine people, and Jahane has known the love and comfort of a kind and loving family."

"But they are not her family. She has a family who has spent sleepless nights worrying about her safety."

"Yes, I suppose you are right. The longer I talk to you, the more convinced I become that she is your sister. The likeness between the two of you is remarkable."

"You said earlier that you had a plan whereby I can meet with Jahane."

"Yes, I do. There is the Fireman's Ball coming up

182

this Saturday. Since the Merediths always attend, I expect they will be there."

"Will I be able to attend the ball?"

"I will have to see if I can get you an invitation." He pondered for a moment. "That should not be too difficult. The hard part will be finding someone to present you to Jahane. I may just have to attend the ball myself so I can make the introduction."

Alexander leaned back in the leather-bottomed chair. "Four days. So near and yet so far."

"You have waited a lifetime, my young friend. What is four more days?"

Chapter Seventeen

Jahane had spent two days lingering in her room, unwilling to face anyone. Cord had knocked on her door, but she had refused to see even him.

Now it was the day she and her mother had been invited to a musicale, and Jahane decided she would no longer hide in her room. If Cord could not love her, then she would put on a brave face and show him it did not matter, for Cord's happiness was far more important to her than her own.

In spite of her determination, Jahane glanced down at her green satin gown, wishing Cord could see her looking her best. The skirt, with its three flounces, was adorned with black lace, which Jahane was sure made her appear older. Her hair had been elaborately dressed and now hung down her back in soft ringlets. She pulled her fingers through black lace gloves and wrapped the matching lace shawl about her shoulders.

Hearing her mother calling from downstairs, Jahane moved out her bedroom door and rushed out to join her.

"You look lovely, dear," Maggie observed, looking Jahane over carefully. "I wasn't sure if the green would be flattering to your coloring, but I can see that it is," she said, carefully avoiding mentioning the circles beneath Jahane's eyes.

Jahane glanced through the door of the sitting room, hoping Cord would be there. When she saw the room was empty, she turned disappointed eyes on her mother. "I suppose Cord is not coming with us."

Maggie pulled on her cashmere shawl. "No, he has other matters to attend to. He did, however suggest he might be able to accompany us to the Fireman's Ball two days hence."

"I was hoping he would be our escort tonight, Mama."

Maggie noted the misery in Jahane's eyes, and the disappointment in her voice, but there was nothing she could do to soothe her hurt feelings. "He did say if he could get away, he would join us later in the evening."

Jahane had somehow known Cord would want to avoid being with her after she had so thoroughly disgraced herself in front of him. When she remembered how brazenly she had proclaimed her love for him, she ducked her head in shame. If Cord had been humiliated by her advances, she herself had been humbled in the dust by his rejection of her.

"I feel sure Cord will not join us," Jahane said regretfully. Dropping her lace handkerchief into her satin handbag, she smiled bravely. "We need no gentleman to escort us. You and I shall just enjoy each other's company tonight, Mama."

Maggie took both of the young girl's hands in hers. "I know how difficult this has all been for you, dear." Tears brightened her eyes. "I shall always feel that you are my daughter, and Cord will always want you to think of him as your brother."

"Cord told you what happened between us, didn't he, Mama?"

185

The older woman turned to the door, reluctant to discuss Cord and Jahane's deep feelings for each other. "All I know is we are going to miss the beginning of the musicale if we don't hurry. Do you think I should take a parasol? It is cloudy and might rain."

Jahane knew her mother was deliberately putting an end to their conversation so she shrugged indifferently. "You always said one should be prepared, Mama, so we shall both take a parasol. If they aren't needed, we can leave them in the carriage."

A smiling Jojo opened the front door for the ladies. When they descended the steps to be helped into the carriage, Jahane saw two of Cord's men standing to the side of the house and she knew they were keeping watch over her.

As the carriage door shut, Jahane glanced at the clouds gathering in the western sky and predicted it would rain before the night was over. To Jahane's way of thinking, the dark thunderheads that hung over the city represented the way she felt tonight. There was no joy in her future—nothing to look forward to, no one to love her as she wanted to be loved.

After she had seen her mother comfortably settled in the seat, she sat opposite her and stared out the window.

Jahane blinked back her tears. If Cord wouldn't have her for his wife, she would never marry any man. She pictured herself as the years passed and she aged into a tragic, wasted figure, dying inside because the only man she would ever love did not love her.

As the horses moved forward with a lurch, Jahane settled back, resigned to the fact that she would not see Cord tonight. She wished she had not agreed to attend the musicale which was being held at the Dunning home.

Mrs. Dotty Dunning was considered to be something of a celebrity. The matriarch snobbishly boasted that her father had been a gentleman-at-arms to Queen Victoria. Dotty Dunning, a narcissistic woman caught up in her own importance, was a patroness of the arts. Musicians of great renown often performed at her home. The people who wished to climb socially in San Francisco's elite society found it difficult unless they became acquainted with Dotty, and then were fortunate enough to be invited to one of her musicales.

As the carriage snaked its way down the hillside, Maggie smiled at Jahane. "I wonder what the entertainment will be tonight? Dotty is insistent on keeping it a secret."

Jahane returned her mother's smile, observing flippantly, "Perhaps Mrs. Dunning will perform herself. Conceivably she may try to walk on water."

Maggie looked shocked for a moment, but when she saw laughter dancing in Jahane's eyes, she smiled. "I wouldn't be at all surprised if Dotty did just that. But you should not be so ready with your comments, dear. It isn't kind."

"I hadn't thought to be unkind to Mrs. Dunning, Mama. But I do think she's often puffed up on her own importance, don't you?"

"Perhaps so, but all the same, you should be more careful with what you say." In spite of Maggie's reprimand, her lips twitched and she smiled. "Besides, I'm sure Dotty would never walk on water unless she had invited all of California to witness her feat."

Jahane's laughter burst forth. "Mama, you are incorrigible."

Suddenly the carriage came to a halt. The door was

opened, and Jahane and Maggie were assisted to the ground by the coachman. As they ascended the steps to Dunning House, they were met by the sound of laughter and music.

Before they reached the front door, Maggie paused and turned to Jahane. "It is a shame that you must attend this function in my company instead of some handsome young gentleman. I'm sure I don't know what is being said about you always being accompanied by your mother."

Jahane linked her arm through Maggie's. "I don't give a fig what others may think. I have no intentions of being bored senseless by some man who would spend the evening pointing out his marriageable qualities to me."

Maggie had no time to reply as the door swung open and they were admitted by a formally dressed butler. Dotty Dunning, smiling and dazzling in blue and silver, greeted the two Meredith ladies.

"I am so glad you could make my little musicale." Her eyes sparkled as she pulled herself up proudly. "You will never guess who is performing tonight."

Before Jahane or Maggie could answer, Dotty continued. "Madame Estraille, the famous soprano from Italy, will be performing 'The Resurrection'. She is quite famous and has sung before all the crowned heads of Europe."

Maggie, without batting an eye, smiled. "Oh, too bad, I had hoped she would perform 'the Walking on Water'."

Dotty's face fell as she looked from Maggie to Jahane with an expression of anxiety. "I am not familiar with that opera." She bit her lips in vexation. "Should I ask Madame to sing your selection instead of 'The

Resurrection"?"

Maggie, feeling guilty for her underhanded slight, shook her head. "No, Dotty, I look forward to hearing Madame's rendition of 'The Resurrection.'"

Dotty, still looking uncertain, spoke in a fanciful voice. "Are you certain?"

"Yes, quite certain," Maggie assured her.

Jahane glanced about the room, nodding at acquaintances, her eyes hopeful as she searched for Cord. When she saw he was not present, she hid her disappointment. Being swept along by the hostess, they were soon seated in the grand salon, and Madame Estraille began her song.

From where Jahane was seated, she had a good view of the front door, so she saw Cord when he entered a short time later. She experienced a sinking feeling when she saw Cord was not alone, but had escorted Nancy Hartford. To make matters worse, Jahane could find no fault with Nancy. She was pretty, shy and unassuming, just the sort of girl who would hang on to Cord's every word. Even from the distance Jahane could see Nancy simpering at Cord, and her blood boiled with jealousy.

Cord caught Jahane's hot glance and nodded ever so slightly.

Since Madame Estraille was already singing, Cord and Nancy stood until she finished her first chorus, then they were seated at the back of the room, out of Jahane's view.

Even though she could not see him, Jahane was aware of nothing but Cord. Her mind whirled, her heart ached. How could Cord be so heartless as to flaunt Nancy in her face? He had to know it was a painful experience for her to see him with another woman.

Jahane was grateful when the last note died away and Madame finished her presentation. All she wanted to do was to flee for home and seek the sanctuary of her room so she could be alone with her misery.

Since the evening was yet young, Jahane was forced to put on a happy face. She had to prove to Cord that she was indifferent to him. That was why she bestowed her brightest smile on Richard Moyer, the eldest son of the owner of the Moyer Bank. Richard had paid marked attention to Jahane in the past. But thus far, she had not encouraged his attentions. Now, however, she would use him to show Cord she was indifferent to him.

"Good evening," Richard said, bowing to Jahane. "I must say, as always, you are the most outstanding beauty in the room."

Jahane noted that Richard was handsome, a fact she had not noticed until now. With black hair and dark eyes, Richard had a certain boyish charm, and, while not dashing like Cord, he possessed a certain sophistication that she found appealing.

"You must be careful that you do not turn my head, Mr. Moyer." She offered him her most beguiling smile. "I am sure you only mean to flatter me."

Richard, who had never exchanged more than a dozen words with this stunning beauty, felt encouraged to go even further. "How can it be flattery, when it's the truth. Surely you know you outshine all others tonight."

Jahane's eyes strayed over to Cord. He gave no indication that he was aware of her conversation with another man, so she turned her attention back to Richard. "I had thought Nancy Hartford was a beauty.

190

Do you not find her so?"

Richard dismissed Nancy with the shrug of his shoulders. "She is considered well enough." His eyes widened in admiration as they swept across Jahane's face. "But yours is a startling beauty that makes men stare at you in wonder."

Ordinarily Jahane would have turned away from such glowing accounts of her beauty, but tonight she needed the reassurance that she was admired, so she dared to go further.

Placing her hand on Richard's arm, she snapped her fan open and smiled. "Would you consider taking a stroll about the room with me? I declare, it is warm, and I would like to stand by the window so I can catch a breath of air."

Richard quickly complied. With her hand resting on his arm, he knew he was the envy of every other gentleman present tonight.

Richard could not believe his good fortune, and he wondered if he were dreaming. "I would be honored to escort you, Miss Meredith." He spoke in a determined voice. "Would you consent to have dinner with me? I am sure Dotty has already made the seating arrangements, but she will not mind placing you and me together."

"Yes," Jahane said, with a toss of her head. "I would enjoy being your partner for the evening."

Even though Cord pretended indifference to Jahane's movements, he was totally concentrating on her. Now he watched her and Richard Moyer move around the room, knowing what he really wanted to do was drag her away from that man who wasn't worthy of her slightest attention.

"Cord . . ." Nancy said, dragging his attention back

191

to her. ". . . don't you agree that Madame Estraille has an exceptional talent?"

"Yes, of course." His voice sounded wooden to his ears.

Nancy noticed where Cord's attention was centered, and she spoke softly. "Jahane seems to be paying marked attention to Richard Moyer tonight. I happen to know he is in love with her. Of course, most every gentleman of her acquaintance is in love with your sister, though she hardly gives them a thought."

"She is too young for him," Cord stated gruffly.

Nancy looked puzzled. "But, Cord, Jahane is my same age. We went to Mrs. Helms's Academy together and celebrated our birthdays but a week apart. Richard is no more than three years our senior."

There was an edge to Cord's voice when he spoke again. "You are more mature for your age than Jahane. She has been too protected by my mother and knows nothing of how to fend off a man's advances."

Nancy laughed. "Oh, there speaks the brother. I am sure you would keep her at home for as long as you can. But she is a beauty, Cord, and before too long she will fall in love and want a life on her own."

Cord's eyes were troubled as he followed Jahane and Richard out the door and onto the terrace. He knew Jahane well enough to realize she was trying to show him her indifference. But did she know the dangerous game she was playing by encouraging Richard Moyer?

Leaning against a marble statue of some long-dead Greek god, Jahane spread her arms in a gesture that was meant to draw Richard's attention. "It is a glorious night."

He smiled and moved closer to the beautiful enchantress. "It looks like rain," he said softly.

192

She glanced up at him, pursing her lips. "I like storms, don't you?"

"I like storms when they are reflected in blue eyes," he admitted, drawing her into his arms.

Jahane had not meant it to go this far. Stiffening in his arms, she pushed against his chest. "Release me at once," she said indignantly. "How dare you think—" Her voice broke off as she saw Cord step out onto the terrace just behind Richard.

With a cunning twist to her mind, Jahane decided to show Cord she could have any man she wanted. She became soft in Richard's arms. Glancing up at him, she forced a smile. "You startled me for a moment," she said almost coyly, playing her part for Cord's benefit. And she could feel his dark gaze on her.

Without considering what she was doing to Richard, she parted her lips, inviting him to kiss her. "So you like the storm in my eyes?" she asked softly.

Poor Richard was undone. He held in his arms the one woman who had haunted his dreams. For so long he had wondered what it would be like just to have her notice him. Now, if he were reading the signals correctly, she was inviting him to kiss her. Slowly, he bent his head, which was reeling with her nearness.

When Richard's lips brushed against her soft cheek, he felt his body tremble. When she turned her head and pressed her lips to his, feelings of delight exploded in his head. He hardly had time to savor those soft lips, for at that very moment a heavy hand fell on his shoulder, and he was spun around to face an incensed Cord Meredith.

"Take your hands off Jahane," Cord ordered in a deadly voice. He pushed Richard aside and grabbed Jahane by the wrists. "Just what do you think you are doing?"

She glanced up at him innocently. "Why, Cord, Richard and I were—"

"I know what you and Richard were doing. Have you no shame?"

Richard, seeing his love being so harshly reprimanded, stepped forward in her defense. "Now, see here, it was all my fault. I forgot myself for the moment, but it will not happen again. Your sister is innocent of any wrongdoing."

"You're damned right it won't happen again," Cord hissed. Before Richard knew what was happening, Cord's fist flew out and caught him in the jaw. The poor man reeled from the stunning blow, and his legs buckled, causing him to fall to his knees.

Jahane rushed to him, only to have Cord drag her back and fling her aside. "Stand up and fight like a man," Cord demanded. "I am not finished with you yet."

"Oh, yes you are," Jahane cried, moving between Cord and Richard. "You have done quite enough for one evening. You have no right to interfere in my life, and you owe Richard an apology."

Cord's eyelids half closed as he gazed down at Jahane. When he saw anger in her eyes, it stopped him cold. Did she not know he had reacted so strongly because he couldn't bear to see her in another man's arms? Couldn't she see that he wanted to be the one to hold her? He wanted only his lips on hers, only his hands to touch her, only his voice speaking love words in her ears. He was eaten up with jealousy, and he had reacted out of pure frustration.

Offering his hand to Richard, Cord pulled him to his feet. "I will not apologize, because you were

194

wrong, Richard. In the future, you might remember tonight and proceed with more restraint. My sister is unaccustomed to a man's advances, and if you ever forget that again it will go hard with you."

Richard looked at Jahane regretfully. "I can only apologize for my impetuous actions, Miss Meredith. Your brother was within his rights to call me to task. If you will forgive me, I shall promise to behave with the utmost decorum in the future."

Jahane knew deep inside it was her fault that Cord had reacted so violently. It was she who had misbehaved and led Richard to take liberties. Now, as she saw the bruise on his chin, her guilt was unbearable. "There is nothing to apologize for, Richard," she said, ducking her head. "You did nothing wrong."

"If the two of you will excuse me," Richard said, turning away.

Jahane did not look up until she heard his footsteps fade in the distance.

"Are you happy that you humiliated that poor man?" Cord snapped.

Jahane's eyes were swimming with tears. "I didn't mean—I never considered his feelings."

She looked so young and vulnerable Cord wanted to pull her into his arms, but he dared not. He doubted if he would be able to control his passions as easily as the luckless Richard Moyer had. "You should keep this in mind for the future, Jahane. A man can only resist a beautiful woman if she holds him at arm's length. You deliberately enticed Richard, and don't deny it."

"I am not denying it," she admitted ruefully. She had only intended to make Cord jealous; she had not considered how violently he might react to Richard kissing her.

Cord's muscles were taut with the restraint he was keeping on his emotions. His heart cried out at the love he was forced to deny. He stared into Jahane's eyes, and she thought she saw something akin to compassion in the dark depths of his eyes.

"I believe you should join Mama now," he said in a kinder voice. "She will be wondering what happened to you. Do not worry that your reputation will suffer from your indiscretions tonight. Richard Moyer, being a gentleman, will use decorum and tell no one what happened."

"Yes," she said, drawing in her breath. "Richard is a gentleman."

Cord stared into her eyes, and she saw remnants of her beloved in the depths of his dark eyes. She reached out to him, but he stepped back.

"You are young, Jahane. You were just testing the waters to see what it was like."

She had a sudden thought. "Do you think that was what I was doing with you the other night?"

"Yes, I'm sure of it."

Misery settled on her shoulders. How could he think she had just been playing games with him. Couldn't he see that she still loved him? If she couldn't have Cord's love, she wished it could be the way it used to be between them—before she confused their relationship.

Never again would Cord come to her as her beloved confidant and friend. No, she had ruined that. She had created her own hell, and she would just have to live with it.

Turning away, Jahane rushed into the house, hoping she wouldn't have to face Richard again tonight. Surely he must despise her for her forward actions.

196

To love Cord had cost her dearly in pride and scruples. Were there no depths that were too low for her to sink in trying to make Cord jealous? When would she face the fact that Cord did not love her—at least not in the way she loved him?

She watched Cord enter the room and make his way straight to Nancy. He whispered something in her ear, and then they both took leave of their hostess, Dotty Dunning. Not once did Cord look in Jahane's direction.

In misery, Jahane wondered if Cord would kiss Nancy tonight, and hold her in his arms. She envied the woman who would capture his heart, knowing it would not be her.

Chapter Eighteen

In her bedroom, Jahane cried until she was exhausted, regretting that she had resorted to common trickery to get Cord's attention. How he must detest her.

Now she fell into an exhausted sleep and tossed restlessly on the bed.

Shadowy figures swirled about in her mind, figures which had no substance or faces. Jahane knew she was about to be embroiled in her recurring nightmare. She fought to wake up, but without success. In terror, she called out to Cord to save her from her nightmare world.

Cord had just removed his jacket and loosened his cravat when he heard Jahane call out to him. He recognized the terror in her voice, and he realized she was having her nightmare.

With quickened steps, he rushed down the hall, opened her door, and silently entered.

The threatened rain pelted the window. Flashes of lightning split through the sky, illuminating Jahane's slight figure as she tossed and twisted on her bed.

Cord sat down beside her and drew her up so her head rested on his shoulder. "Wake up," he said gently. "You are having a bad dream, sweetheart." He talked to her just as he had when she had been a child calling out to him in her fear. "Wake up and the nightmare will go away. I have you in my arms and nothing can harm you, Jahane."

Slowly sleep receded, and Jahane opened her eyes. For a moment she was disoriented and didn't know where she was. Then she realized she was in Cord's arms and smothered a cry against his wide chest.

"The man was after me again. He wanted to show me something, but I didn't understand what he was doing. He—he cut me," she sobbed, holding her scarred hand out to Cord as she had many times before.

"It all happened a very long time ago, sweetheart. You were merely reliving your old dream." He kissed her damp brow. "Take comfort, dearest, you know I won't allow anything to harm you."

As she had when she was a child, Jahane curled up in Cord's arms, feeling as if the whole world could fall apart and Cord would take care of her. "I don't want to have that dream anymore. It frightens me. Why can I not forget it?"

Her hair was plastered to her head with perspiration, and he pushed it away from her face, while still holding her in his arms. "I'm not sure we will ever know the significance of the dream, Jahane. We have discussed this before, and we both agreed that you were reliving something from out of your childhood."

"But I haven't had the dream in a very long time, Cord. Why did it come back now?"

"I suspect it returned because of the scare you had the other day in the market. Try to put it out of your mind. A dream cannot hurt you. The fear is all in your mind."

"Will you stay with me until I fall asleep?" she pleaded.

"Yes, I will not leave you."

"Will you lay beside me as you did when I was a child? I miss that."

He hesitated. "For obvious reasons, and because you are no longer a child, I don't think that would be wise."

"I promise to be good." He could hear the pleading in her voice, and he knew she was still frightened. "Please, Cord, lay beside me until I fall asleep."

Unable to deny her plea, he placed her head on the pillow and lay beside her, cursing himself under his breath for a fool. He tried to maintain distance between them, but she snuggled up to him, needing the reassurance of his closeness. Right now she was like a frightened child, and he had to keep reminding himself that she was extremely vulnerable.

"Go to sleep," he told her in a soothing voice. "I will battle all your demons for you."

A sob escaped her lips, and her body trembled with love for this man. She couldn't understand why he did not return her love.

Jahane's golden hair spilled across Cord's shoulder, and he could smell the sweet scent of her. He felt her sigh inwardly, and then she relaxed. He tried not to think about the soft curves beneath the flimsy nightgown she wore, but he was having trouble blocking them out.

"I think I want to talk about the nightmare, Cord," she said. "The man was somehow sad because he had hurt me. I saw that tonight."

"Think of something pleasant," he urged. "Think of something that makes you feel happy, and the bad memories will fade away."

Jahane was silent for a moment. "I remember the time we were on an outing and I had wandered away. You and Mama couldn't find me. It got dark, and I was in the woods frightened half out of my mind. But even when I was frightened, I knew you would find me."

She raised her face to him, and a flash of lightning revealed the painful twist to his mouth. "I always want to know you will find me when I am lost, Cord. Please don't ever turn away from me."

"I never want you far enough from me to lose you."

She looked bewildered at his confession. "Then you do love me."

He groaned, wanting to take her into his body, to make her so much a part of him she would know how it felt to belong to him. "I need you," he whispered hotly against her ear, feeling his restraint slipping. "I wake up needing you, and I go to bed needing you, Jahane. How can I exist without you?"

Her arms slid around his neck as hope flamed to life within her. "Hold me, Cord. Hold me very tightly and never let me go."

"Sweet, sweet Jahane," he groaned. "You do so test my fortitude."

Jahane pressed against him, and she could feel the hardness of his body. "I want to belong to you in every way, Cord. I have waited for you for a very long time. If you won't have me, I will never give myself to another man."

Cord took a deep, painful breath and let it out

slowly. "I see you will not be satisfied until you have me groveling at your feet, Jahane."

"Who has your heart, Cord?" She remembered the way she had embarrassed him before, and now she was doing it again. "I know you don't love me in the way I love you, Cord, and I don't expect you to."

Her eyes were swimming with tears, and he had never been able to endure the sight of her tears. "Don't do this, Jahane. If you have any pity for me, let me go."

"Cord, you don't have to love me. Take anything you want from me, and I will give it willingly, without asking anything of you in return."

His body trembled from the intensity of his feelings. "You are such an innocent, Jahane. You have no notion what you are offering, do you?"

"I—not exactly. But I know when I'm near you I feel all funny inside and I cannot seem to get close enough to you, Cord."

A hiss escaped his throat, and he grabbed her to him, molding her body tightly against his. "Do you feel what you are doing to me, Jahane? Have you any conception of what torture you are putting me through?"

"I know I am in torment," she admitted. "If you are feeling anything like I feel, could we not find relief from our suffering together?"

He was almost mindless at her suggestion. He gently rolled her over on her back, and his hands slid down her arched neck. With trembling hands, he cupped her face, lowered his head, and pressed his hot lips to hers.

Suddenly he jerked away. "Dear God, how could you

even think I would not want you? Since the time you were given into my care, you have belonged to me. You are flesh of my flesh and heart of my heart. No two people have ever been so much a part of each other as you and I." His voice broke. "Even now I can scarcely take a breath without feeling you inside me."

"Oh, Cord, Cord," she cried. "You do love me, you do."

His mouth found hers, and he pressed her back into the mattress. Cord deepened the kiss until his body trembled with desire.

Jahane was lost in the blissful beauty of his kiss. As innocent as she was, she knew she was again enticing him, but it didn't matter. Nothing mattered but that she was in his arms and he was responding to her nearness.

She was startled at first when his tongue gently swirled around her lips. With gentle pressure, he pried her mouth open and plunged his tongue inside to taste the velvet softness. Shivers of delight hammered inside Jahane's head. She was like a rag doll that had no will of her own, no substance, no willpower.

"You have pushed me too far," he growled in her ear. "I tried to warn you, but you wouldn't listen. Now you must suffer the consequences."

His hand moved down her neck, and she gasped when he cupped her breast, the heat of his hand penetrating her thin nightgown. When he lowered his head and kissed her firm nipples through the gown, she reached up and pushed the gown aside, allowing him access to her bare breasts.

Her body trembled and shook as his hot mouth settled on her breasts, sending rivulet after rivulet of

203

emotions coursing through her body. She wanted to tear her clothing off and press her whole body against his. She ached to feel his naked flesh against hers.

"Cord," she murmured, unbuttoning his shirt and pushing it aside. Her fingers entwined in the rough hair on his chest, and he pulled back in a moment of sanity.

"Sweetheart, what are you doing to me?" he asked in torment. "I want you so badly it's like a pain inside me. Day and night the taste of you lingers with me. I believe I am losing my mind. You never draw a breath that I do not feel it."

"I want you, too, Cord. You know I do."

His hand slipped lower across her stomach, and he hesitated, knowing he was close to paradise, but that she was the forbidden fruit.

"You know I belong to you, Cord. I always have—I always will."

Lower still his hand slipped. He gently spread her legs apart and caressed her tenderly. When she gasped, he moved his hand in a soft, stroking motion.

Tossing her head from side to side, she cried out his name. "Cord, I never knew it could be like this."

His lips fanned hers as he painfully whispered, "This is only the beginning, my dearest love. I will introduce you to—"

He jerked his hand away as if it had been burned. "My God, what am I doing!"

It was as though he was propelled off the bed. He grabbed the bedpost, trying to bring his racing heart back to normal. "Forgive me, Jahane. How could I have allowed it to go this far?" he asked more of himself than of her. "I am your protector, not your ravisher."

She reached out a pleading hand to him, but already she could feel him withdrawing from her. "You did nothing, Cord. It was I who am to blame. Just as before, I shamelessly threw myself at you."

"You cannot possibly know what you invoked in me. Where as I—" He ran his hand through his hair. "I should have known better. You are an innocent."

She sat up and swung her legs off the bed. "I wouldn't be so innocent if you would teach me how to be a woman, Cord."

"I am sure Mama has taught you better than to deliberately entice a man, Jahane. You must know that what happened between us was wrong."

"But who is to teach me to be a woman if not you? How can that be wrong? You said I belonged to you."

His voice had an edge to it. "Jahane, do you know what almost happened between us tonight?"

"No, but I wanted it to happen, Cord. I wanted you to know all of me, so you would love me as much as I love you."

He took several steps backward to put some distance between the two of them. "You only think you love me, Jahane. When you are older, you will know that what you thought was love was nothing more than gratitude."

"No, you are wrong. I will never feel any differently about you than I do tonight."

He still didn't trust his feelings. His nerves were raw, his breathing was still heavy. A part of him wanted to take all she offered, but he knew she didn't really know what she was doing. She thought love was a beautiful dream like some fairy tale he had read her as a child. He would not allow himself to tear down those beautiful illusions. He could not bear to think of the love and trust he saw in her eyes turn to confusion.

"Jahane, you have to promise me you will never do this again."

He remembered finding her in Richard Moyer's arms earlier in the evening and he shook his head. "Dear God, did you act this way with Richard?" he demanded.

"Of course not," she said indignantly. "I only allowed Richard to kiss me so I could make you take notice. I would never allow anyone but you to . . . touch me intimately."

"Jahane, what am I going to do with you?" he asked gruffly. "In the future you might want to act with more decorum than you have displayed tonight. You are too old to go around acting like a little girl searching for someone to heal her bruised knee."

"I never—"

"Be quiet and let me do the talking."

"Are you still angry with me?"

"I am angry with myself, Jahane. I don't know how I allowed this to get out of hand. I promise you it will never happen again."

She stood up and walked toward him. A flash of lightning revealed her beautiful, naked body beneath the thin nightgown, and Cord stepped away from her so quickly he bumped against the wall.

She advanced on him, wanting to feel his arms about her. "All you have to do is tell me that you don't want me, Cord, and I'll leave you alone. Tell me that you despise me and I'll never ask anything of you."

His voice was rough. "I could never despise you, and you know it."

"Love then?"

He avoided answering her question by turning the conversation. "I will tell you this, Jahane. I have met many women, but never one who was more brazen than you."

Her laughter tinkled out. "You have taught me to always go after what I wanted . . . and what I want is you, Cord. Tell me you don't want me, and mean it, then I shall never bother you again."

He could feel her nearness, and he fought to retain control over his body. What he wanted to do was grab her and throw her on the bed, driving his manhood into her so she would beg for mercy. She was a little temptress and she was tearing him apart inside.

With great willpower, he spoke. "When you act like you did tonight, you cheapen love."

She stepped back, and he could hear the hurt in her voice. "You and I have always been honest with each other. You taught me to always share my feelings with you, Cord. While you were away, I grew up, and these are the feelings I have for you. Is it wrong of me to be truthful with you?"

"As I told you before, Jahane, I love you as a brother and I always shall. Do not expect anything more than that out of me."

Jahane stood silently trying to gather her shattered feelings so she could speak. "After the last time I offered myself to you, I vowed I would never do it again. I suppose I just couldn't believe you didn't love me in the way I love you. I have played the fool once too often, and once more I beg your forgiveness."

He knew how proud she was, and he knew how hurt she was by his harsh words. "There is nothing to forgive, Jahane. We shall just go on as if nothing happened between us."

She whirled away from him. "Do you think I will ever forget that I made a fool of myself over you, not just once, but twice?"

"It was my fault," he offered generously. "You didn't know what you were doing."

"No, the blame is mine. Please leave me now, Cord. I want to be by myself."

"Yes, perhaps that's best," he agreed, still not trusting his own feelings. The most difficult thing he had ever done was lie to Jahane about his love for her. The second hardest thing he had ever done was to walk out of her room, knowing she would cry herself to sleep.

As Cord stood looking out his bedroom window, the rain had stopped and he watched the clouds part to let a bright moon shine through. His heart ached, and he felt as if he had just turned away from the best friend he had ever had. Jahane must never know how much he loved her. He had pushed her away and humiliated her, because he could never allow himself to love her.

Brynn spent her days in silent agony, worrying about Prince Alexander's safety. Willa, the woman who now looked after her, was not much for conversation so Brynn could find out nothing from her. One day followed much as the others with no news from the outside world. Brynn thought she would lose her mind if she did not hear something soon.

The night was chilled as Brynn tossed and turned on her bed. The sun had set hours ago, but her mind was so full of questions that she was unable to sleep. Quietly, so she would not disturb Willa, Brynn left the comfort of her bed. Going outside, she breathed in the frosty air before sitting on the doorstep where she listened to the night sounds that came from the nearby woods.

Clasping her arms about her to ward off the chill that crept through her thin nightdress, she glanced up at the crescent moon that appeared to be suspended above the tall trees.

Wherever he was, perhaps Prince Alexander was staring at that same bright moon. Did he ever think of her? No, most probably not. He had said he would come back—but would he?

If Brynn closed her eyes very tightly, and allowed her mind to drift, she could almost feel the touch of his hands on her body. Her eyes were swimming with tears as she stood up to return to her bed. She paused at the door. What if she never saw him again. What if he left her here in this wilderness and never returned.

Brynn knew Alexander had been troubled, and she had realized he was in danger. If only there was some way she could help him. She would not allow herself to think what would happen to him if he fell into his Uncle Reynard's hands. No, that must not happen. Brynn shuddered when she considered what her own fate might be should Count Reynard find her.

With a sigh of resignation she moved quietly across the darkened room and climbed into bed. Sinking into the soft mattress where Alexander had taken her body and stolen her heart, she reflected on what her life had been like at the convent.

Even if she returned to the convent she would never be the same, because she was different inside. No longer an innocent, she loved the man who had been her imaginary childhood companion. Even if she never saw Prince Alexander again, he had given her something to hold on to for the rest of her life. Something to remember and dream about in the lonely days and nights ahead.

Chapter Nineteen

Jahane drew in her breath so Della could fasten the back of her ball gown. The maid stared at her in the mirror, noting how pale her face was.

"You look as if you were going to a wake instead of the Fireman's Ball, Jahane. This has always been your favorite event of the year."

"Not any longer. I wish I didn't have to go at all, Della. But I cannot disappoint Mama, since she has looked forward to the ball."

Amid yards and yards of frilly blue organza, Jahane moved away from the mirror and pulled on her matching blue kid gloves, totally unaware of how beautiful she was.

She had not seen Cord since the night he had come to her bedroom. She had tried to put him out of her mind, but without success. It should have been easy to forget Cord since he was purposely staying on board the *Golden Phoenix* to avoid her.

The door opened and Maggie entered, looking elegant in a deep purple ball gown. "My dear," Maggie exclaimed, "you will be the most beautiful belle at the ball. Turn around, let me see the back."

Obediently Jahanc did as she was told. Could her mother not see that her heart was broken? Couldn't

211

she see that the blush on her cheeks had been artifi-
cially applied to hide the paleness of her face?

"I wish I didn't have to go to the ball, Mama. I
really am not up to dancing with gentlemen whom I
find boring and uninteresting."

"You seemed to enjoy Richard Moyer the other
night, dear. I noticed he paid you marked attention."

Jahane would just as soon forget about that night.
"I cannot think why he would ever want to seek me
out again. I was positively awful to him that night."

Maggie smiled sympathetically, thinking she knew
what Jahane had been going through. "It will do you
good to get out of the house since you have been
cooped up for so long. I myself am ready to jump out
of my skin, because every time I turn around, one of
Cord's men is under foot. I appreciate the fact that
they are guarding the house, but, nonetheless, I will be
glad to spend an evening away from their watchful
eyes."

Jahane breathed in a resigned sigh. "I am ready,
Mama; I just want to place this flower in my hair."

Maggie watched while Jahane attached a sprig of
jasmine to her hair. "Those are lovely, dear. But where
did you get them? We have no jasmine bushes growing
in our yard."

"Jojo said they were brought to the house by a
delivery boy. I assumed Cord sent them." Jahane
frowned. "Although I do not know why he would
bother after— Oh well, I shall wear them all the
same."

"We had best hurry, Jahane," Maggie said, checking
the time by the clock on Jahane's dressing table. "Cord
will be here any moment to escort us to the ball."

"I wasn't aware he was to be our escort," Jahane said, the hurt she was feeling clearly echoed in her voice.

Maggie looked uncomfortable for a moment. "I think I should tell you, Jahane. Cord is also escorting Lorraine Scott to the ball. He will be bringing her to the house so we can all leave from here."

Jahane tried to speak, but no words came to her lips. With the pretense of pressing a wrinkle out of her gown, she lowered her head. Painful emotions tore at her heart, and she felt as if Cord had committed the ultimate betrayal. How could he be so insensitive as to bring that woman to this house, when he knew perfectly well how Jahane detested Lorraine.

Anger tugged at her mind. Now that she thought about it, Cord's total disregard for her feelings made her furious. Never mind that he had been cruel and harsh when he told her he didn't love her; she could even forgive the fact that he had stayed away from her for two days, but what she could not forgive was him flaunting another woman in her face. First it was Nancy Hartford, and now Lorraine Scott. It was too soon after his rejection of her for Jahane to put her hurt aside.

Proudly raising her head, Jahane glanced in the mirror and practiced a calm expression. Yes, she told herself with growing confidence, she would treat Cord with the cold contempt that he deserved. She would show him that she neither needed nor wanted his attentions.

Cord, dressed in dark evening attire, with an elaborately tied cravat, stood stiffly beside Lorraine Scott, wishing himself at the other end of the earth. He had lived through two days of hell, and tonight he was forced to be attentive to a woman who would never touch his heart. He reminded himself that he was doing this all for Jahane's benefit, to make her see there could be nothing between him and her. He wondered how he would ever get through this evening.

Lorraine smiled up at him prettily. "If only we didn't have to escort your mother and sister to the ball, Cord. I would much rather be alone with you." She forced her mouth into a pout. "Besides, Jahane is always so tiresome. When she is around, she requires all your attention. I declare she makes me positively jealous."

Jahane and her mother had just entered the room, and Jahane caught Lorraine's cutting remark so she was burning with indignation. "Have no fear on my account, Lorraine. My brother is yours—you can have him." Jahane's eyes coldly sought Cord's. "I give him to you."

Lorraine was embarrassed for being overheard. She turned first to Maggie. "Good evening, Mrs. Meredith, that is a lovely gown you are wearing. That color is most flattering to you."

Lorraine then looked down her nose at Jahane, not in the least happy that the girl was breathtakingly beautiful. "Jahane, your gown is nice also," she said without feeling. "As for giving your brother to me, you are far too generous."

"Not at all." She looked deliberately past Cord into the woman's spiteful eyes. "I have oftentimes been praised for my charitable nature, Lorraine."

214

Cord had caught his breath when Jahane had swept into the room trailing some sweet, familiar scent. When he looked into her eyes, he saw only contempt, and his heart seemed to shrivel up inside him. He longed to see her smile at him again. One smile from her would fill his heart with happiness. That he would always love her, he had no doubt. If he lived to be a very old man, he would never forget the vision of how she looked at this moment. He wanted to reach out to her and wipe the frown from her face, but he could not.

With deep-seated dislike, Jahane turned to her rival, generously acknowledging that Lorraine was beautiful. Her red hair was immaculately dressed, her skin whiter than Jahane's would ever be, her green eyes most unusual. She was older than Jahane, more sophisticated, and probably Cord found her much more interesting. Though Jahane hated to admit it, she could easily see why Cord would prefer Lorraine Scott to her.

"What unusual flowers you have in your hair," Lorraine exclaimed, knowing she should say something nice to the girl, at least for Mrs. Meredith's benefit. "They do have an unusually sweet scent."

"Thank you very much, Lorraine." Jahane knew it was childish, but she couldn't help this one barb at the woman. "I believe my brother had them delivered to me just in time to wear to the ball tonight."

Cord froze. He now realized why the scent of the flowers was so familiar to him. The flowers were Jasmine, and the scent of them reminded him of Balmarhea!

"Jahane, where did you get those flowers?" he demanded to know.

"I truly thought they were from you," Jahane said, confused. "Did you not send them?"

"No, they are not from me," he stated flatly.

She smiled and shrugged her shoulders, wanting to wound him. "Well, perhaps one of my admirers sent them. I am sure I will find out tonight."

Cord's jaw clamped tightly together. "I'm not sure you should go to the ball tonight."

Jahane pressed her fingers against her temples wishing she didn't have to go, but she didn't want Cord to know that. She did not look forward to watching Lorraine fawn all over Cord tonight.

"I am going to the ball," she stated flatly. "Should we not leave now."

For a long moment her eyes met and battled with Cord's. At last he looked away. "Yes, let's leave now. I believe we can just get there in time to be fashionably late so each of you ladies can show off your new frocks."

Jahane's dance card was filled soon after she arrived at the ball. She accepted dances from gentlemen whom she scarcely knew. She would show Cord that she was not pining away for him. After tonight, he would never have to be embarrassed because she had thrown herself at him.

She danced, she whirled, she teased the men, and she laughed at their amusing stories, knowing she was behaving outrageously. But she did not care.

As she whirled around the dance floor on the arm of a very handsome cavalry officer, she pretended to be amused by his attempt to be witty. Over the man's

216

shoulder, she could see Cord staring at her, and she was glad he looked displeased. Let him think she was now throwing herself at this officer. She hoped he was very displeased with her behavior.

The music stopped and the young major regretfully escorted her off the dance floor begging for another dance, but she showed him her dance card was filled. When he looked so dejected she did promise to drink a glass of punch with him later in the evening.

Jahane was looking for her mother when Cord approached her from behind. His hand fell heavy on her shoulder and he whirled her around to him. She was not prepared for the anger etched on his face. "Just what do you mean by behaving like a strumpet all evening, Jahane." His eyes were dancing with fire. "Do you think to tear my heart out?"

She jerked her arm free of his grasp. "How dare you say such things to me. I do not have to answer to you for anything I do, Cord. You are not the person I always thought you were. I don't even know how to talk to you anymore."

"Don't you?"

"No, I don't."

"You seem to be doing a good imitation of talking to me right now."

"Just leave me alone and go find your redhead, Cord. Perhaps she will hang on to your every word as great pearls of wisdom, but I assure you I will not."

The music had started and Cord realized he and Jahane were becoming the center of attention. Taking her hand, he led her onto the dance floor. "Try to control yourself, Jahane. I will not have some gossipy old woman discussing your bad behavior over her cof-

217

fee in the morning."

Jahane had endured enough from him for one day. "Cord, I am warning you, do not take your anger out on me. I am no longer a little girl, so therefore I no longer have to listen to you." She took a deep breath. "And don't try to order me around, either."

His eyes softened and he wanted to pull her close to him, to erase the hurt he saw in her eyes. He knew why she was striking out at him, and he had no one to blame but himself. He had handled the situation very badly, but it had been agony to let her go. He had been forced to make her so angry that she would turn away from him.

"I am sorry, Jahane. So much has happened, and I am sure I have made grave mistakes with you. But, know in your heart that everything I do is what I believe to be best for you."

She was not appeased. "Did you bring Lorraine to the ball for my benefit?" she asked sarcastically. "I can assure you, Cord, I do not need that kind of consideration."

"I have hurt you and that's the last thing in the world I'd ever want. Can you forgive me, little one?"

"Don't call me your 'little one' anymore, Cord. And, yes, I forgive you, but I don't want to be with you."

His hand tightened on hers. "What can I do to bring the smile back to your sweet lips?"

Once more he was tugging at her heart, but she would not leave herself open to be hurt again. Pride being her only salvation, she looked straight into his eyes. "I will smile for you, Cord. You pull the strings and I will dance for you, but never again ask me to open my heart to you—for I will not."

He smiled sadly. "Have I driven you so far away?"

"We were never meant to be more than brother and sister, Cord. You yourself pointed that out to me. It just took me longer to realize it."

"Jahane, there is more I would say to you, but this is not the place. In the last four days I have had time to do a lot of thinking. There is something very important I want to discuss with you. I have been putting it off, I must tell you soon."

The music had stopped and she turned away from him. When he followed, she spoke to him in a soft voice so no one else would hear.

"You have insulted me in about every way possible. Tonight you called me a strumpet, and you may have been right. I have danced with many men tonight and I have enjoyed it, Cord Meredith! As for any little talk you feel you need to have with me, spare me and yourself. I do not want to hear anything you have to say."

She moved away from him, but he caught up with her. "Take out your anger on me if you want to, Jahane. But we are going to settle this thing between us tonight if we have to talk all night long."

She turned around to face him. "I do not want to talk to you, Cord."

His eyes were blank and unreadable. "But you will, Jahane."

She spun away from him, wishing she could find a place to hide. She had to get away from him.

When Cord caught up with her, she backed away from him. "Why can't you just leave me alone, Cord. What do you want from me?"

"Trust me," he said, feeling the knife turn in his

heart.

"I will never trust you again, Cord. You allowed me to pour out my love for you, then you purposely made me feel like a fool."

"I know," he said in agony. "Tonight when we get home we will finish this conversation, Jahane. At that time I shall tell you my true feelings, and why I cannot love you."

Before she could ask him what he meant, he turned and moved away, leaving her more confused than ever.

Chapter Twenty

Jahane did not see the handsome blond man whose eyes followed her around the room. Alexander watched her every move, her every gesture. Once she looked right past him with unseeing eyes, and his heart ached because she did not seem to know him.

Jahane was trying to catch her breath, and stepped behind a pylon hoping to escape dancing the next set, when Father Estevan came up to her with a smile on his face.

"How exceptional you look tonight, Jahane. "I would seem there are many lovely flowers that bloom at the ball, but I believe you are the most brilliant of them all."

"I did not know you were a poet, Father." She dimpled at the old priest whom she had known for several years. "As always, Father, you tongue is as glib as your wit. Pity you don't dance, for I would rather dance with you than any of my partners thus far tonight."

Father Estevan turned to his companion, whom Jahane had not noticed until now. "You see how it is, Mr. Beaudette. Miss Meredith prefers me to the young men her own age."

The man's eyes locked with Jahane's, and she had

the strangest feeling she had seen him before, but where? There was warmth in his eyes as they ran over her, not in an insulting way, but more in a searching manner.

"If you would allow it, Jahane, my young friend here has asked to be presented to you," Father Estevan said.

Again she dimpled. "Any friend of yours, Father, comes to me on good recommendation."

The priest cleared his throat for the introduction. "Mr. Alexander Beaudette, may I present you to my good friend, Miss Jahane Meredith."

Alexander took Jahane's gloved hand and bowed over it gallantly. "Charmed, Miss Meredith. I hope you will allow me the privilege of the next dance."

She was aware of his French accent, and she found herself wanting very much to dance with him. He was by far the most interesting man at the ball, except for Cord, of course.

"Well . . ." she said, consulting her dance card, ". . . this dance belongs to someone else . . ." She smiled. "But he's not here. Yes, I will dance with you."

With another gallant bow, Alexander took Jahane's hand and led her forward.

Father Estevan watched the two young people dance away, feeling happy inside. Now that he had seen Alexander and Jahane together, he was more certain than ever that they were brother and sister.

Alexander looked into eyes that were very much the color of his own. Her golden hair reminded him of his mother's hair, and he felt excitement throbbing through his body. This had to be his Jahane—but he had to

222

find out for certain tonight.

"I see you are wearing the flowers I sent to your house, Miss Meredith."

She looked at him quizzically. "So it was you who sent the flowers? But why? I don't know you. We have never met before tonight—have we?"

He smiled down at her, thinking what a charmer she was. He could see traces of his little sister in her. "Perhaps I know you better than you think."

Again she had the feeling of familiarity. "Please explain to me what you mean."

"Search your mind, Jahane. Think about the scent of jasmine. Does that invoke any memories in your mind?"

Jahane knew she should be frightened of this stranger, but for some strange reason she was not. She could see by the tender expression in his eyes that he meant her no harm.

"Do you play games with me, sir?" she asked, trying to be coy and flirtatious.

"Nay, Jahane. It is others who play games; you and I merely get caught up in them."

"You are talking in riddles, Mr. Beaudette. Therefore, I have not followed your conversation. But I do thank you for the flowers. They are lovely."

He glanced at her glove-covered hand, wishing he could see her palm—then he would know for certain if this was his sister. "I have many attributes and talents, Miss Meredith, and sending flowers to lovely young ladies is the least of them."

"Ah, Mr. Beaudette, you flatter me. Is that one of your talents?"

His eyes swept over her beautiful face. "It is not

flattery, Jahane. You are most probably the second most beautiful woman I have ever known."

She was intrigued by this man. Most gentlemen would never dare compare a woman less favorably with another woman. She smiled at him brightly. With anyone else this would be a ridiculous conversation. But it was so easy to tease with this man. "Pray tell me, Mr. Beaudette, who can the first most beautiful woman possibly be?"

His eyes swept her face, and she tingled from some long-lost memory.

"She was my mother, and she looked very much like you. I have little doubt, when you are older you will rival her in beauty."

Jahane caught her breath. Suddenly the conversation was no longer humorous. There were hidden meaning in this man's statements. "Your mother?" she questioned.

His eyes became deep and penetrating, and she could not look away. She had a strange feeling that he knew more about her than she knew about herself. When he smiled, it broke the tension and she was relieved.

When he broke eye contact with her, Jahane blurted out, "Why would you compare me with your mother?"

He chose to change the subject. "We were speaking of my attributes earlier," he said on a lighter note.

"So we were, and you were about to tell me of your other talents."

"I can read fortunes," he said, carefully watching her face.

"Indeed. Then pray read mine."

"I would be glad to, but not here. I have to concentrate, and it's much too noisy here. And," he added,

ACCEPT YOUR **FREE GIFT** AND EXPERIENCE MORE OF THE PASSION AND ADVENTURE YOU LIKE IN A HISTORICAL ROMANCE

〰️

Zebra Romances are the finest novels of their kind and are written with the adult woman in mind. All of our books are written by authors who really know how to weave tales of romantic adventure in the historical settings you love.

Because our readers tell us these books sell out very fast in the stores, Zebra has made arrangements for you to receive at home the four newest titles published each month. You'll never miss a title and home delivery is so convenient. With your first shipment we'll even send you a FREE Zebra Historical Romance as our gift just for trying our home subscription service. No obligation.

BIG SAVINGS AND **FREE** *HOME DELIVERY*

Each month, the Zebra Home Subscription Service will send you the four newest titles as soon as they are published. (We ship these books to our subscribers even before we send them to the stores.) You may preview them *Free* for 10 days. If you like them as much as we think you will, you'll pay just $3.50 each and *save $1.80 each month* off the cover price. *AND you'll also get FREE HOME DELIVERY.* There is never a charge for shipping, handling or postage and there is no minimum you must buy. If you decide not to keep any shipment, simply return it within 10 days, no questions asked, and owe nothing.

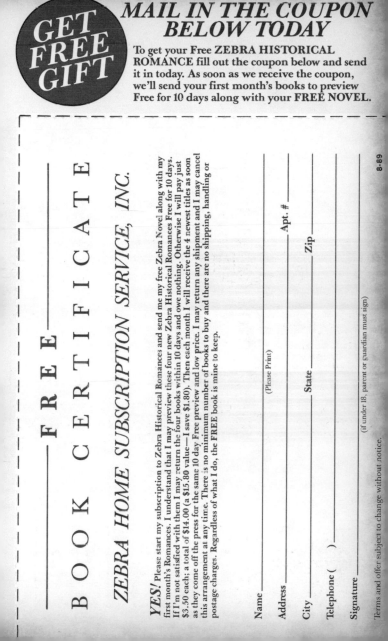

as if it were an afterthought, "I will have to see your palm."

"This is the most extraordinary conversation I have ever had. And where do you propose this little fortune-telling scene take place?"

He seemed undaunted by her mockery. "On entering the ballroom, I saw a small room to the left. It didn't seem to be occupied. Perhaps we could go there."

"You don't really expect me to do that—do you, Mr. Beaudette?"

He smiled. "I thought perhaps you might be intrigued enough to accept."

"I am intrigued," she admitted with a delicately arched brow. "But it would be most unthinkable to go off with a man I have just met."

His expression became serious. "If I asked Father Estevan to accompany us, would you consider it?"

She looked over his shoulder and saw Cord staring at her with blazing eyes and a tight jaw. Was it possible he was jealous of this man? She did not want a repeat of what happened to Richard Moyer. Still, she did want to accept. "I . . . yes, I will do it, if Father Estevan is present."

The music was still playing when Alexander gripped her hand and led her off the dance floor. Stopping before the priest, he spoke hurriedly. "Come with us, Father."

Jahane had no time to reflect on what was happening as the stranger led her past the dancers to the small room near the entryway. Several women occupied the room, and Alexander spoke sharply to them. "I would consider it a favor if you ladies would be so kind as to leave us alone."

225

Two of the ladies looked startled, and one of them was indignant, but they did leave. Alexander looked like a man possessed. He turned to Jahane, and she took a step backward. He still held her arm, and she was about to demand that he release her hand until she detected an urgent plea in his eyes.

Without further delay, he spoke. "Now to tell your fortune, Jahane. But first you must remove your glove."

Her eyes met with Father Estevan's, and he nodded in approval. "Do as he says, Jahane. It will be all right."

Not understanding, but not afraid, she removed her glove and held her hand out to Mr. Beaudette. "What do you see there," she asked nervously.

Alexander took her hand in his and looked for any sign of a scar—but there was none. Discouraged and disillusioned, he released her hand, feeling as if the world had caved in on him. He had been so sure she was his sister.

"But aren't you going to tell my fortune?" she asked, wondering at his strange behavior.

"Alexander, could it not have been her right hand?" Father Estevan suggested.

"Yes, I—of course! I was looking at her left hand." Alexander lifted her right hand, and with a gentle tug, removed the glove. With his heart beating, he turned the hand over!

"Yes, yes," he whispered, looking at her lovingly. "There is the scar!"

Jahane pulled away from him in bewilderment. "What are you talking about? How could you know about—" The color drained from her face. "Who are you?"

For the first time in many years, Prince Alexander felt happiness wash through his body. He had found his sister, he had someone who belonged to him!

"Don't you remember me, Jahane? Search your mind—think back to your childhood."

She took a step back toward the priest. "No, I don't know you. You are frightening me, Mr. Beaudette."

"Father," Alexander cried, wringing the priest's hand. "I will never again doubt the power of prayer. You helped me find her."

Jahane shook her head. "I don't know you. Why are you saying these things?"

Alexander gently took her hand so he wouldn't frighten her. "But I do know you, Jahane, my dearest little sister."

"I . . . what did you say?"

"There can be no mistake, you are my sister. You are Princess Jahane Bcaudette!"

"No, I am . . . Jahane Meredith, or Jahane d'Arcy. I am not your sister!"

"Jahane, you are my sister, and I can prove it to you if you will just give me a chance."

She was dazed. So much had happened to her in the last week; now this stranger that she had never seen was asking her to believe she was his sister. She placed her hands over her ears and backed toward the door.

"No, I will not listen to anymore," she cried. "You are trying to confuse me."

"You are upset now, Jahane. But when we have had a chance to sit down and talk, you will know you are my sister."

"I want to go home," she whispered, taking another

step backward.

"Sleep on what I have told you, and I will call on you tomorrow so we can talk."

Turning around, she fled through the door, wishing she had never met this man. Alexander would have gone after her, but Father Estevan put a restraining hand on his arm. "It is better to let her go for now, my son. I didn't expect your news to be so upsetting for her. We will call at the Meredith house tomorrow morning and set everything straight."

The young prince's shoulders slumped. "I suppose I expected her to be as happy as I was about being reunited with her. Of course, she was so young when we were parted. She probably does not remember me at all."

"Tomorrow you will convince her that you are telling the truth."

"Will you help me convince Jahane of the truth, Father?"

"Of course, my son. Everything will look better to her in the morning. I am sure it was just the shock of it all."

Father Estevan thought about Cord Meredith. The captain of the *Golden Phoenix* was a power to be reckoned with, and he would not easily give Jahane over to Prince Alexander without conclusive proof that he was her brother.

Jahane quickly made her way across the room and searched until she found Maggie Meredith. She would not allow herself time to think about what had just occurred, because she was on the edge of total panic.

"Mama," she said, clutching her gloves tightly in her hand. "I am not feeling very well. Do you think it would be all right if we went home?"

Maggie looked at her with concern, and seeing how pale Jahane looked, nodded her head. "Of course, dear. Let me find Cord and tell him. You wait right here."

Jahane glanced back at the room where she had gone with Father Estevan and the man called Alexander Beaudette. What had the man called her—Princess Jahane Beaudette? No, it was impossible. She was not a princess.

Suppose Mr. Beaudette was in collusion with the man who had followed her at the market? What if he wanted to do her harm?

Suddenly she glanced across the room, and her eyes locked with Alexander Beaudette's. No, he would not harm her. She searched her mind, trying to remember him from out of her past, but it was no use.

He looked at her regretfully, nodded his head in farewell, and turned to follow the priest out of the room.

Something inside Jahane made her want to call out to him, but she dared not. Jahane knew she had not seen the last of that man, just as she knew she had no reason to fear him.

"Jahane, Mama says you aren't feeling well," Cord said, breaking into her thoughts. He took hold of her elbow and turned her to face him. "Are you ready to go home?"

She spoke without looking at him. "I don't want to spoil the evening for you and Lorraine."

The redhead hung on to Cord's arm and smiled sweetly at Jahane. "Don't fret, dear. Cord will take you and Mrs. Meredith home first. Then he and I

229

shall have the whole evening together. Won't that be nice?"

Jahane glanced past Cord. With a shrug of her shoulders, she threaded her way through the crowd, hardly aware of the several gentlemen who called out to her.

Once she was situated in the carriage, Jahane leaned her head back and closed her eyes. She listened to Lorraine's voice drone on and on about what colors went best with her red hair, and how she preferred emeralds to diamonds. Jahane wondered how Cord could stand the woman. By the time the horses made the final leg up the hill, Jahane wrenched open the door.

When Cord helped her out of the carriage, Jahane murmured her good-night, and moved up the steps to the house.

Cord caught up with her, and after helping his mother inside, he pulled Jahane to him. "Don't shut me out, Jahane. I can stand anything but your coldness."

"What do you want of me? You can't keep pushing me away and then trying to pull me back. If you don't want me, let me go, Cord."

"I can't."

Her eyes were unfeeling. "Go back to Lorraine, Cord. There is no need to be rude to her as well."

"Will you wait up for me so we can talk?"

"No, I'm going to bed, and I do not want to be disturbed."

Helplessly he watched her enter the house, realizing she was slipping away from him.

In the morning he would tell her who she was and

lay his heart at her feet. If she would forgive him for being such a fool, then they would turn away from the rest of the world and find happiness in each other.

His face was grim as he got back in the carriage with Lorraine. He listened to her prattle, wishing he had insisted on talking to Jahane.

Chapter Twenty-one

Jahane found it impossible to sleep, so she got out of bed and stood at the window for a long time. Ordinarily, when she was troubled, she would go to Cord, but that was impossible now. She would have to find her own answers tonight.

As she walked slowly downstairs, the hall clock struck two o'clock.

Moving silently into the morning room, she stood before the window that gave her the sweeping view of San Francisco.

In the distance tiny lights bobbed up and down in the bay, and she knew they would be ships swaying at their anchors. Possibly one of the lights was from the *Golden Phoenix*.

Her eyes followed the twisting street where most of the houses were in darkness. She wondered if she was the only person awake at this time of night. But no, some people would still be dancing at the Fireman's Ball.

Dropping down on the floor, she leaned her forehead against the window, her mind too full to see what she was looking at.

Was it possible Alexander Beaudette had been telling the truth? Was he really her brother? Could she be a princess? It was all so confusing.

Again she searched her mind, trying to remember fragments of her childhood. She remembered the man with the dagger, but then that was the one thing she always tried to forget and couldn't.

As always, her mind drifted to Cord. What had gone wrong between them?

If only she had not acted like such a fool and tried to get him to admit he felt something for her that he did not feel, they would still be friends. Why couldn't she have gone on accepting what love he gave her as a brother and have been satisfied with that?

She ached so badly inside, because she wanted more from Cord than a sister would want. She wanted to be his wife, his lover, and the mother of his children.

Jahane heard footsteps coming down the hallway, and she glanced over her shoulder to find a dark silhouette behind her, and she knew it was Cord.

Wordlessly, he dropped down beside her, took her hand, and raised it to his lips. For a long moment they sat there together, silently gazing out at the flickering lights of San Francisco.

"Jahane, have you decided to forgive me?" he asked at last.

"Yes, although now that I have had time to think about it, it is I who beg your pardon. It was so foolish of me to ask you to feel something for me that you couldn't feel. You and Mama have been so good to me. You have taken me in and given me a home. You even uprooted your life in Boston because of me. After all your sacrifices, I acted so badly. Can you ever forget how ungratefully I have behaved?"

A loud, throaty groan escaped from Cord's throat,

233

and he pressed his lips to her hand. Oh, God, how could he explain to her the feelings that ate away at him day and night? He dreamed of her when he was asleep, and she was always in his mind when he was awake. She was in his head, in his heart, and he could not exorcise her ghost.

When she felt him tremble, she misunderstood. "Don't worry, Cord. I no longer have my head in the clouds. Call what happened between us a young girl's foolish fancy—a girl's daydreams. I can assure you it will never happen again."

"But, Jahane, I—"

She placed her finger on his lips to silence him. "No, don't say anything. I don't know why I acted as I did, but I beg you to put it out of your mind and never think of it again."

His voice was deep. "Is that really what you want me to do, Jahane?"

"Yes."

"Then you have changed toward me."

"I know that I have considered you to be something of a hero to me." She smiled and wrinkled her nose at him. "I have decided to overcome all my foolish trepidations. Tonight I took my first step toward becoming an adult."

"So," he said, releasing her hand. "Like the dolls you no longer play with, you have decided to put me on the shelf where I belong."

"Perhaps I have. I always depended on you too much. The time has come when I need to stand on my own and make some of my own decisions."

He could feel her slipping away from him, and there was nothing he could do to hold on to her. "Would you tell me what brought this on?"

"Someone I met tonight at the ball gave me cause to reflect back on my life, and to look forward as well."

"And who might that be?"

"Did you notice the blond-headed man I was dancing with?"

"You danced with so many, but I followed you with each partner," he admitted. "I believe I do know the one you are referring to. He was tall, and I suppose a woman would have called him handsome."

"Yes, very tall, very handsome."

Cord felt a lump forming in his throat. "So, has the tall blond one replaced me in your affections?"

"In a manner of speaking, yes, he has."

He took in a ragged breath. "Is he someone you have known for a long time?"

She tried to think how to tell Cord about Alexander Beaudette. "No . . . yes . . . I'm not sure—perhaps so . . . yes, I suppose he is."

He looked into her eyes, and she could see the reflection of lights in the dark depths of his. "You have me confused, Jahane. Would you care to explain?"

"Cord, the man I am speaking of is Alexander Beaudette. Do you know of him?"

"I am not aware of ever hearing his name. Should I know him?"

"What if I told you he is Prince Alexander Beaudette, would you know him then?"

The silence lay heavy in the room until Cord spoke at last. "How would I know a prince?"

"He claims to be from Balmarhea."

"I see . . ."

"He says I am his sister. Is that possible?"

Jahane expected Cord to deny Alexander Beaudette's claim, but he did not. "It could be. But I would have to investigate the man further before making a decision."

"Is that all you have to say? Is there nothing you are keeping from me, Cord? All these years I have thought I had no family. Only a few days ago you told me you thought I was Chapin d'Arcy's daughter. Were you keeping my brother from me?"

"Jahane, I didn't know you had a brother until just recently. This man may or may not be who he claims to be. Have you thought that he may even be in league with the man who followed you at the market?"

"I know Alexander Beaudette would never harm me. Don't ask me how I know, I just do. Besides, Father Estevan introduced him to me. I got the feeling he believed Alexander is my brother."

"I'm not sure you can trust anyone at this point, and surely not all your own feelings. Perhaps you want this man to be your brother, so therefore you have allowed yourself to believe he actually is."

"No, that's not it. There is something about him that seems familiar. He is my brother!"

"As I said, I shall have him investigated."

She grabbed Cord's arm in protest. "But you cannot do that. If I am in danger, would he not be in danger also? Perhaps even more than I."

"I will be discreet, Jahane. I have ways of getting things done."

"Yes, I suppose you do. But will you tell me who I am? Could I possibly be Princess Jahane Beaudette?"

How could Cord tell Jahane that his mother had

kept this knowledge from the girl all these years. No, he could not put the blame on his mother, for what she did was out of love for Jahane.

"I have only lately come to suspect that you might truly be Princess Jahane."

"Oh, Cord, why didn't you and Mama tell me? I had a right to know about my family. Every time I asked Mama, she would change the subject. And when I would ask you, you would say I was in danger and we couldn't talk about it. I am so confused, Cord, I don't know what to believe."

"You must believe that I care deeply about you and will always want what is best for you."

"I know that, Cord. There was never any question that you and Mama have always put my welfare first, even to the point of uprooting your own lives. Did you think I would expect such a sacrifice from you?"

"I don't know what to say to you, Jahane. For all my blundering, I ask your pardon."

She turned to him and pressed her cheek to his. "Oh, Cord, if only I could have stayed your little girl. You always made me feel so safe and loved. Now things are moving so quickly I don't know where they are carrying me. I wish I could turn back the clock, but I cannot."

His arms slid around her, and he felt the tears on her cheeks. "Jahane, I want to hold on to you, sweetheart, so tightly that you will never leave me." His arms tightened about her. "But already I feel you slipping away."

She looked into the face of the man she loved, and saw torment in his dark eyes. "We are losing each other, Cord. I grew up and lost my best friend and my hero."

He stared at her, wanting to imprint her image in his mind. "Dearest heart, if I can never be anything else in your life, allow me to stay your hero."

Softly she kissed his lips. "You will always be my one and only hero, Cord. No one can ever take your place in that."

"I suppose this Alexander Beaudette made plans to call on us."

"Yes, he will be here tomorrow morning." She glanced at the clock and saw that it was after three. "I suppose it would be today now." She was thoughtful for a moment. "He was hurt tonight when I didn't recognize him, Cord. How sad that I wanted to reach out to him, but I could not."

"I will confront him tomorrow and decide if he really is your brother. Until then, you should put the incident out of your mind. Go to bed and get some rest."

Cord's eyes moved across Jahane's face. She looked so slight and frail, but he sensed a hidden strength in her that he had not been aware of before now. He had always thought of her as his little girl. Now he was confused not knowing what to do about her. His head reeled with a new rush of love that overflowed from his heart.

"What is happening to us, Cord?" she asked, shaking her head sadly. "Is there no way to stop time so I can remain with you forever?"

A low, muffled cry escaped Jahane's lips as she buried her face against his shirtfront. "I can feel myself being pulled away from you, Cord. There is nothing I can do to stop events from dividing us."

His arms went around her and he pulled her tightly against him. So she felt it, too? They both knew time was running out for them and soon they would be torn apart. As their eyes locked, slowly, with Jahane's consent, Cord lowered her backward until her head touched the floor. For a long moment he hovered over her, staring into misty blue eyes. When her hand reached up to trail down his cheek, he closed his eyes at her soft touch.

"Kiss me, Cord," she said in a throaty voice. "Hold me very tightly."

Cord was lost within the depths of the shimmering eyes that held him captive. Unable to fight against the pull of her love, he lowered his head, his lips touched her cheek, slid across her jawline, to find at last the heaven of her soft lips. He allowed his hands to slide down her neck to gently rest against her rounded breasts, wanting to possess her, to keep her within the circle of his arms.

Jahane yielded her body to Cord's caress. She held her breath as he slipped her robe off her shoulders. She closed her eyes, lost in the beautiful feelings he had awakened in her body.

Cord nudged her gown aside and his hot lips closed around the pink tips of her breasts, causing them to harden in his mouth. She felt him shift his weight and his body pinned her to the floor. She reveled in the feel of his hardness pressed tightly against her.

"I cannot think clearly when I'm near you," he murmured in her ear. "You make me forget about my responsibilities. I have this need for you, and I can find no relief from this torment."

"Oh, Cord," she cried, turning her face away from

239

his wandering lips. "This is my fault. I have purposely tormented you, and I'm sorry. I think we both know it's too late for us now."

He stiffened as if she had thrown a dash of cold water in his face. He sat up, and with trembling hands he pulled her gown together. Avoiding her eyes, he held her robe so she could slip her arms into the sleeves. With a regretful smile he tied the sash snugly about her waist.

Silently he stood up, knowing if he stayed with her longer he would not be able to resist taking her in his arms again—only next time he might not be able to stop himself.

Holding out his hand, he helped her to her feet. "Come, Jahane. I will see you to your room."

She clasped his hand, and they walked arm-in-arm upstairs. He stopped at her door and spoke softly. "Remember this, Jahane. No matter where you go, or what you do, I will always care about you."

"With the love of a brother for a sister?" she asked, holding her breath, waiting for his answer, needing him to say he loved her deeply as a man loves a woman.

He smiled sadly. "I no longer have a place in your life, Jahane. You don't need me for a brother, since apparently you have found your own brother."

She stood on tiptoes and brushed a kiss on his lips. Then she slipped through her bedroom door and closed it softly behind her.

She fought the urge to wrench the door open. If she did, would she find Cord waiting for her on the other side? Would he take her in his arms and give her the love she so desperately wanted? No, it was not to be.

Tonight her feet had been set on a path that would

take her away from Cord, and they both knew she would have to leave this heaven that had been the only home she had ever known.

Alexander was too excited to sleep, so therefore he stood in the mission courtyard waiting impatiently for the sun to rise. His thoughts were tumbling over one another. Now that he had found Jahane, the two of them would stand together until they defeated their Uncle Reynard!

Suddenly he thought of Brynn, and he wondered what part she would play in his life. He still believed in her innocence, but who was she?

He thought of the night she had given herself to him, and he felt a tightening in his stomach. He wanted her again, and he would go on wanting her. When he thought of her alone and frightened, he wanted to make haste in returning to Balmarhea. First he would have to convince Jahane that she was his sister and hope she would return to Balmarhea with him.

Brynn entered the cabin and nodded to the servant, Willa. The woman was small in stature, but wide in girth. Her red hair was laced with white, and while she was not unpleasant, she very seldom conversed with Brynn.

In desperation, and needing to know something about her plight, Brynn spoke. "Willa, have you had no news from the outside?"

"No. Why should anyone tell us anything?"

241

"It has been weeks now since I was brought here. I wish I could know what is happening."

Willa was slicing carrots into a stew that bubbled on the open hearth. "I do not know anything about anything. I was paid by the archbishop's gamekeeper to take care of you, and that's what I will do until I am told different."

The girl did not know how much knowledge Willa had of her situation. She wondered if the woman knew about Prince Alexander. Without giving anything away, she decided to question Willa.

Picking up a knife, Brynn helped Willa slice the carrots into the stew. "Willa, do you know who I am?"

The woman gave her a measured look. "No, and I do not want to know."

"No one knows what is happening in Balmarhea these days, Willa. Since I was raised in a convent, I seldom knew what was happening outside those high walls. But this is far worse. Can you not tell me anything?"

The woman put the lid on the stew pot with a forceful clatter. "Humph, I can tell you well enough that nothing good is afoot. The farmers' crops have failed. The fishermen's lot is little better. Since our king and queen were slain, the country has fallen on desperate times. But everyone knows that, though they don't speak it aloud."

Willa leaned toward Brynn and spoke in a hushed tone as if she feared being overheard. "The irrigation ditches King Alfons had dug are grown over with weeds." Her voice now came out in a whisper. "Things have been no good since that black-hearted duke took over. There are even those who say he was behind his brother's murder—'course I don't know myself, and I have never said such a thing."

For someone who had been silent for so long, Willa couldn't seem to stop talking. She looked over her shoulder fearfully and then continued. "Most of the people would rather rise up against the duke than be subject to his rule. I do know most folks are glad the duke cannot find the scepter so he can't have himself crowned king."

"What would the people do if Prince Alexander came back? His body has never been found, you know, so it is possible he might be alive."

Willa looked wistful. "If only that could be. But no—he's dead well enough, as is the little princess. There is no hope for the people. These are terrible black times for us—*black* times indeed."

"But just suppose for a moment the prince did come back?"

Willa was thoughtful. "If by some miracle he arose from the dead—and if he could produce the scepter—the people would joyfully rally around him." The little woman's eyes flamed and then saddened. "But that will not happen. We are all subject to Duke Maxime's orders."

"The people must have loved the royal family very much."

Willa looked at Brynn as if she were addlebrained. "You must have been out of touch with the world if you do not know of the affection we all had for the king, queen, and their children. But then you could have only been very small when tragedy struck, so you can be forgiven."

"So without a leader, the people are content to allow

243

Duke Maxime to make the decisions for them?"

"No, not content, but there is nothing they can do. Every time anyone voices dissatisfaction with the duke, they are taken to the castle and never heard from again. He is a truly evil man."

A heavy rap fell on the door, and Brynn jumped nervously.

"I wonder who that could be?" Willa said, slipping the latch and throwing the door open.

The woman gasped when she saw several of Duke Maxime's soldiers. "W-what do you want?" she asked in a shaky voice. "Why are you here?"

The man who appeared to be the leader pushed the old woman aside and entered. When he saw the young girl, he smiled. "You are the one known as Brynn?"

She backed against the wall. "Yes."

"Then you will come with me."

"No, I don't know you. I will not go with you," she declared.

Before Brynn knew what was happening, the man struck her hard across the face, and she went reeling to the floor. When Willa would have rushed forward to help her, a second man held her back.

Without pausing, the soldier scooped Brynn up in his arms, and in long strides reached the door.

"What shall we do with this old woman?" the second soldier wanted to know.

"She looks harmless enough, let her be."

He then pointed a finger at Willa. "Tell your master that Duke Maxime has the girl." The man gave an evil snigger. "That should send the good archbishop down to his knees to see if he can pull another miracle out of his priestly robe."

Brynn was sure she was living in a nightmare. The man's hands were rough as he pulled her down the path to where others were waiting with the horses.

When he mounted, and then pulled her up beside him, he enfolded her in his cape and she could hardly breathe.

Too fearful to cry out, she closed her eyes, knowing she was in the hands of the evil duke once more. She doubted that Prince Alexander would be able to find her this time.

Chapter Twenty-two

Prince Alexander and Father Estevan waited on the Merediths' doorsteps to be admitted to the house. When the houseboy Jojo opened the door and recognized Father Estevan, he smilingly bowed them inside.

"You wait in here," Jojo announced, leading them into the formal sitting room, then abruptly withdrew.

The priest had often been in this room so he felt right at home. He seated himself on the green leather chair and watched Alexander pace restlessly about the room, guessing at the emotions and feelings the young man was having to deal with.

"I half feared the servant would turn us away this morning and I would have to force my way in," Alexander stated, stopping his pacing long enough to look around at the tastefully decorated room.

"I never had any doubt you would be admitted," Father Estevan replied. "Not after what you confessed to Jahane last night. If I know Cord Meredith, he will be anxious to look you over to determine if you are who you claim to be."

The prince looked toward the door. "What can be keeping them? Is it not considered an insult to keep royalty waiting in this country?"

"America has no royalty," the priest reminded him. "And I do not believe the Meredith family would deliberately insult anyone. Especially someone who is important to Jahane."

At that moment, they heard voices in the hallway, and Alexander stood stiffly, waiting for the Meredith's to enter.

Alexander's eyes locked defiantly with the tall, dark-haired man, and the prince didn't have to be told he was in the presence of Captain Cord Meredith. The men stared long and hard at each other, neither willing to be the first one to break eye contact.

Cord could see the startling resemblance between the stranger and Jahane. They had the same hair coloring, the same blue eyes, even the shape of the head and the tilt of the chin was the same. Except where Jahane was soft and feminine, the man was hard and muscled. There was nothing soft about the man whose eyes defied Cord at the moment.

Maggie Meredith broke the tension when she rushed across the room to Father Estevan. "Father, we are so glad you could be here this morning. My son has told me what is happening, and we will need your guidance today."

The good father patted Maggie's hand while she cast a surreptitious glance at the man who claimed to be Jahane's brother. Maggie had expected to find an impostor, but she had to admit to herself this man looked like he could indeed be Jahane's brother. Her heart was aching because she might be called upon to give her daughter up to this stranger.

Jahane's legs felt like stiff boards as she came down the stairs. She knew the moment she entered the room, where the others were gathered, that she would cease to be Jahane Meredith and would become Jahane Beaudette.

She paused at the doorway, listening to Father Estevan making the formal introductions. With a trembling hand, she pushed a stray curl behind her ear.

The memory of Maggie Meredith crying this morning and begging her not to leave her was still fresh in Jahane's mind. She felt numb, as if nothing could touch her heart at the moment. She dreaded the time when she would have to decide what to do with her life.

Taking a deep, steadying breath, Jahane moved into the room. Standing with her head held high, she watched as everyone's attention became focused on her.

Cord had never loved Jahane so much as he did at that moment. Lovely beyond belief in her lilac gown, with her face molded into a stiff mask, he knew what was going on inside her. He wanted to go to her and assure her that he would stand beside her, but this was a time when she would have to stand alone. He knew it, and she had already admitted it last night.

Jahane looked at each person in the room in turn. She smiled at Cord, reassured by his strong presence. Her heart broke for the tears she saw swimming in Maggie's eyes. She acknowledged Father Estevan by the nod of her head, and then her eyes turned to the man who stood across the room from her, Prince Alexander Beaudette.

Jahane thought he looked very much as she would

have pictured a prince to look: tall, handsome, broad-shouldered, and strong.

As if she had no will of her own, she walked toward Alexander, while his eyes softened with love for her. She caught her breath when she saw a tear roll down his cheek. Without realizing it, she ran the rest of the way across the room and was soon enfolded in Alexander's strong arms.

"My dearest little sister," he choked out, holding her so tightly that she thought he would break her bones. "You do remember me."

A tide of feelings washed over her at that moment, while a dear childhood face flashed through her mind—the memory of a young boy that had lifted her upon his horse and then the two of them had raced across a green meadow where the scent of jasmine filled the air.

Like a curtain rising on scenes of her past, she was aware of vague childhood memories about this beloved face. Then, like a door that had been cracked and then burst open to allow in the light, she was bombarded with memories that included Alexander. He was older now, and not so boyish, but she had no doubt that he was her brother.

"Yes, I know you," she said, crying now herself. Raising her face to him, her tears brightened her eyes. "I remember you, Alexander. You are my brother!"

"Dearest sister," he said, brushing away her tears with his thumb. "You cannot know what it means for me to find you alive and well. For so long we were lost to each other. Now I have someone who belongs to me."

Cord watched the tender reunion with growing apprehension. He was seeing Jahane replace him with this man, and all he could do was stand by helplessly and watch.

Maggie was crying softly while the priest comforted her. She was touched by the tender reunion, but saddened as well, because it meant she was losing her daughter.

Cord was the first to speak with the voice of reason. "I suppose you have proof of who you are?"

The rivals again stared at each other. "The proof is in my sister's eyes. Why don't you ask her," Alexander stated flatly. He was not at all sure he liked this man who had kept Jahane from him all these years.

"Cord, he is Prince Alexander, and he is my brother," Jahane said with assurance.

"Suppose we all sit down and talk until everyone is satisfied that these two are brother and sister," Father Estevan offered logically.

While the others seated themselves about the room, Alexander took Jahane's hands and seated her beside him on the sofa.

"Tell me what you remember about your childhood, Jahane," he urged, needing her to remember more about their life together.

She was thoughtful for a moment while fragments of her past played elusively with her mind. "I remember you taking me on your horse. There was a woman, but I cannot remember her face. There was some kind of festival." She smiled brightly. "How strange, I hadn't thought of that in years. You took me on your horse and we won a race."

250

"Yes," he said, his smile transforming his face to boyish handsomeness. "It was the Jasmine Festival, and I had entered the race. You begged to ride with me, so I took you on my horse. The people cheered us on and we won." His eyes clouded. "The people of Balmarhea have very little to cheer about lately."

Alexander pushed his gloominess aside. "What else do you remember, Jahane?"

Her eyes took on a faraway look. "I remember being very frightened. It was at night and this man and woman . . . I suppose they were my mother and father . . . ?"

"Go on," Alexander encouraged.

"Yes, they were my mother and father." She felt panic as she always did when she had nightmares about that night the man cut her hand. "It frightens me to remember."

"Then allow me to tell you about that night that has obviously caused you pain," Alexander said, smiling understandingly at her. "Most probably you are remembering the night that our parents were killed. Our Uncle Reynard was behind the uprising, and he tried to kill you and me as well as our mother and father Uncle Reynard thought he had killed me, but our Uncle Serafimo, who is Archbishop of Balmarhea, saved me and hid me out in a monastery for all these years."

"But why?" she asked. "If the man is our uncle, why would he want to harm us?"

"Because he is an evil man, and he wanted our father's power. But even though he had our parents assassinated, the power has been denied him."

251

"What about me?" Jahane asked. "How did you and I become separated?"

Alexander's eyes went to Cord. "Our Uncle Serafimo knew he could not protect you from Uncle Reynard, so he gave your safety into the hands of an American sea captain. The rest of your story was played out here in America, and I have little knowledge of your life from that night on. I thought you were lost to me until my Uncle Serafimo sent a man, Everette, to America to locate you. It has taken many years, but finally you were found."

"If this Everette has been following me, could he have been the man that I met at the market?"

"I don't know," Alexander said. "Was the man you saw very slight with a hunch back? Everett always dressed in priestly robes. He was unable to take the vows of a priest, but he always dressed as one."

"No. This man was dressed like a gentleman. But he knew who I was, and he knew I came from Balmarhea."

Alexander squeezed her hand. "Then you were fortunate that the man did not take you away by force, Jahane, for he would have been Uncle Reynard's man. You see, Uncle Reynard has been searching for you every bit as diligently as Uncle Serafimo."

"I do not understand all this talk about your Uncle Reynard and your Uncle Serafimo," Cord broke in. "Am I to gather one brother wanted the rule of Balmarhea, while the other one tried to help you hold on to it?"

"In a way, that is exactly what happened," Alexander admitted. "My Uncle Reynard is an evil man who will

252

stop at nothing to get what he wants; while my Uncle Serafimo, or if you prefer, the Archbishop of Balmarhea, is a godly man who lives for the day that our country will be purged of poverty and unrest."

"But, Alexander, where do I fit into all of this?" Jahane asked.

Alexander laced his fingers through Jahane's, while giving her a look of encouragement. "I know this is all overwhelming to you, but you are the Princess Jahane, and your place is in Balmarhea. Our mother and father died for our country, and they would expect you and I to fight for our people."

Jahane's eyes glowed, for Alexander had infected her with his patriotism. "What can I do to help?"

"You are too young to remember any of this, but our mother and father were well loved by the people. You can ask anyone who was alive at the time and they will tell you that Balmarhea was a paradise under their rule. There was no such thing as hunger for our people. Father was having dams and irrigation ditches built to help the farmers. He would often walk unmolested through the streets and soon be surrounded by crowds of loyal subjects."

Jahane began to feel pain in her heart. "You say that he was a good man? Did . . . he . . . did my father love me?"

"Did he love you!" Alexander exclaimed. "You should have seen his face when Mother brought you to him for the first time. You were his sunshine, and he was so proud of you. I once saw him interrupt a very important council meeting, attended by many dignitaries, just to explain to the members that you were cutting your first tooth and he was asking their advice on how to ease the pain of your swollen gums."

Visions of a tapestry with horses and knights danced through her mind, but she brushed them aside, thinking of her father. "I remember him inflicting pain on me." She glanced down at her hand, and at the white scar that ran the length of her palm. "But you know about the scar, don't you, Alexander? This was how you identified me as your sister."

"I know how it happened." He traced the scar with his finger. "I can only imagine the agony our father must have felt when he did this to you. But you will have to understand that rulers, if they are good ones, cannot live by the laws of other people. They are often called upon to make great sacrifices. That was the case with our father. He had to hide the great scepter where Uncle Reynard could not find it. Since I was not there, he had to show you the hiding place. You, being so young, were bound to forget the hiding place, so he inflicted pain on you so you would always recall where the scepter was hidden."

"Yes." Her eyes brightened. "I recall him saying, 'Remember, Jahane, remember.' "

Alexander glanced at the others in the room and held up his hand. "Say no more about the scepter at this time. We shall talk of it at a later time."

"Alexander, can you tell me the date of my birth, and how old I am?"

He smiled. "Of course. This last January twenty-third, you turned seventeen. When you were living in Balmarhea, you were so loved by the people that the whole country celebrated your birthday with a special feast."

Her eyes were shining. "Did they?"

"Indeed they did. Our father always said you were our sunshine child, and so you were, Jahane."

Cord broke into the conversation. "What do you intend to do about Jahane . . ." He hesitated. "Forgive me, I don't know how to address you. Do I still call you Mr. Beaudette?"

"Mr. Meredith, until I confront my Uncle Reynard and am crowned King of Balmarhea, I am not using my title. You may call me Mr. Beaudette. As for what I intend to do about Jahane, I hope she will return to Balmarhea with me."

"How can you keep her safe there?" Maggie blurted out. "You intimated that you would be in danger in your own country. Wouldn't Jahane be safer here with us?"

"Mrs. Meredith," Alexander said, knowing what the older woman was feeling. "Jahane will not be safe even here if my Uncle Reynard knows of her whereabouts. And I fear he knows. My Uncle Serafimo's man, Everett, was found dead. It is my belief that he was slain by one of my Uncle Reynard's men."

Maggie stared teary-eyed at Jahane. "I cannot bear to see her go."

Jahane stood up and rushed over to Maggie. She then knelt down before the woman she had always thought of as her mother. "I have to go with my brother, Mama. Only I know where the scepter is, and only I can help him regain the throne."

Cord's eyes narrowed. "If this is to be your decision, Jahane, then I shall outfit the *Golden Phoenix* so I can take you there. I will not allow you to go with this man without knowing everything is being done to protect you. You will both sail to Balmarhea with me."

Alexander nodded his head in agreement. "I would feel very much as you do, Mr. Meredith." He turned to Maggie and smiled. "I know if my mother and father were alive today they would thank you for taking such good care of their daughter. On their behalf, may I offer you my deepest gratitude."

Maggie dabbed at her eyes. "It was no bother. She was a true and loving daughter to me."

Alexander turned back to Cord. "I will accept your offer to sail on your ship, Captain. I am most impatient to return home now that I have found Jahane, and I hope we will be able to sail as soon as possible."

"I can have the ship made seaworthy within eight days. Will that meet with your requirements, Mr. Beaudette?"

"Indeed, that will do nicely, Captain." The two men stared at each other, knowing they still had matters to discuss at a later time.

Jahane could sense the animosity between the two men, and she realized the day would come when they would confront each other. She was torn between the two of them, and she hoped their dislike for each other would soon ripen into friendship, for they were both wonderful men.

"Mrs. Meredith," Alexander said, bowing from the waist, "thank you for allowing me to impose on your hospitality this morning." He then turned to Cord. "I will be in touch with you later in the day." His eyes changed and softened when he turned to his sister. "Having only found you, I am grieved to leave you, but there is much to do before our journey. If it is acceptable to you, I would like to call on you tomorrow so we can make further plans for the future."

"I look forward to it," she answered, covering his hand with hers. "And, Father Estevan, thank you for bringing my brother and me together."

"Until tomorrow," Alexander told his sister. Again he turned his attention to Cord. "Will you walk with me outside so I might have a word with you?"

"Of course," Cord agreed stiffly.

Jahane watched the three men leave the room, feeling confused about the future. She had been right last night when she guessed her life would never be the same. It would be difficult to think of herself as a royal princess, and even more difficult to leave this home where she had been so happy.

When Cord and Alexander were on the steps, Alexander spoke. "I just wanted to impress upon you the need to continue protecting Jahane. As I said, my Uncle Reynard has men here searching for her, and I am certain the man Jahane saw at the market was one of his men."

"If you will look to your right, you will see a man beneath the street lamp, he is my man; then just across the street is another of my ship's crew, Mr. Beaudette. I can assure you they will see to it that no stranger gains access to my house. Jahane will be quite safe while she remains inside."

"Then I shall take comfort in knowing my sister is receiving the best of care," Alexander said, turning away and walking down the steps.

Father Estevan smiled at Cord and followed after the prince.

Cord watched until the two men got into a carriage and disappeared down the street. Everything had happened too fast and it was pulling him in different directions. One thing was for certain: he would never allow Jahane to go off with that man alone. He still didn't trust him.

Chapter Twenty-three

With frightened eyes, Brynn's gaze roamed around the cell where she had just spent the most frightening night of her life. When she had been locked in the night before, it had been dark and she had not been able to see her surroundings. Now a faint light streamed in through the high, barred window.

Pushing her tangled hair out of her face, she noticed that the cell was narrow, with a stone floor and stone walls containing only the one door. Other than the straw mattress, the only other objects in the cell were a wooden stool and a metal pail.

Standing up, she stumbled toward the window, wishing she could look out, but it was just out of her reach. She longed to see the bright sunlight because the cell was dark, dank, and cold. She reasoned if she could just see the sun, perhaps she could control her panic.

Pushing the wooden stool beneath the window, she climbed up, her eyes just level with the bottom of the barred window.

From where Brynn stood, she could just make out an inner courtyard. She could see several soldiers marching and drilling, so she surmised she was being kept somewhere near the castle armory.

Stepping off the stool, she lowered herself onto the straw mattress, wondering what her fate would be at the hands of Duke Reynard Maxime. Brynn had decided that if she saw Reynard she intended to inform him that she knew she was not the real Princess Jahane. She had no intentions of playing his game. He could kill her, but she would never agree to allow him to present her to the people of Balmarhea as the Princess Jahane, Prince Alexander's sister.

Her slight body trembled with cold as well as fear. She huddled against the damp wall, wishing herself back at the convent. Why had the duke chosen her as the instrument of his deception?

Feeling alone and miserable, Brynn looked at her dismal surroundings. With a sob, she stood up and moved to the other side of the room.

She tried to think of Prince Alexander and how he had held her in his arms for one glorious night. The touch of him, the smell of him, was burned into her memory, and no one, not even the evil Reynard, could take that away from her.

When she thought of Reynard, Brynn felt her panic return, so she tried to divert her thoughts so she would not succumb to hysteria.

To give herself comfort, she conjured up Alexander's face, and she felt her tears melt away. Closing her eyes, she remembered how wonderful it had been to be with him.

Suddenly Brynn was brought back to reality by the grating of a key in the lock.

The guard approached her with a peevish snarl on his lips. With jerky motions he indicated she was to follow him.

Calling on all her courage, Brynn marched out of the cell ahead of him, wondering where he could be taking her.

"Are you setting me free?" she inquired hopefully.

"Be silent," he ordered in a gruff voice.

They went down long passageways lit with torches, up winding stairs that were cast in shadows.

When at last they stopped before a nail-studded door where two guards stood watch, Brynn knew she was about to be taken before Duke Maxime.

As frightening as it had been to be locked in that cell, she wished herself back there instead of having to face the evil duke, Reynard.

Brynn swallowed hard as the two guards stepped aside and she was forcefully pushed inside the room. She blinked her eyes at the lavishness of the room. Her first impression was one of brightness—of gold and white colors—white rugs, golden wall hangings and bed drapes, and even white satin chairs shot with gold threads.

She stood with hands clasped together demurely and head high as the duke motioned her forward and ordered the guards out of the room.

Reynard was seated at a table laden with food. He waved a rib bone at her, indicating she should come closer.

Brynn saw Reynard smile, but his dark eyes were without warmth. The scar on his face gave him a sinister look, and Brynn felt a heavy hand of fear settle on her.

"I was most distressed when I learned you had been thrown in prison, my dear. Not at all the way a princess should be treated, is it?" He indicated that she

261

should be seated, and when she complied, he raised a goblet to his mouth and took a deep drink of wine.

"Are you hungry?" he asked, waving a mutton joint in front of her.

Brynn's stomach had never felt so empty, but she shook her head. "No. I want nothing to eat."

"Pity, Princess Jahane. You are looking too thin."

"I am not the Princess Jahane and you know it," she stated bravely.

His dark eyebrow arched and his mouth turned down, showing white teeth. "And what has happened to make you draw that conclusion?"

She refused to lower her eyes and stared directly into his. "I just know I am not Princess Jahane. I have known that from the first."

His eyes narrowed. "I will tell you what I know, Brynn—I know that you were discovered in my brother Serafimo's lodge." He arched his hands and placed his fingertips together. "I suspect it was my brother who spirited you away from us. Am I right?"

"No, it was not your brother. I do not even know the archbishop."

He stared at her. "Don't you?"

"No."

"Oh, well, we shall discover all about that later. I had to pity my son, Damerou. As your future bridegroom, he was inconsolable when he heard his bride had disappeared. We are glad to have you back with us."

"It is hardly likely your son grieved overmuch since we are strangers to each other."

Reynard's eyes burned with hidden fire. "Do not play innocent with me, Brynn. You and I both know that my brother was behind your disappearance. What did he say to convince you to go away with him? How did he persuade you to turn your back on all the riches I laid at your feet? I would have placed you on the throne of Balmarhea. What did my brother offer you that would compare with that?"

"I told you I do not know your brother. I have never been introduced to His Eminence."

"Then why were you at his lodge?" Reynard stated with satisfaction gleaming in his eyes. "Serafimo doesn't know that I am aware of his little hideaway. But there is little that goes on in this kingdom that is not called to my attention."

"How many times do I have to tell you that I do not know your brother?"

For the moment Reynard was not listening to Brynn; rather his eyes were moving over her body, taking in every soft detail. She had an innocence about her that intrigued him. Her golden hair tangled down her back, her skin so delicate and white, made his blood run hot in his veins. He had visions of taking her to his bed.

Drawing his eyes away from her soft, curving breasts and back to her face, Reynard realized Brynn had spoken and he had not caught her meaning.

"You were saying, Brynn?"

She twisted her hands together, aware of his hot glance. She ducked her head, and her cheeks burned with embarrassment. There was something about the duke that made her aware of her own body. "I . . . said that a friend took me to the lodge. I was not even aware that it belonged to the archbishop."

His eyes snapped, and the scar on his face became blood-red. "Do you take me for a fool? I know everything about your life, Brynn, and you have no friends outside the convent. Don't you know I have had you watched for years? Your every move was reported back to me."

Wiping his hands on a snowy-white napkin, he stood and walked around the table to loom over her. "You will tell me the truth. You can do it now, and it will go easy on you. Or you can play the fool, and it will go hard on you. The decision rests with you—which is it to be?"

She pressed her back tightly against the chair and gripped the clawlike arms. "I have nothing to tell you, Your Grace. I am but a girl of no importance, so why would anyone want to bother with me?"

Reynard looked into Brynn's eyes and saw fear, but he saw something else as well. There was a stubbornness, a determination about her, and he realized it would not be easy to break her to his will. But he was confident that with the right persuasion he would eventually make her tell him what he wanted to know.

Reaching out, he pulled her up, staring deeply into her frightened eyes.

Suddenly he didn't want her to look at him with fear. He wondered what her eyes would look like when they were softened by love or flaming with passion.

"Tell me what I want to know, Brynn. It would grieve me if I were forced to cause you pain."

He ran his hand down her smooth cheek, and she shivered in disgust. "I don't know what you want of me," she said, closing her eyes so she wouldn't have to look at his face.

Reynard became aware of Brynn's softness, and his grip tightened on her. "I could easily bend you to my will, Brynn. You are such an innocent. You have never known the touch of a man's hand or all the joys that one can experience in the arms of a man with experience."

His hand moved across her back, and she shuddered in disgust, remembering the night Prince Alexander had caressed her body until she trembled in ecstasy.

"You can threaten me with whatever pleases you, Your Grace, but I still have nothing to tell you," she insisted.

He gripped her arm, then flung her away from him with a force that sent her tumbling across the floor.

"Who spirited you away from the convent?" he demanded. "Tell me now, or you will regret it!"

Pain shot through Brynn's body as she scrambled to her knees, her eyes fearfully watching the duke's every move. She would never betray Prince Alexander—never! "I will not tell you," she exclaimed, rising on shaky legs. "You can beat me—you can even kill me, but I'll never tell you what you want to know."

Crossing the floor, Reynard yanked her forward, shoving her down in a chair. "So you will not admit there is something to tell? Oh, I think you will talk, little nightingale. I think you will sing a song that will enlighten me."

She flung her head back and met his eyes. "No, never!"

He smiled down at her maliciously. "I have ways of making people talk that you could not even conceive. Stronger and more determined men than you, a mere girl, have broken under my methods."

She met his eyes bravely. "I . . . will tell you nothing, because I have nothing to tell."

He knelt beside her, looking pointedly into her eyes. "Was it Prince Alexander who took you away?"

She felt her nerves tighten and her stomach lurch in fear. How could he know about the prince? She forced a calm and then bewildered look on her face, vowing she would not betray the prince by the slightest word or expression. "Surely you do not think Prince Alexander's ghost spirited me away? Everyone knows he has been dead for these past years."

Reynard watched her closely, but could tell nothing from her expression. He had underestimated her bravery. He had certainly not credited her with enough cunning to be able to deceive him. He had thought it would be easy to force her into a tearful confession.

His passion for her intensified, and he wanted to rip her gown off and fling her to the floor, taking her maidenhood as his reward. Sanity returned when he remembered what was at risk if his nephew Alexander truly did live. If Brynn did know anything about the prince, Reynard was determined to find out.

He stalked to the door and flung it open, speaking to the guard. "Send Hogarth to me at once."

Leaving the door ajar, he returned to Brynn. "You might be interested in knowing that Hogarth is an expert at what he does. Would you like to know what his craft is?"

"N-no."

"I'll tell you anyway. Hogarth is a persuader. His methods of obtaining information are renowned. I have been a witness when he made grown men beg for mercy." He smiled at her. "They beg for death to release them from Hogarth's . . . shall we say . . . his unspeakable methods of persuasion."

266

She shook her head. "Why are you doing this to me? I am not your enemy, and I have said over and over that I can tell you nothing."

"Cannot tell me — or will not?"

"I am just an insignificant girl who was raised in a convent. Until you took notice of me, I knew nothing of the ways of the world and few people aside from the nuns at the convent."

"I have a feeling you are protecting someone. It cannot be my brother, the archbishop, because if he had part in your disappearance, he would flaunt it in my face. Oh, yes, he would revel in being able to thwart me."

"I have heard that the archbishop is a godly man, and I feel sure he would be appalled if he was aware that you have been planning to present me as the Princess Jahane."

"Ah, so you are on to my little game. Did you decide on your own that you were not my niece, or did someone . . . say my nephew, the prince, tell you?"

Her face was stoic, even though she trembled with fear. "The reason I know that I am not the princess is because I have no recollection of being her. I would know it if I were of royal blood."

The sudden burst of sinister laughter that emitted from the duke's mouth echoed throughout the room. "So you would know if you were of royal blood, would you? Well, my dear, I know very well who you are, and you are not from peasant stock. Think you that I would place a peasant on my family's throne?" His hand tangled in her hair, and he jerked her face up to him. "Perhaps you, my dear, have the blood of nobles running in your veins."

She wondered what new lie he was presenting to her now. "Please," she groaned in pain. "Allow me to return to the convent. I know nothing that would be of help to you."

Before Reynard could answer, someone spoke up from the hallway. "You sent for me, Your Grace?"

The man was huge. He had moved around to stand before the window, and Brynn noticed that he blocked out the sunlight. He had long, stringy black hair and beard. Since he was wearing a sleeveless leather vest, she saw the dark hair that covered the exposed portions of his body. Her eyes were drawn to his hands, and she shivered, thinking of the strength they must possess.

The duke frowned down at Brynn, but his words were for the giant. "Yes, I sent for you. I have a prisoner for you to question. She has some answers that she refuses to give willingly."

Hogarth's mouth set in a severe line. "You can always depend on me, Your Grace."

Reynard ran his finger across Brynn's lips, then down her neck to brush against her breast. "She is a lovely and delicate flower. Try not to be too severe with her. I will want her back undamaged . . ." His eyes moved to the bed suggestively. "I have other plans for her once you have made her talk."

Hogarth smiled, and a nefarious gleam lit his eyes. "You just tell me what you want to know, and I'll see that the little lady tells me."

Reynard's expression became hard. "Find out who lured her away from the convent. Also find out if she knows anything about my nephew, Prince Alexander."

Reynard brought Brynn closer to him. "I have discovered that my nephew did not die. My brother has kept him hidden from me all these years. I think you know more about him than you are willing to tell."

"No, you are wrong," she insisted.

Reynard flung her from him. "Take her below."

Brynn shrank away when Hogarth took her arm and pulled her toward the door. "I have never failed you yet, Your Grace," the jailor said. "I'll not fail you now."

With a last pleading glance at Duke Maxime, Brynn felt unspeakable fear. She trembled as she looked down at the hand with dark hair on the knuckles, wondering if this man was capable of inflicting death. She squeezed her eyes together tightly, hoping death would come quickly, because she would never betray her dearest love.

When she stumbled, the man dragged her up and forced her to walk ahead of him. Brynn realized she was not being taken to the cell she had previously occupied as he led her through dark corridors, down, down, down into the very bowels of the castle.

Hogarth opened a door and thrust her inside. At first it was too dark for Brynn to see, but the man lit several torches and she saw the room was large and round-shaped with moss clinging to the damp walls. She shivered when she saw a rat gnawing on a piece of stale bread someone had dropped. Shackles hung from the ceiling, and Brynn shuddered with panic so strong that she cried out when she saw the unspeakable implements that were apparently for torturing.

She was limp as a rag doll when the man pushed her forward and clapped chains on her wrists. Her head fell forward, but he grabbed a handful of her hair and forced her to look into his face.

"You can talk now and save yourself a lot of pain." His eyes danced with something akin to pleasure. "Of course, I hope it takes a long time for you to break. I don't mind using what persuasions are necessary to get at the truth."

"I will never tell you what you want to know," she said, spitting into his hateful face.

With his fist doubled up, he struck her across the face, and pain exploded in her head.

"You'll talk right enough," he hissed. "You'll talk plenty before I'm through with you."

Brynn was still reeling from his stunning blow when she felt him ripping her gown down the back. She had no time to wonder what he was about as a whip snaked out and cut into her tender skin.

She screamed as the lash cut deeply. Again and again, the whip snapped through the air to lay her back open in deep wounds.

"Tell me what I want to hear," the man demanded. "Talk now."

"No, I will not," she said, bracing herself for another onslaught from the whip. Pain tore at her back, and she felt her head reeling under the impact.

"Talk, damn you. Talk!"

"No," she moaned. "I will tell you nothing."

Brynn's back felt like it was on fire. She clutched her fists so tightly that her nails bit into the palm of her hand. Again and again the whip slashed out to inflict unbearable pain.

At last a dark tide swirled around Brynn and she gave herself to the darkness where there were no feelings and no pain.

With a muttered oath, the man threw the whip aside, knowing when this one regained consciousness, he would have to use other methods to make her talk. A spark of admiration lit his eyes. She was a brave one and had earned his respect. But he would make her talk before he was through.

Three

Balmarhea

Chapter Twenty-four

The Archbishop of Balmarhea moved quickly down the corridor, his eyes reflecting the anger he was feeling. When he entered the antechamber, the crowd of citizens which had gathered to seek Duke Maxime's justice respectfully stepped aside to make a path for the archbishop.

Serafimo moved up the steps where Reynard was perched on the throne, with all the pomp and circumstance as if he were the true king. His lip curled in distaste when he saw the purple robe Reynard wore.

"You have draped yourself in kingly garments, Brother. Pity you cannot give yourself a crown," the archbishop scoffed, his words echoing around the antechamber.

Reynard smiled as he waved a jeweled hand at his guard. "Send everyone away. It would seem my brother and I have important matters to discuss." He motioned for Serafimo to be seated next to him, but the archbishop indicated he would rather stand.

Serafimo waited for the room to clear before he

spoke. When he faced the duke, his voice was harsh. "You knew I would come when I learned what you had done, Reynard."

"Yes, I depended on your coming, but I didn't expect you so soon. Pray tell what brings you to our presence? You usually avoid my company whenever possible."

"You know why I am here. Let us not waste each other's time."

The duke leaned back and studied his younger brother intently. As Serafimo aged, he began to look more like their dead brother. It was sometimes unsettling to look into Serafimo's eyes and see Alfons. Sometimes at night Reynard would have nightmares about Alfons's death, and he would awaken in a cold sweat.

"Well, Reynard," Serafimo cut into his thoughts. "I am waiting for an explanation. And do not play games with me, or mistake me for a fool."

Lately it had not escaped his notice that Serafimo was a favorite with the people. Somewhere in the deep recesses of his mind, he resented Serafimo's popularity. Being a master of masking his feelings, however, he smiled. "I would not have called you a fool, Serafimo. A bit erroneous at times, but, no, not a fool."

"Don't change the subject. Where is she?"

Reynard arched an eyebrow. "Which 'she' are you referring to?"

"You know who I mean. The young girl you thought to pass off as Jahane."

Reynard's face was the picture of calm indifference, but his eyes sparked with elation. "If you've been told this, then you have been badly misinformed. Why should I place a pretender on the throne when I will soon have the real Princess Jahane? We both know she is in San Francisco, Serafimo."

"You will never get your hands on Jahane, Reynard. You have dreams of grandeur, but you will never wear the crown of Balmarhea."

Reynard's eyes narrowed. "So you, too, think Jahane is alive."

Serafimo eyed Reynard. "I never for a moment thought she was dead."

Reynard's malicious laughter resounded around the chamber walls. "Are you still reeling from your great blunder, Brother?" Again his laughter rang out. "For several years you misplaced our niece, did you not? For a time, after the rebellion, I thought you knew where Jahane was. But I soon learned, through unnamed sources, that you knew no more about her whereabouts than I did."

Serafimo glared at his brother. "What did it matter where Jahane was, as long as she was safe from you?"

Reynard spread his hands and studied the ruby ring on his finger. "Are you suggesting I would do harm to our dear niece? Nay, I only want to place her on the throne where she rightly belongs."

Now Serafimo smiled. "If you think to rule through Jahane, I would dismiss the notion if I were you. If she is anything like her mother and father, she would brush you aside like the insect you are."

Reynard's eyes flashed with hidden lights. "Have you ever thought she might be more like me, Serafimo? But then, of course, we would have to find Jahane before we can find out, will we not?"

Serafimo stared into his brother's eyes. "Suppose we stop playing games. We both know Jahane is in San

277

Francisco, but you will not be the one to bring her to Balmarhea. No, I shall be the one to present her to her people. What a glorious day it will be when the true princess comes home at last."

Serafimo could not resist goading Reynard still further. "Can you hear the church bells chiming, Brother? Can you see the crown slipping out of your grasp?"

Reynard's hand balled into fists. "You go too far, Archbishop. I am the one who decides who will rule and who will not. You tend to the people's spiritual needs, and I shall see to their daily wants." Reynard stroked his chin. "Besides, no one will be the true ruler unless they can produce the scepter, and Jahane was only a baby when she was taken away. She cannot possibly know where it has been hidden."

"We can talk about this all day, but you and I both know your time is almost up, Reynard. I stand ready to see to your spiritual needs the day the true heir is set upon the throne of Balmarhea."

Reynard's eyes sparked with an inner glow. "Which one will ascend the throne, Brother. Will it be . . . Princess Jahane or Prince Alexander?"

Before Serafimo could mask his distress at Reynard's mention of Alexander's name, he stared in disbelief. "What did you say?" he choked out. "Surely you cannot think that Alex—"

Reynard cut him off. "Drop the pretense, Brother. I know about Alexander. I admit you had me fooled for a time, but I now know you hid him out at the mountain monastery all these years. Pity he will never live to be crowned king."

Serafimo felt the advantage slipping away from him. He had to protect Alexander from his brother's evil.

"You are just guessing, Reynard. We both saw Alexander fall into the sea when you had him shot."

"All right, Serafimo, play your little game, but I shall come out winner. Not you, and not anyone, will take what belongs to me."

"Yes, you believe because you killed for the throne, that it now belongs to you. In the end, God will have his revenge on you, and you will be swept away just like an annoying insect."

Reynard stood up, his face livid, his eyes bulging out with anger. "You will never live to see me fall, Brother. I have allowed you to stay alive this long only because it amused me to spar with you. The day I tire of our little game of wits, you will draw your last breath."

"You allowed me to live because you already had too much blood on your hands. You knew if I died, you would never be able to control the people's rage. Enjoy the time you have left, Reynard, for vengeance will be twofold."

Serafimo looked calm and superior in his archbishop's regalia, and Reynard's burning desire was to tear him down. "You are supposed to be so saintly, and yet you talk of vengeance. Perhaps you are not so different from me after all, Serafimo."

"It will not be my hand that will strike you down, Reynard. If you believe Alexander is alive, should you not worry about what he might do to you? He knows you are responsible for the death of his mother and father." Serafimo smiled. "Do you sleep well at night, Reynard?"

In spite of his attempt at bravado, Reynard's eyes darted around the room, searching every darkened corner. "I will see you in hell, Serafimo," he swore through clinched teeth. "Mark my words, I shall."

"No, not I. It was not I who killed my brother. Hell is for the depraved and sinful. You are both."

Reynard's face turned red, and he gasped for breath. "Get out, Serafimo, or I shall have *your* blood on my hands. I am your brother, why do you find joy in provoking me?"

Serafimo gave him a contemptuous look. "Why . . . ? Because you have taken the heart out of our people. Where we were once a paradise with peace and plenty, we are now in poverty while your pockets bulge with gold. Now many of the citizens of Balmarhea spy on their neighbors for you just for a crust of bread to feed their hungry families. You have spawned hatred and distrust among the people, and you have sullied our good name. Are you aware that the royalty of Europe laugh at you?"

"Never!" Reynard raged. "No one laughs at me. I will not have it!"

Serafimo was weary of the conversation. "Where is the girl, Brynn? Turn her over to me at once."

By now Reynard had regained his composure. "I think not. I have taken a fancy to her and have decided to make her my mistress. She is a comely little wench, and I shall dress her in clothing that becomes a princess."

"Let her go, Reynard. She is just a poor unfortunate girl who doesn't even have a last name. She just happened to fall into your clutches. What could you possibly want with her now?"

Reynard smiled, and this time his eyes danced with humor. "You think Brynn has no last name? You think she is insignificant? Oh, my brother, think you that I would place an unworthy person on our ancestral throne? If you considered Count Chapin d'Arcy not of the nobility . . ." Reynard was enjoying the bewilderment on his brother's face. ". . . then you could also think of his daughter in that light."

"You lie, Reynard?" Serafimo stated skeptically.

"I have lied on occasion when it pleased me, Serafimo. But in this case, I am telling the truth. You see, the humorous part in all this is the satisfaction I derive from thinking how the good prime minister would turn over in his grave, because his daughter has been under my control for all these years. Yes, her name is Lady Brynn D'arcy. You remember her as a child? You saw her often enough."

"Dear Lord, Reynard. Are you saying that you kept this girl hidden for all these years?"

"That surprises you, doesn't it? Yes, she has been in a convent, not an hour away from the city gates. She fell into my hands when her mother was killed. It took me some years to decide what to do with her. It was only lately that I discovered she had grown into a beauty."

"Can it be true? Is she really Count d'Arcy's daughter? If so, she deserves better than the life you have planned for her. Chapin was a hero; he gave his life for what he believed in."

"Spare me the glowing tribute. I never cared for our brother's prime minister. As for the girl, I assure you she is Chapin's daughter, although the poor child has no notion who she is. I do believe that given time I could have convinced her that she was the Princess Jahane." Reynard shrugged. "Oh, well, perhaps she will be better suited for the role I have in mind for her."

281

"You are a monster, Reynard. You will feel God's wrath one day, and you will beg for mercy for all your many sins."

Since Reynard had succeeded in shocking his brother, he was now in better spirits. "Yes, I am sure that will happen. Add this to my sins, Brother. I was certain that the girl knew about Alexander, so I had Hogarth try to persuade her to talk. You will be happy to know that if she did know anything about Alexander, she kept it to herself. Even Hogarth's methods could not make her speak."

"You devil!" Serafimo ground out. "God have mercy on you, for I will not. You have gone too far this time, Reynard."

"Oh, no, Serafimo, not nearly far enough."

Serafimo realized his brother was deranged. He had to get Count D'arcy's daughter out of his grasp. He owed that much to the dead prime minister. Besides, he had promised Alexander he would protect her. "Let me see the girl," the archbishop insisted.

"No, I cannot do that. You see, since she was so willful and refused to talk, Hogarth was somewhat too rough with her. He inflicted deep wounds on her back, and she is not up to receiving guests."

Serafimo's voice was commanding. "Take me to her at once!"

"Rest assured she is receiving the best of care. I even have my private physician looking after her. He says there will be scarring on her back, but in time the wounds should heal nicely."

Serafimo knew Reynard was not finished with the girl. Feeling sick at heart, he knew he must bargain for her release. "Let us strike a bargain, Reynard," Serafimo said, feeling sick inside.

"I'm listening, but I doubt you have anything I want, Brother."

"I will tell you about Alexander if you will allow me to send my housekeeper to look after the girl. And I want her under my protection."

Reynard's eyes flamed with eagerness. "Done, done."

"All right, what do you want to know about Alexander?"

"He did live after his fall?" Reynard asked.

"Yes. You were right when you said I had him hidden away at the monastery."

"What makes you agree to tell me this now?"

"Because you cannot get to him. He is out of your reach."

"I assume he sailed for America."

"You can assume that."

"Will he return?"

"You can depend on that. I have kept my bargain, now you will keep yours. I will send Mrs. St. John to tend the girl."

Without another word, Archbishop Serafimo turned and walked away, but as he left the antechamber, his brother's laughter echoed in his ears. He had no doubt that the girl was truly Chapin d'Arcy's daughter, and he feared for her life. Reynard was dangerously mad and there was nothing Serafimo could do about him. He was too well protected.

His footsteps quickened. Now that Reynard knew Alexander was alive, he had to make plans for his safe return to Balmarhea. And Jahane — what about her? Would Alexander get to San Francisco in time to protect her from Reynard's men?

283

Brynn felt as if someone had placed hot burning coals on her back. She tried to move, but weakness overcame her and her vision blurred. She noticed she was no longer lying in the cold cell. She was in a room with lace curtains around the bed.

"This is going to hurt, miss," a woman's voice came to her from out of a fog. "This is a healing balm, and it will help you."

Brynn licked her dry lips, and it took a moment for her to find her voice. "Where . . . am I?"

"Do not worry, child, you will be fine," the kindly voice assured her.

She closed her eyes, hoping she would die before the duke's man could torture her again. At least she had the satisfaction of knowing she had not betrayed Prince Alexander. She hoped she never would betray him, but the pain had been so difficult to endure, and she feared if they tortured her again she might talk.

In a swirl of darkness, she felt herself drifting in a sea of pain.

Brynn did not know how much time had passed when she awoke to a woman's voice. "Come, miss, eat just a few spoons of broth. You will never get well if you don't eat."

Brynn glanced at the matronly woman who held the spoon to her lips. "No, go away. I don't want it. Just let me die by myself."

The woman looked at her with sympathetic eyes. "Now, miss, you don't want to talk like that. You being

284

pretty and all, you have so much to live for."

"Beauty is nothing but . . . a curse . . . if . . . he, the duke, wants me." Her eyes showed her torment. "Oh, what shall I do?"

The woman clicked her tongue as if she understood very well what Brynn was feeling. "You are a very sick girl, and no one, not even His Grace, will be bothering you for a long time if I can help it."

"Who are you?"

"Mrs. St. John. I don't know how he arranged it, but I was sent by the Archbishop of Balmarhea to look after you, and no one is going to harm you while I'm here, miss."

Brynn looked into clear blue eyes and knew she had found a friend. Reluctantly, she took a sip of the broth. "The duke . . . will not come here, will he?" she asked hopefully.

"No, not that one." Mrs. St. John declared with conviction. "You are now under the protection of the archbishop, and not even the duke dares defy him."

Brynn took another sip of broth and then turned her head away. "Why would such an important man as the archbishop be interested in my welfare?"

The woman looked astounded that the girl should ask such a question. "Because you have been tormented, and because he is the archbishop."

Brynn did not understand, but she was too weary to think. "I have a feeling Duke Maxime is not finished with me yct," she injected wearily.

"See that cot over by the window?" the woman asked.

"Yes."

"That is where I sleep. Outside the door is the

archbishop's guard. No one gets in or out without his say, not even the duke."

With a pitiful sigh, Brynn closed her eyes. At least she was safe for now.

Chapter Twenty-five

A misty dawn met Jahane's eyes as she pulled the floral curtains aside and glanced at the woods just across the street from the house. Looking down the hill toward San Francisco, she could see people already scurrying about their daily routines, undaunted by the fine mist that dampened the ground.

Her eyes went automatically to where the *Golden Phoenix* should be at anchor, but it was gone! She blinked away her tears. How could Cord have sailed without letting her know? She was confused. Hadn't he agreed to take her and Alexander to Balmarhea?

Nothing was as it used to be; everything had changed—most of all, she had changed. She thought of her brother Alexander. He would be coming today so they could make plans for their future. There was so much she had to think about. It was hard for her to think of herself as a princess. She had been raised as an ordinary girl, and she was frightened to think what lay ahead of her.

It was strange, this strong tie she had felt with Alexander, almost from the moment she saw him at the Fireman's Ball. What she found unsettling was the intrigue and danger that surrounded her as the Princess Jahane.

Alexander had assured her only yesterday when he came to visit that there were people who adored her and would welcome her to Balmarhea with love and affection. He explained about their Uncle Serafimo, the Archbishop of Balmarhea, who had been responsible for her escape from the island that bloody night when their parents had been killed.

Jahane heard Maggie playing the piano in the music room. How she would miss her, for she was the only mother Jahane could remember. It was hard to think that her own mother had met with a violent end.

In her mind, she tried to picture her mother and father, but they were nothing more than shadowy forms.

Jahane turned away from the window and made her way to the music room. She stood in the doorway for a time, listening to Maggie sing. Her heart went out to the woman who had nurtured and loved her all those years. It would be very difficult when the time came to leave her.

She turned away and walked through the house, examining it with new eyes. She wanted to take the memory with her wherever destiny took her. Her fondest times had been spent here in this house. This was Cord's home, and one day he would bring a wife here. No she would not allow herself to dwell on that unhappy thought, because she had always pictured herself as Cord's wife.

Moving through the entryway, she paused at the cherrywood table and picked up several calling cards which were lying in the silver tray. Absentmindedly she saw that several of them were to her from Richard

Moyer. She briefly read one of the notes and saw that he was apologizing for the night of the Fireman's Ball. He went on to beg her to meet him across the street at eight o'clock so he could apologize in person.

Jahane wondered why Richard had not asked to come to the house. She smiled, knowing he would not want to encounter Cord. She glanced at the hall clock. It was almost nine now, but perhaps Richard was still waiting for her. Poor man, he did deserve some consideration from her after the way she had used him to make Cord jealous.

She could hear Jojo moving around in the dining room, so she saw no harm in sneaking out for a while. She would be back before anyone missed her. Reaching for her shawl from the coat rack, she pulled it about her shoulders.

As Jahane stepped outside, she noticed it was still misting, and she wished she had worn her bonnet. Apparently Cord had taken his men with him because they were nowhere in sight. Pulling her shawl over her head, she ran across the street to the woods, knowing she would have to be brief since Alexander would be calling at noon.

Cyryl Dionysos was sure his mission to find and return Princess Jahane to Balmarhea had ended in failure. He dreaded the thought of informing Duke Maxime that he had failed. Duke Maxime had put the royal flagship at his disposal, with instructions not to return without Princess Jahane. After the day Cyryl had encountered the princess at the market, she had been guarded by Captain Meredith's men, and he had been unable to get near her.

Today he had taken up his vigil behind the scrub oak trees, in hopes that he would see Princess Jahane.

Mr. Dionysos watched in disbelief as the door of the Merediths' house opened, and not only was the princess walking in his direction, but she was alone!

He flattened his body against the tree and waited for her to enter the woods so no one could see her from the house. His eyes danced with greed as he pictured the reward he would receive from the Duke Maxime.

Jahane glanced around the woods. Seeing no one, she decided that Richard must have given up on her coming and gone. With a wistful smile, she realized she would never have the opportunity to talk to poor Richard.

The mist had now turned to rain, which was coming down in heavy torrents. She adjusted the shawl about her head, hoping to keep her hair dry. When she turned to retrace her steps, a man stepped into her path. At first, blinded by rain, she thought it was Richard, but when he spoke, she knew it was the man who had pursued her at the market!

"Hello, Your Highness. So glad our paths crossed today. I began to despair of ever seeing you again." The man spoke in French, as he had before.

Jahane took a step backward, answering him in French. "What do you want with me, monsieur? I do not know you."

He bowed from the waist. "I want only to serve you as my sovereign. My name is Cyryl Dionysos."

Jahane's heart was beating with fear. She glanced toward the house and saw Jojo standing on the landing, looking up and down the street. Apparently she had been missed and the houseboy was searching for her.

"Move aside and allow me to pass," she said with a voice of authority.

"I am afraid I cannot do that, Your Highness. You see, I have orders from your uncle to bring you back to Balmarhea."

She could hardly breathe, so oppressive was her fear. "Which uncle?" she asked, hoping it would be her Uncle Serafimo.

"Why, Your Highness, it was your Uncle Reynard who sent me to fetch you home."

Now her fear took on a deeper meaning. She looked into the man's strange yellow eyes. "If my uncle sent you, why then did you not call at my home, introduce yourself to me, and tell me what you wanted?"

"I feared, after I frightened you at the market, I would not be welcomed in the Merediths' home."

"You are right. You would not have been allowed anywhere near me. If you are wise, you will leave now before my brother returns."

He smiled. "I assume you are referring to Cord Meredith as your brother. We both know your own brother, Prince Alexander, has been dead these many years."

She lowered her head so he could read nothing in her eyes, because the man did not know that Alexander was still alive. "Surely you do not expect me to go away with you?"

"I had hoped you would come with me peaceably. Your Uncle Reynard is most anxious to see you after you have been separated from him these many years."

Jahane saw Jojo mincing down the street away from her, and she started to call out to him, but the man, sensing her intentions, stepped forward with a warning in his eyes. "Do not call out, Your Highness. I cannot allow you to alert anyone."

Even though she was frightened, Jahane spoke to the man in a commanding voice. "Move out of my way at once and let me pass."

"No, Your Highness, I cannot do that." He reached out to her, but evidently he had enough respect for her as his princess that his hand fell away. "I'm afraid I am going to have to ask you to come with me now."

She retreated a step. "Where to?"

"I have a coach waiting to take us to the docks where we shall board the royal man-of-war which will take us to Balmarhea."

"Surely you do not expect me to go with you willingly? And you cannot force me to go with you."

Suddenly his eyes became cold, and he grabbed her by the shoulder. "You will come with me, Princess, because you have no choice."

"I could scream," she warned.

Before she knew what was happening, Cyryl's hand slipped up to clamp across her mouth tightly. "I did not want to do it this way, but you force me."

Before she could protest, he swung her up into his arms and tramped through the bushes. "You forced me to be rough with you," he said again. "Why could you not just do as I said?"

Fear invaded Jahane's brain, and she tried to twist out of his arms, but one look into his hostile eyes and she became still.

When they emerged from the woods, he carried her to an awaiting carriage and placed her on the seat. "We got her," he said to the coachman, nodding for him to drive on.

Jahane reached for the door, but Cyryl pulled her back. "Sit still. Do not force me to restrain you, Your

Highness," he warned.

"You would not dare."

"I would not like it, but I would dare it." He assured her. "Do not fret, Your Highness. You will receive only the best treatment when we are on board the ship." His eyes sought hers. "When we reach Balmarhea . . . if Duke Maxime asks how I treated you, I hope you will tell him that you would not come with me so I was forced to bring you along."

Jahane studied the man's face. Why did she see fear in his eyes when he mentioned her Uncle Reynard? "If you don't let me go, I will tell my uncle that you were abusive," she threatened.

His smile was indulgent. "Go ahead. I would have much more to fear from the duke if I allowed you to escape."

While Cyryl was talking, Jahane edged toward the door. When he saw her intention was to jump out of the speeding carriage, he placed his hand on her arm.

Jahane pushed his hand away and searched her mind for a way to free herself. She decided she would scream for help when they descended into the town. But to her dismay, when they came to the fork in the road, the coach turned left instead of turning toward San Francisco.

"Where are you taking me?" she asked, seeing her only chance of escaping slipping away.

"Ah, you thought the royal ship would be anchored in the bay. Not wanting to call too much attention to ourselves, we were instructed to find a secluded stretch of beach. The journey up the coast will take about two hours. If it pleases you, Your Highness, we shall soon be on the ship and you can rest in your cabin."

"Stop calling me 'Your Highness'," she said with ill

293

humor. "I find it offensive."

"I beg your pardon, Princess Jahane, but you are my sovereign, and the heir to the throne of Balmarhea. Appropriately I should be calling you, 'Your Majesty'."

Again, Jahane was thankful that the man did not know about Alexander, for her brother was the rightful King of Balmarhea. "Are you so sure I am this princess?"

"Yes, Your High— Yes, I am certain. I often saw your mother, the queen, and you are very like her."

"Surely you could not have been a friend of my mother."

He shook with laughter. "Regrettably no. But I did admire her from a distance. If you don't mind my saying so, and meaning no disrespect, you will also make a most beautiful queen."

Jahane raised her head with a proud tilt, looking very like the royal princess she was. "If I am to be your queen, should you not obey my slightest command?"

"Alas, there will be those who will gladly be yours to command, Your Highness. But circumstances being what they are, I will leave Balmarhea as soon as your uncle pays me for delivering you to him. So you see, I will be safely away when you are crowned queen."

Jahane turned her face away, no longer wanting to talk to the odious man. She was sure after what Alexander had told her about their Uncle Reynard that he would never allow her to be crowned queen.

She leaned back against the soft headrest, as her thoughts tumbled over one another. Apparently she was in no danger. The most she could hope for was that Cord would find out what had happened to her and come to her rescue. But how would he ever find her?

The rest of the journey was covered in silence. When the carriage pulled up to a rocky cove, Cyryl got out and offered Jahane his hand, which she refused, preferring to get out on her own.

Cyryl said something to the driver, handed him money, and sent him on his way. When he would have assisted Jahane down the steep cliff to the waiting longboat, she again refused his aid.

Jahane made up her mind that she would act the way she supposed a princess would behave. With her head held high, she moved across the sandy beach. Rain was pelting her in the face and she knew she must look a bedraggled sight, but still she would keep her dignity.

When she neared the longboat, she saw men dressed as sailors emerge from behind a huge rock. While Cyryl and the men conversed, she watched the huge waves hammer against the shore.

Suddenly Jahane became aware that the men were silent, and she turned to face them. To her astonishment, the sailors bowed low to her, their eyes reverently fastened on her face.

"Your Highness," one of the sailors spoke up, "our hearts are gladdened that you have been found. We will be honored to be the ones who will escort you home."

Not knowing what was expected of her, she merely smiled. In truth, she was embarrassed by their attention.

"Let us get her to the ship," Cyryl spoke up. "Her Highness will catch a chill if we keep her standing in the rain."

One of the men gallantly offered Jahane his arm. "If you please, Your Highness," he said, his eyes shining.

Jahane placed her hand on his arm while he gently swung her into the boat.

Launching the craft into the waves, the men jumped on board and rowed out to sea.

A heavy mist hung over the sea, and Jahane strained her eyes trying to locate the ship. At last it loomed before her. Jahane was startled when she saw a carved figurehead of a beautiful woman, whose golden hair was flying out about her. Jahane gasped at the resemblance to herself, and, beneath the figurehead, she saw the name of the ship—the *Queen Eleanor*. The ship had been named for her mother.

A rope ladder was thrown over the side, and helpful hands pulled Jahane on board. There was much murmuring among the crew, and she saw the same adoration in the men's eyes when they found out her identity. Apparently those people from Balmarhea loved their royal family, and they had wholeheartedly accepted her as their lost princess.

A man called down from the quarterdeck in French and the others moved aside as he approached. He was a man who looked as if he had been born to the sea. His white-and-scarlet uniform with gold epaulets proclaimed him to be the captain. His coffee-colored hair was swept across a wide brow, and his eyes were steely blue. Jahane thought he was but a few years older than Cord and her brother.

"What is going on here?" the captain demanded. "Who is this woman? Who gave her authorization to come aboard?" He turned to Cyryl with accusing eyes. "If you have brought your doxy on my ship, I'll have you horsewhipped."

Cyryl's eyes were almost gleeful with spite as he

spoke to the man. "Captain Ruel Marceau, I have the very great honor to present you to Her Royal Highness, the Princess Jahane. Your Highness, the captain of your ship."

The captain whirled to face Jahane, his expression skeptical, but when he saw her eyes — her face, which was the image of the figurehead on his own ship, he knew she was indeed the princess.

Ruel's face drained of color, and he swept into a deep bow. "Forgive me, Your Highness," he sputtered. "But I have always thought you more myth than flesh and blood." His look was pleading, for it seemed he could not stop saying the wrong thing. "I beg your pardon. I did not mean to speak so familiarly to you. I am yours to command."

Cyryl snorted. "You could start by showing Her Highness to her cabin."

"Yes, of course," Captain Marceau said. "If you will come with me, Your Highness, I will show you to the royal quarters."

Since the captain seemed so willing to please her, Jahane considered asking him to set her ashore. Then a plan formed in her mind. Perhaps by going to Balmarhea ahead of Alexander, she could help him against their Uncle Reynard.

Silently she followed the captain across the deck and down the companionway, with Cyryl following close behind. When the captain stopped at a door and pushed it open, Jahane stepped in and glanced around. It was decorated in purple and creams, and was as elegant as any bedroom she had ever seen. The bed was draped with purple satin, and a thick cream rug covered the floor. She could see another room with a heavy carved desk and chests. One of the chests was open, and she saw that it contained many gowns.

"I was instructed to obtain clothing for you, Your Highness," Cyryl spoke up when he saw Jahane's inquiring glance. "You see, His Grace leaves nothing to chance. You do not need to be concerned, the gowns are your size."

Her lips curled in scorn. "How would you know that?"

"Because I employed your very own dressmaker to make them."

Her tone of voice held a hint of insult. "I am impressed by your ingenuity, Mr. Dionysos. How ever did you do that, and how did you know I would sail on this ship."

"I merely hoped you would. And I found out that a Mrs. Coolidge was your dressmaker. I instructed the woman to make gowns for every occasion, for a woman of your size and height. She was delighted when I told her to spare no expense."

Jahane did not like Cyryl, and she turned to the captain, speaking to him in French. "The quarters will do nicely, Captain. Is there a lock to the door?"

The captain's eyes searched her face with the same adoration she had witnessed in the faces of the sailors. "Yes, Your Highness. I will find the key and deliver it to you at once."

She removed her sodden shawl and hung it over a chair, deciding if she was to be treated like royalty, she might as well act the part. "Have a bath prepared for me at once."

"Very good, Your Highness. Will you be taking your meals in your cabin?"

She hesitated. "Yes, for the time being."

The captain's face reddened. "I am sorry that we did

not employ a woman to look after your needs. In truth, Your Highness, I did not believe we would ever find you. Can I say how happy I am that we did?"

He seemed so sincere that Jahane could not help bestowing a smile on him. "Thank you, Captain."

Jahane saw that he waited, and she realized he was waiting for her to dismiss him. "You may go, Captain." She looked pointedly at Cyryl. "But wait. Captain, can I assume you will allow no one access to my cabin without my permission?"

Captain Marceau was so overcome by the princess's striking beauty, he did not answer at first. Even with her hair wet and plastered to her head, she was the most striking woman he had ever seen. "Y-es, Your Highness. No one is allowed in this part of the ship without your say. This has always been the royal family's flagship. As you saw, the ship was named for your mother, the queen."

"Will you do something for me?" Jahane said, looking haughtily at Cyryl.

"Of course, Your Highness," the captain said.

"I would like to send a note to my . . . home. Will you see that it is delivered before we sail?"

He inclined his head. "It will be done in all haste, Your Highness."

She quickly moved to the desk and scribbled a note, sealed it, and handed it to the captain. "Please see to this at once. It is the big gray house which is a mile beyond Market Street."

"Yes, I know the house," the captain said. "We will withdraw now, Your Highness. If you wish anything, you have but to pull this cord, and a bell will alert me that you wish something and I will attend you at once."

Jahane walked to the door, indicating the two men should leave her now. When Cyryl bowed to her with a satisfied smile on his face, she ground her teeth together. She just did not like the man.

"Captain," Jahane said, realizing Cyryl would be feeling pleased because she had not begged to be set ashore. "Mr. Dionysos is not to be allowed in my presence for any reason. Is that understood?"

While Cyryl Dionysos's face reddened with indignation, the captain nodded with satisfaction. "It will be as you command, Your Highness."

Before Jahane closed the door, the last thing she saw was Cyryl's angry expression. She found the greatest satisfaction in putting him in his place.

Cyryl turned to Captain Marceau and held out his hand. "I will deliver Her Highness's note, Captain."

"I think not. Since Her Highness entrusted the note to me, I will see that it is safely delivered."

Cyryl's eyes narrowed, and he would like to have protested, but the captain was master here, and he knew he had no authority. He stomped away, with anger burning in his heart.

It was still raining when the wind caught the canvas of the *Queen Eleanor* and carried her out of the cove.

Jahane lay upon the satin bed feeling very alone. She wished she had asked the captain to take her ashore, but her destiny had already been set on a path, and she could not turn back. What awaited her when she arrived in Balmarhea, she could not guess. But the one thing she did know was that she had a friend in Captain Marceau.

Her thoughts moved to Cord, and she wondered

what he would do when he found her missing. She knew it was but a matter of time before he would come after her.

She closed her eyes, imagining Cord was there beside her. She could face anything if he was with her. Even now, she trembled when she remembered him kissing her and touching her so intimately.

"Oh, Cord," she whispered. "I am so frightened."

Chapter Twenty-six

When Alexander arrived at the Meredith house, he noticed the front door was wide open and Jojo was moving back and forth, waving his hands to the heavens in an agitated manner.

It never occurred to Alexander that anything had happened to his sister until he climbed the steps and encountered Mrs. Meredith, her face pale, her eyes teary.

Maggie clutched at Alexander's arm. "Have you seen her? Cord told me he was taking the men who had guarded the house away for the day, since he had to sail down the coast. He said to keep Jahane in the house. How was I to know she would take it in her head to go out alone?"

Alexander's heart plummeted. "What are you saying? Isn't my sister here?"

"You haven't seen her? Dear Lord, where can she be? We have to find her."

Alexander saw the panic in the woman's eyes. "No, I have not seen Jahane since yesterday. Is it possible she is visiting a friend?"

Maggie was wringing her hands and muttering incoherently. "No, she would not do that without telling me first. I don't know where she could be. My only hope was that she had gone to see you."

Alexander tried to keep a clear head, for it was apparent Mrs. Meredith was losing hers. "When did you first discover my sister was missing, Mrs. Meredith?"

"About three hours ago. We searched the house and then the yard, without success. Jojo has made inquiries with the neighbors, but no one saw her."

"Is it unlike my sister to cause you undue distress? Would she have let you know if she went into town or perhaps to the market?"

"Jahane would never have given me cause to worry. She has always been considerate of others' feelings."

Alexander glanced at Jojo. Another Chinese gentleman had just come up, and the two of them were conversing in their language. When the man left, Jojo rushed up to Mrs. Meredith and handed her a note.

"Man say this given him for you, madame. Maybe from Missy, I think." The houseboy's eyes were hopeful as he waited for Mrs. Meredith to read the note.

Maggie's hand trembled as she tore the note open, her breath came out in a gasp, and she started crying hysterically.

Alexander took the note from her and read:

Mama, please do not worry about me. I have been taken aboard the Balmarhean ship, Queen Eleanor. *I am treated with kindness, and am in no danger. I will write you as soon as I am able.*

Alexander felt the hand of dread settle on his shoul-

303

ders. "If my sister was taken against her will, it was by my Uncle Reynard's men. Therefore, she is in grave danger."

"What shall we do?" Maggie asked. "I cannot bear to think of that dear child being harmed."

There was an urgency in Alexander's voice. "When do you expect your son to return, Mrs. Meredith?"

"I . . . this evening."

"I will be at the dock to meet him when he anchors. Try not to worry, madame. You can be sure I will do everything I can to get my sister back safely."

"Yes, find Cord," she urged. "Tell him to sail to Balmarhea at once. I will see that his trunks are packed," Maggie said, needing something positive to do.

Alexander knew his Uncle Reynard would not hesitate to kill Jahane if it suited his purpose. He only hoped it was in Reynard's best interest to keep her alive.

Alexander was impatient to be underway. He hadn't come this far to find his sister only to have her fall into the hands of the man who was responsible for the death of their parents. He blamed himself for not being more cautious with her welfare. He alone knew what deviltry his uncle was capable of. How could the Meredith family know that his Uncle Reynard would stop at nothing to get his own way?

Cord was silent while the *Golden Phoenix* sailed down the coast of California. He had remained on board ship while his men had taken on guns and munitions for the voyage to Balmarhea. He ordered an extra cannon, a twenty-pounder, to be mounted on the quarterdeck. If he were going to take Jahane to Balmarhea, he wanted to make damn sure he could protect her.

It was late evening when the *Golden Phoenix* began her return voyage to San Francisco. Cord stood at the helm, the sea breeze ruffling his dark hair, while his eyes stared at the dying sun.

He had not allowed himself time to dwell on his love for Jahane, knowing it was a bittersweet love and he could never make her his wife. No, she was most likely destined to marry someone from one of the royal houses of Europe. He didn't have to be told that she would never be allowed to marry an American sea captain without a drop of royal blood in his veins.

The thought of another man touching and holding his sweet Jahane was too painful to think about. He remembered how sweetly and innocently she had come to him and offered him her love. He blamed himself for not taking her then. If he had, he would not be losing her now.

"So much for being noble," he muttered under his breath.

"Did you say something, Captain?" Thadeus asked.

"Make ready to come into port," he said, anxious to be home so he could see Jahane.

Inside Cord raged against the fate that had set Jahane above him and so far out of his reach. He dreaded when they would have to say their final farewell, for it was but a matter of time until she would take up her life in Balmarhea.

His eyes darkened with painful memories as he stared at the shoreline of San Francisco. His hands were sure and accurate as he skillfully maneuvered his ship into the bay.

Jahane had always been the most important person in his life. He had been with women, but always he kept them at a distance, never allowing them to touch his inner thoughts and feelings. He now knew what Jahane had known all along. That they belonged together. She had cut her teeth on his heart, and it would always be hers.

Giving the order to drop anchor, Cord wondered if he would be strong enough to let Jahane go when the time came.

Tying off the wheel, Cord watched the lowering of the gangplank. No sooner had the plank fallen into place than Alexander rushed aboard, his eyes searching frantically until they fell on Cord.

"We have to sail at once," Alexander blurted out. "My Uncle Reynard's henchman has abducted Jahane, and she is being taken to Balmarhea! Her life is in great danger."

Without thinking, Cord grabbed the prince by the shirtfront and yanked him forward. "Who is responsible for her falling into your uncle's hands? If you have been lax with her safety, I will—"

Alexander pried Cord's hands away and looked at him accusingly. "If anyone is to blame, it is you, Mr. Meredith. There were no guards around your house to protect my sister. It appears that she went out alone and that monster was lying in wait for her. You knew she was in danger, why did you not have her better protected?"

Cord turned away from Alexander's accusations, calling out to his first mate, "Thadeus, have the ship prepared for a long voyage at once. Tell the crew that where we go, there will be danger. I will excuse any man who does not wish to come along."

Thadeus's eyes were troubled. "What has happened, Captain? Is it your sister?'

"No," Alexander broke in. "It's *my* sister."

"Jahane has been taken by her uncle's men," Cord explained. "I fear she may be in great danger."

The first mate sprung into action. "I'm sure, Captain, the entire crew will go along. They are all right fond of Jahane."

Cord turned back to Alexander. "Do you know how long Jahane has been missing?"

"Since this morning. She sent a note to your mother saying she was unharmed but that she was being taken to Balmarhea."

"Dear God," Cord moaned. "They have a full day's start on us. Tell me exactly what the note said."

"Just that she had been taken aboard the *Queen Eleanor,* but that she was in no danger. I think I should point out to you that the *Queen Eleanor* is the fastest ship in the Balmarhean Navy. We don't have time to stand around talking while they get farther away."

"Come below and look at my maps. I need to chart the quickest route to Balmarhea. They may have had a head start on us, but the *Golden Phoenix* is also noted for her speed."

"Is there any chance you can overtake her?" Alexander wanted to know.

"No, but we will not be far behind her when she arrives in your country."

Jahane stood topside beside Captain Marceau, watching the sun set in the west and feeling very homesick. She wanted to see Cord, have him hold her in his arms and tell her everything was going to be all right.

The young captain stared at his princess with adoring eyes. The dying rays of the sun seemed to be reflected in her golden hair. Balmarhea had been floundering ever since the king and queen had been slain. Of course, everyone knew that Prince Alexander was dead. But there had always been rumors that Princess Jahane had escaped death that night. Until now, the captain had put little value in those rumors. Even when he had been ordered to sail to San Francisco with the hope of bringing the princess back, he had been skeptical. Now he rejoiced in his heart, for no one could deny that the lovely vision beside him was Queen Eleanor's true daughter.

Captain Marceau thought about how the people of Balmarhea had kept their hopes alive that the Princess Jahane might one day return to bring peace and prosperity back to the land. Now that day was not far away.

"Your Highness, might I be permitted to point out to you that you look very much like the pictures I have seen of your mother?"

She smiled. "I have heard that, and it pleases me very much."

"It should please you," he said without thinking how forward he was being. "The queen was very beautiful." His face reddened, and he hastened to add, "Meaning no disrespect, Your Highness."

308

Even though she was gratified that he had compared her to her mother, Jahane chose to ignore his compliment and his discomfort. "I have no memory of my mother, and only vague shadowy images of my father."

"I can recall the king and queen riding through the streets of Montique in an open carriage when I was a young man. At that time, Your Highness, you were a golden-haired angel who smiled and waved to everyone, while your brother, Prince Alexander, always had such a serious expression on his face. Being but a boy myself, I always hoped the prince would glance at me, and one day he did. He looked right at me and smiled."

Captain Marceau's eyes saddened. "The country has been shrouded in sorrow since that awful night when the streets of Montique became a bloodbath."

"Am I to take it that my Uncle Reynard has not made the people happy?"

His honest blue eyes blinked as he wondered how to answer her. How could he tell her that Duke Maxime was unpopular with the people, and that most of the citizens of Balmarhea were suspicious of him. He decided to say as little as possible.

"As you may know, His Grace cannot be absolute ruler without the great scepter; therefore, he has very little power. Especially since your uncle, Archbishop Serafimo, kept hinting that the rightful ruler would one day return." His eyes now brightened with a smile. "Now his prophecy has come true, and you are with us again."

Jahane had much to reflect on. She could not tell Captain Marceau that her uncle had been referring to her brother Alexander. It seemed everyone believed her brother dead, and she would not say differently until Alexander himself decided the time was right. Perhaps with her returning to Balmarhea, it would buy Alexander the time he needed to plan his return.

"Was I wrong, or do the people of Balmarhea love my Uncle Serafimo?"

"You are not wrong, Your Highness. The archbishop is well loved and trusted, but not so with your Uncle Reynard." He looked apologetic. "I beg your pardon, Your Highness, I have often been accused of speaking without thinking. I fear it is a bad failing with me."

She gave him her brightest smile. "I hope you will always speak the truth with me, Captain. I want no one around me to tell me what they think I want to hear."

In a quick move that surprised Jahane, Captain Marceau dropped to one knee, while his bright eyes looked into hers. "I am your man, Your Highness. I pledge my fidelity to you, for now and all times."

She tried to hide her embarrassment at his declaration. She wondered if she would have to grow accustomed to people bowing to her. "Good, Captain, I am going to need trusted friends around me," she said, staring at the last glowing embers of the sun. She said softly, more to herself than to the captain. "I fear for the unknown."

Then, to change the subject, Jahane glanced around the ship. "I am somewhat an authority on ships, Captain, and I find the *Queen Eleanor* a very fine ship. She has a trim line."

"Indeed she does. She was built to your father's specifications. Of course, you already know you occupy the cabins that belonged to the king and queen."

"Does not my Uncle Reynard sail on this ship?" she asked.

"No, not he," the captain said, unable to disguise the scorn in his voice. "The duke does not care for the sea."

Jahane was certain the captain did not like her Uncle Reynard, but she had to find out for sure. "Captain, if you are called upon to obey Duke Maxime over me, what will you do?"

Without hesitating he answered, "I will serve you."

"May I depend on that?"

"Always," he stated with feeling. "I do not believe you have any notion how much loyalty and love await you once the people of Balmarhea know you have returned."

"If that is so, then I fear my Uncle Reynard will not be well pleased."

Tactfully the captain replied, "Your Uncle Serafimo will be overjoyed at seeing you."

"I have another question," Jahane said quietly so she would not be overheard. "If you are so loyal to me, why were you a party to my abduction?"

Horror was etched on his face. "I would never have abducted you, Your Highness. Did you not accompany Cyryl Dionysos on board of your own free will?"

"No, I did not. From what I understood from him, my Uncle Reynard sent him to fetch me home."

Anger burned in the captain's eyes. "Then I beg your pardon, Your Highness. Had I known that was the circumstance, I would have had Dionysos clapped in irons. If you say the word, I shall do so now. If you wish to return to San Francisco, I will take you back immediately."

Jahane breathed a sigh of relief. She had not been mistaken, she had a friend in Captain Marceau. "It would be useless to lock Monsieur Dionysos up. And I am now convinced that returning to Balmarhea is the wise thing to do."

Jahane had begun to realize what her homecoming would mean to the people of Balmarhea. From deep inside her, in some hidden part of her brain, loyalty for her subjects rushed forth with such an intensity it startled her. Inbred in her was the concern for the welfare of her people, and she did not want to see any of them suffer needlessly. Would her homecoming start another civil war?

The captain was thoughtful for a moment, then a slow smile played on his lips. "Just this morning, Your Highness, Dionysos told me that His Grace wanted you brought to the castle under cover of darkness, and as secretly as possible." His eyes danced with mirth. "I wonder what would happen if we debarked in early morning, when the streets are always crowded with women going to market. What do you suppose would happen if we sent a runner ahead to announce to all the citizens along the way that the Princess Jahane had returned?"

Her laughter danced on the air. "Captain, I believe you have a devious mind."

He smiled. "I do, Your Highness."

"Yes," she said thoughtfully. "Let us see if we can thwart my Uncle Reynard's plans, whatever they might be."

"It will be as you say, Your Highness."

Captain Marceau looked away, aware that he had been staring at the princess. He wondered where she

312

had been all these years, what kind of life she had been living. Knowing he was in no position to satisfy his curiosity, he trained his eyes on the restless waves that slapped against the ship. All he needed to know was that she was his princess, and he was sworn to obey her commands.

The captain did not trust Duke Maxime, so he vowed to stay beside the Princess Jahane until he saw her safely under the protection of her uncle, the archbishop.

Chapter Twenty-seven

Brynn now felt well enough to get out of bed. Although the welts on her back were still very painful, and it was painful for her to move around, she found joy in going out into the palace garden.

Often she would take out her memories of the night she had spent with Prince Alexander and relive every moment. It was hard to know when she first started loving him. Perhaps it had been while growing up lonely and alone at the convent, when he had been her make-believe playmate. Or perhaps it was the night he had abducted her.

She was glad she had not betrayed him, and she wondered if Duke Maxime would torture her again to find out what he wanted to know.

Brynn had not lost her fear of Reynard, but thus far he had left her alone. Of course, the archbishop's housekeeper, Mrs. St. John, still guarded her like a mother hen.

As Brynn walked along the garden path, she stepped over a puddle of water. There had been a morning shower, and the rain had washed everything clean. Brynn paused to breathe in the wonderful aroma of the rose garden.

It felt good to be alive, and she glanced up at the bluest sky she had ever seen, thankful she was able to be out in the open and not locked in that dark dungeon. She doubted she would ever take the sunlight for granted again.

Behind Brynn, a deep voice cut through her troubled thoughts.

"Good morning, my child. I am gladdened to see you are up and about at last. It is hoped that you are enjoying renewed health."

She spun around to face the Archbishop of Balmarhea. She had seen him once before when he had arrived at the lodge to visit Prince Alexander. At that time, his voice had been gruff, and she had the feeling he was displeased with her. Now he smiled warmly, and she wondered what had happened to change his opinion of her.

Her eyes shone with reverence as she faced her bene-factor. "Your Eminence," she said, dropping to her knees. "I am so in your debt. How can I ever repay you?"

Serafimo took Brynn's hands and pulled her up to a standing position.

"Dear child, my reward is in seeing you returned to health. You are feeling better, I am told."

"Yes, Your Eminence. Each day I improve."

Serafimo had been told by Mrs. St. John that the girl would always bear scars on her back from the beating she had received at the hands of that black-hearted Hogarth. Inside, he shook with rage that Reynard had treated Chapin d'Arcy's daughter so cruelly.

He clasped his hands behind his back and looked

her over. She was pretty, even though her eyes were almost too big for her small face. She was so small-boned and delicate, he could not believe anyone would dare harm her.

"Are you comfortable here, child? Is there anything you require?"

"I require nothing, Your Eminence. I have nothing but thanks in my heart for your kindness and Mrs. St. John's attentiveness. I thank you from the bottom of my heart, but I do not know why a man of your importance would bother with me."

"Why is it you do not think of yourself as important? My dear child, God believes all his creatures are important. It has always been my theory that some are less worthy than others, but fortunately for humanity, the Divine Father does not share my views."

She smiled at the archbishop, feeling grateful that he had the ability to put her at ease. She could see why the citizens of Balmarhea loved him. "I will always remember that you thought me worthy of your consideration, Your Eminence."

Serafimo looked into the face of the young woman, trying to see some resemblance to Count d'Arcy. Yes, she had the same hair and eye coloring as the count, but there was very little else about her that resembled D'arcy.

"Tell me, child, do you recall anything about your parents?"

"No, Your Eminence. I only remember a woman, I think she was my mother. I was torn out of her arms . . . and . . ." She glanced at him sadly. "I saw her cut down. To this day I remember her screams."

"So you have no notion who you are? I am sorry to

316

hear that."

"None. But I do know that I am not your niece, Princess Jahane."

"No, you are not she. I am grieved that you have been used in such a loathsome scheme to defraud the people. Have you any notion what my brother had in mind for you?"

She turned teary eyes to him. "I am ashamed, Your Eminence, that I was involved in such a scheme."

He patted her kindly. "It was not your fault, Brynn. For what it's worth, child, I would never have allowed my brother's plan to succeed."

Suddenly, without thinking, she grasped the front of his satin robe. "Will Duke Maxime have further use of me? Do you think he will want to have me tortured again?"

"No, my dear. I will not allow that to happen."

The archbishop enfolded her in his arms as her slight body trembled with fear. The daughter of Count Chapin d'Arcy deserved much better than she had received. When it was safe to do so, he intended that she be recognized as the great man's daughter. But for now, it was better not to tell Brynn her true identity. On the day when Alexander would be set upon the throne of Balmarhea, many things would be put right.

"Try not to worry, child. Sometimes the darkest clouds have the sweetest rain."

Brynn realized she had been far too familiar with the archbishop. Fearing he would think she was taking advantage of his kindness, she moved away from him. "Must I stay here in the castle, Your Eminence? Could I not return to the convent?"

"I have extracted a great concession from my brother

to allow me to bring Mrs. St. John to look after you. I have not been able to persuade him to give your welfare into my keeping."

When he saw her face fall, he hastily added, "However, Mrs. St. John will remain with you indefinitely. Does that make you feel safer?"

"Yes, Your Eminence. Thank you," she said gratefully, taking his hand and planting a kiss on his ring. "You have been so kind to me."

"Nonsense, child. Someday you will know that Balmarhea owes you a great debt."

She looked at him, puzzled, but he only smiled. "Never mind about that now." His expression became serious. "I know you were tortured to make you reveal what you know about my nephew, Prince Alexander. I also know you told Hogarth nothing. You are a credit to your country, and your . . . family would be proud of you. You are a brave girl."

"I was not brave, Your Eminence. I was so frightened I prayed for death."

"But you told nothing about Prince Alexander."

"I never would—no, never." Her eyes sparkled with fire. "I would take his secret with me to my grave."

"That will not be necessary, my child. The time will come when Balmarhea will need all her loyal citizens."

He smiled. "I must take my leave now, but do not fear for your safety. I have a watchful eye on you."

Brynn bowed her head, not wanting him to see the grateful tears that washed down her face.

After the archbishop's footsteps had faded away, she glanced again at the sun, feeling hope in her heart. She had wanted to question the archbishop about Prince Alexander, but she dared not, because she did not want to know anything about him that she could be forced to reveal under torture.

Alexander was impatient to reach Balmarhea before Reynard had time to harm Jahane. As he watched Captain Meredith issue orders to unfurl the sails, he knew he would have to be patient.

As he gazed at the flock of sea birds that flew into the horizon, he imagined he could see his Uncle Reynard's face as it had been on their last meeting, twisted and distorted with hatred. Alexander knew Reynard still bore the scar from their last confrontation. He was glad that every time his uncle looked in the mirror he would be reminded of him.

He thought of his beautiful sister, Jahane, so young and innocent. His hand clenched the ship's railing at the thought of Reynard getting his hands on her.

Hearing footsteps approach, Alexander glanced up to see Cord Meredith.

"The wind has picked up, so we are able to increase our speed by two knots. The problem is that the *Queen Eleanor* will have the same wind," Cord observed, joining Alexander at the rail.

"I cannot tell you how imperative it is that we make it to Balmarhea as quickly as possible. My Uncle Reynard is an evil man, and if it suits his purpose, he will not hesitate to kill Jahane."

"I have done everything I can to gain on the *Queen Eleanor*," Cord said, grim-faced. He took in a ragged breath. "I feel the helplessness of the situation, just as you must. But I can tell you this, any man who harms one hair on Jahane's head will answer with his own life, be he prince or pauper."

Alexander snorted. "You have not the means to even get near my Uncle Reynard, American." There was scorn in his voice. "Most probably you have lived your life in your safe little world, never knowing what it was like to lose your mother and father in a power struggle with your uncle. What do you know of sacrifice?"

Anger sparkled in Cord's eyes. "Apparently you don't know that my father lost his life the same night your mother and father died."

"But I do not think your father—"

"Let me finish. My father lost his life, saving Jahane from your Uncle Reynard. So don't speak to me of sacrifice, because I was there, and I saw my father fight for a child he did not even know. I have resented your attitude ever since we met. If you were worthy to be called a prince, you would at least be grateful to my mother for giving up her life and moving away from her friends and family to an unknown place so your Uncle Reynard could not find Jahane. Have you thought about the sacrifice my mother made?"

Prince Alexander stared into the eyes of the man he had believed had deprived him of his sister, realizing how mistaken he had been. He owed the Meredith family gratitude and much more, for they had indeed kept Jahane safe for all these years.

"I do so humbly beg your pardon, Captain Meredith. If you were to toss me overboard, I would not blame you. I must seem an arrogant and ungrateful bastard to you. I have criticized you, when I should have been praising you. In my own defense, I can only say that I have spent years of my life believing my sister was lost to me. When I finally found her, I struck out at you unjustly, thinking you had kept her from me."

Cord looked into eyes so like Jahane's that his anger melted away. "I can see how you might have thought that. Until a few short days ago, I thought she was the daughter of my father's friend, Count Chapin d'Arcy."

Alexander shook his head. "D'arcy also died that awful night. He died trying to protect me."

"It seems there were many heroes that night," Cord observed. "I wonder if their stories will ever be told?"

"Yes," Alexander cried with conviction. "When I am king, the whole world will know of the valiant men who died that night."

Long after the sun had gone down, the two men talked. Alexander told Cord how Reynard had tried to kill him that night. He also told him how he had grown up in a monastery, where his Uncle Serafimo had hidden him.

Cord told Alexander what Jahane's life had been like growing up in San Francisco. Soon they were talking like old friends and had developed a mutual respect for each other.

"I can see you as my ally, Captain Meredith. We are both concerned for Jahane's safety, and I know you will do everything to help me find her. You have been like a brother to her, and I am sure she is quite fond of you."

"Yes," Cord said, looking past Alexander. "I believe it is only fair to tell you that what I feel for Jahane transcends brotherly affection. I love her . . . as a man loves a woman."

Alexander stared at Cord before he spoke. "And how does she feel about you?"

"She has said she loves me."

"As her brother, I feel bound to ask you how far this has gone between you and my sister?"

Cord raised his head, looking long and hard at Jahane's brother. "She is as chaste and innocent as she ever was. Do you think I could look after her all these years, and then . . ." He shook his head. "I have tried to discourage Jahane from loving me. After my mother told me she was not Count d'Arcy's daughter, but the Princess Jahane, I have known she can never belong to me."

Alexander nodded. "That is true, Cord," he agreed, calling him by his first name. "Should this all end in victory for us, Jahane will not be allowed to marry you. No matter how much we would wish it otherwise, she can only marry into royalty."

Pain throbbed in Cord's voice. "Have you ever loved a woman, Prince Alexander?"

Alexander remembered all too well how Brynn had felt in his arms and how he had made passionate love to her. "Yes, I have," he admitted. "I also know how it feels to love a woman whom I cannot make my wife. I, too, shall have to choose a wife who is of royal blood."

A long moment of silence fell while both men were lost in their own thoughts. Finally Alexander spoke. "When do you think we shall reach Balmarhea?"

"If these winds continue, we should sight Balmarhea three days hence."

Again silence fell. This time Cord was the first to speak. "Do you think Jahane will be safe on board the

Queen Eleanor?"

"Yes, she will come to no harm until she reaches Balmarhea."

"Can we be sure?"

"No one on board the ship would dare raise a hand to her."

"I have been tortured by what they might do to her."

"Put that fear aside. Uncle Reynard will have given orders that she is to be treated with respect. He will want to see her, question her, and find out if she knows where the scepter is hidden. Of course, he is not aware that I am alive, so therefore, he believes she is the rightful queen."

Cord could feel the distance between him and Jahane yawn like a deep cavern. Even if they did manage to save her, she was lost to him forever.

Chapter Twenty-eight

A heady wind snapped the sails of the *Queen Eleanor,* and the ship glided smoothly across the water in the wake of white-crested waves.

Captain Marceau was leaning over his log book, charting the day's progress, when a rap fell on the door. Murmuring to whomever it was to enter, he did not look up until he had made the last entry.

He was not surprised to see Cyryl Dionysos looking agitated.

"You wanted to see me about something?" he asked, knowing very well what the man wanted. Since they were nearing Balmarhea, he had been expecting this visit.

Reynard's man lowered himself in a chair and studied the young captain. "You have surely become Princess Jahane's man, haven't you, Captain?"

The captain knew the man was trying to find out how deep his loyalties were to Princess Jahane. "Of course. As a citizen of Balmarhea, I am honor-bound to serve the princess—as are you," he answered, giving nothing away.

"Yes, of course. But it may not be in your best

interest to be too attentive to her."

Ruel Marceau closed his log book and stared at the man, Cyryl. "What do you mean?"

Cyryl played with the frayed cuff of his jacket. "I mean, if you are Duke Maxime's man, you could find yourself financially able."

The captain looked pointedly at Cyryl's well-worn jacket. "Like you?" he asked.

The barb went right over the man's head. "Of course. I have been the duke's man for many years. He treats me very well. And with every bit of useful information I bring to him, he rewards me."

"So you are Duke Maxime's informant, and you are asking me to do the same?"

"You would not regret it if you became devoted to the duke. You will not find him ungenerous, this I can assure you."

"I see what you mean. And since you apparently have Duke Maxime's ear, suppose you tell me what he would require of me at the moment."

"It's all very simple. Just put in at Balmarhea after dark so I can sneak — ur . . . take Princess Jahane to her uncle unobserved."

Captain Marceau picked up his quill pen and twirled it between his fingers. "Therein lies a problem, Cyryl. You see, I have already pledged my loyalty to Princess Jahane, and we all know that a man cannot serve two masters."

Cyryl's eyes narrowed with a cunning light. "What do you intend to do?"

The captain tossed the pen aside and leaned forward, fixing the man with a cold stare.

"I intend to do whatever Princess Jahane asks of me. And I do not feel compelled to discuss her wishes with you. If you serve Duke Maxime, you cannot be loyal to the princess as well."

"Surely you will not openly defy Duke Maxime. It is your duty to help me see that the princess is transported to the palace in the least conspicuous manner."

"I'm afraid the princess will make her journey to the castle without you. You see, she has taken a definite dislike to you, and it is her wish that you do not accompany her at all."

Anger twisted Cyryl's face. "As soon as we reach Balmarhea, I intend to go directly to the duke and inform him of your lack of cooperation."

"I'm afraid you won't be allowed to do that, either. You will remain on board the *Queen Eleanor* long after the princess has departed the ship."

"You would not dare go against Duke Maxime's wishes. Are you mad? He is the power in Balmarhea."

"For the moment, he is the power. But what do you think his chances are to rule the people once they have laid eyes on their lost princess? I think most of them will follow Princess Jahane, don't you?"

Cyryl's face drained of color, and his eyes bulged out. "Surely you do not intend to show her to the people. That is not at all what Duke Maxime wanted for her." Suddenly his eyes became wild with fright. "If you do this, my life will be in jeopardy. Have you thought how you would explain it to the duke?"

The captain shrugged his shoulders. "I would be grieved should the duke take it in his head to reprimand you. But such is the price for serving the wrong master."

Cyryl stared at the captain with hatred in his eyes. "I will see you dead for this, Captain. You have gone against the duke, and no one can save you."

"A groundless threat since you are in my hands at the moment, and 'your duke' is nowhere in sight."

Captain Marceau walked to the door, flung it open, and called to his man that had been stationed outside. "Take Monsieur Dionysos below and have him confined. I don't believe chains will be necessary, but see that a guard is posted at his door and he is unable to leave his cabin."

Cyryl's eyes glinted like frozen ice. "You will live to regret this, Captain. You will rue the day you went against the duke."

Captain Marceau laughed with satisfaction. "Your threat would be a bit more credible if you were not my prisoner, Cyryl." He turned back to his man. "Take him away, and until further notice, he will remain under lock and key."

Cyryl hissed angrily as the sailor escorted him out of the captain's cabin. When silence fell over the room, Captain Marceau had time to think.

Since Cyryl had been so insistent that Princess Jahane be taken to the castle under a cloak of secrecy, he would carry through with his plan to take her to the castle amid great fanfare.

Duke Maxime would not dare harm her if the people were made aware that she had returned.

Balmarhea Harbor

At Captain Marceau's suggestion Jahane wore her golden hair free of any restraint. Dressed in a gown of royal purple, she surveyed herself in the mirror. Yes, she did resemble the figurehead on the ship.

She moved up on deck, where several sailors stared

327

at her in open awe. Each time she would catch one of the crew's member's eyes they would bow to her. It was a new feeling, having people treat her with special consideration, and Jahane was not at all certain she liked the attention. But she would do what she must to help Alexander.

She hoped by drawing everyone's attention to her, it would enable Alexander to slip into Balmarhea unobserved.

She glanced up on the quarterdeck where Captain Marceau was issuing orders that would bring the ship into port. Walking slowly to the railing for the first sight of her country, Jahane drew in her breath at the sight that met her eyes. Balmarhea was beautiful. Everywhere there were flowers in bloom, their fragrance sweet and inviting.

Gentle winds touched her face, bringing with it the sweet smell of wild jasmine. Palm trees dotted the white sandy beaches. In the distance, she could see the tall cupolas of a castle. She shifted her gaze to the docks where men were loading and unloading cargo, while the women wearing brightly colored clothing moved about, selling fruits and vegetables to the departing ships.

An unexpected feeling of homecoming washed over her, and she was surprised at the tears that gathered in her eyes. These were her people, and this was where she belonged. This was the home of her ancestors. Her mother and father had given their lives for Balmarhea, and she might be called upon to do the same.

Wiping her tears away, Jahane wished with all her heart that Alexander could be here to share this moment with her.

Raising her face, she allowed the feeling of tranquility to inhabit her whole being. With the smell of jasmine on the air, her lips curved in a smile. Yes, she had come home.

Jahane turned to face Captain Marceau, who had just walked up beside her. He drew in his breath, thinking no one woman was as lovely as the princess. He could only guess how her subjects were going to love her.

"Your Highness, it is almost time to disembark. You have already won the hearts of the captain and crew of the *Queen Eleanor*. Suppose we go ashore and let you win the hearts of your other subjects."

Jahane was overcome with momentary fear and uncertainty. What would she do if the people rejected her as an impostor? Would she be able to bravely face her Uncle Reynard, knowing he desired her death?

When the gangplank swung into place, like the true princess she was, Jahane raised her head and smiled at Captain Marceau and said, "Shall we go?"

Captain Marceau returned her smile. "Not just yet, Your Highness. If you will allow me to make a suggestion, it is my belief that the time is right to inform the people that you have arrived." Deviltry danced in his eyes. "Now we play our high card, and hope we take the game."

She nodded her head just the slightest bit. "I defer to your military proficiency, Captain."

He proffered his arm to her and led her onto the gangplank so she could be clearly seen by those on shore.

The captain then moved down the gangplank, talking in a loud voice to catch the dockworkers' attention. "I will see what has gone wrong, Your Highness. I am sure whoever is to blame will be called to task."

Stepping before several men, he played his part. "Monsieurs, look lively," his voice boomed out. Reaching into his pocket, he tossed a gold coin at the nearest worker. "Would you be so kind as to run to the castle and find out why the royal carriage has not been brought around to transport the princess to the castle."

The dockworker, a man in his late fifties, glanced from the captain, up the gangplank, to the golden-haired beauty with her hair blowing in the wind. His faded blue eyes brightened at a sudden memory of his dead queen, and in his expression was hope. "What princess would that be, Captain?" he wanted to know.

"Why, monsieur, have you not heard? This is your Princess Jahane grown into a woman and returned at last to Balmarhea."

Worship and admiration sparkled in the man's eyes as he looked up at Jahane. With the sun shining on her golden hair, her image brought back memories of the beloved Queen Eleanor, and the man fell to his knees, his hand reaching up to her.

"Praise be to God," he said in a shaky voice. "Our princess has come home to us at last. Now we will again be blessed with peace and prosperity."

Jahane clasped her trembling hands behind her as several men dropped to their knees and looked up at her with reverence. Still others had gathered around the captain, and he was informing them that Princess Jahane had returned.

Before now, Jahane had not considered the people of Balmarhea, for they had not been real to her. But now, the rugged-faced men, the brightly dressed women, seemed to reach out to her with such love that the intensity of it made her want to cry out

330

in anguish.

Without thinking, she moved slowly, regally down the gangplank. When she stepped onto the pier, a swelling crowd moved aside to make a path for her. Hands reached out to her, but stopped short of touching her.

She saw tears in the people's eyes, and she was now crying openly herself. Impulsively, she reached out and took the hand of a frail old man, while his tears splashed on her hand. The crowd fell silent as the old man spoke.

"God bless you, Your Highness. You have the look of your mother, the queen, and the kindness of her, too."

When a deafening cheer rippled through the crowd, Jahane was overwhelmed with feelings that surrounded her like a soft hug.

Glancing up, she saw a hint of tears on Captain Marceau's face just before he bowed to her. He was conveying to her that she had come home in triumph!

Reynard stood on the second-floor balcony, which gave him a good view of the bay. He had been informed that the *Queen Eleanor* had docked. That had to mean his niece had been found and brought home, because he had ordered Cyryl not to return until he had the princess with him.

When he heard the noise of the crowd, he swore angrily. The fool Cyryl would pay for not carrying out his orders. Had he not ordered him to sail into harbor under the cover of night!

"Surely this is a glorious day, Brother." A familiar voice spoke up from behind him. Serafimo beamed with good humor. "Do you not think so?"

"In what way?" Reynard asked sourly.

"I'm sure that you have heard that our niece has returned. I would have gone to meet her, but I have been told that no one can get close to her, since the citizens of Balmarhea are surging around her like a protective shield."

"It might not be her," Reynard said coldly. "It might be an impostor."

Serafimo chuckled. "No. Have you forgotten you had the impostor, so therefore this one must be the true princess."

The archbishop was enjoying himself immensely at his brother's expense. Poor Reynard's plan had gone awry, and the princess was now in the hands of loyal subjects who adored her.

"Have done, Serafimo. I have not decided it is Jahane."

Serafimo's chuckle turned into deep laughter. "It matters not if you have decided, Brother. Listen—the citizens have decided for you."

Reynard's hands gripped the railing. "This was not supposed to happen."

"But it has. This is truly a happy day for Balmarhea. Listen, can you hear the people cheering? May God bless our niece, for already she is being blessed by her subjects."

"Impossible," Reynard snarled. "I will have someone's head for this."

"How can you say so, Brother? Was it not your orders that sent the *Queen Eleanor* to San Francisco to bring the princess to Balmarhea? I do not know about you, but I am going to the main steps to welcome her home. Shouldn't you come with me? It will look odd if you do not pay your respects."

The ever-increasing crowd cleared enough to allow a carriage through to the dock. Captain Marceau helped Jahane inside and then climbed in with her.

After ordering the top lowered on the carriage so everyone could see the princess, he nodded to several of his men to walk beside the carriage in case there should be any trouble. Not that he expected trouble. It was all too apparent that if anyone tried to harm the princess the crowd would tear them apart.

Seeing the surge of faces, and as an ever-increasing number joined the procession, Jahane looked at Captain Marceau with a stunned expression.

"I never realized how much a royal family is loved by its subjects, Captain."

"I do not know about other countries, Your Highness, but here in Balmarhea, your subjects have been hoping for a miracle. To them, you are the miracle."

By now the carriage was having trouble moving through the crowded streets. Word of Princess Jahane's homecoming had spread throughout Montique. People came from their houses, from their shops, from every corner of the city to pay homage and hopefully get a glimpse of Princess Jahane.

Jasmine-scented blossoms rained down on Jahane as she waved to her subjects. With feelings of love, she reached out to the people, and in return they reached back to her.

She could hear bits of their conversation as the buggy proceeded. "Looks like our beloved Queen Eleanor," one woman was heard to say. "Now everything will be as it once was," another remarked. "Glorious day," another added.

She turned to Captain Marceau, and when she spoke there was a catch in her voice. "I am unworthy of so much love." She knew Alexander should be here—he should be the one receiving the people's outpouring of love. "If only . . . if only . . ."

The captain's eyes adored her as he shook his head. "Nay, Your Highness. You are the worthiest of monarchs."

Chapter Twenty-nine

When the carriage carrying Princess Jahane and Captain Marceau came to a stop inside the castle courtyard, hundreds of people pressed forward, trying to get a better look at their princess.

Jahane glanced up at the steps leading to the castle, and her heart stopped beating when she realized both men awaiting her were her uncles.

Her eyes went first to the man wearing the robe of an archbishop, and she knew he would be her Uncle Serafimo. The archbishop's blue eyes softened as they met hers, and she returned his glorious smile.

Now both men started down the steps to greet Jahane, and her eyes shifted reluctantly to the man dressed in black velvet, knowing he was her Uncle Reynard. Yes, from somewhere a long way back in her memory she could remember those cold eyes staring at her with hatred, just as they were now.

Although Reynard smiled, Jahane shivered. The scar that ran the length of his face stood out a vivid red.

When Jahane could no longer stand to look into his eyes, she glanced back to her Uncle Serafimo.

The archbishop descended the steps with his arms

outstretched. As he approached Jahane, the crowd watched in silence to see if their archbishop accepted this woman as Princess Jahane.

Jahane smiled brightly and held her hand out to her Uncle Serafimo. "I would know you anywhere, Uncle Serafimo, even if you were not dressed in your regalia."

"My dear child," Serafimo said, aiding her to the ground. "I would also pick you out of a crowd, for you look very like your mother did at your age."

For a long moment Serafimo stared at Jahane, thinking no one could look so like the late queen and not be her daughter.

Still, he must be certain . . . and he knew that there was only one way to know for sure—if she had the scar on her hand, then she would be Jahane—but that would have to wait until they were away from the crowds. For now, he would treat her as if she were the true princess.

Embracing her in his arms, he felt her tremble, and he realized she was frightened. "Fear not, child. I will not allow anything to harm you," he whispered with assurance.

She gave him a weak smile, as a dark shadow fell across her face. Reynard hovered above her like a dark bird of prey, and she shivered at the coldness she sensed in him.

"Jahane, my dear. How can we impart to you how truly wonderful it is to have you back with us again." His voice was silky, his manner stiff.

"Hello, Uncle," she said through trembling lips. It occurred to Jahane that Reynard would not know how to love anyone.

"Dear niece, we have long awaited this day." Rey-

336

nard's voice was deep and held no trace of warmth, and she was chilled to the bone. When he held his hand out to her, she declined to offer him her hand.

"Uncle Reynard," she said in a strong voice that carried around the courtyard. "How very nice of you to welcome me home."

Jahane's eyes met and locked with Reynard's, and she saw something she had not expected to see in the dark depths. He was afraid . . . but of what? Surely not of her. She decided to press her advantage. "I have been welcomed by my subjects, and now by you. What a glorious day this is."

His eyes almost seemed to drain of color as he raised his head and looked down his nose at her. "Your subjects?" he asked in a voice that challenged her right to the fidelity of the citizens of Balmarhea.

"Yes, my subjects," she answered, knowing she had to meet this man without faltering. "Am I not the throne princess?"

Her eyes moved to Serafimo's, and she saw humor dancing there. "Indeed, the whole of Balmarhea belongs to you today, Jahane. Come, we cannot keep you out here talking in this heat," Serafimo declared.

When the archbishop would have led Jahane up the steps, she turned back to the carriage where Captain Marceau was waiting.

"Please," she said, leaning closer to her Uncle Serafimo. "Would it be possible for the captain to accompany me? I have found him to be a true and loyal friend. And I do not want him to be punished for that loyalty."

"Was it his idea to arouse the mob and bring you into the city by daylight?" Serafimo asked.

"Yes, it was. He is very clever."

337

"Then he is a valuable man." Serafimo motioned for Captain Marceau to fall in behind them. "We can use all our friends for what lies ahead," Serafimo whispered in Jahane's ear.

Reynard followed the procession as it entered the castle compound, his scowl darkening when the castle servants dipped into a curtsy at Jahane's approach.

"Everyone seems willing enough to accept you as their princess," Reynard observed when they entered the throne room. He turned to Serafimo. "Have you no doubts, Brother, that this is the real Jahane? I noticed you have not set the cathedral bells to chiming, so therefore you must also have doubts. Even the people in the streets wait to hear the church bells so they might know this is the true princess."

Serafimo turned to Jahane and said softly, "There is one way that will be proof positive that you are my niece. Do you know what proof I ask?"

"And what would that be?" Reynard challenged. "I know of nothing that would prove who she is."

"But I do. It is very simple. You see, the true Princess Jahane has a mark that I can identify her by—a mark no one knows about, save one other besides myself," Serafimo stated. Again he asked of Jahane, "Do you know what mark I speak of?"

Before she could speak, Reynard scoffed. "What mark? I know of no distinguishing mark on our niece."

Serafimo smiled. "No, you would have no cause to know about the scar, but I do."

Jahane smiled slightly and stripped off her white kid glove, offering her hand to Serafimo.

"Could this be what you want to see?" she asked, knowing the scar on her palm had been important to

338

Alexander.

Serafimo held his breath as he took her hand and turned it over. He stared at her hand so long that the people in the room began shuffling their feet and murmuring.

When the archbishop glanced at Jahane, she saw there were tears in his eyes. "My dearest, dearest child, you are indeed my niece."

This time Jahane was embraced warmly, and he placed a kiss on her forehead. Keeping her near him protectively, he turned to his aid. "Go to the cathedral, and to all the churches throughout the land. Ring the bells loudly so all may know the Princess Jahane has come home at long last."

Reynard stared at Jahane, and a slow smile curved his thin lips. "So, she is truly our niece. This is good news. We must prepare a feast and in'ite all the dignitaries in the land. We have much to do to prepare for your presentation to the people, dear Jahane."

"She has already been presented to the people," Serafimo reminded him.

"But not in a grand manner which befits her station." Reynard rubbed his hands together, and his eyes gleamed from the new scheme he was planning. "I have much to do on your behalf, Jahane. You will need personal servants—a man-at-arms."

Jahane spun around and looked at Captain Marceau. "I would like the captain to accompany me if he is agreeable," she said, fearing he would be punished by Reynard for his loyalty to her.

Reynard looked down his nose at Ruel Marceau, thinking this man had much to answer for. "He cannot be your guard since he holds rank in the royal navy."

"Of course he cannot," Serafimo said in an airy

voice, his dancing eyes giving evidence that he was still enjoying himself at his brother's expense. "But I have been looking for a good man to add to my guards, and I shall assign him to look after Princess Jahane."

"You cannot do that," Reynard said angrily.

"Of course I can, if Jahane approves," Serafimo insisted, without giving Reynard time to think. His arched brow dared Reynard to defy Jahane's wishes. "I shall have the papers drawn up at once," Serafimo stated, glancing at the captain. "Is this acceptable to you?"

Captain Marceau quickly agreed, for he could see the archbishop was trying to thwart his brother, though he could not see what means the archbishop would use. "I would consider it a great honor, Your Eminence."

"Good, it is settled then," Serafimo stated. "Captain Marceau, with her approval, you will be Princess Jahane's personal guard." When the archbishop looked into Jahane's eyes, he saw her slight smile, and knew with her quick mind, she had realized that he had just outmaneuvered Reynard and saved the captain from his retribution.

Jahane smiled at Captain Marceau. "Yes, I would like that."

Captain Marceau gasped at the honor. He quickly inclined his head, since he had not been called on to speak.

"Yes," Serafimo agreed. "I will see that the commission is drawn up at once."

"Hold," Reynard stated between clenched teeth, not willing to allow his brother any part of his power. "Since I am the head of the council, I will attend to it."

340

"If that is your wish," Serafimo agreed, only too willing to allow Reynard this one concession. "Now Jahane will need a servant. Might I suggest the girl who is under my protection. Actually, because of Brynn's rank, she should be a lady-in-waiting, as her mother was lady-in-waiting to Jahane's mother."

Reynard looked as if he might protest, but thought better of it. He would give in on small matters, since he had something else in mind. "So be it," he mumbled. "Now, as to where Jahane will reside . . . Since I am occupying the royal apartments, I would be willing to vacate them immediately."

"No, please do not do that," Jahane said, looking to her Uncle Serafimo for guidance. She would much rather return to the safety of the ship, but she knew there was no going back. She had come this far and had to go the rest of the way. "I would rather not inconvenience anyone," she said.

"Let her stay in the garden rooms," Serafimo suggested. "They are light and airy . . ." and he added, looking at his brother pointedly, ". . . easy to defend against intruders. Surely you have no objections to that arrangement."

Reynard's eyes half closed, and he smiled slightly. "Then I shall keep the royal apartment until Alexander returns . . . if he returns."

Jahane's eyes widened in fear, and she glanced quickly at the archbishop. She had thought Reynard did not know her brother was alive.

Serafimo patted her hand reassuringly while he spoke to Reynard where only he and Jahane could hear. "Yes, Brother, enjoy your last bit of power, for the time is close at hand when the rightful king will come forward."

Reynard spoke through clenched teeth, no longer pretending politeness. "There is no rightful king without the royal scepter."

Serafimo glanced down at Jahane. "It may be that the hiding place of the scepter will soon be revealed to us all."

Unconsciously Jahane's eyes ran searchingly around the walls of the room. There were several tapestries, but not the depicted knights and horses. Could her remembrance of that night be at fault? Or had her father shown her a hiding place behind one of the tapestries?

Serafimo took Jahane's arm. "I am certain that our niece is weary after her long voyage, Reynard. I will show her to the garden rooms."

"Yes, do that," Reynard answered, almost absentmindedly. He moved over to the window and stared down into the courtyard. His face became a mask of fury when he saw the people still waiting in hopes Jahane would reappear. This was not the way it was supposed to happen, but he still had the power of the council behind him.

When the church bells began to peal, Reynard balled his fists. He was not going to lose this kingdom to a girl unworthy to rule, or to her brother, who by rights should be dead.

As the archbishop led Jahane from the room, Captain Marceau fell in behind them at a discreet distance.

Jahane turned troubled eyes to her uncle. "Uncle Serafimo, does Uncle Reynard know about Alexander?"

He glanced about him before he answered. "Yes, he knows that Alexander lives, but he does not know where he is. I suppose your brother contacted you in San Francisco. But what I don't know is why you are here."

"Yes, I saw Alexander. As to why I am here, Uncle Reynard's man, Cyryl Dionysos abducted me."

"A crafty, sly man," Serafimo admitted.

Jahane smiled. "Yes, but not as crafty and sly as Captain Marceau. The captain outfoxed the man and is now holding him prisoner on board the ship."

"Well done. We shall see that the good captain is rewarded. Meantime, I want him to stay near you, for your safety. And I suspect for his own safety as well. If I could, I would take you out of the castle, but if you leave, the people will believe that Reynard had succeeded in driving you away. We must keep you here at all costs."

"Uncle Serafimo, I do not understand all this struggle for power. It should be simple to tell the people that Alexander is their true king and he is alive. Would that not solve everything?"

By now, they had stopped before a door, and Serafimo gripped her by the shoulders. "I wish it were that simple, but I fear it isn't. If Alexander were here, and we could produce the scepter, then, and only then, would our troubles be over."

"I see—or think I do."

"I have to ask, Jahane, do you recall where the scepter was hidden?"

"I . . . think I might be able to find it—but I'm not certain."

Serafimo held up his hand. "Say no more. Keep your secret until the right moment. Tell no one—not even me."

The archbishop motioned for Captain Marceau to come forward. "Have you a gun?" he asked.

"Yes, Your Eminence."

"Then do not be afraid to use it. Take up a position in front of this door and do not allow anyone inside besides myself or a woman named Mrs. St. John and a younger woman by the name of Brynn. Is that clear?"

"Does that include Duke Maxime?" the captain asked.

The archbishop quickly removed his ring of office and shoved it on the captain's hand. "Show this to anyone who wishes to cross this threshold, and tell them you have my orders not to admit them. This ring will protect you, even from my brother." He smiled at the young man. "Are you concerned for your ship and crew?"

"Yes, Your Eminence."

"Do not be. I will attend to them for you." Suddenly he laughed aloud. "I will also release your prisoner."

The captain did not know if he should join in the laughter, since he had never been in the company of the archbishop, so he merely nodded.

"Tell me, Captain. Have you any men on your ship that you trust without question?"

"Yes, there are several that I would put my trust in, Your Eminence."

"Give me their names, for I shall send them to you so you might enlist them in protecting the princess." He turned back to Jahane. "I do this because Reynard would never allow more than one of my guards in the castle at once."

Jahane reached out and placed her hand on Captain Marceau's. "For all your devotion, I am grateful. I will feel safe knowing you will be guarding me."

"I will give my life for you, Your Highness."

"Do not dare," she said, smiling. "I want you alive."

Captain Marceau's eyes became troubled. "Pardon me, Your Highness, but I could not help overhear you speak of Prince Alexander. Is it possible that he lives?"

Jahane exchanged glances with her Uncle Serafimo. "We can trust him, Uncle."

Serafimo nodded. "Yes, Captain. Prince Alexander is indeed alive. But I would caution you not to mention this to anyone. His very life may depend on your secrecy."

"I will tell no one," the young captain vowed earnestly. His eyes were bright as he stood at attention.

Serafimo laughed. "Enjoy your last day of freedom, Captain. Tomorrow you will be in charge of the princess's safety."

Jahane smiled at the captain as her uncle opened the door to her chambers and led her inside. When the door was closed behind him, he spoke. "Tell me, my dear child, is there news of your brother?" he asked softly, as if he feared being overheard.

"I was preparing to sail to Balmarhea with him when I was abducted, Uncle Serafimo."

"Will he come soon, do you think?"

"I believe he will. Cord Meredith, the man whom I . . . lived with as his sister for all these years, is captain of his own ship. I do not believe he will allow many days to pass until he comes after me."

"You trust this Cord Meredith?"

"With my very life. He is the bravest, the most honorable—"

Serafimo held up his hand. "I understand, my dear. Now I would like to tell you a little about the girl, Brynn, who will be coming to be your servant. She was once in Reynard's hands, and he was preparing her to present to the people as . . . you."

"What?"

"Yes, he thought to use her as he uses everyone to his advantage. She is a sweet girl, and deserves your kindness, for when she refused to tell Reynard what she knew about your brother, she was severely tortured."

"That monster. I shudder to think how many people have fallen under his evil guidance. I am afraid of him, Uncle."

He kissed her cheek and smiled at her. "You are safe for now. And even though I must leave you for a time . . ." He squeezed her hand reassuringly. "Have no fear, I will not allow anything to happen to you."

"Trust no one, Jahane, with the exception of your Captain Marceau, my housekeeper, Mrs. St. John, and Brynn. If we surround you with enough loyal subjects, Reynard would not dare harm you."

Jahane placed her hand on her uncle's, wishing he didn't have to leave. "It is very unsettling to believe my own uncle would wish to harm me."

Serafimo became grave. "Believe it, Jahane. Reynard will try every trick he knows to stay in power. He realizes either you or Alexander knows where the scepter is located. Be warned that he will do anything to get his hands on the scepter. Until your brother arrives, forget you know where it is hidden. At the right moment, we shall reveal its hiding place."

Jahane watched the archbishop walk away, wishing he would take her with him. When the door closed behind him, she felt more alone than she had ever felt in her life. Even though she knew Captain Marceau was standing guard outside the door, she was frightened.

Looking around the room, she saw that it was very luxurious, but cold and impersonal.

She longed for her home in San Francisco, for the gentleness of the woman she had always called Mother. She wanted more than anything to feel Cord's arms around her—comforting her—and to have him assure her that everything was all right.

Moving across the room, she stood at the door that opened out into a secluded garden.

The events of the day had been very unsettling to her, and she felt drained.

If only she could see Cord and have him assure her that everything would be all right.

Chapter Thirty

Jahane sat in the garden beneath a clear blue sky trying to visualize what her life would have been like if she had grown up in this castle. But then she would never have known Cord if she had lived her life here.

Even though this was her ancestral home, she felt it belonged to her Uncle Reynard.

Glancing toward the western horizon she saw the gathering of dark storm clouds and shivered. Closing her eyes she breathed in the sweet smell of Jasmine. Vaguely, in the back of her mind, she remembered a beautiful golden-haired woman who also smelled like Jasmine. She remembered the woman speaking softly to her and Jahane knew this was her first clear remembrance of her mother. She supposed her homecoming and the smell of Jasmine had brought back memories she had blocked out since childhood.

Jahane was so caught up in her thoughts she did not hear the two women who now stood before her.

Opening her eyes Jahane was startled to find she was not alone.

The elder woman, dressed as a servant in a white

mob cap and stiff white apron, was the first to speak. The woman's eyes sparked with excitement as she swept into a deep curtsy and addressed Jahane.

"Your Highness, I am Mrs. St. John, and I have been sent to you by the archbishop to serve you." She pointed to the young woman beside her. "This is Brynn, and she is also to serve you."

"Thank you, Mrs. St. John, Brynn." Jahane nodded to each in turn. "I have been told to expect you."

For a moment, Jahane's eyes lingered on Brynn. Was she mistaken, or was the girl avoiding her eyes.

Mrs. St. John spoke up. "Your Highness, I am to tell you that the archbishop desires all the food you eat to be prepared only by myself, and it will come from the archbishop's own kitchens."

Jahane could not keep the horror out of her eyes. "Does my uncle fear I will be poisoned?"

"It is his wish that we not take chances with your health." The elderly woman smiled. "I will be like a hawk, Your Highness. No one will be allowed to serve you, other than Brynn or myself."

"Did my uncle say anything else?" Jahane asked wearily.

"He cautions you are not to go anywhere without either myself or Brynn or Captain Marceau."

Again Jahane looked at Brynn. Now the young woman was staring at her so hard, and when her eyes met Jahane's, she ducked her head.

"Brynn is such a pretty name. Are you a friend of my Uncle Serafimo's?" she asked, remembering that her uncle had said the woman had suffered because she would not betray Alexander.

"I have not known your uncle long, but he is a wonderful man," Brynn answered shyly.

"Hush, girl," Mrs. St. John cautioned. "One must not refer to the archbishop as a man. Go into the small room we shall be occupying and unpack your belongings, child. I shall send for you if you are required."

Jahane watched with a puzzled expression as Brynn departed. She sensed something very sad about the young woman and wondered what it was.

"Your Highness, the reason I sent Brynn away was so I could speak to you alone. The archbishop asked me to tell you about Brynn's plight so you might keep a protective eye on her."

"My uncle told me something about her. But, yes, tell me what you know."

Mrs. St. John's mouth set in a severe line. "She was extremely ill-treated, Your Highness. Evidently she is a friend of your brother, the prince. For that reason, Duke Maxime had her beaten and tortured. But I must add," the housekeeper went on, "she told the prince nothing, although she was horribly beaten."

Jahane gasped, her hands balling into fists. "You can be sure I will not allow my Uncle Reynard to get his hands on Brynn again."

The housekeeper curtsied, and a smile covered her face. "This is a happy day for us, Your Highness. You have given us renewed hope. And when your brother comes home, we shall rejoice anew."

"You spoke of my brother. It was my understanding that most of the people believe he is dead."

"That is so. Only a few know he survived that awful night. Unfortunately, Duke Maxime is one who knows."

When Mrs. St. John departed, Jahane sat for a long moment in silent thought. Looking to the west, she saw the distant clouds had darkened the sky and were blocking out the dying rays of the sun. Today had been her homecoming, but somewhere deep inside, she felt a loneliness so painful that she cried out.

Again she glanced at the gathering storm, and she felt trouble brewing like the dark clouds that swirled and boiled in the distance.

The wind and the rain pounded the *Golden Phoenix*. Her timbers creaked and groaned with each violent wave that slammed against her hulk.

Cord stood at the helm, bringing her into the same secluded lagoon where his father had anchored on that bloody night so long ago. He was glad for the storm, for no one would be expecting them to come ashore in such tumultuous weather.

After Cord gave orders to drop anchor, the ship pitched and rolled drunkenly on the waves.

With urgency in his dark eyes, Cord ordered all lights extinguished and the longboat lowered.

Since no one on board the ship knew Alexander's true identity, Cord had been referring to him as Mr. Beaudette, and he did so now. "Thadeus, Mr. Beaudette and I are going ashore, and I am leaving you in command. If the storm becomes too violent, you might want to sail away from land. I shall leave it up to you, since you are capable of making that decision."

"But, Captain, sir, it isn't safe to go ashore on such a night . . ." Thadeus's voice trailed off when he saw the determined look on Cord's face. "But, then, you always know what's best, Captain."

Suddenly Cord remembered another night when his father had made the decision to go ashore on this very beach. "If anything goes wrong, Thadeus, and I don't come back, you must sail for home. You know what to do."

Before the first mate could answer, Cord turned to Alexander. "I hope you know how to row, because it's to be only two of us in the longboat."

Alexander buckled his ancestral sword about his waist and nodded grimly. "I learn quickly."

Both men went over the side, climbed down the swaying rope ladder, and dropped into the boat below. With every ounce of strength they possessed, they rowed in the direction of the distant shore.

At first it was difficult going, since the waves slapped them back against the hulk of the ship. With the rain peppering their faces and the wind tearing at their clothing, the two men soon set the right rhythm and rode the waves to shore.

When they touched shore, Cord motioned for Alexander to help him hide the boat behind a clump of bushes. After this was accomplished, he spoke. "I have brought us thus far, Alexander; now it is up to you to take us the rest of the way."

The storm intensified as Alexander led them inland. Silently, they moved beneath the cover of trees and bushes, keeping well away from the main path that led to Montique.

Soon the rain was so heavy and the wind so strong, they had to stop to seek the shelter of a large tree. Alexander saw a dim light glowing in the distance. "It must be a farmhouse," he yelled out to be heard above the storm, motioning for Cord to follow him as he walked toward the lights.

Cautiously, Alexander led them around the house to the barn. When he pushed the barn door open, it creaked on rusty hinges, but the fury of the storm drowned out the sound.

"We will just borrow the horses," Alexander stated, feeling his way in the dark until he came to the horse stalls.

"A prince who is a horse thief," Cord said, as he felt along the wall until he found the bridles.

"I have no time to ask the farmer's permission tonight," Alexander supplied. "The farmer will be repaid later."

Handing Alexander one of the bridles, Cord quickly slipped his over the head of one of the horses. Hastily, both men led the horses out of the barn, then leaped on their backs and headed toward the city at a fast pace. Pulling their cloaks about them for protection from the raging storm, they thundered on into the night.

It was almost midnight as the two weary travelers reached the city of Montique. Since the hour was late and the storm still raged fiercely, the streets were deserted.

The impact of the horses' hooves striking the wet cobblestones sparked fire, and the echo was swallowed up by the thunder that shook the ground.

There was no happiness in Prince Alexander's heart at returning to the city of his birth; there was only fear for his sister, and an urgency to find her. He had planned to come home at the head of a great army, not riding through the deserted streets like some thief in the night.

The bell tower of the cathedral loomed ahead of them, and Alexander spurred his horse onward. Riding through the archway of the cathedral, the prince slowed his horse and motioned for Cord to dismount.

"We will lead the horses to the back and put them

in my Uncle Serafimo's stable in case we are being watched."

Cord nodded, following Alexander's lead. Both men were anxious and troubled, their minds on the golden-haired princess they both loved.

The chapel was deserted but for the lone figure who knelt before the altar. The candles burned low in their sconces as the Archbishop of Balmarhea bowed his head in prayer. He had been on his knees for hours, and his bones ached and his back hurt. He raised his tear-stained face to the golden cross, a whispered prayer on his lips. These were troubled times, and he was not so sure he could protect Jahane from Reynard.

Serafimo felt the cold of the stone floor work its way into his whole body as he beseeched God to keep Jahane safe from Reynard's evil plans and to bring Alexander safely home.

The archbishop was so deep in prayer he did not hear the opening and closing of the heavy door. Something, a sound or a feeling, alerted him to the fact that he was not alone. He glanced up when a shadow came between him and the flickering candlelight.

"Are you praying for me, Uncle?" Alexander spoke up from the shadows.

Serafimo's eyes blinked, and he rose shakily. His cheeks were still wet with tears, but there was a spiritual light in his sparkling eyes. He stared at Alexander for a long moment, then he beamed with great joy. "At the moment, you look more like a drowned rat than crown prince of Balmarhea." He moved forward, embracing his nephew, unmindful of the young man's dripping cape. "Welcome home, sire. You have been sorely missed."

"I came as quickly as I could, Uncle."

"God be praised! First your sister is back with us, and now you. My prayers have been answered."

"Is Jahane safe?" an urgent American voice spoke up from the doorway. "Is she here with you?"

The archbishop glanced into worried brown eyes, and he knew this must be Jahane's Cord Meredith. "My niece is safe enough for the moment, but unfortunately she is not here with me." He answered in English, then he switched to his native tongue. "Do you speak French?"

"Yes, I do," Cord said, answering him in kind.

"Uncle, this is Cord Meredith. I could not have come so soon if he had not brought me aboard his ship," Alexander explained, smiling at the captain who had become his friend and companion.

"I assumed as much," the archbishop said. "Jahane has spoken of you, Captain Meredith."

"I want to see Jahane and know she is all right," Cord said in an urgent voice.

The archbishop stared for a moment at the American, then he spoke in a warning voice. "Regrettably, that will not be possible tonight." Serafimo then turned to his nephew. "Your sister is in the castle."

Alexander's face paled. "Surely not under Uncle Reynard's protection?"

"I have done all I could to ensure her safety, but I could not take her from the castle." Serafimo's eyes danced. "You should have seen how readily the citizens accepted Jahane when she came through the streets on her way to the palace. She was received with waves of love."

"But could you not have brought her here with you,

Uncle?"

"No. She could not have abandoned the castle to Reynard once she had established herself as Princess Jahane. Be assured that Reynard is not so foolish as to harm her yet. But, he will soon decide on how she can best serve his purpose. And that is when we must worry."

"When can I see Jahane?" Cord insisted. "I need to know for myself that she is unharmed." His eyes grew wild. "She will be frightened." Now his eyes were beseeching as he turned them on the archbishop. "You see, she has this recurring nightmare, and if no one is there to comfort her . . ."

"I am sorry, my son, but it would look too suspicious if we were to go to the castle tonight. Reynard will have his spies about, and they will report my activities to him."

Serafimo looked into the American's anxious eyes. "Every move we make from here on out must be thought out and the consequences weighed," Serafimo stated. "I believe I can get you into the castle tomorrow. But you will have to do everything I tell you."

"I will do what I must to help Jahane," Cord assured him.

"I want to see Jahane also," Alexander declared. "Would it be possible for me to go with you tomorrow?"

"No, you cannot!" the bishop said in a booming voice. "Reynard will be on the lookout for you. He will set traps for you, and try every trick he can to have you under his power. We must be more clever than he, and we must keep your presence a secret until just the right moment."

"I suppose," Alexander admitted in a surly voice. "I

had hoped the long years of waiting were over."

"They are, my young king. Just a few more days. Can you wait that long?"

Alexander's eyes locked with his uncle's. "I can wait."

There was satisfaction on the archbishop's face. "I see you have learned to curb your impatience, Alexander. That is one of the best qualities a monarch can have."

Cord glanced at Alexander with sudden awe. He had not thought of Alexander as a king, but then he had been having as much trouble thinking of Jahane as a princess. "Is there no way I can see Jahane tonight, Your Eminence?" he wanted to know.

"No, my young American friend. You might want to learn patience also. Your life would be forfeit if my brother discovers your identity." The archbishop smiled again. "But come. We must get you out of your wet clothing. I have many questions to ask, and much to tell you. And, we have plans to make."

Thunder rattled the windows in Jahane's bedroom, and sleep eluded her. She was feeling frightened and alone. If she had been back at home in San Francisco, she would have gone to Cord's room and he would have comforted her. But, no, not anymore. Cord had comforted her for the last time. She would now have to put her fears aside, or face them, once and for all.

She got out of bed and moved to the window. Throwing back the curtains, she opened the window and allowed the pelting rain to hit her in the face. A sudden gust of wind whipped up, and the lamp flickered and almost went out.

Jahane had no sense of direction here in Montique, but she looked toward where she thought the sea might be. Cord was out there somewhere in that storm. But not even the storm would stop him from coming to her rescue.

Now that she had met her Uncle Reynard, she experienced great fear for Cord and her brother. Reynard was a dangerous man, and someone had to stop him.

Closing and locking the window, she moved back to her bed and lay down. She was shivering and didn't know if it was from cold or fear.

After extinguishing the lamp, she squeezed her eyes together tightly, wishing she could sleep.

Finally, in the early morning hours, she did fall into a restless sleep, and the old familiar dream came to her.

The dream was drawing her back under its spell, and she was pulling back the tapestry of the horses and removing the shiny object from its secret hiding place. Then there was pain, oh so much pain.

Jahane did not realize she had cried out. Suddenly, soft hands rested on her brow, and a gentle voice came to her from out of the darkness.

"Do not fear, Your Highness. It's Brynn, and you were having a nightmare. Shall I sit with you until you are feeling better?"

Jahane clutched at Brynn's hand. "Yes, please sit with me, talk to me—do anything that will help me forget that horrible dream."

Brynn lit the lamp and pulled a chair to the side of the bed. Jahane was still frightened, and she reached for Brynn's hand.

"It was only a bad dream, Your Highness. I have them all the time."

358

Jahane looked into soft blue eyes and saw concern. "It is a nightmare that comes to me from out of the past. I have come to believe it will never go away."

"Perhaps you would like to talk, Your Highness. That sometimes helps me when I am frightened," Brynn suggested. She looked timidly at Jahane. "Actually, I pretended a lot as a child, and when I was frightened, I would pretend I was talking to a friend."

Jahane plumped up her pillow, feeling her fear receding. She remembered what this woman had suffered, and smiled kindly at her. "Tell me more about your childhood," she urged.

Brynn's eyes were troubled. "Your Highness, I hope you will not find it presumptuous of me . . . but I . . . when I was small, imagined Prince Alexander as my friend and confidant."

"I do not find that presumptuous. But when you were a child, did you not think my brother was dead?"

"Yes, Your Highness, and that made it all the more tragic, for I kept him alive in my heart. When I saw His Highness for the first time, and knew he was alive, I knew boundless joy."

Jahane glanced into Brynn's eyes, seeing them soften at the mention of Alexander's name. "You love my brother, don't you?"

Brynn took a deep, ragged breath. "Yes, Your Highness, but he does not know, and I would not want him to think . . . that I . . . that I . . ."

Jahane's eyes clouded with anguish as she thought of her own bittersweet love for Cord. "I will say nothing to my brother, Brynn, for I know how hurtful it is to love a man whom you can never belong to."

Brynn shook her head in disbelief. "Oh, no, Your Highness, not you. Any man would consider it an

359

honor to be loved by one as beautiful as yourself."

Jahane only smiled sadly, remembering her Uncle Serafimo telling her that Brynn was supposed to have been presented to the people of Balmarhea as their princess. Oh, how she wished Brynn was the princess of Balmarhea. Then Jahane would be free to marry Cord, and he would be allowed to love her.

Chapter Thirty-one

The storm had moved away, and the heavy rains left behind a sweet aroma of cleanly washed earth.

Cord was alone in the archbishop's study. He was seated on the window seat, looking across the city to the castle beyond.

From his vantage point, the castle appeared to be an impregnable fortress. He felt helpless, knowing that somewhere in that giant of stones and mortar his love was being held captive and there was nothing he could do to free her.

"Jahane, Jahane," he whispered. "We are so near, and yet you are so out of my reach. I will not rest unless you tell me you are where you want to be."

He had not heard the soft footsteps that carried the archbishop in his direction. "Jahane may not be where she wants to be, my son, but for the moment we cannot get her out."

The archbishop smiled. "But be of good cheer. Remember you shall see her in a few hours."

"Is there some way I can be with her? To protect

her? I don't like the thought of her being in that place without protection."

Suddenly laughter emitted from the archbishop's lips. "I believe you have something there, Captain. I think I may be able to set you up as Jahane's guard. Yes, I will surround her with a wall of those who are devoted to her. That should keep her safe for the time being."

"Can you do that?" Cord asked, hope coming alive within him.

"Yes, but only if you do exactly as I say. As I have already told you, Reynard will have his spies, and if you show any undue attention to the princess it will be reported back to him. You must act as if she were a person that you revere, but would never dare address, unless she speaks to you first. Will you be able to do that?"

"I — yes."

"And you will not forget to speak in French? Actually, it would be better if you spoke as little as possible, since you do not speak like a native of Balmarhea."

"If it will get me in that castle to see Jahane, I will agree to anything you say."

"Don't be too hasty, my young friend. You cannot possibly understand the intrigue you will be walking into. Never let your guard down for one moment. And remember to keep a cold distance between yourself and Jahane. If my brother suspects who you are, you will be in peril."

"I'll take that chance," Cord said, unconsciously slipping back into English.

"In French," the archbishop cautioned. "Speak only in French."

Serafimo turned away and moved to the bell pull. "Now, you must retire for the night—or what is left of it. I will have a servant escort you to your sleeping quarters."

Serafimo's expression became grim. "These are dangerous times we are living in, my son. In the balance hangs Alexander and Jahane's lives. You will do exactly as I tell you, and we may just be able to save them both from my brother."

"I will do whatever you think is best if it will help Jahane. And I have come to admire Alexander . . . er . . . the prince."

"In another time and place, you and Alexander would have been very good friends. On observing the two of you this evening, I can see you are very much alike."

"I have a great deal of respect for his courage, Your Eminence."

"And he has spoken well of you. I was grieved when he told me of your father's death. You see, I was the one who handed Jahane over to your father on that night he died. Your father was a very worthy man. Someday, when we have the time, I will sit with you and tell you what a courageous man your father was."

"I would like that, Your Eminence."

The archbishop saw the tired lines under Cord's eyes, and he spoke kindly. "Go and rest now, Cord Meredith, and one day when this is all over, I will tell you how grateful my country is that you and your mother have kept Jahane safe for all those years. It is a pity you had to sneak into our city. Because if the citizens knew of your deeds, you would have been welcomed as a hero."

"I only want to know that Jahane is safe, Your Eminence." Cord moved to the door. He had much to think about tonight. His heart was a little lighter, for he would see his beloved later in the day. Of course, he would have to treat her in a cold and impersonal manner, and that would be the hardest of all. It would be worth any sacrifice, though, to look upon her face. Just to be near her would be his recompense.

The night was silent as Serafimo entered his nephew's bedroom. Finding the prince standing by the window with a meditative expression on his face, the archbishop sat down and motioned for Alexander to do the same.

Staring at his uncle, the prince shook his head. "I have waited for a long time for this day to come, and now that it is here, I have no plan, no loyal soldiers to follow me. I do not know what to do, and I have not the means to take back what belongs to me."

Serafimo nodded in understanding. "I learned yesterday that you will not need soldiers to take back Balmarhea, Alexander. You will have the people behind you. It is the people who deny Reynard the right to rule. Did you not hear me tonight when I told you how the citizens of Balmarhea rallied around your sister? Do you think an army of trained men could have accomplished what they accomplished?"

"What do you mean?"

"I mean that the people have held Reynard away from the throne for years. He tried torture, starvation, and every kind of force he had at hand, and yet still they did not recognize him as their leader. Without the scepter he has been unable to obtain his fondest wish."

"But—"

"Such a glorious sight it was today when your sister came through the streets, cheered on by her loyal subjects. Merciful heavens, Alexander, how readily they accepted her, and how eager they will be to have you ascend the throne."

Alexander was still not convinced. "My subjects have long thought me to be dead."

"There have been rumblings and rumors for years that Prince Alexander is not dead but only waiting for the right moment to return and lead his subjects to victory. Every time the rumor would begin to die down, I would make sure it was stirred up once more."

"But, Uncle, will they know and accept me as their rightful king?"

"They will believe me when I tell them that you are Prince Alexander, because they know I am always truthful to them. And they will believe Jahane when she shows them you are her brother."

"What I do not understand is how Uncle Reynard holds his position at the castle. Has no one challenged his right to administer the laws?"

"The strongest and most powerful men in our country are either dead or imprisoned, because they challenged him. Then there are men like that viper, Count Arville, who carries out Reynard's orders without question. Reynard has cleverly surrounded himself with those loyal to him, and it has been impossible for the people to unseat him without a leader. The best I could do was to make certain there was always a council of Reynard's peers to balance his power."

Serafimo laced his fingers together. "And, of course,

the people of Balmarhea have always looked to our family to lead them. Reynard is of the royal family, which offers him a certain amount of deference."

Serafimo noticed the tired tilt to his nephew's head, and he stood up. "We have much more to discuss, but there are difficult times ahead of you. It is best if you rest now."

"Uncle," Alexander called out, stopping Serafimo's departure, "have you any word of the girl, Brynn? Is she still at your hunting lodge?"

A light of regret hardened the archbishop's eyes. "No. Not long after your departure Reynard's men found her and took her to the castle."

For a moment Alexander felt the pain of loss, and then skepticism creased his brow. "Was she taken, or did she go with them willingly?" He had been unable to forget about Brynn, and now the thought that she was once more under his Uncle Reynard's domination hardened his heart against her. He had expected her to be waiting for him, and the fact that she was not, made him suspect her of being on Reynard's side and against him.

"She was forcibly taken," Serafimo said with assurance.

Doubt added a chill to Alexander's voice. "She could have escaped into the woods. She went with them willingly enough."

"We will talk of Brynn at another time. You look ready to fall over, and I want you to get some rest." Without giving Alexander time to protest, Serafimo was out the door, and closing it behind him.

The young prince moved to the bed and lay back. Yes, he was so weary, and he did not want to remember Brynn tonight. He did not want to think about how soft her skin had been, or how sweetly the fragrance of her hair had haunted him. No, he would not think about the sweetness of her lips when he had— With a smothered oath, he turned his back to the window, striving to block out his memories of Brynn. He wondered if she had betrayed him to Reynard. Had she told his uncle that he was alive?

In the throne room Reynard ranted at Count Arville. With a jeweled hand stabbing the air, his voice came out in an angry roar. "What do you mean my son has left the island?"

Lord Arville lowered his eyes, unable to bear the duke's heated glance. "I was told that your son, along with several of his friends, took ship for Spain. It is said that on hearing of his cousin Princess Jahane's triumphant entrance into the city, he fled. The viscount swears never to return to Balmarhea."

Reynard's face was a mask of bitterness and rage. "The sniveling coward. How could such a weakling come from my seed? If Dameron ever does return, I shall have his limbs torn from his body and his remains fed to the buzzards."

"He never has been willing to serve you as I have," Arville said, seeing his chance to ingratiate himself still further into the duke's confidence. "I am always ready to do whatever you ask. You will find no other as loyal to you as I, Your Grace."

Reynard sneered. "You are like all the rest of them. You will be loyal to me as long as I line your pockets with gold. I have strived to form a kingdom of strong, worthy subjects, and instead I am surrounded by fools and cowards."

Lord Arville swept into a deep bow. "My aim is only to serve you, Your Grace."

Reynard studied Count Arville. The man had to be in his sixties, and he was not of any great wealth. "How can you be of any use to me? I had hoped to marry my son to the Princess Jahane, and I certainly cannot marry her to you." Suddenly Reynard's eyes brightened. "How old is your son, Gillis? As I recall, he has never married."

"Nay, my son, Gillis, has never married because he is simpleminded and is content to remain on my country estate. His only interest is raising hunting hawks."

Reynard's eyes gleamed with a sinister light. "How old is Gillis?"

Lord Burgess was baffled for a moment. "I'm not sure. I believe he is somewhere in his forties."

Now Reynard smiled, the scar on his face curling his lips in a sinister expression. "Yes, it might be to my advantage. Your son comes from a good family. If I recall, your wife was from a noble French family."

"That is so," Lord Arville admitted, wondering why Reynard was being so inquisitive about his family.

"By God, we will do it!" Reynard cried, bringing his fists down hard on the arm of his chair. "Go at once to the country and have your son made ready. Bring him here as quickly as possible!"

When Reynard saw the confused look on Count Arville's face, he spoke in an irritated voice. "Well, hurry, man. We have little time if this is to work."

Neither Reynard nor Arville saw Mrs. St. John as she passed in the hallway. When she heard the duke's

368

voice, she pressed her back to the wall and listened.

"I am not certain what you want me to do, Your Grace," Lord Arville said in a befuddled voice.

The duke gave the man an intolerant glance. "What do you think I have been saying? Go to the country and prepare your son for a wedding. Gillis is going to marry Princess Jahane!"

Shock registered on Lord Arville's face. "But Gillis is incapable of being any woman's husband. The princess would never consent to marrying him."

"She will marry him, because she has no choice. Through her, I shall rule Balmarhea."

"But you cannot without the scepter, Your Grace," the count reminded him.

"It's true Jahane cannot be crowned without the scepter, but the people will want her to be the figure-head. I, of course, will be the real power."

"But what of Prince Alexander? You know he is still alive."

"He may be alive for now, but I will soon deal with him. Did you not have guards at all ports?"

"Yes, Your Grace. If the prince comes back to Balmarhea, it will be impossible for him to slip past us."

"Have someone keep an eye on the cathedral. I want my brother the archbishop watched day and night."

Mrs. St. John did not stay to hear more. She was trembling with fear as she hurried along the corridor, down the steps, and out into the bright sunshine. She had to get to the archbishop and tell him of the plot the duke was hatching. Feeling sick inside, she stopped to catch her breath. She had never known such wicked-ness existed. The duke must not be allowed to carry through with his evil plan. Surely the archbishop would be able to stop him.

Serafimo moved through the castle garden until he saw Jahane sitting near the fountain. With a smile on his lips, he hurried to her. She was trailing her hand in the clear water, and thinking she was alone, had given in to the loneliness she was feeling.

Seeing the wistfulness in her expression, Serafimo spoke. "My dear child, surely you grow more lovely each time I see you. Apparently the air in Balmarhea agrees with you."

She smiled up at him. "I have seen little of Balmarhea, Uncle, save on the way from the ship."

"I assume you are feeling a bit homesick for your California."

She nodded. "Yes, I confess I am. I know this is the country of my birth, and I want to do what is expected of me, but I do so miss the only family I can remember."

"That is as it should be, child. The Merediths were good to you. I would be disappointed in you if you did not remember them with fondness."

"Have you had any news of Alexander?" she asked hopefully.

"Before I answer that, I wonder if you would come with me," he said, taking Jahane's hand and pulling her to her feet. "We can be observed here, and there is something I want to show you that I do not want others to see."

"Yes, of course, Uncle," she said, curious as to what he wanted to disclose to her.

The archbishop led Jahane down the rock walkway, to a corner of the garden that was enclosed by flowering hedges. With a warm smile, he pushed her forward. "Go on, my child. There is someone who wishes to see you."

Jahane's heart was pounding as she slipped behind the hedge. When she saw Cord, a deep sob escaped her lips and she raced across the distance to throw herself into his arms.

Tears were flooding down her cheeks as he held her in his arms. "You are here," she sobbed. "Oh, Cord, I knew you would come for me."

"Jahane, Jahane," he murmured over and over, crushing her to him so tightly she could scarcely breathe. "My dearest love, I feared I would never see you again."

Looking up into his face, she saw his eyes were shining with adoration. Perhaps it was only the love a brother would have for his sister reflected there, but there was no denying he cared for her.

"You are wearing the uniform of one of my Uncle Serafimo's guards," she stated, not knowing what else to say.

"I had to so I could slip past your Uncle Reynard's guards."

Her eyes clouded. "This is a troubled country, Cord. Danger lurks at every turn, and yet it is my country. You do know that whatever happens I will have to remain here?"

"Yes, I do know that." The admission tore at his heart. "I know our lives will never be the same, Jahane, and the day will come when we will be parted."

She clung to him. "Until that day, stay beside me,

Cord. Be my friend and my strength. For with you near, I have always been at my best."

His lips rested against her cheek, and he allowed love to flow through his body to hers. "I will stay near as long as you need, my dearest one."

"Mama, how is she, Cord?"

"She is stronger than I thought. Before I sailed, she accompanied my trunk to the dock." He pulled away from Jahane and reached into his pocket. Handing her the pouch that contained the ruby, he smiled. "Mama thought you might need this."

Jahane clutched the stone in her hand, fighting against her tears. "I wish . . . I wish . . ."

His eyelids flickered in pain. "I know, Jahane. I wish I could take you home with me, too, and that we could pick up our lives as before. But we both realize that can never be."

Her lips curved in an almost smile. "I assume Alexander sailed with you."

"Yes. Your uncle has convinced him to remain hidden in the cathedral. He sends his love to you."

"I hope you will caution him to be careful. I have met my Uncle Reynard, and he is a frightful man."

"The archbishop will make sure that your brother remains hidden," Cord assured her.

"How long can you stay, Cord? Shouldn't you leave before someone discovers you here?"

He enfolded her in his arms, wishing he could whisk her away from the dangers. "You will be seeing quite a lot of me, Your Highness. For I am to be one of your guards."

She pulled back and stared at him in disbelief. "You?"

She stepped back and surveyed his green-and-gold uniform, thinking how handsome and dashing he looked. Jahane saw that the jacket fit snugly across his wide shoulders, while the pantaloons outlined his long, muscular legs. He clicked the heels of his black knee-high boots and bowed gallantly, a smile on his lips. "Do you not think I will pass as the archbishop's guard?"

"Indeed I do," she beamed, knowing she would feel safe with Cord looking after her.

Before they could say more, Serafimo joined them. "You must go now, Cord. Stand guard at the front door, and remember from here on out, when you see Jahane, you will treat her like a princess and nothing more."

Cord stared into Jahane's eyes for a long moment. "I never lose sight of the fact that she is a princess," he said at last. With a sad smile, Cord turned away, moving out of the garden.

"Will Cord be in danger?" she asked her uncle.

"We are all in danger, my dear. But I suspect your American would have it no differently."

"He is truly wonderful, Uncle Serafimo."

The archbishop grinned at the golden-haired beauty. "I can see that he is not exactly indifferent to you, either, Jahane."

"Yes, but we both know nothing can ever come of our love. I do not believe Cord would want me for his wife, even if circumstances were different. He loves me as a sister. While I . . . while I . . ."

"Perhaps it is just as well, Jahane. For he would never be allowed to reach so high as to touch the hem of your garment. You are a royal princess, and no commoner may ever hope to wed you."

"I wish it were not so, Uncle."

He took her hand and squeezed it. "So do I, child. So do I."

Chapter Thirty-two

Alexander lay on the curtain-draped bed, trying to curb his impatience. He and his Uncle Serafimo had talked for hours and made plans for the moment Alexander would at last face his Uncle Reynard.

What Alexander wanted to do was walk boldly up to his Uncle Reynard, denounce him to his face, and take up his rightful place as king. But, as he had learned, justice was slow in coming, and there were many preparations yet to be made.

First of all, they had to arrange for Serafimo to take Jahane on a tour of the castle without rousing Reynard's suspicions. They hoped something would trigger Jahane's memory and she would recall where their father had hidden the scepter. Alexander realized that to face Reynard without the scepter would be foolhardy indeed.

A fierce smile curved Alexander's lips as he thought of the pleasure it would give him to run his Uncle Reynard through with his sword.

He was so deep in thought he did not hear the soft rap on his door. When the rap came again, this time more forcefully, he muttered, "Come in."

Alexander shot up from the bed when Brynn shyly stepped into his chamber.

At first the two of them could do no more than stare at each other. Then Alexander remembered that Brynn had been with his Uncle Reynard, and his lips turned down in a scornful frown.

"So, you have discovered my hiding place, Brynn. Do you come here so you can report back to my Uncle Reynard?"

Her face fell, and she shook her head. "No, Your Highness, I would never inform on you. Mrs. St. John reluctantly told me that you were here . . . and I . . . wanted . . . to be sure you were well."

"A likely story," he scoffed. "Why would Uncle Serafimo's housekeeper give my hiding place away to you when she is loyal to me?"

He nodded at the door. "Are Uncle Reynard's guards waiting outside the door to take me into custody?"

A tear trailed down Brynn's face. "No, Your Highness. No one accompanied me here. As for your Uncle Reynard, I would tell him nothing."

Alexander advanced toward her, and Brynn cringed at the steely look in his blue eyes.

"I thought about you often enough," he admitted. "I had hoped when I returned, I would find you waiting for me at the lodge." He reached out and touched her soft cheek. "But you didn't wait, did you? How long after I had gone did you wait before you betrayed me to my Uncle Reynard?"

"I told you, I did not—"

Alexander allowed his hand to drift down her neck and across her breasts, pleased when he felt her tremble at his touch. "Did my uncle also test the delights of your body? Did you allow him the liberties you allow me?"

She shook her head, wondering why he was being so accusing and cruel. "I would sooner die than have your uncle touch me, Your Highness."

"How easily you lie. You even have my Uncle Serafimo convinced of your innocence. He believes you were forcefully taken away from his lodge. He has been taken in by your innocent looks, just as I once was."

Her slight body quaked. "Why are you saying this to me? I . . . why?"

Alexander was not listening to her words. His hand had drifted up to tangle in her golden hair, and, against his will, he brought her forward, resting his face against hers. "You have woven your way into my brain, and if I am not careful, I will give up a kingdom just to possess you again. You are the best weapon my uncle could send against me, for you almost make me forget everything but the feel of your body and the sweetness of your kiss."

"Your Highness, please, no. Do not shame me with your words. I am not the way you think."

He jerked her head up and stared at her lovely face. "Are you not? What secrets are locked behind those soft eyes? What lies are spoken from those soft lips, Brynn? How many men have fallen under your spell? Did my foolish cousin Damerou experience the joys of your body?"

"No, no!" she cried. "You know I never saw him."

By now Alexander was eaten up with jealousy and beyond reasoning with. "Why could you not wait for my return, Brynn? I would have given you anything you wanted — wealth, power, recognition."

She wanted to run from him, to flee to a quiet place where she could cry out her pain, but she did not. She tossed her head and looked into his eyes, ready to defend herself against his insults. "Are you offering me marriage, Your Highness?"

He looked at her with an expression of irritation. "No, you know that would not have been possible. But I would have elevated you so high, no one would have dared look down on you."

"Your mistress, perhaps?"

"Yes . . . no, more."

"What could be more?" she taunted.

"I could have cared for you, Brynn." His voice was almost accusing.

She drew in her breath and looked into his blue eyes. "You could have?" she asked, her heart beating a wild tempo.

"Yes. But now —" His hand moved to the laces at the front of her gown. Slowly and deliberately, he unlaced the tie. When Brynn made no motion to stop him, he pushed her gown over her shoulder, then moved forward, pressing his lips against her creamy skin.

"Please, no, Your Highness. Not like this," she pleaded, taking a step backward.

Her plea went unnoticed. His eyes were wild with passion as he glanced back at her. Pulling her to him with a smooth motion, he pushed her gown to her waist. When she only stared back at him with blank eyes, he hooked his finger through her chemise and pulled it down, exposing her upper body.

He was so overcome by her beauty he could not

look away. His eyes moved over her silken skin, and he could hardly control his need for her.

"What does it matter if I take you on a small cot deep in the woods or in a silk-draped bed?" His voice was unsteady. "I will have you, Brynn."

She reached out and touched his face, saddened by the torment she felt in him. How could he believe she would betray him? "You will regret later if you do this, Your Highness."

"Regret, never. You can give me what I want or I will take what I want. It is of no matter to me."

Her eyes were swimming with tears. "I will give you whatever you want, Your Highness. But afterward, I will never want to see you again."

Alexander was beyond hearing her words. With a quick tug, he yanked her gown, and it fell in a satiny heap at her feet.

Brynn cried out when he lifted her in his arms and carried her to the bed, where he quickly removed her remaining clothing. With an exclamation of impatience, he stripped his clothing off and joined her on the bed.

She backed away from him, ashamed that he might see the horrible lacerations on her back that had been left by Hogarth's whip. She did not want him to see what she thought was a horrible disfigurement.

Alexander's eyes softened, and he reached out, drawing her to him. "Brynn, do not fear me. You should know I will not harm you." His voice deepened. "I just want to bury myself inside you and stay there forever."

Blood ran hot in Brynn's veins at his suggestion. Raising her arms, she laid back against the pillow and welcomed him to her.

Alexander closed his eyes, filling his mind with the satiny body he held close to him. As he sunk into her, he felt his body come alive as never before. All he took from her, he returned with soft-spoken words, a gentle kiss, a caress.

Brynn watched Alexander's face as he made love to her. She wanted to remember his golden body long after this day, long after he had ascended the throne and chose a queen to sit beside him.

Her lips softened under his hot kisses, and she wished she could stop time so she could hold on to Alexander for eternity.

Suddenly Alexander's lovemaking became intense. He drove into Brynn with a punishing force. His lips smothered her protests as he satisfied his animal needs. Brynn's pain quickly turned to pleasure, and she clutched him more tightly to her. She tore her mouth away from Alexander's, and a deep groan of pleasure escaped her lips.

When Alexander brought his desire to the very pinnacle of human pleasure, he knew she belonged to him as she would never belong to another man.

For a moment, they were both caught in the lingering effects of their lovemaking. At last Alexander raised up on his elbow and gazed down at her through half-closed lashes as his doubts and accusations returned.

"Now, Brynn, you can go to my Uncle Reynard and tell him you have just been ravished by a king. That is something he will never be."

She saw the mocking glint in his eyes, and she tried to twist away from him. To her relief, he released her, and she slid off the bed, pulling the coverlet about her.

"If you are finished with me, sire," she said with as much dignity as she could manage, "I will be leaving now."

Alexander came to his feet, pulling his pants on. "I have very definitely finished with you, Brynn."

He turned away from the hurt he saw in her eyes, wondering why he should feel so guilty. She deserved what he had done to her.

Moving to the window, he kept his back to her. He could hear her pulling her clothing on, and he wanted to turn back to her, but he did not.

Without a word, she moved to the door, opened it, and closed it behind her softly.

Brynn moved quickly down the hallway, out through the back garden and toward the archbishop's stable. Surely she could be forgiven for borrowing one of the archbishop's horses.

No one attempted to stop her as she selected a mare and heaved herself on its back. With fear that Alexander would come after her, Brynn urged the horse forward, not daring to breathe easy until the stable was far behind her.

Riding out the gates of the city, Brynn did not care where she was going. Her spirit was crushed, and her heart felt like an open wound. She could feel the blood running down her back and staining her gown, and she realized her wounds had opened up again.

Blinded by tears, Brynn raced down the roadway, unmindful of where her thundering steed was taking her. She only wanted to put as much distance as she could between Prince Alexander and herself.

Alexander was still gazing out the window when Serafimo entered his room a short time later.

The archbishop, seeing the scattered coverlet on the floor, picked it up and was about to toss it on the bed, when he saw the tumbled state of the bed and the bloodstains on the sheets. He turned quickly to his nephew with an inquiring glance.

"What is this, Alexander? Where did the blood come from?"

Alexander's eyes followed his uncle's gaze, and his brow furrowed into a frown. "What blood?"

Serafimo pointed to the sheets. "There."

Alexander was puzzled. He had not physically harmed Brynn. He certainly had not hurt her so she would bleed.

"You might as well know, Uncle Serafimo. Brynn was here, and I am not sorry for what happened between us."

Serafimo stared at his nephew, as realization sunk in. "Do you mean you took Brynn?" he asked in amazement. "That innocent girl who has been so misused by Reynard? I suspected what happened between the two of you at my hunting lodge. But now . . . how could you do this to her?"

This was the first time Alexander could ever remember his uncle's anger being directed at him. "I did not force her, if that's what you think. She was willing enough after a while. And I have no notion where the blood came from."

"I am ashamed of you, Alexander. How could you not see the pain you were inflicting on her? Do you know what you have done?"

382

Guilt did not set well with the young prince. Inside, he was devastated that his lovemaking could have caused Brynn pain, but evidently it had, though God knew he could not think how.

On the defensive, Alexander raised his head haughtily, nodding at the bloodstains. "I am not responsible for that."

"No, not directly. But how could you have been so intimate with her and not known about her suffering?"

"What suffering?"

"You do not even know about that." Serafimo took in a deep breath, trying to find patience. "I told you that Reynard's men had taken Brynn."

"Yes, but I told you I thought she went with him of her own free will. You have been taken in by her look of innocence, as I once was."

"You are either a fool, Alexander, or you are trying to dismiss your guilt by making it appear as if Brynn was the guilty one."

The prince's eyes flamed. "Careful, Uncle. I may be many things, but I am neither a ravisher of women nor a fool."

"Alexander," Serafimo declared in exasperation. "Brynn was forcibly taken from my lodge. When Reynard questioned her about you, she would tell him nothing. She was beaten and tortured, and still she would tell him nothing about you. It was only by my agreeing to tell Reynard that you were still alive that I was able to gain her release!"

Alexander felt all the life drain out of him as he glanced at the bloodstained sheets with better understanding. "She was beaten?"

"Brutally beaten."

"My God, what have I done?" he whispered in agony. "What have I done to her?"

"I suppose you can be forgiven for desiring Brynn, but why did you not see she was injured?"

"Uncle Serafimo, she did not cry out or indicate that she was . . . hurt. The cuts on her back must be very deep if they bled so profusely."

Alexander's eyes grew suddenly tormented. "I have to find her, Uncle. I have to make her understand why I did what I did. But then I don't understand myself, so how can I make her understand?"

"I think I understand your reason, Alexander," his uncle said kindly. "I do not condone what you did, but I know when a young man is in love, he sees every man as a threat to his woman. Your father was always possessive of your mother."

The young king raised his head and met the archbishop's eyes. "I felt betrayed by Brynn. I thought she preferred my Uncle Reynard to me. There is no excuse for what I did, but I have to find her and beg her forgiveness."

Serafimo's eyes softened with understanding. He realized Alexander was of a kind disposition, and he would never intentionally harm a woman.

"What mood was Brynn in when she left, Alexander?"

The prince's eyes clouded with misery. "I had the feeling she never wanted to see me again. I now understand why—after the accusations I flung at her."

The prince picked up his shirt and pulled it on. "I am going to find her."

Serafimo placed a restraining hand on his shoulder. "You cannot leave this room. I will send someone to search for her. It could be that she has returned to the castle to be with Mrs. St. John. Pray that she does not fall into Reynard's hands again."

"Make sure she is found and brought to me at once."

"It will be as you say. But now I have something else to discuss with you. It has just come to my attention that Reynard is calling together all the nobles to meet at the castle two days hence."

"But why?"

"I am not sure why. I have been thinking about it, and have decided there could not be a better time to have you come forward and face Reynard than before the assembly of the nobles."

"How could I come forward without the scepter, Uncle?"

"You cannot. Jahane has only two days to remember where your father hid the scepter."

"You must take her around the castle at once. We have little time left to us. But if you feel she is in danger, remember my sister is more important than the scepter."

"Yes, that is what I think."

"I feel so helpless. I should be the one to find Brynn. And Jahane should not have to go through this alone. I do not feel like a king—rather I feel like a fool hiding out and allowing others to do everything for me."

"But you are the rightful king, sire. All that is lacking are the scepter and the crown. The final and most dangerous move will be yours."

Serafimo smiled and turned to the door. "You will have time enough to thank Jahane, and time enough to admit your faults to Brynn once you are king."

Leaving the room, the archbishop's footsteps quickened when he saw Mrs. St. John rushing down the corridor. When Serafimo called out to the housekeeper, she turned frantic eyes upon him.

"Oh, Your Eminence, thank goodness I have found you. There are grave happenings at the castle. Duke Maxime has evil plans for Princess Jahane!"

Chapter Thirty-three

Jahane moved across the room, her blue silk gown swaying gracefully over the wide hoop she wore. Standing before the mirror, she brushed her hair and secured it to the back of her head with two ivory combs.

She glanced at the clock, wondering where Mrs. St. John and Brynn could be. They had both been gone most of the day, and it was not like them to leave her alone for so long.

Unable to endure the loneliness any longer, she moved to the door, hoping Cord would be on guard there. Even if it was dangerous to be seen talking to him, she needed the comfort of seeing him.

To Jahane's disappointment, instead of Cord, she encountered Captain Marceau. His new uniform announced that he was in the archbishop's guard, instead of the royal navy.

"Good afternoon, Captain." Jahane smiled. "Have you been on duty long?"

The captain stood at attention, only too aware of his duties to watch over the princess. "Yes, Your Highness. I have been at my post for three hours."

She glanced down the long, dimly lit corridor. "Have

you seen Mrs. St. John?"

"No, Your Highness. I have seen no one."

Jahane tried not to think about the oppressive loneliness that waited for her on returning to her quarters. How could she sit here for days doing nothing, when it was so important that she find the scepter for Alexander?

A sudden gleam lit her blue eyes as an idea grew in her mind. Why could she not move through the castle on her own and search for the tapestry she had seen in her nightmares? If she located the scepter would it not help Alexander in his fight against their Uncle Reynard?

But that would be impossible because the castle was enormous. Down the corridor, she could see many twists and turns that led in several different directions. How would she ever find her way around?

"Captain, are you familiar with the layout of the castle?" she asked hopefully.

"Not to any great extent, Your Highness. But now that I am your personal guard and have come under the archbishop's household, I am allowed access to this wing and many of the rooms on the first level."

"Then you could guide me through the common rooms and the antechambers?"

He looked doubtful. "If that is your wish, Your Highness. But my orders from His Eminence were to pay particular attention to your safety. I am not certain it would be—" His voice broke off as he realized it was not his position to instruct the princess.

Jahane was silent as she weighed the consequences. "Since knowing you, Captain, I have always been safe in your company." She closed the door to her quarters and glanced up the corridor. "I put great trust in you. Shall we go?"

The captain would honor the princess's wishes, even though it was against his good judgment. He would rather not have allowed her to be exposed to danger or placed in a situation where she could encounter Duke Maxime.

"I will guide you, Your Highness," he agreed.

As they walked along, Jahane searched her memory to recall anything she could about the room her father had taken her to that night. All she could remember was that it was a huge room, but when one is small, everything seems enormous, she reasoned.

"Captain, I want only to see the chambers which are of significant size."

Although she was frightened, Jahane put on a brave face as she walked beside Captain Marceau down the long, twisting corridor. She knew it was not wise to wander through the castle without the protection of her Uncle Serafimo, but was not discovering the scepter worth the risk? she reasoned.

They walked past great arched doorways which meandered off in different directions, and Jahane realized she would never have found her way without the guidance of Captain Marceau.

When they came upon the landing where wide marble stairs led down to the first floor, Jahane tried to push her apprehension aside.

She remembered entering the castle the day of her arrival. She had been too frightened then to take notice of her surroundings, but now she saw the magnificent grandeur of the castle and its furnishings. The rug runners her feet sank into were deepest blue. There was heavy wooden furniture, with chairs covered in delicately woven materials. Gold, silver, porcelain, and crystal were on display in every room they passed through. To Jahane's way of thinking, the castle was more like a museum than a place of residence.

Captain Marceau paused before an open doorway. "This is the main antechamber, Your Highness," he explained.

Jahane peeped around the door, and finding the room empty, stepped inside. The room was enormous. With couches and chairs covered in heavy, dark-blue material, it appeared to be a room for entertaining.

Quickly Jahane's eyes ran the length of the walls, searching for the tapestry of the horses. But, to her disappointment, the walls were decorated only with shields, swords, battle axes, and weapons from long-dead kings.

"Let us see another room, Captain," she said, feeling trepidation rising up inside her. She had to find the tapestry—she just had to!

Captain Marceau led Jahane to several other chambers. Some of them were ballrooms, and still others were for receiving guests and dignitaries. In each room, Jahane's eyes would search the walls, but without success. Fourteen years was a long time. What if the castle had been redecorated and the tapestry moved?

In a panic, she wondered if her dream had only been a fabrication and not real at all. But no, her Uncle Serafimo had told her dreams had been based on reality. Why had she not asked her uncle which room her father had taken her to on that fatal night?

"And to what do we owe this unexpected pleasure," a sinister voice spoke up from behind Jahane.

Recognizing Reynard's voice, she spun around to face him, her eyes locking with his. Dropping her eyes, so her uncle would not read the revulsion she felt for him, she took a step closer to Captain Marceau.

Reynard was dressed in black, his fingers circled with jewels, and Jahane found him not only a strutting peacock, but an odious man. There was something about the way he watched her that made her cringe inside.

"Good afternoon, Uncle Reynard," she said through stiff lips. "I had a desire to see the castle. After all, I was born here."

"Of course. I made a suggestion to Serafimo just the other morning, that I give you a tour of the castle, but my brother has become very possessive of you, my dear. He seems to think he can keep you to himself." Reynard appeared calm outwardly, but a muscle which twitched in his tightly clamped jaw revealed his agitation. "We shall just have to take Serafimo to task for his selfishness, shan't we, my dear?"

Jahane mentally pulled away from this man who repulsed her. How could she be civil to the person who was reputed to be responsible for her parents' death. "I have seen little of Uncle Serafimo, but I do not find selfishness to be a fault of his."

Reynard laughed knowingly. "Ah, yes, he is regarded as a most saintly man. But I know how often he visits with you, Jahane." His voice deepened with feeling. "You see, I have ways of following my brother's movements." Reynard added as an afterthought, "As he does mine." He stared down his nose at her, while ignoring Captain Marceau. "But tell me, Jahane, how can I be of service to you?"

He reached out his hand to her, and she stepped back with alacrity. "No," she said hastily. "I only wanted a glimpse of some of the rooms. After all, this was once my home."

He pretended not to notice her aversion to him. "It still is your home, my dear."

"That is a lovely old tapestry," she said, changing the subject and turning away to look at an aged yellow-and-blue tapestry hanging above an arched doorway.

"Yes. At one time we had many fine tapestries in the castle. But many of them were so old and delicate, I had them packed away."

Jahane felt her heart sink. If the tapestry of the knights and horses was one that had been removed, she would never find the scepter. "I am very interested in family heirlooms, Uncle Reynard, and tapestries in particular. We have nothing like these in America, where I was raised."

"Then you should see the great hall, for that is where we display the more spectacular needlework." He offered his arm to her. "Would you allow me to escort you there?"

Jahane tried not to look at the hideous scar on his face, but she was also reluctant to look into his hard, cold eyes. She balked at being in close contact with him, and yet she had to see the grand hall. Even now, she feared the secret of the scepter might be lost forever, and therefore her brother would never be crowned king.

"Yes, please, Uncle," she said, placing her hand on his proffered arm. She glanced back to make sure Captain Marceau would accompany them. "I would like very much to see the great hall."

As they moved along the well-lit corridor, Reynard studied Jahane intently. She was very like her mother, and that alone was unsettling to him. If he had regretted giving the order to put anyone to death that fateful night, it had been the order to slay Queen Eleanor. She had been so like every man's dream of what a queen should look and act like. Yes, Eleanor had been a very beautiful woman, and she was one of the few people who had ever been kind to him.

Thrusting his dark thoughts to the back of his mind, Reynard smiled amicably. "I am glad to have this chance to converse with you, Jahane. I have made special plans to ensure your future happiness. I hope when I reveal them to you, that you will find them agreeable."

She glanced at him suspiciously. "I would have to know what the plans were before I could be agreeable."

"I will tell you about it all in good time, Jahane." He pushed open two double doors that creaked on their hinges. Then he led her into a huge room that was in shadows and without benefit of light. Strange multicolored patterns fell across the floor from the enormous stained-glass window high above their heads. The room had a musty smell, as if it was never in use.

"What a strange room," Jahane observed, shivering from some unknown dread.

Reynard looked at her through narrowed eyes. "As you may have already suspected, this room stays shut up. If any ghosts inhabit the castle, they will have chosen this great hall."

She already sensed the reason, but she had to have

it confirmed. "Why, Uncle?"

Now Reynard looked into Jahane's beautiful face, thinking how much she and her brother had cost him. He wanted to strike out at her, to break that haughty calm that reminded him so much of her dead mother.

"The great hall is not used because this is where your mother and father were killed." He took pleasure in the gasp that escaped Jahane's lips and the color that drained from her face. "Yes, this is where it happened, Jahane. So, therefore, no one wants to be reminded of that grim fact by entering this room."

Jahane felt her throat close off, and she took a step backward, clutching at the door handle to keep her balance. When she glanced at Captain Marceau, she saw the anger on his face as he openly glared at Reynard.

"Why did you bring me here?" she asked accusingly, meeting Reynard's eyes.

"Why, my dear," he said in innocence. "It was you who expressed an interest in the tapestries. I was merely satisfying your curiosity." His dark brows came together above the middle of his nose. "You did want to know where your mother and father died, did you not?"

Suddenly Jahane knew terror so strong that it seemed to rip the air from her body, and she felt her legs go weak. "I am not feeling very well," she said, reaching out her hand to Captain Marceau. "Please help me back to my room, Captain."

The captain rushed forward to her aid, but Reynard stepped in front of him. "But since you are here, Jahane, should you not see the tapestries?"

She met Reynard's cold glance with one of her own,

suddenly knowing it was important that she not show her fear. "Yes, since I am here, Uncle. Show me around the room."

Reynard set the pace to walk slowly around the room, explaining to Jahane about each lovely ancient needlework. But, with growing apprehension, her footsteps quickened as she moved from one tapestry to another, feverishly searching for the one that had haunted her dreams.

After every tapestry had been carefully examined, she felt her spirits plummet. The one she searched for was not here. Knowing she must not arouse Reynard's suspicions, she decided to give up the search for today and search another time with her Uncle Serafimo.

"I have seen enough for one day," she said, allowing herself a sweeping gaze of the room that had known so much violence. It cut at her heart to think her parents had come to a brutal end here. She tried not to think of the scene of blood and suffering that came to her mind.

Jahane did not realize her face had whitened. She stumbled toward the door, but Reynard took her arm and turned her to face him. "My dear, this has been an upsetting day for you. Had I known you were of such sensitive nature, I would not have told you the history of this room."

Jahane saw the delight in his eyes. He had deliberately tried to frighten her. "It is not often a girl is shown where her mother and father were murdered, Uncle. I would have thought you more sensitive to human feelings."

Their eyes met and battled. The white scar stood out on Reynard's face, and his eyes became even colder.

Jahane felt rage in the deep recesses of her brain. She wanted to fling the guilt of her parents' death into this hateful man's face. She wanted to scream at him that she knew him for an evil man. But calm reasoning prevailed, and her good judgment returned. She asked pointedly, "By whose hands did my mother and father die, Uncle Reynard? Have you found and punished their murderer?"

"Jahane!" Archbishop Serafimo cried, coming into the room and rushing to her side. "When I discovered you missing and the guard gone . . ." Serafimo enclosed her in his arms while he stared at Reynard. He noticed that the anger he had seen in Reynard's eyes when he first entered the room had now turned to caution.

"Why have you brought Jahane here to the great hall?" the archbishop questioned.

Reynard shrugged his shoulders. "I found Jahane wandering around, Serafimo. And when she expressed an interest in the wall hangings, naturally I brought her here. I merely helped her satisfy her curiosity."

Serafimo directed Jahane toward the door. "I will be taking her back to her quarters now." He flung back over his shoulder, "You might have spared her this room."

Jahane leaned gratefully on her Uncle Serafimo, also comforted by the fact that Captain Marceau walked just behind her.

"Uncle," she whispered so only Serafimo could hear. "Reynard is a truly evil man. I was so frightened of him."

"And well you should be, Jahane. Whatever possessed you to go alone into the lower level of the

396

castle?"

"I . . . know it was a mistake. I only hoped I might locate the tapestry of my dreams."

"Child, child, you do not know what danger you faced there today."

"I felt . . . he, Uncle Reynard . . . hates me."

Serafimo paused and looked down at her. "You might as well know right now, Jahane. Reynard will stop at nothing to get what he wants. Now that the people of Balmarhea have poured out their love to you, he will try harder than ever to defeat you."

Taking her arm and leading her up the steps, the archbishop wondered how he would tell Jahane of Reynard's latest scheme. "The reason I came to call on you this afternoon was an urgent one, Jahane. We have to do something at once!"

Serafimo glanced back to see that Captain Marceau was following at a discreet distance. "We have to act tonight, Jahane, or it will be too late."

"I do not understand."

By now, they had reached Jahane's quarters, and Serafimo turned to the captain. "Do not allow anyone to interrupt us, Captain. We have grave matters to discuss."

Without giving Jahane a chance to consider his words, Serafimo pulled her in the room and closed the door behind him. When she would have spoken, he placed his finger to his lips and led her out into the open garden.

"Uncle, you are scaring me. What has happened? Has anything happened to Cord or Alexander?"

He gripped her by the shoulders and shook his head ruefully. "Nothing has happened yet." He searched for a delicate way to tell her what he must. Seeing no other way, he blurted out, "You must be married soon . . . tonight, Jahane."

"I . . . what?"

"I will perform the ceremony in secret, and tonight the marriage must be consummated. Yes, that is the only way we can stop Reynard."

Jahane looked at her uncle as if he had lost his mind. "You had better explain what you are talking about. I will do many things for you, Uncle. But you might as well know right now, I will not marry against my will."

He smiled at her kindly. "Forgive me, Jahane. I have been babbling senselessly. It is just that Reynard has plans of his own for your marriage."

The color drained from her face. "Tell me what has happened!" she insisted.

He let out his pent-up breath. "I have news of a sinister plot that Reynard is hatching." He touched her face and endeavored an encouraging smile. "He has made plans to marry you to Count Arville's son. The man is somewhat dim-witted, and he could easily be manipulated by Reynard."

Jahane's mouth flew open in disbelief. "I will not have it! No one can make me marry someone I do not want to marry." Her eyes became defiant, reminding Serafimo of Queen Eleanor. "Not even for you will I do this, Uncle."

"Of course not," he agreed. "Alexander and I have discussed this all afternoon, and your brother has decided upon a plan that I think you will approve. We will beat Reynard to the altar. You will be married to a man of our choice."

Jahane shook her head in disbelief. "Whether it is a man of Alexander's choosing, or of Reynard's choosing, I will not be manipulated."

The archbishop smiled and pulled her into his arms. "But, child, your brother is not heartless. I shall marry you to the man of your heart."

"Cord?" she asked breathlessly.

"Of course, Jahane. You did not think your brother and I completely unfeeling, did you?"

"But I . . . what has Cord said to this?"

The archbishop's eyes looked past Jahane as if he saw something she could not. "I have not told him yet, but I am certain when he learns of Reynard's devilish plan, he will be only too willing to comply."

"No," she moaned, feeling as if her life was being controlled by everyone. "I will not have Cord. You do not understand; he does not love me in that way."

"Jahane, you do not have any choice. This is not San Francisco, where in polite society men and women woo and wed at their own discretion. These are dark times. For each move Reynard makes, we have to make a countermove. If you are not married to Cord Meredith tonight and the marriage consummated so it cannot be annulled, you will find yourself married to a stranger, and one who has no other interest than to please Reynard."

Jahane clasped her hands together, her eyes desperately searching the archbishop's. "I know you would not do this if it were not necessary. But you forget, Cord is not a citizen of Balmarhea, and he is not bound by our laws or by Alexander's decision."

"This is true, Jahane, but he seems to be fond of you."

"Of course he is fond of me! But fondness is no reason to marry someone. No, it is utterly impossible. I refuse to allow you and Alexander to use Cord."

"Suppose he is willing?"

"How can you ask Cord to marry where he does not love?"

"Many have started marriage with far less. At least you will admit he has a great fondness for you. Your own mother and father saw each other only the day before their wedding, and yet they grew to love each other deeply."

"This is different. I do not want Cord to be involved in the plots and intrigues of my country."

"He has already involved himself, Jahane."

"Suppose he agrees to help me, but only if he can have his freedom later on. Can you do that?"

"I am not an archbishop for nothing. After all this is over, and if Cord Meredith is dissatisfied with the arrangement, I will find a way to obtain an annulment."

Jahane drew in a deep breath. In coming to Balmarhea, she had entered a world she did not understand, a world where people were like pieces on a chessboard, to be moved and controlled to suit the players.

In her head she had a vision of how Reynard had looked when he told her about the deaths of her mother and father. A game or no, she was but one of the pawns. And, oh, poor Cord would become an unwilling participant. She wondered if he would agree—and if he did, would he regret it afterward?

"All right, Uncle Serafimo, if Cord is willing, I will be married to him tonight. But only if you assure him he can be free when this is all over."

"That I can do, child."

Jahane realized that Cord would probably agree because he was a wonderful man and he would never allow her to be married to one of Reynard's puppets.

She turned away from her uncle so he would not see her tears. Suppose Cord was repulsed by her when the time came to consummate the marriage? She did not want to think of being rejected by him again, for she did love him so desperately.

"Jahane," Serafimo spoke up, "I am sorry to have to leave you, but there is much to do."

"I will await word from you, Uncle."

He patted her shoulder. "It will be all right, Jahane. It is far better to marry you to your sea captain than allow Reynard to have his choice of grooms thrust on you."

Jahane heard his retreating footsteps, feeling no joy in her heart that this would be her wedding day and she would be marrying the man she loved.

Chapter Thirty-four

Jahane was in a daze as Mrs. St. John placed a wreath of jasmine blossoms on her golden head.

"You look lovely, Your Highness. Just the way a bride should look."

Jahane glanced down at the white gown she wore, trying to realize that within the next hour she would be Cord's wife. Still not convinced this was happening, she looked at the archbishop's housekeeper.

"Tell me again, Mrs. St. John, what my Uncle Serafimo said to you about the wedding."

Mrs. St. John pursed her lips and studied the angle of the jasmine wreath, then tilted it more to the front of Jahane's head. "The archbishop instructed me to have you prepared for a wedding as quickly and as secretly as possible. He said to tell you that he and Captain Meredith would be here at eight. So nothing will appear out of the ordinary, Captain Meredith will be dressed as one of His Eminence's guards."

"Did you see Captain Meredith?"

"No, Your Highness. I saw only your brother and

His Eminence."

Jahane paced the floor. "If only I could be certain I was doing the right thing. I dislike being forced into marriage, and most of all, I loathe the notion that Cord is being forced to be my bridegroom."

Mrs. St. John's eyes were soft with understanding. "Your Highness, I know how difficult this must be for you, and if I might be allowed to give you a word of warning, it is far better that you marry your American than to marry the groom the duke has in mind for you."

Jahane pushed her doubts to the back of her mind, knowing if she examined her feelings too closely she would fall apart inside. "What time is it now, Mrs. St. John?"

The housekeeper glanced at the watch she had fastened to her apron pocket. "It is almost time to go, Your Highness."

Cord stood by the open window, allowing the warm night breeze to fall on his face. His eyes moved over the others in the room. There was the archbishop, of course, who would be conducting the ceremony, and the archbishop's assistant whose priestly regalia cloaked his identity. He had been told that Mrs. St. John would also be in attendance. Not at all the kind of wedding he would have chosen for Jahane and himself.

Cord could feel himself being drawn tighter and tighter into the politics of Balmarhea. When the archbishop had explained to him the situation Jahane faced, he had not hesitated to agree to take her as his

403

wife.

What he really wanted to do was take her back to San Francisco where she would be safe. But he reminded himself that she had not been safe there. The archbishop had told him that Jahane would not be safe until her brother sat on the throne of Balmarhea.

Serafimo joined Cord at the window. "It is a nice night for a wedding, my son."

Cord looked past the archbishop to the priest who stood silently before the garden door. "I could have found a more reasonable time to marry Jahane."

Serafimo laughed and clapped Cord on the shoulder. "I have to agree these are not the ideal circumstances." He glanced at the clock on the mantel. "The time for objections is now. You can still change your mind."

"You know I will not do that, Your Eminence."

Cord, standing stiffly before the archbishop, allowed his eyes to wander toward the bedroom, where Jahane was dressing for their wedding. He wore a white uniform with the gold epaulets on the shoulders. At that moment, he would gladly have exchanged the dress uniform of the archbishop's guard for his own captain's uniform.

Cord now knew why bridegrooms always confessed to being nervous before their weddings, because it was an unsettling experience for him even though he wanted nothing more than to make Jahane his wife.

The archbishop smiled understandingly. "Just think what an anxious state you could have worked yourself into, my son, had you known when you arose this morning that you would be a bridegroom before the day ended. This way, you had very little time to ponder the situation."

Cord stared down at his shiny black boots, weighing his answer. "No amount of preparation could have prepared me for the way I feel inside, Your Eminence. As you said, it is just as well that I had no time to think."

"But this is what you wanted, my son. I recall you telling me that you loved Jahane. Have you changed your mind about that?"

"No, I will never change in my feelings toward Jahane. I just do not approve of forced marriages. I can only imagine what she must be feeling at this moment."

"Have no concern for Jahane. As I have often pointed out to her brother, they have the blood of kings flowing in their veins. It is my belief that you can take one of royal blood and raise them as a common citizen, and they will still be royal underneath."

"That may well be, Your Eminence," Cord agreed, "for Jahane has always possessed a quality that could not be put into words. But whatever it was set her apart from other young women her age."

"Do you have the ring?" the archbishop asked, glancing at the clock.

Cord fished in his pocket and drew out the ring the archbishop had handed him earlier in the evening. On examining it, Cord saw that one solitary diamond danced and sparkled as if it were alive.

"This was my mother's ring," Serafimo explained. "I thought it appropriate that Jahane should wear her grandmother's ring, since she was named for her."

Cord pushed the ring back into his pocket and glanced once more at the bedroom door. "I recall very clearly that you and Alexander both told me that I could never marry Jahane. You indicated that she could only wed into the nobility."

"If these were normal times, that would be the case. But since so much rests on tonight's ceremony, we are forced to overlook the fact that you are a commoner."

Cord arched an eyebrow, and he saw the humor in the situation. "Of less than royal blood, perhaps, but never common."

Serafimo smiled slightly at Cord's attempt to make light of his predicament, then his expression became grave. "Alexander and I have taken steps to ennoble your station, Cord Meredith. We are only waiting for your bride to appear before we enact those rites."

"I do not think I understand what you are saying."

Now the monk, who had been silent all evening, spoke. "Allow me to explain," Alexander said, throwing off his black cowl and facing Cord.

"But it is dangerous for you here," Cord said, stating the obvious.

"Did you think I would allow my sister to be married and not attend?"

At that moment, the door was opened and Mrs. St. John came into the room. She smiled at Cord and dabbed at the tears on her cheeks. "We are ready, Your Eminence," she said to the archbishop, stepping back to stand with her hands clasped in front of her.

With a rustle of silk, Jahane came through the door. She was dressed in a white dress that billowed over a wide hoop. Her only adornment was the wreath of

406

jasmine that rested atop her golden hair. Like the princess she was, she was dazzling and beautiful. Every eye was on her, and all were silenced by her striking beauty.

Cord felt his heart thunder inside him as she gave him a look that conveyed remorse. He gave her that special smile he had always reserved for her alone.

Jahane stood hesitantly for a moment, unable to take the last steps across the room to Cord. She was grieved that he was being trapped into marriage, but she would make certain he knew he could have his freedom later, if he so desired.

A strong hand reached out and gripped her wrist, and she gasped when she saw it was Alexander. Bending, he touched his lips to her cheeks, and whispered, "You should have known I would be here."

"But it is so dangerous."

His smile silenced her. "Come, I will deliver you to your bridegroom."

There was no music, but Jahane's heart was singing. There were no large crowds in attendance, but everyone Jahane cared about, other than Cord's mother, was present.

As she closed the distance between herself and Cord, she was aware that the one missing ingredient in this marriage would be Cord's love.

Now Jahane and Alexander were even with Cord. But instead of Alexander handing her over to Cord, he left her beside his uncle. Jahane gasped when her brother withdrew a sword from the folds of his robe and rested the tip against Cord's shoulder. Then it occurred to her what he was doing.

407

"Kneel down, Cord Meredith; you are about to be knighted," the young king stated solemnly. "It is necessary that I elevate your station in life so you can marry my sister."

"Is this necessary?" Cord asked. "This was not part of the agreement."

"Cord," Alexander said with patience. "You must understand that in the event that something happens to me, Jahane will be crowned queen. Therefore, she must have a husband who will be acceptable to the people. We Balmarheans are a snobbish lot; we do like our royal lineage to be pure."

"I will not consent to this," Cord stated stubbornly. "As I see it, all the royal houses of Europe would benefit from a dose of pure American blood."

"Must you do this?" Jahane asked. "Can you not just go on with the wedding?"

"No, Jahane," the archbishop spoke up. "This is as important as the marriage." He looked at Cord. "Will you not do this for Jahane's sake?"

With grim determination, Cord dropped to his knees.

Alexander, with the solemnness of the situation reflected in his eyes, raised the sword so the shiny blade shot out prisms of light. Touching each side of Cord's shoulder, he recited the ancient rites. "I dub thee Lord Cord Meredith, First Baron of Devenue. Rise and accept your title."

Cord stood up, his eyes on Jahane's. He saw the teardrop playing on the tip of her lashes, and he knew this night was more of an ordeal for her than it was for him.

Alexander took Jahane's hand and placed it in Cord's. The archbishop waited for their attention, and then he started the ceremony.

As Jahane rested her hand on Cord's arm, she could feel the taut muscles, and knew he was holding himself rigid. She could only guess at the thoughts that were going on in his mind as the noose of the marriage knot was tightened about his throat.

"Do you, Baron Cord Meredith, take the Princess Jahane Isabeau Beaudette, as your lawfully wedded wife?"

The ceremony went by in a blurred haze. Words were spoken—answers given—and then it was over.

Jahane stared in disbelief as her uncle pronounced that she and Cord were man and wife. When she looked into Cord's dark eyes and he ducked his head to place a chaste kiss on her lips, she was stunned.

Was that all there was to it? Was she really Cord's wife?

There were no shouts of congratulations, only a sudden feeling for haste. Alexander kissed Jahane's cheek. "I have only recently found you, and to loose you so soon." He shrugged. "I shall have to keep you near me all the same."

Her Uncle Serafimo had taken Cord to the other side of the room, and the two of them had their heads together. Alexander slipped his black hood over his head and waited at the door to be joined by his uncle.

In a flurry of good-nights, the door was opened. Mrs. St. John, Alexander, and Serafimo passed through, closing the door behind them. Cord and Jahane were alone.

Slowly, Cord advanced across the room to her. Jahane could read nothing from his dark eyes, but she was so nervous she blurted out the first thing that came to her mind.

"So . . . what did you and my uncle talk about just now?"

Cord, by now, towered above her. His lips curved into a smile, and he raised her hand to his lips. "Your uncle was advising me to consummate the wedding at once," he said in a deep, meaningful voice.

Chapter Thirty-five

Jahane felt hot blood pumping in her veins as Cord took her hand. "I never wanted you to be involved in this, Cord. I am sorr—"

He placed a finger over her lips and smiled down at her. "I have been involved in your life for a very long time, dearest Jahane. Did you think I would allow you to marry another man when I could be your husband?"

Her eyes were earnest as they sought his. "No, Cord. I knew when Uncle Serafimo told me about Reynard's latest plan that you would come to my rescue. You have always come to my aid; why should now be any different?"

He pretended seriousness. "Indeed, it was a difficult thing I was called upon to do tonight."

"Oh, Cord," she cried, turning away from him so he could not see her distress. "It must appear to you that I was bound to have you. I hope you do not think that I contrived—"

His amused laughter cut her off in midsentence, and she whirled around to face him. "Why are you laughing at me?" she asked with indignation.

He reached out and pulled her into his arms, allowing her sweetness to fill his whole being. "It's just that you looked so adorable when you tried to explain about the wedding." He raised her chin and stared into her blue eyes, loving her to the very depths of his being. "Don't you know how I feel about you?'

Her eyes filled with misery. "Yes, I believe so."

"Suppose you tell me."

She was encouraged by the warmth in his dark eyes. "I have never doubted that you cared about me, Cord. My mistake all these years was in believing you loved me in the way I loved you. But I learned differently the night I went to you in San Francisco."

His eyes drank in her delicate beauty. "What do you suppose I feel for you, Jahane?"

"You told me that you felt about me as you would a sist—"

"Don't," he said, touching his lips to her smooth cheek. "Now that I look back, I believe I never thought of you as a sister. It's hard to explain, but you were mine from the very beginning. You had not been given to my mother, but to me."

She loved the feeling of being held securely in his arms. "I have always felt that, too, Cord. That is why, when you came home from your last voyage, I thought you would feel . . . I wanted you to . . ."

His body shook with laughter. "How adorable you were that night, and how tempted I was to make you mine. You cannot imagine how difficult it was to send you away."

She smiled sadly. "You always did have a way of

making me feel good about myself, Cord. I know that is what you are doing now."

His lips curved into a half-smile. "Do you think so?"

"Yes. You and I both know what must happen between us tonight, and you want to make it easy for me."

His eyes flamed. "But who will make it easy for me, Jahane?"

There was a catch in her voice. "Will it be so difficult for you to make love to me?"

He moved away from her and turned to the table where a wine bottle and two glasses had been conveniently placed. "You cannot imagine how degrading it is for a man to be called upon to perform for an audience."

There was a puzzled frown on her face. "I do not follow your reasoning. There is no one here but the two of us."

He offered her a glass of wine, and when she refused with a shake of her head, he drank it down. "That's where you are wrong, Jahane. Your uncle and brother may not be here in the physical sense, but they are here all the same."

"I begin to understand your meaning, Cord. This must be all very abhorrent to you."

He set his glass down and picked up the bottle, carrying it with him. "I will need this," he murmured, taking her hand and leading her toward the bedroom.

When they stood in the bedroom, a cheery lamp gave off its light. The bed had been turned down invitingly, and Jahane's nightgown was draped over the foot of the bed.

Now that she was alone with Cord, Jahane felt nervous and shy. As she glanced up at him, she noticed he was removing his jacket and draping it over the back of the chair. When he loosened his cravat, she felt the prickle of something unknown running the length of her spine.

"I . . it's a warm night," she observed unnecessarily. She moved to the window and drew the curtain aside. "No clouds, so I don't think it will rain."

She felt Cord behind her, but she dared not turn around. "I wonder what Mama would think of all this, Cord."

His arms slid around her waist, for he knew how unsure she was feeling, and he knew he would have to woo her slowly. "If Mama knew about the marriage, she would be glad, even though in her practical mind, she would never understand the haste of it. She will think we could have waited to invite her to the ceremony."

Now Jahane did turn to Cord. "I miss her, Cord. This is the first time I have been parted from her, and I have wished so often for her love and good advice."

He cupped her face between his hands, feeling her hurt like a knife thrust into his heart. "I know, Jahane. So much has happened to you. If only I had been able to see ahead, I would have taken Mama's advice that night and taken you away."

"It's too late now, Cord."

He trailed his hand down her cheek, to the clasp on her wedding gown. Pausing for only a moment, he unhooked it, then moved to another. Something rose up inside him, and he felt as if Jahane's brother and

414

uncle were indeed looking over his shoulder. With a smothered oath, he turned away, unable to go farther.

"This is all too bizarre," he muttered. "How can a man be expected to function under these circumstances? Am I to behave like some lustful animal?"

His words cut Jahane to the quick. Was it so difficult for him to make her his wife? Was the notion of making love to her so distasteful to him? She remembered well the two different occasions she had offered herself to him and he had turned away from her. Now, he was turning away from her again.

With a firm resolve to make it easier on him, but with her heart broken, she reached up and unhooked her gown. She would have to be the one to seduce him, and she had no notion how that act would be accomplished. "I know the sooner this is over, the sooner you can go on with your life, Cord. I am certain my uncle will not require you to stay with me more than just this one night."

Only half hearing her words, Cord picked up the bottle of wine and took a deep drink to fortify himself for what lay ahead.

When he turned back to Jahane, she stood before him dressed only in her chemise. The instinct ran deep to turn away from her nakedness because she had been his to protect for so long. But already his eyes ran the length of her body, and the sight of her soft curves left him shaken with desire.

"So you need wine before you can make love to me?" she said in a painful voice.

Cord watched as her hand went to the hook on her chemise, and he placed the wine bottle down and slowly walked to her.

"I need nothing to help me make love to you, Jahane. I need someone to keep me from ravishing you."

Bending his dark head, he blew out the lamp, casting the room into darkness. When his eyes became accustomed to the dark, he moved to Jahane. Standing before her, he expertly unhooked her chemise and slipped it over her shoulders.

Jahane felt Cord move away from her, and she realized he was undressing. Her body trembled with fear of the unknown. This was a Cord she did not know, and she realized that after tonight she would never think about him in the same way.

He lifted her in his arms, carrying her across the room, where the only pinnacle of light in the room fell across the bed. When he placed Jahane on the satin coverlet, the silver moonlight played across her body, and he saw how really beautiful she was.

Wild madness controlled his thinking—she was no longer the little girl he had adored and protected, she was the woman he loved and desired. Thoughts of her had haunted his mind, robbed him of sleep. Now she was his, and he would have her!

Jahane's flesh tingled as Cord lay down beside her. Unashamed, she stared at his magnificent body, muscled and hard. This was as she had imagined them together. Her eyes widened when he reached up to remove the jasmine wreath from her head.

"My little wife," he said, stroking her long golden hair. "Soon you will really belong to me."

Jahane's innocent look was replaced by one of burn-

416

ing desire. With the age-old instinct of Eve, she quivered at the dark look in his eyes. Waiting expectantly for him to touch her, she placed her hand on his face, loving him so desperately and wanting the closeness that his dark eyes promised.

To her it felt so right that she and Cord should be lovers. This was what she had always known would happen, although, in her innocence, she did not know to what extent he would claim her body.

Cord kissed her cheek, then nestled his lips against the lobe of her ear, slowly pulling her body to his. He fought to keep his own burning desire under control, while he prepared her virginal body for his ultimate penetration.

He removed one of the fragrant jasmine blossoms from the wreath that rested on her pillow. At first he brushed the blossom against her lips. Then he bent his head so his lips would lightly touch where the blossom had caressed her. He could hear Jahane's fast intake of breath when he trailed the blossom down her neck, then softly and sensuously across her breasts—first one and then the other. He lightly touched his lips to the path the blossom had taken.

Passion, like a wildfire out of control, shot though his body. He trembled from the tight restraint he was keeping on himself. Smoothly, he allowed the blossom to move down Jahane's ribcage, across her stomach, his lips following the same path.

Jahane felt her body quake, and she felt like Cord was liquid fire, burning her everywhere he touched.

"Cord," she whispered, "I do not want to disappoint you."

"Jahane, sweetheart," he murmured against her lips. "I am on fire for you." He smothered her groan with a kiss that seemed to pin her to the bed with its intensity.

Her hands moved up his back to his muscled shoulders, feeling as if she wanted to hold him to her forever.

When he broke off the kiss, she stared into his dark eyes, seeing something she had never seen there before, a softness, and yet an uncertainty. His hand trembled as he trailed the jasmine blossom down her stomach; then, gently moving her legs apart, stroked the blossom across her quivering flesh.

Jahane's eyes were luminous, and Cord knew she was ready to receive him. Never had he wanted a woman as he wanted her, but his mind cautioned him to take her gently.

A passionate moan ripped from Jahane's lips as Cord moved above her. With patience and gentleness, he positioned himself to enter her. Slowly he moved forward, slipping into her tightness. Now, with the hot joining of their bodies, came the joining of the minds and, ultimately, the joining of their hearts.

Cord stoked Jahane's body like a furnace. From his masterful lovemaking, she gave in to the beautiful feelings that whirled around her. She was shaped, honed, and introduced to the leaping flames of passion.

In the silvery moonlight the two lovers were united in body and soul. When the ultimate pleasure came, it left Jahane's body quivering and breathless. She clung to Cord as if she were going under a dark wave and he was drawing her up to the sunlight.

As passion receded, they gazed into each other's eyes, caught in the wonder of what had just happened to them.

Jahane did not need to be told that she had given Cord pleasure; she could see it in his eyes and sense it in the gentle touch of his hand.

"Did I hurt you?" he asked at last, pushing a damp curl from her face.

"No, it was wonderful, Cord. Just as I always knew it would be."

He looked at her, smiling. "How could you have imagined anything like this?"

"I . . . no, not like this, but I always knew if our bodies could be joined, so would our hearts." She looked at him, searching to see if there was denial on his face. "I believe I know what you are feeling."

He touched her lips and trailed his finger down her neck. "There is no possible way you could know how I am feeling right now." His voice deepened. "I am a man who has just been handed his heart's desire, and I am still reeling under the impact."

She looked into his eyes. "Me, Cord?" she whispered.

He took in a deep breath, and his voice came out in a whisper. "Yes, you, Jahane. How could you know the torment I have been living through these last weeks?"

"Are you saying you love me as your wife?"

"I love you in every way it is possible for a man to love a woman." A possessive light came into his eyes. "Now that I have you, I will never let you go. Your uncle and your brother may as well grow accustomed to having this common American in their family, because I will never give you up."

Joy ripped through her heart as he drew her to him possessively. "I will never allow anything to separate us, Cord. Never!"

There, among the scent of jasmine, Cord lowered his head to cover her lips with a hot kiss. When he raised his head, he spoke in a choked voice. "Every time I catch the scent of jasmine, I will remember this night, Jahane. But then, you have always reminded me of the jasmine flower."

She pressed her cheek to his chest, comforted by the steady drumming of his heart. "My Uncle Serafimo has told me that although the jasmine bush can grow as high as a tree, its stems are not strong, and it always needs support." She looked deeply into his eyes. "I am like that, Cord. Without you, I cannot flower and grow."

Closing his eyes, Cord's arms went about her protectively. He could feel the danger closing in all around her. If it meant watching over her day and night, he would fight to keep her from being swallowed up by that danger.

Jahane ran her fingers through the mat of hair on his chest. "Cord?"

"Yes, sweetheart."

"Now, if my nightmare returns, I will only have to reach out for you to comfort me."

He shook with laughter. "Yes, how convenient it will be now that we share the same bed, Your Highness."

He raised her chin, and his lips descended, robbing her of speech. "Now," he said, pushing her back

420

against the pillow, "the first time I took you, it was at your uncle's insistence. This time, I will take you for myself."

She laughed and slipped her arms around his shoulder. "How can I resist an offer like that? What is a princess to do when her knight in shining armor, turns out to be a knight."

Clasping her to him, Cord's wonderful hands worked their magic, and she was again drawn under his spell.

Chapter Thirty-six

Cord was awakened to a loud rapping on the bedroom door. He glanced down at Jahane and smiled. She was curled up to him, and the soft rise and fall of her breasts showed she was in a deep sleep.

Again the rapping came, and Cord carefully moved off the bed so he would not awaken Jahane. Pulling the coverlet over her nakedness, he put his pants on and hurriedly slipped his arms into his shirt.

When he opened the door, he saw Mrs. St. John standing there with a nervous expression on her face. "I am sorry to wake you, my lord, but His Highness wants you and Princess Jahane to attend the high chamber meeting this morning. The archbishop has sent this gown along, and it is his wish that Her Highness wear it to the meeting."

Cord shook his head, trying to follow the housekeeper's instructions. "What time is it now?" he asked.

"Just half past nine, sir. The high chamber meeting convenes in one hour."

"What kind of meeting is this?"

"His Eminence believes that Duke Maxime has called all the nobles together to announce his plans to marry

Princess Jahane to the man of his choosing."

"Then Jahane could be in danger when the duke realizes his plans have been foiled?"

"His Eminence will take every precaution to protect her."

Cord's eyes flared. "Well, that is not good enough for me. Assist the princess in dressing, and tell her I have gone to see the archbishop. I will be back in time to accompany her to the assembly."

Jahane had never known such happiness. As she wound her long golden tresses around her head in the shape of a coronet, she remembered the night before and how Cord had made her his wife. She blushed when she recalled her own daring.

The housekeeper helped Jahane into a beautiful wine colored gown which had been elaborately embroidered with gold threads.

"Wherever did you come by this lovely creation, Mrs. St. John? It is the most beautiful gown I have ever seen."

"His Eminence ordered it made up just for this occasion. There are seven women who worked on the gown throughout the night so you could wear it this morning."

"Important events must be about to happen," Jahane said, moving away so she could see her entire length in the mirror. "Do you think the council will accept me as their true princess?"

Tears sparkled in the older woman's eyes. "You look so like your mother, the queen, God rest her soul, how could they not accept you? Queen Eleanor will be remembered by most of the lords in the council today.

His Eminence is sure when they see you, they will know you are her daughter."

It seemed that something was happening at last. Would today be the day when Alexander would take his place as king? she wondered. "Mrs. St. John, will my uncle present my brother to the council today?" she asked, putting her thoughts into words.

"Alas, no, Your Highness. His Eminence has said that would not be wise until you remembered the hiding place of the great scepter."

Jahane was thoughtful for a moment. "How well do you know the castle, Mrs. St. John?"

"As well as some, better than most. In your grandmother's time, I was a downstairs maid."

Hope sprung to life within Jahane. "Perhaps you can help me. Do you ever recall a tapestry of knights and ladies on a blue background? And, oh, yes, there was a crown in the background also."

The housekeeper's eyes sparkled to life. "But of course. Your grandmother had a great interest in the old tapestries, and she had them all catalogued. Since I had a fair hand at writing, I was allowed to help the chamberlain who catalogued them. That one was my favorite."

Jahane grasped the housekeeper's hand. "Can you recall where it hung?"

"Of course." She was thoughtful for a moment. "Now that I think of it, I have not seen it in several . . ." Her voice trailed off. "Yes, I know now. Duke Maxime had that tapestry removed and packed away." Her eyes gleamed, and her excitement grew. "He replaced it with a banner of his coat of arms!"

Jahane felt her excitement rising. "In what room is this?"

Mrs. St. John looked uncomfortable for a moment. "Why, Your Highness, in the great hall where your mother and father were murdered."

"This is too important to make a mistake, Mrs. St. John. Are you certain the tapestry has been replaced by Reynard's coat of arms?"

"Yes, Your Highness. There is no mistake."

"How will I know Reynard's coat of arms?"

"It is a raven in flight against a green background."

"Listen to me very carefully, Mrs. St. John. This is what I want you to do: Go to my Uncle Serafimo at once and tell him it is imperative that the council meeting take place in the great hall. I do not care what miracle he has to call forth to bring this about, but the assembly *must* be held in the great hall. Then impress on His Eminence the importance of having my brother attend the meeting, disguised in any manner he deems necessary. Tell them I now know the location of the scepter!"

Jahane's voice rose with excitement. "If all goes well, today is the glorious day that we see Alexander ascend to the throne of Balmarhea!"

The housekeeper dabbed at her eyes. "I'll see to it at once, Your Highness." She rushed away, then turned back at the door. "This will be a wondrous day indeed!"

Brynn felt like a wayward child as archbishop's guards escorted her back to the city. In her hurt and frustration at Alexander's cruelty, she had sought the only sanctuary she knew, the convent where she had grown up. Now, it seemed the archbishop had located her and was bringing her back to the city.

She rode along, feeling bruised and battered. In her heart she still loved Prince Alexander. But if she could only be to him someone he would have to keep hidden from the eyes of the world, then she would rather never see him again.

Brynn held her head high as they rode through the gates of Montique. To her surprise, the guards did not take her to the cathedral, but turned instead toward the castle.

She reined in her horse. "Why are you taking me to the castle?" she demanded. "You said it was His Eminence who sent you after me."

The captain of the archbishop's guards merely shrugged his shoulders. "I am following the archbishop's orders. He wanted you brought to the castle, and that's where I'm taking you."

Brynn's mind was in a quandary. Why had she been brought back at all? She only wished to be left in peace. She had even considered taking the veil and becoming a nun and devoting her life to doing good deeds for others.

With head held high, Jahane walked along the corridor with Cord at her side. They were flanked by six of her Uncle Serafimo's guards.

She caught the loving glance Cord gave her, and her lips slightly curved into a smile. As they descended the grand stairway to the lower level, she was astounded to find that the hall was lined with citizens of Balmarhea. As she approached them, they bowed low before her.

Jahane looked neither to her right nor to her left, but raised her head higher and stiffened her back. Evidently her Uncle Serafimo had invited the people to the castle today, and she smiled to herself, thinking it was a touch of genius on his part.

Cord was astounded at the outpouring of love he felt directed toward Jahane from the people. For the first time, he realized how important she was to this country. He had never loved her more than he did as she regally walked down the hallway, masking the fear he knew she was feeling.

As Jahane reached the great hall, her footsteps lagged, and she realized what a tremendous ordeal lay ahead of her. Taking her courage from the pressure Cord applied to her hand, she entered the room.

The council members seated in rows of chairs came to their feet when they saw Jahane. Scrafimo watched Reynard's face as Jahane walked toward the dais where they were seated. He saw the angry twitch in Reynard's eyes. His brother had not been pleased when Jahane had ordered that the great hall be opened for the meeting. But Reynard had relented, having no reason not to comply.

There had been little time to properly air the room, so it still smelled damp and musty. Serafimo closed his eyes, remembering the scene that had been played out in this room so long ago. Because of his bad memories of this room, this was the first time he had been able to come here since that night. He could still picture in his mind the stricken look on Queen Eleanor's face and the brave lift of his brother Alfons's head. Today, perhaps the queen and king would be avenged.

He heard the excited murmurs that ran through the crowd as the council members came to their feet at Jahane's approach. The lords bowed to her as she ascended to the dais. Reynard, as the ruling head of the council, came forward and took her hand, seating her between himself and Serafimo.

As Serafimo had instructed, Cord had merged with the crowd so no one would notice him until the time he would be called to come forward.

The citizens who could squeeze into the room pushed forward to stand behind the roped-off area where they were allowed to watch the proceedings. Jahane hid a smile when she saw that her Uncle Reynard's face was murderous as he glanced in the direction of the citizens.

Reynard raised his hand to indicate silence. "My lords, fellow council members," he began, smiling at Jahane, "as you are all aware, Princess Jahane has miraculously been restored to us."

Shouts of joy rippled through the room, and Jahane forced herself to stare straight ahead, for, in truth, her heart was pounding with fear. She realized Reynard had been talking for some time, and she had not heard one word.

"And," Reynard continued, "I have a proposal to put before you that I am sure you will find satisfactory. We all know Princess Jahane will need a consort so the royal line can continue. She must marry, and soon."

Serafimo moved to his feet. "I challenge my brother on this."

Reynard smiled, seemingly indulgently, at his brother, as if he had expected this. "My brother, the archbishop, was bound to object on one ground or another. But, as you all know, I have the last say in these matters, and I will have to overrule his objections."

"Not this time, Reynard," Serafimo insisted. "You

cannot marry Princess Jahane to anyone, because she is already married."

Reynard swung around to look at his niece, as if he would be able to read the truth in her eyes. "Preposterous," he roared, for this had taken him by surprise. "How could that be? I challenge you to produce some proof of this allegation, Serafimo."

"I am the proof, Reynard, because I officiated at the ceremony myself."

Reynard's face reddened. "When did this take place, Brother?"

"Last night," the archbishop said innocently.

Reynard's eyes went again to Jahane. "Then the marriage was—"

"Consummated," Serafimo supplied. "Yes, that was also last night."

"Produce the bridegroom," Reynard thundered.

Serafimo nodded. "Will Baron Devenue please come forward."

All eyes were on Cord as he moved out of the crowd and up the steps to stand before Reynard. The two men's eyes met, and Reynard's eyes narrowed with hatred. "I know of this man," he hissed. "He is not a baron, he is an American."

"While it is true that he is an American," Serafimo intervened, "it is also true he is a baron."

"I know not of this," Reynard stated doubtfully.

"It is true," Jahane said, standing up and deciding it was time for her to be the princess she was. She placed her hand on Cord's. "My husband was endowed with the title of baron last night before we were married."

Reynard's eyes traveled around the room, and he saw doubts on many of the council members' faces. "No

429

one among us has the power to create a baron. Not even you have that power, Your Highness," Reynard said, knowing Jahane had overstepped her bounds.

"That is not true," a deep voice spoke up from the right side of the dais. One of the monks that had accompanied Archbishop Serafimo to the hall now stepped forward. "There is someone who can perform that deed."

"Have this man removed," Reynard said. His eyes locked with the young monk's, and he felt his calm slip. It had been many years since he had looked into the eyes of his nephew, Prince Alexander, but he knew he faced him at that moment. Reynard began to feel trapped, and he looked around at the sea of faces where everyone watched him expectantly. "Guards," Reynard said with an urgency, "take the intruder away at once."

"Hold," Jahane cried out, stopping Reynard's guards in their tracks. "Allow this man to approach me."

The guards looked to Reynard for guidance, but his attention was still on the monk. Slowly Alexander advanced across the room, removing his disguise as he walked. First he dropped the cowl on the floor; next he pulled the black robe over his head and tossed it aside.

When the prince walked slowly up the steps of the dais, he smiled at Jahane, and in a clear voice, he called out so all might hear.

"I say *I* had the right to make my sister's husband a baron, for I am the rightful king of Balmarhea. I am Alexander, and I have come here to take back my throne."

Silence hung tensely in the room. Then urgent whispers could be heard.

Jahane laced her fingers through Alexander's, and she spoke. "If you believe me to be Princess Jahane, then believe my words. This is my brother, Prince Alexander, your true king."

Now Reynard smiled with satisfaction, silencing the murmuring with a raised hand. "If this is the true king, have him produce the great scepter. Only then will we know he is who he claims to be."

"Come with me, Brother," Jahane said, walking slowly down the dais. She had already spotted the banner bearing Reynard's coat of arms, and she moved to stand beneath it now, praying there would be no mistake. All eyes were on her as she nodded to Alexander to take down the wall hanging.

When this was accomplished, Jahane ran her fingers along the stone wall until she found a place where the stones did not fit together smoothly. Her father's words echoed in her mind. "Remember, Jahane, remember . . ."

"Can you remove this, Alexander?" she whispered, knowing everyone was watching her, and none so intently as her Uncle Reynard.

No one spoke as Alexander was handed a dagger by one of Serafimo's guards. With applied pressure, the stone moved. With a sharp tug, Alexander pulled it out, leaving a gaping hole in the wall.

Jahane's hand trembled as she reached inside the carved-out stone. Her heart was beating wildly as she touched the cold scepter. Since it was gold and very heavy, she had a difficult time removing it. Tears blinded her as she relived the scene of that night when her father had shown her the hiding place. She now realized why he had been forced to cause her pain. Had he not done that, she would not have remembered the hiding place.

Her fingers ran lovingly across the scepter, knowing her father's hands had been the last to touch its smoothness.

Among gasps, tears, and murmurs, she extended the golden scepter to her brother Alexander. "This is for you, my brother, my king. A gift from our dead father."

Alexander was fighting hard not to cry himself. Taking the scepter, he raised it above his head, and his shout echoed throughout the great hall. "I proclaim I am your rightful king. If there be any among you that dispute this claim, let him step forward now," he challenged.

Alexander turned to Reynard. "Do you concede that I am your rightful king?"

Chapter Thirty-seven

Reynard edged away from Alexander, feeling a deep dread. The day he had always feared had come to pass. Still he hoped to discredit his nephew. "You have the scepter, but I could not help noticing one of the rubies are missing. Perhaps the scepter is an imitation. In the charter, it states that the scepter shall have twelve perfectly matched rubies."

Jahane stepped up to her brother and extended her open hand. There, nestled in her palm, was the twelfth ruby. "My father gave this to me on the night he died, so all would know that it was his hand that hid the scepter. This is my brother, Prince Alexander, son of my father and your true king."

The people, who were now pressing forward, dropped to their knees. Most had never seen the great scepter and had only heard of its existence.

Now the archbishop moved forward, and his voice seemed to have a calming effect on the people. "I charge you to go to your homes and tell your families and neighbors to rejoice in this day, for I can testify that this is your true king. It was I who drew him out of the ocean when he was badly wounded. I have kept

him hidden all these years, for fear of his own safety."
His voice softened. "Now we are a united people, and
we have a king!"

Serafimo fought against tears. He had almost finished what he had vowed to accomplish — almost, but
not quite. "Clear the room, please," he said, looking at
Reynard's stricken face. He did not want anyone to
witness his brother's final disgrace. "There is much that
needs to be done, citizens of Balmarhea. I will see
that you are kept abreast of what happens, but for
now the royal family needs to be alone."

The archbishop's guards began clearing the room of
the people, and when this was done, the council members rose as one body, and as they left the great hall,
every member bowed to Alexander, demonstrating their
acceptance of him as their king. At the archbishop's
command, his guards disarmed Reynard's confused
guards and led them from the room. Soon, only the
family members and Captain Marceau remained.

Reynard was never so vocal as when he was cor-
nered. His eyes traveled across the faces of his family.
Jahane stared at him coldly. Serafimo's eyes were sad.
It was Alexander's eyes that sent a chill down his
spine, for there was hatred in the young king's eyes,
and Reynard feared him most of all.

"I always swore I would one day stand before you,
Uncle," Alexander said in a smooth voice. "The time
has come when you must answer for all your sins."

Reynard arched his dark brow. "Surely not all. Not
even you have that power, Nephew."

"You killed my mother and father, and thought you
had killed me also."

Reynard seated himself and stared back at Alexander

434

with open hatred on his face. All need for pretense was gone. "If I had succeeded in killing you that night, we would not be having this conversation, would we, hmm?" Reynard's eyes moved to Jahane. "So you were the one who knew where the scepter was hidden. If only I had known that . . ." He shrugged. "Oh, well." His eyes moved to the hollowed-out wall that had all these years held the scepter. "It was here all the time, and hiding behind my own banner." He glanced at Serafimo. "You see, Brother, perhaps there is justice after all."

Alexander nodded to Captain Marceau. "Take Duke Maxime below and lock him up until I decide what is to be his punishment. Also, locate Count Arville and Hogarth, the man who is in charge of the dungeon. Have them all locked away to await the king's justice."

When Captain Marceau would have forcibly removed Reynard, the duke pulled away and looked at him with an imperious air. Serafimo nodded at his guard. "He will follow you. There is no need for force."

At that moment Reynard turned toward Jahane and Alexander, who were embracing. To him they represented everything he hated. They had robbed and humiliated him, and for this they would both die.

In the flicker of a second, Reynard reached inside his breast pocket and produced a gun. Whirling away from Captain Marceau, he pointed the gun first at Jahane.

"I have nothing to lose by killing you both," he hissed, his eyes wild with hatred, "because I know my punishment will be death in any event. I have decided the both of you will precede me."

"No," Serafimo cried. "There is already too much

blood on your hands. Do not do this, Reynard!"

Evil laughter rolled off Reynard's lips. "Pray for all our souls, Brother."

At that moment, a shot rang out, and everyone thought Jahane had been hit. Serafimo reached for her, but there was a puzzled look on her face, and she watched Reynard crumple to the floor, blood soaking his shirtfront just where his heart was located. Then all eyes moved to Cord Meredith, who dropped his smoking pistol and rushed to his wife, enfolding her in his arms.

Jahane laid her head against Cord's shoulder while tremors of fear shook her body.

Silently Serafimo bent over his brother's prone body and discovered Reynard was indeed dead! The archbishop raised his head in prayer, and felt the pain of regret in his heart. He had always hoped Reynard would somehow redeem himself, but that had not happened.

"Remove the body," Alexander said coldly to Captain Marceau. "I no longer want to look upon his face." Alexander saw only the death of a traitor and an assassin. There was no regret in his heart. At last his mother and father had been avenged!

Alexander moved to Cord and Jahane. Shaking Cord's hand, he smiled. "I owe you a great debt, Cord Meredith. One that I can never repay. I thank you for standing beside me and my sister, and for saving her life just now. How can I reward you?"

Cord smiled down at Jahane. "You have given me reward enough when you gave your sister to me as my wife."

Brother and sister stared long at each other, and

then Jahane went into Alexander's outstretched arms.

Alexander chuckled. "I don't know why anyone would want this obstinate woman for his bride. You will have your hands full with her. Did you see the way she manipulated the council today? I fear she will manipulate you in the same way, Cord. Do not say you have not been warned."

"I will take my chances," Cord said, his eyes wandering lovingly over his wife's face.

Jahane beamed up at her brother. "We did it, Alexander! We avenged our mother and father."

"You did it," he said with feeling. "You are the one who made it all possible."

By now Serafimo had joined the young people. He pushed his sorrow to the back of his mind and felt gladness that Jahane and Alexander had found their rightful places. This was his family, and he felt good inside for the first time in many years.

"Well, my children," the archbishop said, beaming at all three, for indeed they were his children. "There is much to do. We have a king to crown and a country to heal."

Brynn sat in the front row of the assembly, beside Princess Jahane and her handsome American husband, wondering why she had been asked to attend, and why she was allowed to sit with the dignitaries who had gathered to honor valorous deeds of several citizens.

As Brynn's eyes rested on the golden head of the newly crowned king, her heart swelled with love for him. She never doubted that Alexander would do well as king, for there was about him an air of greatness.

Brynn had not seen Alexander since she had been brought to the castle by the archbishop's guards—but then she had not expected to see him again. He was king, so why should he seek out someone as insignificant as herself?

Brynn had convinced herself that she would have to be content with seeing him from a distance on rare occasions.

The great hall had been opened to the public today, so common people mingled with lords and their ladies. This was the day that had been set aside by the new king to honor the people who had given their lives, or those who had acted bravely in the defense of Balmarhea.

King Alexander stood up and smiled at the attendance. Brynn was almost certain his eyes settled on her for a brief moment, but she must be mistaken.

"We are gathered here today to honor those who are worthy of being recognized by a grateful nation," Alexander began. "First, I would like to call your attention to one who was not born on our shores, but still a man who gave his life for this country the night my mother and father were killed. Had it not been for the man's bravery, that ultimately cost him his life, my sister would not be here now. That is why I award the Cross of Bravery to the late Captain Jonah Meredith."

Cord stepped forward, feeling proud that his father's bravery had been recognized. He only wished his mother were here to see this day.

"Now," Alexander said, "I would like to honor another man with the last name of Meredith—my sister's husband, the Baron Devenue." Alexander held out his hand. "To a land that is grateful for all your deeds of valor, and to also pay homage to your father, I bestow on you all the lands, estates, and properties that go with your title, Baron Devenue."

Brynn watched the proceedings with the rest of the citizens. She was awed by the king. She searched his face for some sign of the Alexander she had known as a lover, but no, he was every inch a king, and so far out of her reach. She listened as he honored a Captain Ruel Marceau for his loyalty to Princess Jahane, and made him admiral of the Royal Navy.

Brynn's eyes never left Alexander's face, because she wanted to press his image on her heart forever. She loved him so deeply, and the pain of seeing him look so remote was almost unbearable.

"And now," Alexander continued, "let me say there have been many heroes honored here today, but I will now honor the greatest of them all."

In a move that shocked Brynn, the king turned to her and held out his hand. "Brynn, will you join me?"

Too astonished to move, Brynn felt Princess Jahane take her arm and help her to her feet. "Come," Jahane whispered, knowing Brynn was aware that all eyes were on her. "It is but a short walk."

Brynn's hand was trembling as King Alexander pressed it in his. He bestowed a soft smile on her and then spoke again. "I would now like to posthumously acknowledge a man who deserves our consideration. Without a thought about his own safety, he gave his life so I might live."

Brynn stood woodenly beside the king, wondering why she was here. As the king spoke, she glanced at Princess Jahane and was comforted somewhat by the smile of encouragement the princess bestowed on her.

Alexander continued. "I would like the history books and the people of this country to recognize a great hero, Count Chapin D'arcy, faithful prime minister and adviser to my father, and . . ." He drew Brynn closer to him. ". . . and father of my future bride, and your future queen, the Lady Brynn d'Arcy."

The crowd cheered. Amid uproarious shouting and applause, Brynn looked bewildered. There were tears of disbelief on her face as Alexander handed her the nation's most coveted award, the Balmarhea Cross. What had he said? Surely he could not think she was Count D'Arcy's daughter. No, it was not possible. Count D'arcy had been a great man. Had the king said she would be his queen? No, that must be another mistake.

When Alexander saw the confusion in Brynn's eyes, he gathered her close to him and whispered, "Smile, my love. Let the people see how lovely their future queen is."

"But, Your Majesty—"

Still the crowd was noisily showing their happiness, which gave Alexander another chance to whisper in Brynn's ear. "Will you have me for your husband, Lady Brynn?" he asked. "You have my heart, why not take my name? I once told you I would raise you above all women."

Tears now ran freely down her face. "I do not understand any of this. Why did you say I was Count d'Arcy's daughter?"

"Because you are his daughter." His eyes softened with love. "If you do not believe this, ask my uncle the archbishop, for it was he who told me this."

Brynn glanced across the room and met the archbishop's eyes. He nodded to her.

"Will you become my queen, Brynn?"

Her eyes were shining bright. "Oh, yes, Your Majesty. For I love you so dearly."

"You had better, because I love you."

Alexander turned back to the crowd and held up his hand, and silence fell across the room. "The lady has said 'yes'." He smiled. "This council is now concluded."

Epilogue

Jahane's footsteps quickened as she reached her chambers, for she knew Cord would be there waiting for her. Opening the door, she rushed into his outstretched arms.

"Did you see Brynn settled in her new apartment?" he asked.

"Yes, and she is such a wonderful person. I believe my brother has chosen well. Of course, she is a bit overwhelmed with all the attention she is receiving as Alexander's future wife. But her sweetness will make her a very worthy queen."

Cord had hardly seen Jahane in the last few days. Her duties had kept her busy, and Alexander had kept him at his side. "Do you suppose we could sneak away and find a place to be alone for a few days? Since our marriage a week ago, I have hardly had you to myself."

She smiled up at him with a devilish light in her eyes. "How would you like to visit one of your distant estates? I understand from Uncle Serafimo there is one on the south side of the island that borders the sea."

"Can you get away?"

"Yes. I have already told my brother that I am going on a honeymoon with my husband, and we do not want to be disturbed for any reason."

Cord smiled down at her. "And what did His Majesty say to that?"

Jahane laughed. "After a little persuasion, he said yes. Of course, I had to assure him we would return for his wedding."

Suddenly Jahane's eyes clouded over. "You are an American, Cord. Will you be content to remain here on Balmarhea? Will you not miss the adventure of the sea?"

"I want only to be where you are, Jahane. I know this is your country and you are needed here." His eyes took on an excited light. "Since your brother has appointed me his minister of trade, I have ideas that will bring great prosperity to your island. Before too long, Balmarhea will be successful in the export business."

"My brother chose wisely when he chose you, Cord. Everything is so wonderful . . . but . . ."

"But what?"

"I miss Mama."

His laughter was warm. "I have sent the *Golden Phoenix* to San Francisco with instructions for Thadeus to bring Mama here. I suppose I will be forced to live under the same roof as my mother-in-law," he teased.

She suppressed a smile. "But, Cord, she is *your* mother."

His laughter was now amused. "It is a strange situation, is it not? If you will recall, my mother did not think I was worthy of marrying you."

Jahane felt joy in her heart. It had been difficult for her and Cord to overcome the obstacles that had stood between them. But with their love, they had managed to reach across two worlds to find each other. But they belonged together now. They always had—they always would.

Archbishop Serafimo walked across the stone walkway to an incline where he could look down on Montique. In the distance, the blue sea sparkled like a precious jewel. He could see the men and women milling around, and the sounds of their laughter carried to him.

Balmarhea was no longer an oppressed country. One could almost breathe the exhilaration of freedom in the air. The people loved their royal family, and most especially their king, who was proving to be wise and just. Balmarhea had a great future, and Serafimo thanked God he would be alive to see it happen.

Serafimo only wished that King Alfons and Queen Eleanor had lived to see both their children grown, for they would have been so proud.

The archbishop smiled and reached out his arms to embrace the day. They knew—somehow, they knew.

LOVE'S BRIGHTEST STARS SHINE WITH ZEBRA BOOKS!

CATALINA'S CARESS (2202, $3.95)
by Sylvie F. Sommerfield
Catalina Carrington was determined to buy her riverboat back from the handsome gambler who'd beaten her brother at cards. But when dashing Marc Copeland named his price—three days as his mistress—Catalina swore she'd never meet his terms . . . even as she imagined the rapture a night in his arms would bring!

BELOVED EMBRACE (2135, $3.95)
by Cassie Edwards
Leana Rutherford was terrified when the ship carrying her family from New York to Texas was attacked by savage pirates. But when she gazed upon the bold sea-bandit Brandon Seton, Leana longed to share the ecstasy she was sure sure his passionate caress would ignite!

ELUSIVE SWAN (2061, $3.95)
by Sylvie F. Sommerfield
Just one glance from the handsome stranger in the dockside tavern in boisterous St. Augustine made Arianne tremble with excitement. But the innocent young woman was already running from one man . . . and no matter how fiercely the flames of desire burned within her, Arianne dared not submit to another!

MOONLIT MAGIC (1941, $3.95)
by Sylvie F. Sommerfield
When she found the slick railroad negotiator Trace Cord trespassing on her property and bathing in her river, innocent Jenny Graham could barely contain her rage. But when she saw how the setting sun gilded Trace's magnificent physique, Jenny's seething fury was transformed into burning desire!

Available wherever paperbacks are sold, or order direct from the Publisher. Send cover price plus 50¢ per copy for mailing and handling to Zebra Books, Dept. 2726, 475 Park Avenue South, New York, N.Y. 10016. Residents of New York, New Jersey and Pennsylvania must include sales tax. DO NOT SEND CASH.